SECRESY

Or

The Ruin on the Rock

Eliza Fenwick (?–1840) was one of a group of radical women who used the novel to investigate women's issues. She was a friend of other radical women such as Mary Hays and Mary Wollstonecraft and she was with Wollstonecraft when she died in childbirth in 1797. When her husband John Fenwick fled London to escape his debts, she was left to support herself and her family. For a time she worked with William Godwin, producing reading schemes and educational tales for children. She also worked as a governess in Ireland and when her daughter, an actress in Barbados, was deserted by her husband and left with four children to fend for, Eliza Fenwick joined her and together they established a school which did not succeed. They travelled to America where Eliza Fenwick worked as a schoolteacher and experienced further misfortunes in the deaths of her daughter and granchildren. She died in Rhode Island.

Janet Todd was born in Wales and educated at Newnham College, Cambridge, and the University of Florida. She is the author of several books of criticism including *Women's Friendships in Literature* (1980), *A Dictionary of British and American Women Writers, 1660–1800* (1985), *Sensibility* (1986), *Feminist Literary History* (1988), and *The Sign of Angelica, Women, writing and fiction, 1660–1800* (1989). She is a fellow of Sidney Sussex College, Cambridge.

MOTHERS OF THE NOVEL
Reprint Fiction from Pandora Press

Pandora is reprinting eighteenth-century novels written by women. Each novel is being reset in modern typography and introduced to readers today by contemporary women writers. The following titles in this series are currently available:

Self-control (1810/11) by Mary Brunton
Introduced by Sara Maitland

Discipline (1814) by Mary Brunton
Introduced by Fay Weldon

The Wanderer; or, Female Difficulties (1814) by Fanny Burney
Introduced by Margaret Drabble

Belinda (1801) by Maria Edgeworth
Introduced by Eva Figes

Patronage (1814) by Maria Edgeworth
Introduced by Eva Figes

Helen (1834) by Maria Edgeworth
Introduced by Maggie Gee

Secresy; or, The Ruin on the Rock (1795) by Eliza Fenwick
Introduced by Janet Todd

The Governess; or, Little Female Academy (1749) by Sara Fielding
Introduced by Mary Cadogan

Munster Village (1778) by Lady Mary Hamilton
Introduced by Sara Baylis

The Memoirs of Emma Courtney (1796) by Mary Hays
Introduced by Sally Cline

The History of Miss Betsy Thoughtless (1751) by Eliza Haywood
Introduced by Dale Spender

A Simple Story (1791) by Elizabeth Inchbald
Introduced by Jeanette Winterson

The Canterbury Tales (1797/99) by Harriet and Sophia Lee
Introduced by Harriet Gilbert

The Female Quixote (1752) by Charlotte Lennox
Introduced by Sandra Shulman

The Wild Irish Girl (1806) by Lady Morgan
Introduced by Brigid Brophy

The O'Briens and The O'Flahertys (1827) by Lady Morgan
Introduced by Mary Campbell

Adeline Mowbray (1804) by Amelia Opie
Introduced by Jeanette Winterson

Memoirs of Miss Sidney Bidulph (1761) by Frances Sheridan
Introduced by Sue Townsend

Emmeline (1788) by Charlotte Smith
Introduced by Zoë Fairbairns

The Old Manor Home (1794) by Charlotte Smith
Introduced by Janet Todd

The companion to this series is *Mothers of the Novel: 100 Good Women Writers Before Jane Austen* by Dale Spender, a wonderfully readable survey that reclaims the many women writers who contributed to the literary tradition. She describes the interconnections among the writers, their approach and the public response to their work.

SECRESY

Or
The Ruin on the Rock

ELIZA FENWICK

Introduced by Janet Todd

Disguise! I see thou art a Wickedness,
Wherein the pregnant Enemy does much.

Shakespeare

PANDORA

LONDON   BOSTON   SYDNEY   WELLINGTON

This edition first published by Pandora Press, an imprint of the Trade Division
of Unwin Hyman, in 1989.

Introduction © Janet Todd, 1989

PANDORA PRESS
Unwin Hyman Limited
15/17 Broadwick Street, London W1V 1FP

Unwin Hyman Inc
8 Winchester Place, Winchester, MA 01890

Allen & Unwin Australia Pty Ltd.
PO Box 764, 8 Napier Street, North Sydney, NSW 2060

Allen & Unwin NZ Ltd (in association with the Port Nicholson Press)
60 Cambridge Terrace, Wellington, New Zealand

British Library Cataloguing in Publication Data

Fenwick, Eliza, *d. 1840*
    Secresy, or, The Ruin on the rock.
    —— (Mothers of the novel).
I. Title II. Series
823'.7 [F]
ISBN 0-86358-307-5

Printed and bound in Great Britain by
Cox & Wyman Ltd, Reading

CONTENTS

CONTENTS

Introduction

Sensibility is the most exquisite feeling of which the human soul is susceptible: when it pervades us, we feel happy . . . . It is this quickness, this delicacy of feeling, which enables us to relish the sublime touches of the poet, and the painter; it is this, which expands the soul, gives an enthusiastic greatness, mixed with tenderness, when we view the magnificent objects of nature; or hear of a good action.

Mary, A Fiction

Civilized women are . . . weakened by false refinement . . . . Ever restless and anxious, their over-exercised sensibility not only renders them uncomfortable themselves, but troublesome, to use a soft phrase, to others. All their thoughts turn on things calculated to excite emotion and feeling, when they should reason, their conduct is unstable, and their opinions wavering . . . . Miserable, indeed, must be that being whose cultivation of mind has only tended to inflame its passions!

A Vindication of the Rights of Woman

Mary Wollstonecraft wrote these two contrasting passages. The first comes from a novel of 1788 praising the feminine association with admired sensibility or emotional sensitivity. It was written before its writer had come into contact with those revolutionary ideas that would bear such fruit in the feminist *A Vindication of the Rights of Woman* (1792), from which the second passage is taken. The latter work extended the 'rights of man' to women, and denied the absolute importance of sensibility; indeed the peculiar association of femininity and sensibility later seemed to Mary Wollstonecraft a form of mental binding, a snare for the potentially thinking woman.

The two passages together summarize the debate over women's nature current in the decade of the French Revolution, a debate to which Mary Wollstonecraft's friend Eliza Fenwick contributed with her novel *Secresy* in 1795. One question was whether women were naturally more sensitive and tender than men – as well as more irrational and stupid – or whether these assumptions were clogs to female progress towards intellectual equality with men. A related question concerned education, whether girls should be given the same rational and practical training as boys, designed to be independent adult beings, or whether they should be raised 'innocently' in nature, out of reach of corrupting society. With this upbringing they could become simply virtuous, supportive and obedient wives.

Eliza Fenwick joined other women of the 1790s in wanting to use her novel to investigate the female issues of the day. In particular she wanted to embody the problems in a story which would consider what might happen if a woman were given a 'natural' education away from social corruption, what could occur when feminine sensibility was encouraged by a training that avoided strengthening the reasoning faculties, what might befall a woman who rebelled against such an education, and what might result if she followed her sensitive and compassionate feelings into forbidden sexual activity.

In the non-fictional *Rights of Woman* Mary Wollstonecraft had taken the rationalist view and opposed any celebration of peculiarly feminine sensibility as well as any female education that accepted subordination. But in fiction it was not so easy. For it was especially in the romantic novel, so firmly associated with women as readers and writers, that the construction of sensibility was most elaborately made. In this construction the sensitive, tender and palpitating woman was concerned with romantic love with her entire being, and her story was inevitably either the sad one of virtue in distress, ennobled by an heroic death, or virtue rewarded by an aristocratic marriage and sweetened by extraordinary husbandly devotion.

By 1795 when Eliza Fenwick published her novel there already existed a strong tradition of female fiction. This fiction had established conventions which carried very specific messages for contemporary readers. For example, *Secresy* is subtitled *The Ruin on the Rock*, which clearly conjures up a Gothic location. The Gothic novel was becoming extremely popular by 1795 and such a setting would immediately suggest some interest in the problem of the mind's construction, a staple of Gothic fiction, as well as indicating an interaction between a powerful and frightening male environment and a naive young heroine. Another convention of the novel was the pairing of women, as in Jane

Austen's *Sense and Sensibility*, a book also written during these years. In the 1790s this convention was often used as a teaching device in which contrasting girls either stood for good but often austere qualities or bad but appealing ones. Finally there is the device of letters, so associated with novels of sensibility, but becoming less popular in the 1790s; this literary device allowed a concentration on the inner life and responses of the letter writers, rather than insisting that they be judged and placed by an outside authority.

In the novel it was not easy to bend such conventions in order to make them openly oppose sensibility and mistaken feminine education in the manner of Mary Wollstonecraft's non-fictional *A Vindication of the Rights of Woman*. Nor, as revolutionary ideas grew more appalling to the British, was it any longer easy to use the conventions straight forwardly, as they had once been used, to exalt superior feminine feeling, since sensibility was becoming unpopular both as an identity for women and as a potentially anti-social libertarian force. So there was often an ambiguity in novels of this time, well exemplified by *Secresy* with its shifting views and messages.

For example, Eliza Fenwick's apparently conventional use of the letter form to convey an inner world becomes so inward that there seems to be no outlet at all beyond words or unheroic death for the desiring, feeling and thinking woman. So, too, with the device of the two heroines: a reader expecting a simple separation of good and bad qualities would be disappointed. For if the friend represents sense and social knowledge and the heroine sensibility and an education in nature and isolation, it is by no means clear that the book sides with the former. Like Mary Wollstonecraft in her fiction, Eliza Fenwick herself remains both for and against a sensibility which she found politically dangerous but emotionally attractive. At one point the commonsensical friend remarks to the isolated intense heroine, 'With such an education, unless you had been a mere block without ideas, it was impossible you should not become a romantic enthusiast.' Obviously such a character is of little use in the real world. And yet, if men had been similarly motivated by romantic ideals and had lived by the same compassionate codes as women, there would have been little problem with this identity. So, although it is ineffective, perhaps this enthusiastic feeling is in fact rather splendid in the midst of a debased world.

One of the few comforts in the bleak environment of secrecy and betrayal is the friendship of other women, a friendship that gives a defensive solace in a threatening male world, as well as providing an opportunity for sincere self-expression for both friends. The two women in the novel find their happiest moments in writing to each other and in openly expressing an affection that seems impossible in any other relationship.

In her own increasingly arduous life after 1795, Eliza Fenwick herself would find much comfort in female friendship, for she had married an impecunious and unsupportive man. As she struggled to earn a living for herself and her children through writing, lamenting the unsentimental misery of composing in a noisy and over-filled room, she gained great solace from complaining to other independent friends like Mary Hays and, before her death in 1797, Mary Wollstonecraft. Such women were trying to earn a literary living for themselves without the help of the adoring men which romantic fiction had taught them to expect and without much room for the indulgence of that sensibility which was once supposed to have been woman's glory. As Eliza Fenwick ruefully wrote to her friend Mary Hays:

> On Monday I was sadly disposed to compare the present with the past & make discomfort more uncomfortable, but I soon found crying encreased my head-ach & I got as fast as possible into a better mood.

The latter part of Fenwick's life was dismal. After her husband fled debt-ridden from London in 1799, she formally separated from him and worked for a time with William Goodwin, Wollstonecraft's husband, on his Juvenile Library, contributing books for children. Her daughter, an actress in the West Indies, was abandoned there with four children so Eliza Fenwick and her son decided to join her and help her set up a school. Tragedy followed with the death of her beloved son, and the school foundered. Mother, daughter and grand-children then travelled to the United States where first the daughter died and then the two older boys drowned. One of her granddaughters was with Eliza Fenwick when she herself died in Rhode Island.

JANET TODD

Cambridge,
December 1987

ELIZA B—

WHAT does the world care about either you or me? Nothing. But we care for each other, and I grasp at every opportunity of telling it. A letter, they may say, would do as well for that purpose as a dedication. I say no; for a letter is a sort of corruptible substance, and these volumes *may* be IMMORTAL. Beside, it is perhaps my pride to write a dedication and your pride to receive one. I desire the world then to let it pass; for, to tell them a truth – you have paid me for it beforehand.

VOLUME I

LETTER I

FROM CAROLINE ASHBURN

TO

THE HONOURABLE GEORGE VALMONT

SIR,

I am by no means indifferent as to the opinion you may form of me, in consequence of my abrupt, and, in a degree, rude conduct, when you so peremptorily denied the boon I would have begged on quitting your castle. If the reasons which guided your refusal were such as fully satisfied yourself, however incompetent they might be in my judgment, I was wrong in being offended, and in shewing my resentment by something like invective. Ere we had travelled two miles I became sensible of my pride and injustice; and it is from our first resting place I thus present myself to acknowledge my fault, to ask other favors, and to tell you that I have no pleasure in view equal to that I expected to enjoy in the society of Miss Valmont.

But though you denied me the charm of associating with your niece, you will not also refuse me her correspondence? A letter, Sir, cannot waft down your drawbridges; the spirit of my affection breathed therein cannot disenchant her from the all-powerful spell of your authority. No. And you surely will not forbid an indulgence so endearing to us, while unimportant to yourself. Already I feel assured of your consent; and, with my thanks, dismiss the subject.

As your seclusion of Miss Valmont from the world is not a plan of yesterday, I imagine you are persuaded of its value and propriety, and I therefore see nothing which should deter me from indulging the strong propensity I feel to enquire into the nature of your system; a system so opposite to the general practice of mankind, and which I am inclined to think is not as perfect as you are willing to suppose. Remembering your contempt of the female character, I am aware that you may possibly treat this part of my letter only with neglect or disdain. Gladly would I devise a means by which to induce you to lay aside this prejudice against us, and in the language of reason, as from one being to another, discuss with me the merits or defects of your plan; which from its singularity, on the first view, excited my curiosity; and has since, from my observation of some of its consequences, interested me by worthier feelings than that of mere curiosity. If Miss Valmont's education, treatment, and utter seclusion were most valuable for her, why should she, yet so young, and removed from the common misfortunes of life, why should she be unhappy. You, Sir, may not have perceived this effect of your system; for, although shut within the same boundary and resident under one roof, you seldom see her, and when you do see, you do not study her. I believe I know more of her mental temperament in our seven days intercourse than you have learned in seven years, and I affirm that she is unhappy. Yet it is only from her sudden wanderings in conversation, and that apparent restlessness of dissatisfaction in her, which seeks change of place because of all places alike are irksome, that I ground my opinion, for having flattered myself that you would permit her to accompany me from your castle, I passed the days of my abode there, in closely observing Miss Valmont, rather than in endeavouring to gain her entire confidence; and have perhaps made but little progress toward obtaining a friendship, to which my heart aspires with zeal and affection.

In the hope of a speedy and candid answer from you,
I remain, Sir,
  Your well wisher,
    And humble servant,

                                    CAROLINE ASHBURN

LETTER II

FROM SIBELLA VALMONT

TO

CAROLINE ASHBURN

I am come from Mr. Valmont's study. – Can it be? – Oh yes! I am
come from Mr. Valmont's presence, to write a letter – a letter to you!
– Ah, Miss Ashburn! – to write a letter to you by my uncle's——Can
command ever be indulgence? – No, no. I will not believe that: –
No, not even would I believe it, though, when my heart expands
with swelling emotion, he were then also to command me to——.
Miss Ashburn, the command of Mr. Valmont in this, as in all other
instances, is stern and repulsive, but, as his commands are odious to
my acceptation, so, in equal degree, is the action of writing a letter
to you grateful, delightful, overwhelming!

How came it? – How have you prevailed? – Oh teach me your art
to soften his power, to unloose the grasp of his authority, and I will
love you as——I believe I cannot love you better than I do; for have
you not cast a ray of cheering light upon my dungeon? – Have you
not bestowed upon me the only charm of existence that I have known
for many and many a tedious day?

But why did you do so? Do you love me as I love you? You never
told me so. Seven days and seven nights you lived in our castle; and
you walked with me by day, you wandered with me by night. I talked
to you almost without ceasing. – You spoke infinitely less than I did.
– You pressed my hand as it held yours: but you never said, *I love
you! – I love you, Sibella, with all my soul.* – Nor did you ever quit your
rest, amidst the darkness of the night, to hover near my chamber, as
I have done near yours. – Yes, Miss Ashburn, when at night you had
retired from me, I beheld only solitude and imprisonment; and I have
waited hours in that forlorn gallery, that I might catch the whisper of

your breathings, that the consciousness of being near a friend might restore me to hope, to hilarity, to confidence.

Yet now I recollect it, and you do love me; for you asked the imperious, the denying Mr. Valmont, to let you take me from the castle. Oh, you did urge – you did intreat. – You do love me. – I am writing a letter to you; and perhaps, one day, I shall have all my happiness.

I wish Mr. Valmont would shew me the letter you wrote to him. He has charged me to answer it, and I have been obliged to walk a great while, and to think a great deal, before I could remember a word of what he said I was to repeat to you; and now I do not think I recollect the whole. I would return to his study and ask him to tell it me again; but he has an aversion to trouble, and perhaps, irritated by my forgetfulness, might say, I should not write to you at all. – Ah, if he were to say that, Miss Ashburn, and if it were possible for me to send a letter out of the castle in defiance of his commands, do you think I would obey him? – No, no.

Andrew came to me in the wood, to bid me attend my uncle in his library; and I went thither immediately. He was but just risen; and a letter, which I suppose was your letter, and which must have arrived yesterday, was laying open on the table beside him; and when he spoke to me he laid his right hand upon the letter.

'Numberless are the hours, child,' Mr. Valmont said to me soon after I entered, 'that I have employed in pondering on your welfare: – yet you are not the docile and grateful creature I expected to find you.'

'Sir,' I said, 'if in all those hours of pondering you never thought of the only means by which my welfare can be effected, am I therefore forbidden to be happy? – Am I to be unhappy, because I and not you discovered how I might be very, very happy?'

Mr. Valmont raised himself more erect on his chair; and he frowned too. 'Always reasoning,' he said: 'I tell you, child, you cannot, you shall not reason. Repine in secret as much as you please, but no reasonings. No matter how sullen the submission, if it is submission.'

I replied, 'I do not think as you do.'

'Child, you are not born to think; you were not made to think.' He turned the letter on the table, as he spoke, and took a leaning attitude.

'But I cannot ——'.

'Silence, Sibella!' cried my uncle. He fiercely recovered his upright posture; and then, for I was effectually silenced, he gradually and slowly fell back into his reclining station. Indeed, Miss Ashburn, I am in some instances still a mere child, as Mr. Valmont calls me; and yet, I wish you would account for it, for I do not know how, I feel every day bolder and bolder. I can speak to him when I first meet him, as calmly as I can to Andrew; and I can oppose him a little. And when I have not opposed him as much as I wish to do, and have ran away from the fight of his face, and the sound of his voice, I take myself to talk, and say, foolish Sibella! Can a frown kill you? – Can your uncle, though he should be tenfold angry with you, do more to you than he has already done? And, when my throbbing heart denies the possibility of that, I resolve the next time to tell him every thing I feel: and then I wait, and long, and wish that the next time would arrive. When it does arrive, I begin without fear; or, at least, I have only a weak trembling, which I should soon lose, if he did not call up one of those frowns which infallibly condemn me to silence and to terror. But I know, and he knows too if he would but own it, that I do think; that I was born to think: – and I will think.

Oh dear, dear Miss Ashburn, I am writing a letter to you! And what was it but my power of thought, which gave birth to that affection which would impel me on with a rapidity that my pen cannot follow? It seems to me that my thought dictates volumes in an instant; and that, in an instant, I have said volumes. Yet I have only a few pages of paper under my eye and my hand. If Mr. Valmont tells me, I cannot cut the air with wings, I will answer – 'Tis true: but in imagination, I can encompass the vast globe in a second. Hail thought! Thought the soul of existence! – Not think! – why do not all forms in which the pulse of life vibrates, possess the power of thought? – Have I not seen the worm, crawling from his earthy bed to drink the new-fallen dew from the grass, swiftly shrink back to his shelter, his attentive ear alarmed by my approach? – The very insect, while sporting in the rapture of a sun-beam on my habit, is yet wary and vigilant, and will rather leave his half-tasted enjoyment, if apprehension seize him, than hazard the possibility of my inflicting injury upon him. And what but thought, imperceptible yet mighty thought, could make a creature so infinitely diminutive in its proportions, so apparently valueless in the creation, shun the hand of power, and seek for itself sources of enjoyment? – I could tell you, Miss Ashburn, how I have imagined I met sympathy and reflection in that flower which enamoured of the sun mourns throughout the term of his absence, droops on her stalk, and shuts her bosom to the gloom and darkness which succeeds, nor bursts again into vigour and beauty till cheered by his all inspiring return. It is not for you, happy you, who live with liberty, live as free to indulge as to form your wishes, I say it is not for you to find tongues in the wind. It is for the imprisoned Sibella to feed on such illusions, to waft herself on the pinions of fancy beyond Mr. Valmont's barriers, within which, for the two last years, her setters have been insupportable: – for two years, except when she saw you, has she been joyless. I could talk of those two years: but then I should want also to tell you, Miss Ashburn, of the previous hours, the days, the months, the years that came, that smiled, and passed away.

I wonder if I should tire you? Surely I think not: yet I have already written much, and I have also my uncle's words to deliver. —— Ah! to quit such a theme for my uncle!

I told you, Mr. Valmont silenced me by his frowns. He was some time silent himself. He took the letter from off the table, and appeared to read parts of it at length he said, 'Miss Ashburn has very properly apologised for her behaviour to me the morning she went hence. Doubtless, child, you also were much disappointed, that I did not consent to your going with her and her mother.'

'No, sir.'

'No!' my uncle said, seemingly surprised; 'and why not?'

'Because I did not expect you would suffer me to go.'

'Methinks it was a mighty natural expectation.' My uncle looked angry. He presently added. 'Did you wish to go with them, child?'

'O yes, sir, I did indeed wish!'

'It was natural enough, Sibella, that you should wish for such an indulgence;' and he said this very mildly: but I alone am capable of judging of its propriety. Miss Ashburn, I believe, has been little used to disappointment. I pity her. Perhaps a miserable old age is in store for her.'

'Impossible!' I exclaimed; but the exclamation was swift and low; and my uncle, absorbed in contemplating his own designs, did not hear me.

And at last he told me, after many pauses, many slow speeches, that you may write letters to me, and that I shall write letters to you.

I would have kissed him, for I had seized his hand, but his eye spoke no encouragement; and I sat down again to glow, and to tremble.

Part of what followed has escaped me, as I feared it would. I remember that my uncle said, 'Tell Miss Ashburn from me, Sibella, that, like all other females, she has decided with more haste than judgment.'

Thus much for Mr. Valmont. And now for myself, Miss Ashburn; – no, dear Caroline, adieu!

SIBELLA VALMONT

LETTER III

FROM CAROLINE ASHBURN

TO

SIBELLA VALMONT

Thankful to Mr. Valmont for his consent to my request, and more and more endeared to you, my Sibella, by the joy with which you receive his consent, I am impatient till I have explained the motives that withheld me, while in the woods of Valmont, from saying – '*I love you: – I love you, Sibella, with all my soul.*' To have these motives fully understood by you, it is necessary I should made a sketch of my education, the incidents of my life, and their consequent effect upon my character. Yet I know you will continue to read with avidity. Ask yourself if the ear of affection is easily satiated with the communications of a friend, and wonder that you should have repressed your wishes, when they incited you to unfold to me, with minute attention, the feelings of your heart. The breaks, the allusions in your letter, led me for a time into the tormenting and silly practice of forming conjectures. Now I have ceased to conjecture; but I have not ceased to be desirous of being admitted to your utmost confidence, to the full participation of your remembrances, whether of joy or of sorrow.

You have seen my mother, Sibella, but people of a superior class must have superior forms; and the endearing name of mother is banished for the cold title of ceremony. Mrs. Ashburn, as I am now tutored to call her, was the very fashionable daughter of very fashionable parents, who died when she had attained the age of twenty-three, and left her in possession of the most aspiring longings after splendor and dissipation, but destitute of every means for their gratification. Among the many friends who came to pity or advise, one offered her his assistance. His proposal was abrupt and disgusting, but there was no alternative. He would equip her to go in search of a wealthy marriage among the luxurious inhabitants of India; or, with her other professing friends, he would leave her to the poverty which lay immediately before her. The offer, after little deliberation, was accepted. Rather than be poor, she humbled the pride of her birth and pretensions; she strengthened her nerves for the voyage; and, having safely arrived in India, her recommendations, but above all her personal charms, secured her the addresses of Mr. Ashburn, who, though he was neither young nor attractive, had gold and diamonds in abundance. A very short interval elapsed between the commencement of their acquaintance with each other, and the celebration of their marriage.

After my birth my father bowed to no other idol than me; for, although my father had gained a very handsome wife, and my mother almost the wealthiest of husbands, yet happiness was still at a distance from them. Indolent in the extreme, he abhorred every species of pleasure which required a portion of activity in its pursuit: he equally abhorred solitude; and expected to find, in his wife, a lounging companion; a partaker of his habits; something little differing from a mere automaton. She, on the contrary, was laborious in the pursuits of pleasure and dissipation. She had pride and spirit to maintain her resolution of gratifying her own wishes. He was too idle to remonstrate: and theirs was an union as widely removed from the interruptions of bickerings and jealousies, as from the confidence, esteem, and endearments of affection.

From me then my father expected to gain the satisfaction his marriage had failed to afford; nor were his hopes better founded than heretofore. Admired, adored by him, flattered by his slaves, incited by indulgencies showered upon me without distinction to make demands the most extravagant and unattainable, I oftener tormented my father by my caprice than delighted him by my fondness. But still every species of advice or of restraint was withheld; and I continued fruitful in expedients for the exercise of my power, continued the discontented slave of my own tyranny. Happily for me, I met with an adventure when I was little more than thirteen years of age that wrought miracles upon me.

Near to a seat of my father's, as near as the cottage of poverty dare rise to the palace of opulence, lived the wife and family of a poor industrious European. The blue eyes of one of their children had spoken so submissively once or twice, as she viewed me passing, that I became enamoured of her interesting countenance, and demanded to have her for a playmate. Day after day Nancy came, and my fondness for her increased daily. If the turbulence of my temper sometimes broke loose in the course of our amusements, I afterward endeavoured, by increased efforts of condescension, to relieve Nancy from the terror my pride or violence had excited; and, to impress her with a strong sense of my attachment to herself, in her presence I affected to be more than commonly overbearing and insolent to those around us, while to her I was attentive and obliging. At length I became resolved to have her wholly at my command; and, without troubling myself to enquire whether or not my father would object to my plan, I rose earlier than usual one morning, and dispatched a messenger for Nancy; and, while he was absent, pleased myself with anticipating what answers she would make, and what joy she would evince, when I should tell her that henceforward she should live with me, and should have as fine cloaths, as fine apartments, and as many slaves to obey her as I myself possessed. My messenger returned alone. He told me Nancy was ill. What a disappointment! How insolent, methought, to be ill, when I wanted her more than I had ever wanted her before. And so much did she appear to merit my resentment, that I gave orders she should be forbidden to see me again, and that all the valuable trinkets I had heaped upon her should be taken from her by force, if she would not yield them when demanded. But no sooner were the toys brought into my presence than I relented, sent them back with many additions, and wept while I delivered messages, intreating - that she would be well by the next day. On the morrow, still no Nancy came; and I passed the day in alternate paroxisms of rage and sorrow. The third morning I hastened to the cottage; and the first object I beheld was Nancy blooming as health could make her.

The insolence with which I reproached the mother of Nancy on this occasion may be easily imagined; but I shall relate minutely to you, Sibella, the good woman's answer; I have never forgotten it.

'Miss,' she said, 'I might as well have told the truth at once, for out it must. Nancy is not sick in body, Miss; and if I can help it, she shan't be sick in mind. Your papa is a great rich man, and you will be a great rich lady. You, Miss, who are so high born and so rich, need not care if people do hate you; but my Nancy is a poor child, and will never have a penny that an't of her own earning – she never used to fleer, and flout, and stamp at her little brothers and sisters, as she does since she came to your house, Miss. And so, Miss, as she will never be able to pay folks for saying she is good when she is bad,

I, who am her mother, must make her as good as I can. You may be good enough for a great lady; but Nancy will never be a great lady; and, be as angry as you will, Miss, indeed she can't come to your fine house any more.'

Yes, Sibella; she persisted, in defiance of my resentment and its probable consequences, the worthy woman persisted in preserving her child from the infectious example of my vices. Her lesson had awakened in my mind a true sense of my situation; nor could anger or disdain once force me from the painful conviction that people were hired and paid to lavish on me their insincere encomiums. All the instances of attention or kindness I could recollect I believed had been mine only because I was rich and powerful. I imagined I saw lurking hatred and loathing in every eye; and, though I ceased to command, I resented with an acrimony almost past description every effort that was directed towards increasing my pleasures or convenience. These ebulitions of a wounded vanity insensibly wore away, while I considered how much of amendment and happiness was yet in my power; and, at length, I began seriously to remedy the defects which had made me unworthy to be the companion of Nancy; but, ere I had courage to demand again the society of my little friend, her parents had removed to a distant part of the country, and in this instance frustrated the end of my labours. Yet the labour itself had become delightful, and was amply rewarded by the satisfaction betrayed in the eyes of my numerous attendants; but who, however, as I was a great lady and a rich lady, durst not openly rejoice in my amendment. I longed to hear them burst into praises. I almost sickened for the accents of well-earned commendation; but shame of my former unworthiness, and perhaps a remaining degree of pride, withheld me from encouraging such an explanation: and they continued silently to receive the benefits of my reformation.

And now, Sibella, I must bring you back again to my mother, with whom in these years of childhood I have been but little acquainted. She hated children; their noise and prattle and monkey tricks threw her into hysterics. For a few minutes after dinner, I was sometimes admitted, hushed to silence with a profusion of sweetmeats, and dismissed with a kiss or a frown, just as the avocations and pleasures of the day happened to fix her disposition. As I grew older, I was occasionally allowed to sit in her dressingroom, or to take the air with her in the same carriage; and on those occasions I reached the highest pinnacle of her confidence, and used to listen while she poured forth her longing desires to return to England. As I had been frequently disgusted at witnessing the malignant feuds existing among the Europeans resident in the East-Indies, it was easy for her to interest me in the first of her wishes, namely, that my father would return to England. She spoke of this island as of the abode of pleasure. She described an almost innumerable circle of friends, amidst whose society delights would abound. My imagination gave a stronger colouring to her pictures: I indulged the visionary theme till I also panted to become an inhabitant of this climate of peace, joy and felicity.

No sooner had I adopted the project than my father's lethargic indolence gave way to his desire of gratifying my wishes. He vigorously completed the necessary arrangement of his affairs; and we were in daily expectation of quitting India, when he was attacked by the malignant disease of which he died.

My mother was now the uncontrouled mistress of a world of wealth; and, placing her remittances in a proper train, we speedily set sail for our land of promise.

Safely arrived in London, I expected Mrs. Ashburn would instantly fly to the embraces of her friends. But no: a sumptuous house and equipage were first to be prepared; and, while she exulted in preparation, I repined at her want of sympathy for the feelings of those who I imagined were expecting her with fondness and impatience. Alas, Sibella, I had not followed my mother three times into her circles of friendship, ere I discovered that the enjoyments she had looked forward to, during so many years, consisted only of triumphing with superiority of splendor over those who formerly with the same motives had triumphed over her.

Here my enthusiasm in the search of sincere and uniform friendship would have been extinguished; but that my hopes yet rested on Mrs. Valmont. Of Mrs. Valmont my mother had spoken as playmate, schoolmate, and the confidant of juvenile secrets. Separated, said I to myself, near twenty years, what emotions must a first interview produce! The fire of youth in Mrs. Valmont and Mrs. Ashburn will be, for some moments, renewed; and I shall anticipate the effusions of my own heart when it finds a friend.

After exhibiting our pomp at every place of resort in the metropolis, we began our tour; and passed by several invitations to pay our first visit at Valmont castle. What a freezing sensation crept in my veins, as we waited for the raising of your uncle's draw-bridges, as we rolled along his dark avenues! Such gloom, such menacing grandeur brought into my mind a feeling totally opposite to the hilarity, the glow of expectation I had cherished on the journey. Many persons had spoken in my hearing of Mr. Valmont as the most absurd ridiculous misanthrope of his age; but I had not the highest respect for the authorities from which the information was derived, and I had also conceived with much more fancy than judgment of the delights of a life of solitude. I, in my dream, had forgotten the name of Castle, and the ideas associating with the name; my imagination in its reveries had blended elegance and simplicity, nature and art with their most fascinating productions; when, instead of smiling lawns and gay parterres, without, I found moats, walls, and drawbridges, frowning battlements that looked as uninviting on the friend as threatening on the enemy, turrets all cheerless, all hostile, and discouraging to the wandering stranger. The castle's Gothic magnificence within reminded us at every step of the dignity of the Valmont race; the apartments received their guests without welcome; the domestics were obedient, but neither chearful nor attentive. Through carved saloons and arched galleries, into which the bright sun of spring can only cast an oblique ray, we were conducted to Mrs. Valmont's dressing-room.

My Sibella, can you not imagine, you hear your aunt mingling complaint and compliment, langour and restlessness, and labouring to interest real sensibility by moans of imaginary disease? Can you not imagine my mother secretly urging her triumphs over the immured Mrs. Valmont, by lamenting the slavery of pleasure to which she herself is perpetually compelled? And can you not see your disappointed, disgusted Caroline Ashburn viewing caresses without warmth, hearkening to professions without sincerity?

Your uncle entered the room for a moment. Appearing to act, to speak, to look according to some rule settled for the hour, I deemed his character too much assumed to be quickly understood. From the solemn pride which sat on his brow, I judged, however, that he was fitted for his castle, and his castle fitted for him.

Here, thought I, in this place and with these people have we promised to remain for seven long days; and I quitted Mrs. Valmont's dressing-room, to search for amusement and variety in the park and surrounding woods.

I must have been devoid of taste and feeling, if in viewing the exquisite scenery of the park, I had not forgotten the gloomy entrance and the dreary building. I found a seat on the margin of that fine sheet of water which is skirted by *your* majestic wood; and I rested there till twilight began to spread itself over the horizon. Who would not, Sibella, although evening had cast its misty shade over the tall trees and impressed an awful serenity on every surrounding object, who who would not, I say, like me have ventured into the wood rather than have returned to Mr. and Mrs. Valmont and their castle. I found the paths so admirably contrived in their breaks and windings, that I could not forbid myself to proceed. Every now and then I had an imperfect view of something dark, rugged, and mountainous. On a sudden, I caught a glimpse of a rude pile of stones, seemingly carried to a tremendous height, which as suddenly vanished from my fight, amidst the intercepting branches; a few steps further, it was again before me as a wild ruin tottering on the projecting point of a rock. Silence, solitude, the twilight, the objects filled my mind with a species of melancholy. Fancy had become more predominant than judgment. I slackened my pace: I breathed heavily: when, suddenly turning into a new path that I expected would bring me to the foot of the rock, I beheld a female form, cloathed in white, seated at the foot of a large oak. Her hair, unrestrained by either hat or cap, entirely shaded her face as she bowed her head to look on a little fawn, who in the attitude of confidence and affection was laying across her lap.

The names of Wood Nymph, Dryad and Hymadriad, with a confused number of images, arose in my memory; and I was on the point of reverently retreating, but a moment's pause prevented the romance of the fence from thus imposing on my reason, and I resolved to examine whether the face like the form bespoke more of divinity than of mortal.

As I approached nearer, away bounded the fawn – up sprang the nymph. Again, Sibella, I stood still, unknowing whether to fall at your feet or to clasp you in my arms.

Such was our first romantic interview. There was something wild in your air; your language was simple and concise, yet delivered with an impressive eloquence, and I thought you altogether a phenomenon. My heart could not help partaking the transport with which you received my promise of staying with you in the wood. Yet it was to me incomprehensible how you could talk so familiarly of roaming in woods at night, without seeming to know any thing of the ideas of loneliness and apprehension generally supposed to belong to such situations.

But my habits would not so suddenly yield to your's. You saw that the damp and darkness affected me, and you instantly led the way to the castle: but you became silent: you sighed: you walked at a greater distance from me: and I began to fear lest you could only submit to be pleased in your own way. The instant we entered the outer court of the castle you seized my hand; and, having pressed it forcibly to your bosom, you darted through a small side door in the building, and closed it after you. I was going to follow – 'This way, if you please, madam,' said the servant who had been sent to search for me in the park. 'I will accompany Miss Valmont,' said I. 'Miss Valmont does not see company, madam,' replied the man, 'her uncle does not permit it.'

I suffered myself to be conducted to the supper room, where I related the manner of our meeting, the information you had given me of your relationship to Mr. Valmont; and finally I spoke of the singular way in which you had quitted me, and expressed my surprise at not finding you of the supper party.

Mrs. Valmont said, you were a strange unformed child. Mr. Valmont would gladly have been silent; but, as I continually addressed myself to him, he could not rid himself, without gross rudeness, of the necessity of answering me. He spoke mysteriously of his systems, and his plans, of his authority, his wisdom, and your dependence, of his right of chusing for you, and your positive duty of obeying him without reserve or discussion. At last, with tones and gestures, by which I was to understand that he went to the extreme of condescension in my favour, he consented that, provided no other company came to visit him in the time, you should associate with us while we remained at Valmont castle.

Your very extraordinary seclusion and your extraordinary self, occupied my mind during the greatest part of that night. I had found you highly interesting; and I believed you to be infinitely amiable. I thought I might embrace you as the first choice of my affections; but I doubted whether you might not, if now exposed to the glitter of the world, lose that vigour of feeling which in solitude made you appear so singular, so attractive. I longed to make the experiment, for my hopes of you were stronger than my fears; and, as I had so far prevailed on Mr. Valmont, I flattered myself I should also prevail on him to suffer me to conduct you from the castle. And these were the motives, this the expectation, dearest Sibella, that withheld me from confessing in Valmont woods – *that I loved you with all my soul.*

The seven days I remained at the castle I forbore, although with difficulty, to ask you questions, that I might gradually develope your character, as surrounding circumstances should operate on your feelings. Sometimes, I saw you devoted to me; sometimes, I saw your imagination soaring as it were beyond the bounds prescribed to your person, in search of a remoter object. Why, dear Sibella, are you so pensive? Why do you gaze on that portrait of yourself with so much earnestness? And why do you caress that little fawn, who wears a collar inscribed with the initials – C.M. – till your eyes fill with tears?

Let me be the partaker of your unrestrained emotions; while I, who have a wider range of observation, will place my opinions before you without check or limit. Our next resting place is to be the seat of a nabob: Sir Thomas Barlowe's, amongst whose laboured pleasures I shall wish to return to gloomy Valmont, where I found a felicity of which I have no promise in the scenes I am now destined to partake. Adieu! adieu!

                                        CAROLINE ASHBURN

LETTER IV

FROM SIBELLA VALMONT

TO

CAROLINE ASHBURN

Was I pensive, did I gaze, did I sigh, did I weep, when you Miss Ashburn were with me – what do I know when I have only for companion the faithful, the exquisite, but torturing representation of memory? Can I do more than gaze, and sigh, and weep? O yes, I can: for, Miss Ashburn, I can raise altars on a thousand spots in these woods, which were once hallowed by the footsteps of him I love!

Two years have elapsed since he bade me farewel: therefore did you see me pensive.

That picture of me was painted by himself: therefore do I gaze on it.

The fawn he took from a dying mother; by him she was nourished into familiarity. Nina has ceased to mourn the absence of her benefactor; she is satisfied with my caresses; but the heart of Sibella Valmont, nor now, nor ever, can find any substitute for her Clement Montgomery.

I was nearly six years old when they told me that I had lost my father. He had travelled a twelvemonth before to foreign countries, for the benefit of his health; and I knew not that his death more than his absence would deprive me of my happiness, till my uncle Valmont came and carried me away in his coach from my governess, my maid, and all the domestics who loved me and whom I loved, of my father's household.

Then, indeed, I mourned; and my uncle attempted to soothe me. He said, I must be happy, for I was now dependent upon him; and it was my duty to love him, obey him, and be satisfied. My swelling heart revolted against being commanded to be happy; and I found not one person at the Castle who could supply to me the want of my kind governess and kind maid, except a little dog that on my first entrance had fawned on me as if he wished to make me happier. Him I carried incessantly in my arms; and I told him, whenever we were alone, how I longed to get back to my father's house and to carry him along with me.

In a fortnight after I arrived at Valmont, the affectionate little animal died; and I remained inconsoleable. I was sitting weeping on the hall steps when my uncle came to me. He wiped away my tears; bade me be chearful; and said he had procured me a better playfellow than Fidelle. My uncle led me with him into the library; and presented me to a boy three years older than myself, blooming, blushing, beautiful. 'Clement is my adopted son, Sibella,' said my uncle. He will henceforth live with you in the castle. Take him out child; and shew him where you find the prettiest flowers and the ripest fruit.'

Ah! need I tell you how we advanced from shyness to familiarity, from familiarity to kindness, from kindness to love, all powerful, all potent! The castle then seemed no prison; the moat seemed no barrier. Sometimes my uncle carried Clement abroad to visit him, but then I was sure of his return. Even the hours of instruction I shared with him. He had a good, an amiable tutor, who delighted in teaching to me also every science he taught to Clement; and if Mr. Valmont frowned upon me or checked my industry, Clement was still at my side and I smiled through my tears.

Thus passed away the years from six till sixteen. On the day that I became sixteen, we had run races with our little fawn; and, having wearied ourselves with exertion, we had lain down to rest in each other's arms, at the foot of that oak where you, Miss Ashburn, first beheld me. My uncle broke our happy slumbers. He came to the oak; and sternly commanded Clement to rise and follow him.

I followed too. My uncle sat down in his library; and appeared to meditate; while we looked on each other with love and pity, and on him we looked with suspicion and affright.

When my uncle began to speak, Clement trembled; but all my emotions were chained up in astonishment: for I heard him say that Clement should that day quit the castle, that he should seek new companions, new countries, new climates.

'Never! never!' I cried. I folded my arms round my lover – 'Thou shalt not go, Clement,' I said. 'We have world enough. No: thou shalt not go, my Clement!'

Mr. Valmont furiously bade me desist; but he had awakened a dread in my mind more powerful than my dread of him. For a time, I expostulated with vehemence and courage; but I could not repress my tears – and, while I was compelled to listen to my uncle, his tone, his words impressed me with my former awe of him and rendered my remonstrance timid and useless.

To Clement he said, 'You are now to leave these boyish follies, and learn the duties of a man. You shall mix with society; but remember that you are not to be attracted by its specious appearances. Scrutinize into its follies and enormities, as I have done; and let my precepts and instructions be your guide and law. Remember, Clement, that I took you from poverty and obscurity. Remember too that, on your duty and gratitude depends your security. That child,' he pointed to me, 'mind me, sir, that child is in future to be considered only as your sister.'

'As for you, Sibella,' he said to me, 'your duties in life are easily performed. I have chosen a part for you: and nothing is required of you but obedience. You have heard me declare to Clement, and I now repeat it to you, that to Clement Montgomery you are to be no more than a sister.' This day he quits us. When he shall return, I have not determined.'

Yes, Caroline, my Clement went. Two years has he roamed in a world which I am forbidden to know. But, alike in viewing the palace or the cottage, the burning mountain or the fertile plain, must the idea of Sibella accompany him. Our minds, our principles, our affections are the same; and, while I trace his never to be forgotten image within my breast, I know how fondly he cherishes the remembrance of mine.

Caroline, adieu! I go to the oak. On that consecrated spot, mountains, seas, continents dissolve, and my spirit unites with his!

SIBELLA VALMONT

LETTER V

FROM CAROLINE ASHBURN

TO

SIBELLA VALMONT

Yes, dearest Sibella, charming Sibella, in that one short but rapid sentence, you have taught me to understand your progress, *from shyness to familiarity, from familiarity to kindness, from kindness to love, all powerful, all potent.* Oh! be that love happy in its continuance, as at its commencement! Be it the pure garb of your Clement's soul, upon which vice shall leave no spot nor wrinkle! Be it, as you say, That *your hearts, your affections, your principles are the same*; and I would trust this lover amidst allurements such as virtue held seldom rejected, had seldom turned from without contamination.

Your uncle, my Sibella, I perceive, intended you for your lover, and your lover for you. His project, then, was to place a second Adam and Eve in the garden of Eden. Well, Sibella, innocence remains with you. Your Eden will yet bloom; for, trust me, innocence and happiness cannot long be separated.

Why will that uncle of your's so strenuously uphold his mysterious reserve and silence? I long to ask him a million of questions; and he knows that I do, and he wishes that I should. It is not because he is altogether convinced of the wisdom and utility of his plans, that he does plan; it is, that he will oppose himself to general customs and general experience. It is singularity and not perfection that he is in search of; and, since experience formerly taught him, that even the renowned name of Valmont might mix undistinguished with a herd of less illustrious names, he now bravely resolves to enforce the wonder of his compeers, if he cannot claim their reverence.

Perhaps, with the flattering promises of success, he sometimes soothes the rancour of his solitude. And occasionally, indeed, his existence is remembered, and his whimsies are made the subject of ridicule, contempt, and laughter; but some novel circumstance, such as the gay Mrs. Ashburne's visit to his gloomy retirement, must call them into this remembrance, or the name of Mr. Valmont would rest as undisturbed as does, in every memory but his own, the deeds of his forefathers.

It is to my mother's excursion to Valmont castle, that I owe the felicity of calling you my friend, it is to her escape from thence, as she herself terms it, that I owe my knowledge of Mr. Valmont's history. Surrounded, on her arrival at the house of Sir Thomas Barlowe, by a crowd of visitors, as gay, profuse, and dissipated as herself, she hastens to communicate her joy at the agreeable change, and to inveigh against the morose Mr. Valmont and his insipid wife. A conversation ensued of some length for such a subject, during which I discovered that two of the party, the Earl of Ulson and Colonel Ridson were once the intimate companions of Mr. Valmont. The former of these gentlemen appeared eager to place his defects in the strongest point of view; while the latter, with less zeal, to be sure, but with a sweetness of temper infinitely endearing, was willing to smooth the rugged parts of Mr. Valmont's character, and to place a vice behind the glare of a virtue. By setting aside, to the best of my judgment, the Earl's exaggerations, and making also some allowance for the palliative temper of Colonel Ridson, I had succeeded in learning as much of Mr. Valmont's history as enables me to form some, and I believe no inaccurate estimate of his worth, abilities, and character.

Your grandfather, Sibella, a being quite as eccentric tho' lets whimsical than your uncle, lived in the castle you now inhabit. Nor would he, of his own free will, have quitted that castle for heaven itself. Every stone of the building that had kept its station in times of turbulence and discord against the attack of an enemy was to him an idol. If he was thoughtful, it was in recalling the great deeds of his ancestors; if he was talkative, it was on the same theme; if he had wishes, they were that he had lived in those glorious days when fighting well was the most eminent of virtues, and a strong fortified castle and obedient vassals the most valuable of possessions.

As is the established practice in families of such renown and dignity, as that to which you, my friend, appertain, the first born son of your grandfather was the only hope, the only joy, the only object of the careful solitude of his anxious parents; while your father, coming into the world two years after his brother, was adored, flattered and spoiled by no creature but his nurse. Your uncle, I understand, received a stately kind of education within the castle walls; and your father, happier because of less consequence, passed his early years with other young men of fashion at school and at college.

Mr. Valmont was not a whit behind his father in his veneration for high birth, but he could not boast so unqualified a love of fruits of armour; nor did he think that civil war was the only time when a man could gather honours worthy of a distinguished name. No sooner was your uncle emancipated from the fetters of his minority, than he resolved to repair to court, where he expected to find only his equals, and those equals alive to and exact in the observance of all that haughty decorum, which Mr. Valmont deemed indispensably necessary to the well being of social institutions. Poor man! he feels himself lost in the motly multitude, sees his high-born pretensions to notice and deference pushed aside by individuals obscure in their origin, but renowned for artful intrigues, for bold perseverance, and dazzling success! Shocked at the contaminating mixture, he had fled back with precipitancy to his castle, but love detained him, for he had made an offering of his heart to a woman of rank and fashion. Nothing could be more unfortunate than this passion. Nothing further from congeniality than the minds and manners of Lady Margaret B—— and Mr. Valmont: he, just risen, as it were, from the tomb of his progenitors, loaded with the punctilio of the last age, recoiling from the salute of every man who could not boast an unblemished pedigree, and lastly, and most worthily, possessing refined ideas of female delicacy, of honourable love, and of unchanging fidelity; and she, on the contrary, a graceful coquette, without an atom of real tenderness in her heart, and valuing her rank merely as it gave her opportunities of extending her conquest. Lady Margaret B—— was highly diverted with Mr. Valmont's formalities; and, in spite of the torture her dissipated coquettish manners inflicted on him, she had sufficient power to make him the most ardent of her lovers. In fine, she rejected him, laughed at him, despised him.

I could not hear this anecdote, nor can I repeat it, without a sensation of pain, so strongly do I enter into the irritable feelings of your uncle, when, hitherto accustomed only to receive homage and obedience, he is at once foiled in his ambition by low born courtiers, and betrayed in his love by a high born jilt.

Mr. Valmont consulted no other guide than his passions; and instantly drew an angry and false picture of mankind. With such people as I have spoken of he could not associate; for their vices he abhorred; but his mind had not fortitude enough, had not comprehension enough, to cast aside his own prejudices; and, instead of attempting to reform mankind, he retires to rail at them; and carries with him the pride, selfishness, and love of power, in which all the vices of society originate.

Wrapped in the impenetrable selfishness of high birth, Mr. Valmont denies the possibility of eminent virtue existing without rank. Who shall presume to arraign his principles, to sit in judgment upon his actions, to teach him his duty? I stand, cries Mr. Valmont, within the sacred verge of nobility! Look on that coat of arms! I derive from the Normans! Wisdom in rags – keep off!

True: his ancestors conquered, that he should be wise! – Oh, cede to him the palm! Bind his brows with the laurel!

After a few months retirement, Mr. Valmont ventured once more into the heterogeneous multitude, in search of a wife: for, I suspect he found himself as ill qualified for solitude as society. Beside, he had formed the virtuous project of instructing a new race, to put the old world out of countenance.

I cannot but pause, to reflect upon your uncle's toils in search of his help mate. He must have a wife, whose pedigree his future sons might place beside his own; and he must have one, of a temperament and character opposite to that of lady Margaret B——; and his good stars, his ill stars, or whatever else you please, led him to the feet of Mrs. Valmont.

It is true, your aunt was neither as coquettish nor had she the sprightly wit nor the mischievous gaiety of lady Margaret, but she loved crouds, detested solitude, and was a votary of dissipation; to convince her how much he had studied her inclinations, and how much he meant to gratify them, no sooner was Mr. Valmont in possession of his bride then he snatched her from the scenes where her existence was alone valuable to her, and buried her amidst obscurity and horror at Valmont castle.

What is the consequence? she had no mental accomplishments in reserve for their mutual benefit and delight; nor had he mind enough to steal fire from heaven and animate with life the marble. From the struggle of tempers, and the warfare of words, she droops into an hypocondriac; he degenerates into a cynic, proud of himself alone.

Among the disappointments produced by this marriage, the want of children was the most offensive to Mr. Valmont. Your father, who had pursued a course of life quite different from his brother, tasting all the excesses of dissipation; died; and, very improperly in my opinion, left you to the guardianship of your uncle. That Mr. Valmont should adopt a son from the lowly condition of a cottager's child, has occasioned much wonder and many surmises; however, as I do not find any thing material either to you or me in the conjectures, I have listened to on this occasion, I shall not be at the pains of relating them.

But how comes it to pass, my dearest Sibella, that when your uncle had the means of gratifying his darling wish in educating two children, and one of them a female, to whom according to his creed, nothing should be granted beyond what the instinct of appetite demands, how comes it, I say, that you possess the comprehensive powers of intellect? from what sources did you derive that eager desire of knowledge of which I find you possessed; and how came you to be learned on subjects, which, in the education of females, are strictly with-held, to make room for trifling gaudy and useless acomplishments? tell me by what miracle I find you such as you are, and let me cease to wonder at you, but never let me cease to love you.

Tell me too, how came you to be dependant on your uncle? Does your dependance only mean the protection due from him who stands in the place of a parent to you? I wish to be informed what explanation Mr. Valmont and yourself affix to the term of dependant, when it is applied to you; for colonel Ridson talks so familiarly of the fortune you must possess from your mother, and also the wealth of the Valmont family which he says is yours by heirship, that I must own I am puzzled. I care little about your being rich, but is seems unnatural and unjust to have you a dependant on your haughty uncle.

Ah, my dear Sibella, how often in a day do I feast my imagination by allowing it to bear me back to you; and yet perhaps, our separation gives a spur, a stimulus to our friendship. I am not convinced, indeed, but that temporary separations are even useful between lovers; and that Mr. Valmont may have acted rather wisely than otherwise, in parting you and your Clement for a season. Why he should bid you remember him only as a brother, is really too far plunged into obscurity for me to discover.

Do not, however, suppose for an instant that my affection for you would decay were I at liberty to enjoy your society as I wish; on the contrary, I am persuaded that every hour I should pass with you would add something to my improvement, and render us more valuable to each other. My expression arose from my being at that moment in idea a partner of your seclusion, and feeling that I should want in the same situation that energy and activity which is the support of your solitude. I am fond of society; and, indeed, I find myself most excited when I have most opportunities of observing the various characters and pursuits of those around me. Gladly would I possess the power of selecting my society. From that happy privilege I am debarred. But I seldom make one of a circle in which I do not find some novelty of character, and something either of excellence or absurdity from which I may draw improvement.

Yet, a two month's visit at the villa of Sir Thomas Barlowe is rather a hard trial of my patience; and, unless we are enlivened by new visitors, I fear the company here will afford me but a trifling harvest of observation. I shall soon be glad to turn from them to my own resources; and fly, even oftener than I now do, to the ever vivifying remembrance of my Sibella.

Sir Thomas Barlow has risen from some very obscure station to the wealth and dignity of a nabob. He has risen too, I greatly fear, by the same depredating practices which the unfortunate natives of India seem destined constantly to suffer from those who perfidiously call themselves the protectors of the country. Sir Thomas Barlow's riches have become his punishment. Each morning, his fears awaken with his faculties, lest that day should bring tidings of the dreaded scrutiny; and, when evening arrives, and he struggles to yield himself to mirth and wine amidst the circle he has assiduously gathered round him, a word, a look, or the most remote hint or allusion gives his watchful terrors an alarm. A sudden turn of his head, perchance, discovers his shadow on the wall. Legions of threatening phantoms then crowd upon his apprehension; and the evening, yet more miserable than the day, concludes with an opiate, administered to lull the feeble body into lethargy, and hush the perturbed conscience into silence.

And my mother can look on this existing fact with indifference, while I shudder. Those enormous sums of wealth she lavishes away, that cluster of pearls she triumphantly places in her hair, those diamonds heaped into different ornaments, how were they obtained? Thousands perhaps——Oh, Sibella! I have laid aside my ornaments! A dress plain as your's supersedes them.

Lady Barlowe is a composition of a very curious kind. She is about forty years younger than her husband, is tolerably pretty, and has a shewy talent of repartee that she mistakes for a sublime genius; and her inclinations are perpetually at warfare, without being able to decide whether she shall be most renowned as a wit or a beauty. She is extravagantly fond of admiration, which she formerly enjoyed unlimitedly, being the head toast of a small county town, till she became the wife of a nabob. Prosperity has not increased her happiness; for in the great and gay world she has found rivals of such magnitude that malice and envy have strung up within that bosom which till now owned no inmate but vanity.

These are our host and hostess. The first in precedency among the visitors ranks the Earl of Ulson: an antiquated gallant, who, in public, affects not to feel the approaches of age; and, in private, broods over the consciousness of its effects till he sickens with ill nature. The countess of Ulson hates her husband; nor has she over much charity and good-will towards other men. She talks largely, indeed, of her piety, and the strict performance of her manifold duties.

This amiable pair are attended by their son and two daughters. Lord Bowden is so perfectly satisfied within himself, that, if you will take his word for it, there is not a more amiable and accomplished young man in England. His eldest sister, lady Mary Bowden claims no praise beyond what is justly due to the complacency of her temper; she is at once too giddy and too indolent to aim at meriting a more enlarged praise; she loves dress, company, cards, and scandal; and indulges herself in the use of the latter as a mere matter of course, without entertaining the smallest particle of ill-will towards the very persons she helps to vilify. I have endeavoured to convince lady Mary of the folly of this practice, and she acknowledges, that what I say appears very much to the purpose, but then how can she cease to do what every body does.

All the beauty that exact regularity of feature, and transparency of complexion can bestow, is in the possession of the Earl of Ulson's youngest daughter, lady Laura Bowden. Beyond this description, I hardly know what to say of her. I can perceive she entertains a very hearty contempt for her sister; and perhaps, she may hold me in as little estimation; but a woman so perfectly well bred as lady Laura does not display such sentiments if she entertains them, unless some species of rivalship should unfortunately call her passions into action. I do not think her either witty or wise, yet I have been told she bears the reputation of the former, and is poet enough occasionally to pen a rebus or an acrostic. It may be so. I have not been favoured with her confidence. A delicate langour pervades her manners, and this is generally honoured with the name of sensibility. I am apt to call it affectation; for the sensibility that I understand and admire, is extreme only in proportion to the greatness of the occasion; it does not waste itself in vapours, nor is it ever on the watch for wasps and spiders. Colonel Ridson assures me that Lady Laura Bowden is admired by the whole world, and that he must be the happiest of men on whom her ladyship bestows a preference.

Colonel Ridson loves his white teeth, and his epaulet. He likes every body, praises every body, is attentive to every body; lives without attachment; and will probably die in the same torpid state, without ever knowing felicity, or ordinary misfortune.

The colonel hitherto has been the only unmarried man amongst us, except Lord Bowden, who really is so assiduous in remembring his own recommendations that no one else finds it necessary to remember him or them at all.

But we are now to be enlivened. It seems we damsels are to be excited to call forth our charms, for the conquest of a youth of no common value, as his fame goes here. Sir Thomas Barlowe's nephew, Mr. Murden, arrived at the villa this very day.

I know not why I should be particularly selected from the party, by Sir Thomas Barlowe, to listen to his encomiums on this nephew. From the most insignificant occurrences, the Baronet has constantly occasion to say – 'Ha! Ha! Miss Ashburn, if my nephew Arthur was but come!' If I praised a dish of fruit at table, the nabob's nephew Arthur had certainly done the same thing. Let me speak of walking or riding, let me complain of hail, rain or sunshine, Arthur was still my promised chaperon, the future knight-errant of all my grievances.

'Tell me something,' said I one day to Colonel Ridson, 'of this Mr. Murden, this hope of the family.'

'He is very handsome,' replied the Colonel.

'But is he good?'

'Assuredly.'

'And amiable?'

'Infinitely!'

'And wise?'

'To a miracle, madam,' replied the Colonel.

Good! amiable! wise! – Who could desire more?

Lady Mary Bowden stood beside me one afternoon, while the baronet was reminding me of his dear Arthur. 'Sir Thomas I believe intends,' said I to her, 'that I shall be in love by anticipation. You know Mr. Murden. What is he?'

'Oh!' cried Lady Mary, lifting up her right hand, to enforce the spirit of her emphasis, 'he is the most abominable rake in the universe!'

I absolutely started. 'It is possible, Lady Mary, you should mean what you say?' I asked after a moment's pause. 'Yes! certainly!' replied her ladyship, quite gaily; 'every body knows of hundreds with whom he has been a very happy man.'

'I do not want, ' said I, 'to hear what every body says. I want, Lady Mary, to know your own sincere opinion of Mr. Murden. If you have already told me a fact, my situation to be sure will oblige me to be sometimes in his company; but, in that case, there exists not a reptile, however noxious or despicable, from whom I should shrink with more abhorrence than from this boasted nephew of the nabob.'

'Good God!' cried Lady Mary: 'Why! what did I say? I protest I have forgotten, already. I am sure I know no harm in the world of Mr. Murden.'

'Did not you tell me he was an abominable rake?'

'They say so,' replied Lady Mary. 'He certainly is very engaging. He admires fine women. But I don't know whether he has ever made serious addresses to any one. Miss Ashburn, I'll tell you a secret.'

'You had better not. I don't keep secrets.'

'Oh, all the world knows it, already. Lady Laura is quite fond of Murden. You would have laughed to have seen her last winter, as I did, plunged over head and ears in sentiment and sensibility. Well, I do hate affectation.'

'And you do love good nature.'

'So I do,' said she smiling; 'and I hope with all my heart that my poor sister may now secure her conquest, unless indeed, Miss Ashburn, it should interfere with you.'

Neither the baronet's hints, the colonel's all good, all wise, nor the motley dubious character given by Lady Mary Bowden of Mr. Murden, would have tempted me to devote thus much of my paper to him. I have other inducements. I have heard that the domestics of Barlowe Hall anxiously expected the day of his coming. A gardener, who has been discharged for no worse fault, I believe, than his being too old, assures himself, that the prosperity of him and his family will be restored when Mr. Murden arrives. I have heard also, that the neighbouring cottagers bless him. Such a man must have worth. Agnes, who is zealous to tell me all the good she can of any one, has related several anecdotes of Mr. Murden, from which I learn, that he possesses sympathy and benevolence. I cannot tell how such qualities can exist in the mind of a man who is, either in principle or practice, a libertine. Yet, Agnes also had been told that Mr. Murden was a libertine. I bade her enquire more; and she could hear of no particular instances wherein the peace of individuals or families had been injured by him. Still those with whom Agnes conversed, bestowed on him this hateful title. I fear the reproach may belong to him. Young men are frequently carried into these excesses, from the pernicious effect of example, sometimes from vanity, and from a variety of other causes, all which tend to one uniform effect, to destroy the understanding, deprave the heart, corrupt the disposition, and render loathsome and detestable a being that might have lived an honour and a blessing to his species. If Mr. Murden is indeed devoted to this error, farewel to his benevolent virtues, to his sense of justice; and farewel to the pleasure and instruction I might have gained in the society of a virtuous man.

I said Mr. Murden was already arrived; but I have not seen him. He paid his duty to his uncle, in the Baronet's own apartment; and he then retired to dress before he would present himself in the breakfast parlour. Lady Laura appeared impatient; she was adorned in a new morning dress, perfectly graceful and becoming. The hour came in which I was to write to my Sibella; and I would not sacrifice that employment for twenty such introductions.

Farewel, my friend! Close to your altar of love, raise one of friendship, and I also will meet you at the oak.

CAROLINE ASHBURN

LETTER VI

FROM SIBELLA VALMONT

TO

CAROLINE ASHBURN

A confused recollection sprang up in my mind when you questioned me concerning my dependence. On the day of his last departure, my father caressed me fondly; he held me a long time in his arms; and he shed tears over me. He spoke, likewise, at intervals; not, perhaps, with any expectation of being understood by me, but to relieve the weighty pressure of his thoughts. I well remember that he named my uncle. He had many papers on a table before him; and I think there was a connection in his discourse between them and me. I believe he spoke of some disposition of his fortune; but the time is now remote, and the idea is indistinct. I cannot clothe it in expression.

I do not possess a fortune; for my uncle calls me dependent, talks of obligations I owe to him for the gratification of my wants. He talks of obligations, who denies me instruction, equality, and my Clement. He provides me food and raiment. Are there not thousands in the world, where you and Clement live, who supply such wants by labour? And I too could labour. Let Mr. Valmont retire to the shelter of his canopy, and the luxury of down! I can make the tree my shade, and the moss my pillow.

Mr. Valmont calls himself my father; and *calling* himself such, he there rests satisfied. Cold in his temperament, stern from his education, he imagines kindness would be indulgence, and indulgence folly. Ever on the watch for faults, the accent of reproof mingles with his best commendations.

He demands my obedience, too! What obedience? the grateful tribute to duty, authorised by reason, and sanctioned by the affections? No. Mr. Valmont, here at least, ceases to be inconsistent. He never enlightened my understanding, nor conciliated my affections; and he demands only the obedience of a fettered slave. I am held in the bondage of slavery. And still may Mr. Valmont's power constrain the forces of this body. But where, Miss Ashburn, is the tyrant that could ever chain thought, or put fetters on the fancy?

I charge you, cease to repeat my uncle's useless prohibition, that I should remember Clement otherwise than as a brother. Let him give his barrier to the waves, arrest the strong air in its current, but dream not of placing limits to the love of Clement and Sibella!

Do I weary you with this endless topic? You read the world: I, my own heart. Imprisoned, during so many years, within the narrow boundary of this castle and its parks, the same objects eternally before me, I look with disgust from their perpetual round of succession. Nature herself, spring, summer, autumn, degenerate into sameness.

Where must I turn me then, but to the resources of my own heart? Love has enriched it; and friendship will not reject its offerings.

Yes: they are many, my Caroline; various and increasing. Shall my uncle tell me that my actions are confined to the mechanical operations of the body, that I am an imbecile creature, but a reptile of more graceful form, the half finished work of nature, and destitute of the noblest ornament of humanity? Blind to conviction, grown old in error, he would degrade me to the subordinate station he describes. He daringly asserts that I am born to the exercise of no will; to the exercise of no duties but submission; that wisdom owns me not, knows me not, could not find in me a resting place.

'Tis false, Caroline! I feel within the vivifying principle of intellectual life. My expanding faculties are nurtured by the passing hours! and want but the beams of instruction, to ripen into power and energy that would steep my present inactive life in forgetfulness.

Bonneville, when shall I cease to love thy memory, to recal thy lessons? It was thou, Bonneville, who first bade me cherish this stimulating principle; who called the powers of my mind forth from the chaos, wherewith Mr. Valmont had enveloped them. Thou, Bonneville, taught me that I make an unimpaired *one* of the vast brotherhood of human kind; that I am a being whose mistakes demand the conviction of reason, but whose mind ought not to bow down under power and prejudice.

He of whom I speak, Miss Ashburn, was chosen to be Clement's tutor. Can you conceive the sensations which swell within my breast while I recal the memory of this friend of my infancy? My friend, ere I lost Clement, ere I knew you, Caroline. Methinks I hear his voice; I see his gestures. Again, he enters the wood path. Again, I behold that countenance beautiful in age, radiant in wisdom. – He speaks. My soul hangs on his utterance. All my lesser affections fade away.

Ah, no! no! no! Bonneville is gone for ever! Clement is torn from me! You are interdicted! and I am alone in the wood path!

I hailed him by the name of father. He called me his child. He was enervated with disease. The chill damps of evening pierced him. The wintry blast shook his feeble frame. Still, would he endure the damps of evening, and tremble under the cold blast, rather than Sibella should be sunk in ignorance and sloth; for her cruel uncle had forbidden her an entrance into that apartment where Bonneville gave Clement his daily instruction.

Five days passed away, and Clement had not met his tutor in the library. Five long evenings, Clement had taken his usual rides with Mr. Valmont, yet no Bonneville had visited the oak. My mind anticipated the hour of his approach, and mourned its disappointment. My questions accumulated; I stored up demand upon demand; I recalled the subject of all our conversations; I carefully selected for another investigation, those parts which I had not fully comprehended; I arranged my doubts; and, perhaps, had never so prepared my mind for improvement, as when I heard that Bonneville was in bed, ill, dying. I flew to his apartment. Clement followed me. We saw him die. 'My father! my father!' I cried. 'You will not leave us! We are your children! Better were it that we should die with you than be left without you. My father! my father!'

Sobs and tears could not delay the inexorable moment; and my life seemed to fade from me, when I found that his lips were closed for *ever*.

Would you believe that my uncle——Yes, you would believe, for you know his haughty sternness, – but no matter, 'tis past, and ought to be forgotten.

But a few days, and not an eye save mine, wept for the absence of Bonneville. Clement was satisfied with a new tutor. The new tutor was wise, good, and kind; for Clement said so; but he strictly obeyed Mr. Valmont, and Sibella was abandoned of guide, of father.

Death, an object new, hideous, and awfully mysterious was now ever before me. Multitudes of dark perplexing ideas succeeded each other in my mind, with a rapidity which doubt and dissatisfaction created. 'Why is it?' said I to myself, 'and what cause can produce an effect so overwhelming? Throughout life, the mind invariably rules the functions of the body. It transports itself from, and returns to its abode at pleasure; it can look back on the past, or fly forward to the future; it passes all boundary of place; creates or annihilates; and soars or dives into other worlds. Yet, in one moment, its wearied tool, the body, had extinguished these omnipotent powers, and to me quenched its vast energies for ever.' I wrung my hands in bitterness, and in anguish of heart; and I called loudly on the name of my lost instructor, for I had now no instructor.

Caroline, do not expect me to speak again of Bonneville. The tumult, the perplexity returns; and no solution is at hand to soothe or to cheer me.

Seventeen days, Mr. Valmont, his steward, and their labourers have occupied my wood.

My uncle himself gave me a command not to appear there during the day. – I said, 'At night, Sir, I am I hope at liberty.'

'You are, child,' my uncle replied; and I failed not to avail myself of the privilege. On the rising ground of the broad wood path, and nearly opposite to my oak, I found the earth dug away, and preparations made, of which I could not give an explanation; but from the progress of a few days labour, a small beautiful edifice of white marble gradually rose under the shade of a clump of yew trees, whose branches were reflected on the polished surface as in a mirror.

Its structure appeared to me beautiful. I was charmed with it as a novel object. I rejoiced that it was so near my oak. But I stood utterly at a loss, when I attempted to form an opinion of its design or utility.

Perhaps when you were at the castle, you became acquainted with the defects and singularities of the two attendants whom my uncle assigned me. Andrew, almost inflexible in silence, attempts (when I put him to the trial) to explain himself by signs. While his daughter possesses not, that I could ever discover, in the smallest degree the faculty of hearing. Andrew often looks on me with affection; but Margaret, who has a most repulsive countenance and demeanour, appears, even while I endeavour to conciliate her by kind looks, to be scarcely conscious that I am in existence. With such companions intercourse is rigorously excluded. In cases of peculiar uncertainty, I sometimes venture to apply to Andrew, as I did on the morning after

I had seen the beautiful edifice in the wood path compleated. Andrew said, ''Tis a tomb.'

Shortly after, I called at Mrs. Valmont's door to inquire of her health, for she is now recovering slowly from a severe indisposition. Very unusually, she desired I might be admitted. I stood while I spoke to her, for the wood was at liberty, and I was impatient to be gone. The surprise of Andrew's concise information was new in my mind, and I began to describe the structure in the wood path. I perceived Mrs. Valmont's attendant directing strange looks and gestures to me, and I paused to ask her meaning. She positively denied the circumstance, and I proceeded. When I mentioned the name of *tomb*, Mrs. Valmont started forward on the couch where she sat. 'Raised a tomb!' cried she. 'For whom?' And then, again falling back in seeming agony, she added without waiting for my reply, 'Yes, I know it well, he has opened a tomb for me.'

'For you, madam?' I said, 'you are not yet dead.'

'Barbarian!' exclaimed Mrs. Valmont, looking fiercely on me, 'not yet dead! – Insolent! – Be gone, I shall be dead but too soon. Be gone, I say, the very sight of any of your hated infidel race destroys me.'

I wished to understand how Mrs. Valmont's anger and agitations were thus excited, for she began to utter strange assertions, that my uncle intended to murder her, and that he had made me his instrument. She groaned and wept.. One of her attendants urged me to withdraw; and I complied. From thence, I visited the tomb. Again I admired its structure and its situation; but I could not devise why a receptacle for the dead should be reared amidst the living.

At this time Mr. Valmont himself, followed by his steward and by Andrew, came to inspect the tomb. Methought he looked pleased, when he saw me resting upon it. He viewed it round and round, walked to the foot of the rock, and contemplated it at that distance. Mr. Ross did the same, but Andrew stood still some yards on the other side. My uncle spoke thus at intervals.

'No doubt strange reports will circulate, throughout the neighbour-hood, of this monument.'

'The vulgar fools, who lend so ready a belief to the ridiculous tales of that Ruin, will now have another hinge on which to turn their credulity.'

'Sibella, take again the attitude I saw you in when I entered the wood. There, child; keep that posture a short time, your figure improves the scene.'

'Does the monument excite much wonder, Ross?'

'It does indeed, Sir,' the steward replied. 'They wonder at the expence, they wonder more at the object; and, still more than that, they wonder at the unconsecrated ground.'

'And my impiety is, I imagine, the topic of the country.' The steward remained silent. 'Andrew remember my orders, and repeat them to your fellows: I will have no idle tales fabricated in the servant's hall.'

'What are the opinions of other men, concerning holy and unholy, to me? It belongs to men of rank to spurn the prejudices of the multitude.'

Shortly after, my uncle addressed himself to me.

'A strange message, child, has been sent me from Mrs. Valmont, which you it seems have caused. What have you been saying to her?'

I repeated the conversation. My uncle smiled in scorn.

'Contemptible folly!' said he, 'The vicinity of a tomb becomes a mortal disease. It is hard to judge whether the understanding or the frame of such animals is of the weaker texture. Child, you have killed your aunt, by reminding her that she may one day happen to be buried.'

I was startled with the phrase of, *I had killed my aunt*; and I began eagerly to speak. My uncle interrupted me with saying:

'There is no real harm done, child. These nervous affections are tremendous in representation, but trifling in reality. You will, however, do well to remember, that I do not approve of your frequenting Mrs. Valmont's apartments.'

My uncle then left me, not quite satisfied with myself nor with his representation of Mrs. Valmont's case. Yet, on a careful review of the past, I did not feel that my words, my manner, or my information could justly tend to produce uneasiness either to her or me. Yet Mrs. Valmont persists in holding me culpable; and has twice rejected the messages I have sent by Andrew.

Still, Caroline, I do not understand why my uncle should have expended money to rear a marble tomb, when any spot of waste ground might serve for the receptacle of a lifeless body; nor can I understand how Mrs. Valmont is injured by the knowledge of the circumstance. My uncle's conversation with Mr. Ross is for the most part beyond my comprehension. I observe too, that every part of the family, more carefully even than before, now shun the wood. Last night, when Nina and I had held our evening converse at the oak, till the moon shone at her height, Andrew came in search of me; he stood at an unusual distance; and, having beckoned me to return, he with a soft quick step, hastened before me to the castle.

Thus, dearest Caroline, I pass from the weight of a tedious uniformity, to view and wonder at the mysterious actions of mysterious people. Oh, speak to me then, my friend. You I can understand. You I love, admire, revere. Speak to me often, Caroline. Bring the varieties of your life before me. Awaken my feelings with your's, and let my judgement strengthen in your experience.

SIBELLA VALMONT

LETTER VII

FROM CAROLINE ASHBURN

TO

SIBELLA VALMONT

My dearest Sibella,

To all that I yet know of you, I give unmixed praise. Your own rectitude, your own discernment, and your reliance on my sincerity, satisfies you of this truth; and I am assured that I have your sanction when I speak less of yourself than of frailer mortals.

On casting my eye over the foregoing lines, I smile to perceive that I felt as if it were necessary to apologize for the strong propensity I have to begin this letter as I concluded my last, namely, with Mr. Murden; whom, in the moments of my best opinion, I cannot wholly admire, nor, at the worst of times, can I altogether condemn.

As he is, then, or as I think he is, take him. Colonel Ridson, you know, said Mr. Murden was handsome. So say I. At times, divinely handsome; but only at times. His figure, it is true, never loses its symetry and grace; but his features, strongly influenced by their governing power the mind, vary from beauty to deformity; that is, deformity of expression. What would Lady Mary, Lady Laura, or the two Miss Winderhams, who are lately added to our party, say to hear me connect the ideas of Murden and deformity? Yet in their hearing, incurring the terrible certainty of being arraigned in their judgments for want of taste, of being charged with prudery, affectation, and I know not what besides, I shall dare repeat, that I have looked on Murden, and looked from him again, because he appeared deformed and disgusting. The libertine is ever deformed; the flatterer is ever disgusting.

His daily practice in this house justifies me in bestowing on him the latter epithet. I own, and I rejoice to own, that of the justice of the former I have my doubts. Vain he is. That he is gratified by, encourages, even stimulates the attention of fools and coquettes, I cannot deny; and when I view him indulging a weakness so contemptible, so dangerous, I am almost ready to believe he may be any thing that is vicious; and that, having taken vanity and flattery for his guides, he may attain to the horrid perfection of a successful debauchee.

Yet, what man, plunged in the whirlpool of debauchery, ever retained delicacy of sentiment and pungency of feeling? I think Murden possesses both. What man of debased inclinations would preserve that perpetual delicacy, that happy medium between neglect and encouragement, by which Murden regulates his conduct to Lady Laura Bowden? Lady Laura, celebrated as a wit and beauty, betrays to every observer her passion for Mr. Murden. I dreaded, on such an occasion, to see a vain young man, insolent in pity, or barbarous in neglect; but Lady Laura has not a particle more or less of his admiration, his flattery, and his services than any other lady of the circle.

Ah, I feel already that my description languishes. The Murden before me is a being of more vigour and more interest than the Murden on my paper. I have failed in discriminating the contradictory parts of his character; and I give up description; leaving those circumstances I may, on further acquaintance, select from the round of his actions to speak for him.

These insatiable devourers of amusement tear me from my pen. The morning, which in my mother's house in town I possessed uncontrouled, is no longer my own. The days are wasted in the execution of projects that promise much and perform nothing; and I made a whimsical attempt the other day, to convince my good friends here that we ought at least to be rational one half of one's time, if we would find any pleasure in being foolish the other half. But while I am complaining to you, Sibella, the party are perhaps complaining of me. Adieu for a short time. I go to taste *simplicity*. Not the simplicity of a golden age; but the simplicity of gold and tinsel. On the banks of a charming piece of water we fish, under a silken awning. Horns, clarionets, and bassoons are stationed in a neighbouring grove, with their sweet concords occasionally to soothe our fatigues. Ices, the choicest fruits, and other delicate preparations for the refreshment of the palate are at hand; and, notwithstanding all this costly care, it is very possible we shall pass a listless morning, return without any increase of appetite, or animal spirits, and be mighty ready to bestow loud commendations on the pleasures of a morning, from which we derive no other secret satisfaction than the certainty of its being at an end.

A summons! The carriages are at the door. You understand, I hope, that this is a *rural* expedition therefore a coach and a chariot attends, Mr. Murden drives one phaeton, Colonel Ridson another, and Mrs. Ashburn, who has arisen from the voluptuous luxury of the palanquin, and eight slaves, to the more active triumph of a high seat, reins, and long whip, will drive Lady Laura Bowden in her curricle.

It would be vain for me to attempt to sleep, for I endure at present a very considerable portion, though from a different cause, of those restless feelings which so often, my Sibella, urge you from your bed.

I believe I shall not go to bed this night, yet I have not to tell you, that I am roused to this wakefulness by events strikingly removed from the ordinary course of our lives. On the contrary, the accidents of the day, though new in their form, are by no means of an uncommon character. It is, alas, no novelty for some people to be inconsistent, and for others to imagine that rank and riches, as it places them beyond the reach of the common misfortunes of life, gives them full privilege to censure the weak and contemn the unfortunate. I hope benevolence is not a novelty. I would not subtract from the due praise of any individual; but I feel it as it were a tacit reproach upon human nature, or rather upon human manners, when we loudly vaunt the benevolent actions of any single man. I love the man, be he whom he may, who will perform the offices of a brother to the weakest, the most despised of his fellow creatures; but I lament that the example should be so unusual; and, when seen, rather vaunted than valued; and speedily forgotten.

I have no reason to accuse myself of a want of penetration. Our morning was any thing but pleasant. The air from the water chilled Sir Thomas. Lady Barlowe could find no scope amidst the very small talk for one single repartee. The Earl of Ulson had the tooth-ache. The Countess detests the music of wind instruments; and my mother found out that she hated fishing. The young ladies lost their spirits and temper, by losing Mr. Murden, whose absence occurred in such a way as put me out of temper, and out of spirits also.

As we were on the road to the destined spot of diversion, a pretty country girl on a horse loaded with paniers drew up to the hedge-side, while the cavalcade passed her. I was in Mr. Murden's phaeton; and we were the last carriage but one. The girl, in making her awkward obeisance to the company, no sooner lifted her eyes to

Mr. Murden, than she blushed deeper than scarlet. It was a blush of such deep shame, of such anguish, that I felt a sudden pain like a shock of electricity. The time of passing was so instantaneous, that I could not see what effect the blush had at the moment on Murden's countenance; but when I did look on him, I found him lost in thought, from which he presently started, to gaze back upon the girl, while she continued in sight. It was palpably obvious, that in this incident Murden had a concern more powerful than any interest he took in the party, for he remained dispirited and absent; and, after refusing to angle, and walking a few turns to and fro on the banks of the water, he said he should join us again before we returned to dinner, mounted his servant's horse, and disappeared. Thus were we left without one satisfied person of the party, except the ever-satisfied Colonel Ridson, and the self-satisfied Lord Bowden. We saw no more of Mr. Murden, till late in the afternoon.

I must now, my dear Sibella, call your attention to the history of an unfortunate woman, who, in occupying the greatest part of this afternoon, gave scope to the display of that hard-heartedness, and that benevolence to which I alluded in a former passage of this letter.

When Sir Thomas Barlowe left the East Indies, he retained in his service a young Creole as secretary. At that time, the youth, who was sanguine enough, and young enough to believe that his situation would increase in gain, and be permanent in favour, wrote to his mother, whom he contributed to support, saying it was his wish she should come to England. He expected she would wait for a remittance from him to pay her passage; but the mother, impatient to join her only child, sold her little property, borrowed on her son's credit the remainder of the money for her passage, and set sail from Bengal much about the time that her son, with whom the climate had disagreed, and whom Sir Thomas had discharged, set sail from England.

Arrived in London, she hastens to Sir Thomas Barlowe's house, to meet this beloved son. The family are in the country; the porter surlily assures her that her son is gone. She will not believe him; demands the name of Sir Thomas Barlowe's country seat; returns to her lodging with trembling limbs and an aching heart; writes a letter to Barlowe Hall, which probably was never sent; and falls ill of an ague and fever. Eight weeks the unhappy woman languished in the extreme of misery and disease; receiving no tidings from her son, having no friend, no acquaintance, either to pity or relieve her. Her money all spent, her clothes almost all sold, she availed herself of a small recruit of strength, and begged her way, half naked, to Sir Thomas Barlowe's seat, kept alive, no doubt, by the feeble hope that she should yet find her son.

At Barlowe Hall, the tidings of her son's departure was confirmed. Despair gave her strength. In spite of the servants opposition, she forced her way into the dining parlour, ere the desert was yet removed. She designed to have thrown herself at the feet of Sir Thomas; but on whom did her eye first fix? on no other than Mrs. Ashburn, whom, in her own land, in her happiest days, she had served in the capacity of housekeeper. Had the apartment held the first potentates of the earth, I firmly believe they would have been as so many straws in the poor woman's way when she rushed forward to Mrs. Ashburn. She clasped her knees, kissed her hands, her gown, the very chair on which she sat, and was so wild and extravagant in her joy, that I do not wonder at the result. I only wonder that her intellects survived.

It was in vain the company expressed their disgust at so miserable an object; in vain my mother and Sir Thomas commanded her to rise and withdraw. She would, in her imperfect language, curse the climate of Britain. She would intreat them to send her back to her own country. She would relate the history of her griefs, till combined recollections, or perhaps the frigid countenances of those around her, wrought a passionate flood of tears; and she then quietly suffered the footman to conduct her from the room.

The rigid Countess of Ulson instantly began a severe investigation of the folly of the young Indian, who sent so far for his mother, while his own prosperity was yet wavering and uncertain. Lady Barlowe and the young ladies appeared disconcerted. The Earl of Ulson had dined in his own chamber. Colonel Ridson often shifted his seat. Mrs. Ashburn and Sir Thomas Barlowe gave their assent to the invective of Lady Ulson, adding at the same time all the shades of imprudence in the mother's enterprise. They agreed, however, in the necessity of affording her some relief. Two guineas from Sir Thomas, and two from Mrs. Ashburn was the *vast* sum contributed; and, with this four guineas, the servant was ordered to deliver the following commands: That she should immediately go back to London, where she might easily find employment for her support, till her son should know she was in England, and remit money for her return to India.

Colonel Ridson stole to the door after the servant, and gave into his hand a benefaction for the widow.

I had only waited the conclusion of the nabob's and my mother's determination; and I now left them.

The Indian did not, as before, attempt to rush into the parlour; but in the hall, she wrung her hands, gnashed her teeth, tore her hair, exclaiming, she must go back, she could not work, she could not live in a climate that would kill a dog. My remonstrances she could not hear. I might as well have spoken to the dead.

It was then that Mr. Murden returned home. Astonished at the frantic agonies of the poor distressed woman, he enquired the cause from the servants, whom pity had drawn around her. He threw his whip out of his hand, and coming up to the Indian – yes, Sibella, this *seducer* perhaps, this very elegant, fashionable, handsome, and admired Murden immediately lifted in his arms the poor miserable despised object, from whose touch others had revolted, carried her into an apartment, and seated her by himself on a sopha, still holding his arm round her to prevent her relapsing into those violent excesses.

'You shall go back,' cried Murden. 'I swear by the God that made me, you shall go back to-morrow, to-day, this very hour, if you will but be calm.'

She looked on him steadily – it was such a look, Sibella!

'See,' said Murden, 'Miss Ashubrn says, you shall go back. You know Miss Ashburn? Ay, and you love her too. I know you do.'

In a fainting voice, she said, – 'Then I shall die with my poor Joseph at last.'

Her head fell upon Murden's breast; and he suffered it to remain there, till he found she had become insensible; he then requested the housekeeper to see a bed prepared for her; and, by his kind speeches and charming tones, he rendered every servant as eager to do the poor woman service as he himself had been.

All this time, I forgot the country girl.

While I attended the Indian to her bed, Mr. Murden visited the drawing room and when I also went thither, I found Murden's face in a glow. He was debating with his uncle on the danger that might befal his sick patient, by removing her from Barlowe Hall to the next village, and the danger of Sir Thomas might incur by allowing her to remain where she was. The nabob recollected she had spoken of her fever in London; and, already, he saw himself in the utmost danger, and half his family dead or dying of the mortal disease. Any sum of money, any thing in his house that could tend to her accommodation she might have, so that she was but removed. He absolutely shook with apprehension; and Murden was at length compelled to yield the point. A post chaise was accordingly got ready; two maids went in it with her, to support her, for successive faintings had reduced her to the weakness of an infant. Murden, although it was a rainy evening, walked by the side of the chaise to the village, to see that she was there taken proper care of.

In the drawing room, the interval between this arrangement and the time of Murden's return from the village was passed in a most irksome state. The weather would not allow of walking, or riding. No casual visitors arrived. Every common topic of conversation languished; and each individual dreaded lest some other of the party should begin to speak of the Indian, whom they were one and all laboriously urgent to forget. The entrance of tea and coffee was an immense relief. Their cups were received with unusual complacency, and their drooping spirits revived.

The card-tables were just arranged, when Murden entered. Good God, what a charm was diffused over his countenance! He was pale with fatigue, and want of food; his linen soiled; and his hair disordered with the wind and rain; but there was such a sweetness in his eyes, that no heart could resist it. Every one pronounced his name at once.

'Dear Murden!' breathed Lady Laura in the melting voice of love: then, covered with confusion, she added, 'Dear *Mr.* Murden, you will kill yourself!' At the same time, she made an involuntary motion for him to seat himself between her and her sister. He did so, his heart was open to the reception of all tenderness. He could not reject Lady Laura's tone. He took her hand. I saw him press it. He said something low and soft, and her cheeks were instantly suffused with a burning colour.

Ah that country girl! thought I. I could not help sighing for her. I sighed too for Murden. 'Would,' said I to myself, 'that he could suffer me to possess his confidence, would suffer me to advise, exhort, and intreat him to be worthy of himself!'

Perhaps, while these and other such reflections occupied my mind, my eyes were fixed upon Murden, for suddenly I perceived that his cheek took a stronger glow than even Lady Laura's; and he sprang up from his seat.

'James, bring me some biscuits and a jelly,' said he carelessly; 'Egad! I believe I have not dined to-day.'

This was enough to rouse Sir Thomas.

'There now!' cried the nabob.

'Was ever any thing like it? You have had no dinner! And here you are all this time in wet clothes! Lord, have mercy upon me! Call your valet!' and he began to ring the bell furiously.'I am sure, Arthur, you will be ill. You will have a fever. You will certainly kill yourself, as Lady Laura says.'

I had too much compassion to look at Lady Laura; and so had Murden, for he crossed the other side of the room, and immediately withdrew.

As Murden shut one door, a servant opened another, and gave into my hands your last dear letter. I retired to my own chamber to read it.

You are a glorious girl, Sibella, you elevate, you excite me! You awaken my mind to more and more love of those fervid qualities that shine so eminent in you. Had your Bonneville lived – Well, fear not my love. The day of your liberty will come. There are perhaps other Bonnevilles in the world, who will like him delight to give you that instruction for which your mind pants. Already, you possess energy, fortitude, and feeling; and those qualities, now kept alive and fostered by your love, may one day be called into action by objects of higher magnitude, of far higher value, (forgive me) than love, though it were the love of a Sibella.

I stood at my window to read your letter. The rain and wind had ceased; there was not even breeze enough to shake away the drops that yet rested upon the leaves. The dim, grey, melancholy remains of day, just afforded sufficient light to read by; and, when I had finished your letter, I threw up the sash and leaned out, thinking of you, my Sibella, in my imagination seeing you, seeing your fawn, your wood, your oak, your black angry looking rock, your solemn ruin, your clumps of yew trees, your white marble tomb. And these objects engrossed my whole attention, while those which surrounded me became hid in darkness.

Footsteps passed underneath my window through a path leading to the stables.

One voice said, 'Many and many a hard day's work have my poor dame and I done since, and have gone to bed to cry and moan all night for Peggy's naughtiness. We were ashamed to shew our faces in our own parish. But your honour assures me you won't forget her.'

Another voice answered, 'All that I have promised I will perform, depend on it.'

The latter voice was Murden's. Now I felt the chill air of evening, and I shut down my window.

'Won't you have candles brought, Ma'am?' asked Agnes, entering my chamber. 'Only think, Ma'am,' continued she, 'if that good Mr. Murden is not going to send one of the grooms eight miles for a physician to come to the poor Indian, because the laundry maid, who is just returned from her, told him she is not any better. I believe there never was such a young gentleman.'

'Do you know where he is now?' said I.

'Gone to the stables, Ma'am, to hurry away the groom.'

'Is any one with him?'

'Only an old farmer, who has been in his dressing room while he dined. I dare say Mr. Murden has been doing some good thing or other for him too.'

'I hope he has,' replied I. *All that I have promised, I will perform, depend on it*, – I repeated to myself. 'Light me down stairs, Agnes,' said I. 'I hope, indeed, Mr. Murden has done him some kindness.'

Agnes looked at me attentively, and did not reply to me. I returned to the drawing room, divested of that pleasurable glow of feeling which I enjoyed before the voices spoke underneath my window.

As I entered the room, Lord Ulson was saying to my mother, 'such a reference as you propose, Madam, would be unpardonable from me, nor can we possibly expect the lady will be sincere.'

I was surprised to understand, from the Earl's bow, that I was the subject of their conversation; and I requested, that, if his Lordship meant me, he would hereafter never expect to find me insincere; and I begged to know I had merited the accusation.

Mrs. Ashburn and the Earl mutually explained. His Lordship was persuaded, it seems, that a letter exciting such visible pleasure as that did which the servant delivered to me must be from a favoured lover. My mother was certain the effect was produced by my *romantic friendship*, to use her own expression; and, as the Earl was incredulous, she was desirous of referring the decision to me. Lady Laura affectedly begged I would defend the *sweet powers* of friendship; and my mother sneeringly observed, that I had a fine scope for my talents in the present instance.

I took your letter from my pocket. i unfolded and spread it open in my lap. 'This is the letter,' said I.

'A pretty hand,' said Colonel Ridson.

'Nay, it is not a female character, Miss Ashburn,' the Earl said.

I asked if I should read it; the Earl professed to admire my condescension, but my mother yawned.

I selected two passages from your letter, and read them. Lord Ulson, who had only chosen this subject for want of something to do, was now perfectly satisfied and convinced; for Sir Thomas had invited him to piquet. The Colonel thought your stile very charming. Lady Barlowe thought it very dull; and, as no one contradicted her ladyship's opinion, the subject would here have ended, had I not as I put the letter again into my pocket, told my mother that her friend Mrs. Valmont had lately been ill.

A poor inanimate vapoured being, Mrs. Ashburn called her friend; dying, she said, of diseases whose slightest symptom had never reached her, a burden to herself, and a torment to every one else; nevertheless her fate to be pitied, lamented, and deplored without bounds. Then it became your uncle's turn; and his sum of enormities was divided and subdivided into multitudes of sins, so that I was ready to ask myself if I had really ever known this Mr. Valmont. No one spark of pity remained for him. No: he was neither pitied by Mrs. Ashburn, nor prayed for by the Countess of Ulson.

When my mother had exhausted her topic, I said to her, 'Your pictures are vivid to-night, madam. Suppose you finish the family. Miss Valmont, what say you of her?'

'I leave her to you,' replied Mrs. Ashburn; 'I only think her a little handsome, a little proud, a little ignorant, and half insane. You can tell the rest.'

'Pray do, Miss Ashburn,' cried Lady Mary Bowden. 'I dearly love to hear of queer creatures.'

'I am to add,' said I, 'all that remains of a *queer creature*, already declared to be proud, ignorant, and half mad. – To the best of my judgment, I will. This——'

The door opened, and in came Mr. Murden; and the poor Indian, the country girl, and the old farmer who had wept sleepless nights for *Peggy's naughtiness*, together rushed upon my imagination. Again, Lady Laura made room for Murden; and again, he took his seat on the same sopha. I said to myself, as I looked at him, where are the signs of remorse? There are none. Not even the softened eye of new-born virtuous resolutions. Strange, that I read of nothing in that face but inward peace and freedom!

'Do go on, Miss Ashburn,' cried Lady Mary.

I did, Sibella, I began once more to speak of you; and, in a little time, I called back a part at least of the vigour and warmth which Murden's entrance and a train of fugitive thought had chased from me.

I began with your beauty: I omitted nothing which I could devise to make the picture worthy of the original. I spoke of the first sight I had of you; the impressive effect at that moment of your face, your form, your attitude, your simple attire. I appealed to my mother, to testify the singular beauty of your eyes, your forehead, your mouth, your hair. I told them that your hair had never been distorted by fashion; that, parted from the top of the head and always uncovered, it fell around your shoulder, displaying at once its profusion and its colour, and ornamenting, as well by its shade as its contrast, one of the finest necks that ever belonged to a human figure.

Lady Laura now grew restless in her seat; for Murden listened, he had even dropped a shuttle he had taken out of Lady Laura's hand, and either inattentively, or quite unconsciously, had allowed her ladyship to stoop to the ground for it herself. Still he listened.

'Thus adorned by nature,' said I, 'in what way shall I further recommend her? Art has disclaimed her. This *queer creature*, Lady Mary, never out of her uncle's castle since she was six years old, has been left utterly without the skill of the governess and waiting maid. An old tutor, indeed, gave her some singular lessons on the value of sincerity, independence, courage, and capacity; and she, a worthy scholar of such a teacher, as indeed you may judge from the specimen I read of her letter, has odd notions and practices; and, half insane, as Mrs. Ashburn says, would rather think herself born to navigate ships and build edifices, than to come into a world for no other purpose, than to twist her hair into ringlets, learn to be feeble, and to find her feet too hallowed to tread on the ground beneath her.'

'Stop!' cries Murden, bending eagerly forward, 'tell me, Miss Ashburn, of whom you speak,'

'Of a Miss Valmont,' said Lady Laura, peevishly. 'Miss Valmont!' rejoined Murden, 'Miss Ashburn, do you really speak of Miss Valmont?'

'I really do, Mr. Murden.'

He did not reply again; but, folding his arms, he leaned thoughtfully on the back of the sopha. Lady Laura, now quite out of temper, began to complain that he was an incumbrance; and, forgetting to offer the least apology, he instantly sprang up, and took a distant chair.

I should tell you that, by this time, my mother, Sir Thomas, the Earl, and the Colonel, were at cards, so that I had only Lady Barlowe and the younger part of the company for my auditors.

'And how,' asked Lady Mary, does this odd young lady (I must not again say queer creature) employ her time?'

'Playing with cats and dogs, and chattering with servants, I suppose,' said Lady Barlowe.

'No, Lady Barlowe,' I replied, 'the resources of her mind, *various* and *increasing*, to use her own description, furnish better expedients. She wishes for communication, for intercourse, for society; but she is too sincere to purchase any pleasure, by artifice and concealment; she is too proud to tempt the servants from their duty, all of whom, except two, are forbidden to approach her. A grey-headed unpolished footman, brings her breakfast and supper to her apartment. If she is there, it is well; if not, he leaves it, be the time longer or shorter till she does come. Her female domestic, deaf and deformed, would attend if summoned; but Miss Valmont finds her dress simple enough, and her limbs robust enough, to enable her to perform all the functions of her toilet. A true child of nature, bold in innocence, day or night is equally propitious to her rambles; and always mentally alive, she has the glow of animation on her cheeks, the fire of vivacity in her eye, alone in a solitary wood at noon-day or at midnight.'

'At midnight!' Lady Laura exclaimed, 'surely you did not go alone into the woods at midnight?'

I removed the idea her Ladyship and others perhaps had of its impropriety, by informing them your wood was of small extent, not distant from the castle, and inclosed within the moat, which, by means of a canal, had been carried round the park as well as castle. 'No human foot,' said I, 'but those admitted over the draw-bridge, can enter this wood, which though small is romantic, and though gloomy has its beauties. It rises on the side of the canal, and terminates at the foot of a rock. It contains a tomb. On one part of the rock are spread the tottering ruins of a small chapel and hermitage, and these objects serve to invite Miss Valmont to her wood, while they check the approach of diseased imaginations.'

I spoke further, Sibella, of your favourite lonely haunt, the flying speed with which I have seen you bound there, the affectionate caresses of your little fawn, and numberless other circumstances. Lady Laura was resolved neither to be amused by the novelty, nor seduced by the merit I had attributed to you. She found you more whimsical than pleasing; more daring than delicate. She wished you all manner of good things; and, among the rest, that you might not at last fall in love with one of your uncle's footmen.

I smiled and replied to her Ladyship, that your uncle's wisdom and foresight had provided against that misfortune. You already had a lover worthy of you.

'Good God! Are you acquainted with Clement Montgomery?'

It was Murden from whom this exclamation burst; and I looked at him without power to reply. It almost appeared miraculous, to hear any one in that room name Clement Montgomery.

'Is that the Mr. Montgomery,' Lady Barlowe asked, 'you went abroad with, Murden?'

'Yes, madam.'

'Then,' said I, 'you know Clement Montgomery intimately.'

He replied that he did.

'How could you be so cruel,' said I; 'why did you not interrupt me long since? You, who know Miss Valmont's lover, must know Miss Valmont also. Why did you not take the voice of that lover, and paint, as you must have heard him paint, her attractive graces, her noble qualities? Oh it was barbarous to leave that to be done by monotonous friendship, to which the spirit of love could alone do justice!'

Methinks his answer was a very strange one; so cold, so abrupt! I felt displeased at the moment; and checked myself in some eager question I was about to ask respecting Clement Montgomery. Murden's reply, Sibella, was, – That I had done enough: and he withdrew, too – immediately withdrew, as if weary of me and my subject.

At supper, his place at table was vacant. His valet alledged he was writing letters. Sir Thomas would be positive he was ill; we heard of nothing but *the fever*, and it is highly probable the house would have been presently half filled with physicians, and Sir Thomas really in need of them, if Murden had not come smiling and languishing into the supper room.

This time I had the honour of his chusing his seat next me; and, as I saw that he only pretended to eat in order to appease his uncle, I told him in a low voice I believed he was ill.

'My mind is my disease,' he said.

Ah, then, thought I, he does perhaps repent! I longed to talk to him, but I could think of no subject, no name but *Peggy*; and Peggy I had not courage to mention.

I made an aukward remark upon our ride to the water side; then I introduced as aukwardly, and to as little purpose, the time of my leaning out of my chamber window. Murden, unconscious of my meaning and allusions, heard me composedly; and I ended only where I began. He found me absent and embarrassed; and, though little suspecting that *his mind was* also *my disease*, his attentions were more exclusively mine, than I had ever before experienced them to have been.

A few minutes before the company separated, Murden said to me, 'I am informed, Miss Ashburn, that you intend visiting our poor Indian to-morrow morning.'

'Yes,' I said, 'I had ordered my horse early for that purpose.'

'I should request your permission to attend you, madam; but I am in some sort engaged to eat my breakfast on brown bread and new milk at a farmhouse.'

'A farm-house!' said I.

'Yes, madam,' rejoined Murden, as calmly as though he had carried content and joy into that farm-house, instead of remorse and misery; 'Yes, madam, the most charming spot in this country. My constant house of call in the shooting season. Many pleasant brown bread breakfasts and suppers have I eaten there.'

So unblushing, so hard-hearted a confession absolutely startled me. I had already risen to retire, he rose also, and said, 'Will you, Miss Ashburn, allow me to ride with you in the morning?'

'And neglect the farm-house, Mr. Murden.'

He replied, 'the time is of little consequence, I can go there afterward.'

'Oh, but it is,' said I, '*now* of infinite consequence. Not for the world would I be the means of your dispensing with one title of your promises to that farm-house. Pray,' said I, turning back, after having bade him good night, 'Mr. Murden, do you correspond with Clement Montgomery?'

Again I became reconciled to him; again I was persuaded, that he repented of his error, and that he is not hardened in his transgressions, for he understood the fullest tendency of my question. His countenance instantly expressed shame, surprise, and sorrow too; and his voice faultered while he said –

'Why, Miss Ashburn, why should you wish to know that?' And when he added, 'I do indeed madam correspond with Mr. Montgomery,' he looked from me.

My *good night* was more cordial than the former one; and I hope, that, if Murden finds his breakfast at the farm-house less pleasant than heretofore, its usefulness will encrease, as its pleasure ceases.

Day-light bursts into my chamber. In another hour, I shall prepare to visit the Indian. My Sibella, farewel!

CAROLINE ASHBURN

LETTER VIII

FROM CLEMENT MONTGOMERY

TO

ARTHUR MURDEN

Infidel as thou art toward beauty, and indolent as thou art in friendship, whence dost thou still derive the power to attract the homage of beauty, and the zeal of friendship.

That Janetta, the Empress of all hearts, but callous thine, possessed sensibility, susceptibility, or even animation, thou, infidel Arthur, didst deny. Yet Janetta can sometimes torture her admiring Clement by the repetition of thy praises.

Four letters of mine, long letters, letters to which I yielded hours that might have been rapturous in enjoyments, those letters lie, the last as the first, unanswered, unheeded in thy possession.

I devoutly thank the star that shed its influence over the hour of my birth, that it gave me a temperament opposite to thine, Arthur: for, have I not seen thee more than insensible, even averse to the offered favours of the fair? Have I not seen thee yawn with listlessness at an assembly, where rank and splendor, the delights of harmony, and the fascinations of beauty, filled my every sense with extasy? Give me the sphere of fashion, and its delights! Fix me in the regions of ever varying novelty!

Mine is life. I sail on an ocean of pleasure. Where are its rocks, its sands, its secret whirlpools, or its daring tempests? Fables all! Fables invented by the envious impotence of snarling Cynics, to crush the aspiring fancy of glowing youth! Thy apathy, Murden, I detest. Nay, I pity thee. And I swear by that pity, I would sacrifice some portion of my pleasures, to awaken thee to the knowledge of one hour's rapture.

Soul-less Arthur, how couldst thou slight the accomplished L——? How could thou acknowledge that she was beautiful, yet tell me of her defects? – Defects! Good heaven! Defects, in a beautiful, kind, and yielding woman! – Arthur, Arthur, in compassion to thy passing youth, thy graceful figure, and all those manly charms with which thou art formed to captivate, forget thy wild chimeras, thy absurd dreams of romantic useless perfections; and make it thy future creed, that in woman there can be no crime but ugliness, no weakness nor defect but cruelty.

Every day, every hour, Janetta brings me new proof that thy judgment is worthless. She has tenderness, she has sensibility; she does not, as thou didst assert, receive my love merely to enrich herself with its offerings; and constancy she has, even more boundless than I (except for a time) could desire; for she talks of being mine for ever, and says, wherever I go thither will she go also.

And I will soothe her with the flattering hope. Why should I damp our present ardors, by anticipating the hour when we must part? Why should I suffuse those brilliant eyes with the tears of sorrow; or wound that fondly palpitating heart, by allowing her to suspect that she but supplies the absence of an all-triumphant rival?

Ah, let not my thoughts glance that way! Let not imagination bring before me the etherial beauty of my Sibella! Let it not transport me to her arms, within the heaven of Valmont wood! or I shall be left a form without a soul; and be excluded from the enjoyment that I now admire, as being in absence my solace, my happiness.

I expected I should have been dull without thee, Murden; but I hardly know, except when I am writing, that thou hast left me. I dress, I dance, I ride, I visit, I am visited. My remittances bring me all I wish, in their profusion. I adore, and am adored; the nights and days are alike devoted to an eternal round of pleasures; and lassitude and I are unacquainted.

'Read the hearts of men,' says Mr. Valmont. I cannot. I am fascinated with their manners. I pant to acquire the same soft polish; and their endearing complaisance to my endeavours.

That graceful polish is already thine; and, there, I envy thee. I envy too thy reputation; but I hate thy cold reserve. Why, if these triumphs which are attributed to thee be really thine, why conceal them? Others can tell me of thy successes, can shew me the very objects for whom thou hast sighed, whom thou hast oqtained. When I alledge that I found thee constantly dissatisfied, contemplating some imaginary being, complaining that too much or too little pride, defective manners, or a defective mind, gave thee an antidote against love, I am assured that it was the mere effect of an overweening vanity. Seymour, who pretends to know thee much better than I do, declares thou art vain beyond man's belief or woman's example. He is thy sworn enemy; and well he may, provided his charges against thee be true, for the other night in the confidence of wine, he assured me, that thou art the seducer of his mistress. A mistress, fond and faithful, till she listened to thy seductions. Is it possible, Murden, thou canst have been thus dishonourably cruel? I doubt the veracity of Seymour's representation; for, I think thou are not only too strict for the transaction, but too inanimate to be assailed by the temptation.

Prithee, Arthur, banish this thy ever impenetrable reserve; and tell me truly, whether thou art inflated with victory; fastidious from change; or, whether, as I deem thee, thou are not really too cold to love; whether thou hast not cherished the indolent caprice of thy temper, till it has deadened thee into marble?

Once more, I thank heaven I am not like thee. Ever may I thrill at the glance, the smile of beauty! Ever may I live, to know no business but pleasure; and may my resources ever be as unconfined as my wishes!

CLEMENT MONTGOMERY

LETTER IX

FROM SIBELLA VALMONT

TO

CAROLINE ASHBURN

It is now a week since, one evening at sun-set, I carried your letters, and that portrait painted by Clement in the days when we knew no sorrow, into the wood; where, shutting out every remembrance, save those of love and friendship, I was for a time wrapped in the sublimity of happiness. Is the mind so much fettered by its earthly clog the body, that it cannot long sustain these lofty flights, soaring as it were into divinity, but must ever sink back to its portion of pains and penalties? For, this I have before experienced; and, at the time of which I speak, pain and grief suddenly burst in upon me. I rushed from the foot of my oak to the monument; and, resting there, wept with a bitterness equal in degree to my former pleasure.

Nina was at my side – and her flying from me into the wood, was a signal that some one approached. I raised my head; and beheld, descending from the Ruin on the Rock, the tall figure of a venerable man, with a white and flowing beard. He was wrapped in a sort of loose gown; a broad hat shaded part of his face; his step was feeble; he frequently tottered; and, when he had come near to me, he leaned both hands on his staff, and addressed me thus.

'Fair virgin, weep not! The spirits of the air gather round you; and form a band so sacred, that the malignant demons hover at a distance, hopeless of approach. Your guardian angel presides over this grove. Here, Mildew, Mischief, and Mischance, cannot harm you. Fair virgin weep not!' He paused, I said, 'Who are you?'

'Once,' he continued, 'I was the hallowed tenant of yon ruined mansion; once, an inhabitant of earth, it was my lot to warn the guilty, and to soothe the mourner. Well may such tears as thine draw me back to earth. I come, the spirit of consolation. Fair virgin, why weepest thou?'

'I know,' I said, 'that the sleep of death is eternal. That the grave never gives back, to form and substance, the mouldering body; and it indeed matters little to me who or what you are, since I well know you cannot be what you would seem.'

I stepped down from the monument; and turned up the wood path, leading to the castle.

'Stay,' cried he. 'Do you doubt my supernatural mission? – View my testimony. Behold, I can renovate old age!'

I looked back, the beard, the hat, the mantle were cast aside; and a young man of graceful form and fine physiognomy appeared before me.

I stood, an instant, in surprise; and then, I again turned toward the castle. He stepped forward, and intercepted my path with outspread arms.

'Fear me not,' said he. 'I ——'

'No,' I answered. 'I do not fear you, though I know of no guardian angels but my innocence and fortitude.'

He folded his arms, fixed his eyes upon the ground, and I passed on without further interruption.

When Andrew brought supper into my apartment, I asked if there were strangers in the castle; and Andrew shook his head, by which I understood that he did not know if there were any.

The following morning, I expected my uncle's commands to absent myself from the wood; and though no message came, I did absent myself, both on that day and on the succeeding day and their nights, confining all my walks to the open ground behind the castle and the lawn.

During these two days, I was attended only by Margaret. Poor Andrew was indisposed. Banished from my oak, deprived of my Nina's society, excluded even from the slight intercourse the table afforded with Mr. and Mrs. Valmont (for my uncle has lately determined, that it is an indelicate custom to meet together at stated times for the sole purpose of eating; and refreshment is now served up to each in our separate apartments) it is nearly impossible to tell you, Caroline, how much *alone* I felt myself, while these two days and two nights lasted.

The third day was bleak and stormy; the wind roared; and showers fell frequently. Every one of this household seems at all times loath to encounter such inclemencies, and I imagined that to me alone these were things of little moment. I went, therefore, to the wood; but, ere Nina had expressed half her joy, the stranger appeared.

'Why fly me,' he said, 'if you do not fear me?'

'I shun you,' replied I, 'because I do not understand you.'

'But, if you shun me, you cannot understand me.'

'I do not deem you worthy of enquiry,' I said; 'for you came with pretences of falsehood and guile, and those are coverings that virtue ever scorns.'

'Fair philosopher,' he exclaimed, 'teach me how you preserve such vigour, such animation, where you have neither rivalship to sustain, nor admiration to excite? Are you secluded by injustice from the world? Or, do you willingly forsake its delights, to live the life of hopeless recollection? Say, does the beloved of your soul sleep in that monument?'

The supposition, Caroline, was for an instant too agonising; and I called twice on the name of Clement, with a vehemence that made this man start. His face flushed with colour; he retreated a few steps, and looked every way around him.

'No,' said I, as he again approached, 'my beloved lives. Our beings are incorporate as our wishes. The sepulchre need not open twice. No tyranny could separate us in death. But who are you,' I added, 'that come hither to snatch from me the moments I would dedicate to remembrances of past pleasure, and to promising expectation?'

'Is then your heart so narrowed by love, that it can admit neither friendship nor benevolence?'

I answered, 'To my friendship you have no claim; for, we are not equal. You wear a mask. Esteem and unreserved confidence are the only foundations of friendship.'

As he had done on the former day, he again intercepted my path; for I was going to quit the wood.

'Stay,' he said, 'and hear me patiently; or I may cast a spell around you!'

He interrupted the reply I was beginning to make, thus – 'I do not bid you fear me. My power is not terrible, but it is mighty. Tell me, then,' he added, 'have you no sense of the blessings of intercourse? Have you never reflected on the selfishness of solitude, on the negative virtues of the recluse?'

'I find you here,' said I, 'in Mr. Valmont's wood; and I expect, there-fore, that you already know my seclusion is not the effect of my choice.'

'But from whom, other than yourself, am I to learn why it is the effect of your submission?'

This was a question, Caroline, which I had never steadily put to myself; and I stood silent some moments before I found my answer.

I said, 'I am not yet convinced that the time is arrived when my submission ought to cease.'

'Ah, rather, honestly confess,' he replied, 'that you shun a stern contention with that power which here detains you. But there are other means. A secret escape. If you resolve to exert yourself for that purpose ——'

'No,' I said, 'I am not weak enough to descend to artifice. Did I think it right to go, I should go openly. Then might Mr. Valmont try his opposing strength. But he would find, I could leap, swim, or dive; and that moats and walls are feeble barriers to a determined will.'

'Oh, stay, stay in these woods for ever!' he vehemently exclaimed. 'Go not into the world, where artifice might assail and example corrupt that noble sincerity. Or if, as I think, your courage, your integrity, are incorruptible, Oh yet, go not into the world! View not its disgusting follies! Taste not its chilling disappointments!'

My answer was: 'I am accustomed to listen to inconsistencies. You just now, spoke of the pleasures and blessings of society.'

As he did not reply, but stood as though he was musing, I thought I could pass him, which I attempted to do. He immediately knelt on one knee before me; spread one hand on his bosom, and said –

'You are above my controul. I would not dare profane you, by the single touch of my finger. But I beseech you, by that firmness, that innocence which holds distrust and danger at defiance, I beseech you listen to me a few short moments longer.'

'Have you any thing to impart which can interest me? I asked him.

'I have that which ought to interest you.' – He rose from his kneeling posture, and appeared to hesitate. 'Alas,' he then added, 'I have many many faults! I am unstable in wise resolutions; and yielding, as childhood, to temptation. I wanted a guide, a monitor. I fought one in the world, and found only tempters. I have quitted the world. I have chosen my abode in that Ruin. There I would fain learn to amend myself. I want to learn to be happy. But I come not to that Ruin, to banish you from this wood. This is your selected spot; and that is mine. Only a few paces divides them. Yet, if you say it must be so, the distance shall be as impassable as though entire kingdoms lay between us. Ah, reflect a moment before your single word forms this immense barrier! – A moment did I say? – No: reflect a day. Leave me now in silence; and return to-morrow, the next day, when you will, and then tell me, if you could not sometimes find me a more sympathising auditor than trees and marble, when you would breathe complaint, or utter joy. Go then. But ——'

A second time he hesitated; and, when he spoke again, his articulation was changed from its clear decisive character to a thicker lower utterance.

'Be aware,' he said, 'that there are certain requisites necessary to form the utility of my solitude: Uninterrupted retirement, and perfect secresy.'

Was I unjust, Caroline? but his mention of secresy instantly filled my mind with a supposition that his words wore one form, and his intentions another. I warned him to depart. I told him, I despised concealment; that I had ever scorned to separate my wishes from my acts, or my actions from my words. I said, his caution pointed out my duty. I bade him, as I then thought a final adieu.

I proceeded immediately to the library, to relate this conversation to my uncle. There I was told, that my uncle was gone from the castle, not to return till four days were past. I then requested to be admitted into Mrs. Valmont's dressing room, and she received me.

Her conduct disgusted me extremely at the time; and I have since thought it very extraordinary, that Mrs. Valmont should doubt my veracity. Scarcely had I described the manner in which the person in the wood first came to me, than Mrs. Valmont broke my narration by asking me over and over again, I know not how many times – 'Had I indeed seen a hermit come out of the Ruin? - Was I quite sure I had seen him? - Could it really be true! Not disposed to hear such offensive repetitions, I declined entering any further into the story; and merely said, that, if the person was a visitor in the castle, it might be proper for her to signify to him that his intrusion in the Rock and wood would be displeasing to my uncle, and highly inconvenient to me.

I went to my own apartments.

On the next morning, I rose as I frequently do, at the first dawn of day – Do you recollect the situation of my apartments? You will certainly remember, that the south-west wing is rather distant from that part of the body of the castle where most of the family inhabit. You know too that my rooms open into a long gallery; but you never explored this gallery. My hours with you were rich in pleasure and variety; and I thought not then of the solitary haunts to which I fly, when I seek amusement and find none.

This gallery, at the remote end from the body of the castle, closes with a stair case. These stairs descend into a narrow and winding passage of the West Tower, and lead to the door of the Armoury. It is probable you never saw either the West Tower or the Armoury. They are both out of repair, and altogether out of use; nor do I recollect any that I ever saw one of the family enter them but Clement and myself.

In very tempestuous weather, the Armoury was a favourite place of resort for us. The various implements and cases of steel with which it is furnished, were subjects of wonder and conjecture; besides, it is a hall of large dimensions, and we possessed it so free of interruptions, that it served better for play and recreation than any other apartment we were allowed to frequent within the castle.

At a very early hour on the succeeding morning, as I before said, I rose and left my chamber, to walk in the Armoury. After I had gone down the stairs, and as I had nearly reached the end of the dark stone passage, I heard a sudden creaking noise; but whether or not it proceeded from the Armoury I could not be certain. I entered the Armoury. The door closed heavily after me. There was scarcely light enough to distinguish the surrounding objects. – I stood still. – But all was silent.

I walked about; and other thoughts entirely effaced an impression of something unusual in the noise; till, again, and in a louder degree, it assailed me. I hastened toward the door, but the voice I had heard in the wood called me to stay. I turned round, and the same figure was before me.

Andrew interrupts me. My uncle is returned home; has something to communicate; and expects me now. I go.

In continuation.

Farewel, thou precious resemblance I must part with thee. From yesterday, until the present hour, thou hast been mine. Farewel, then, exquisite shadow!

Caroline, I left my letter unfinished, yesterday; and hastened to the library.

'Come hither, child,' my uncle said as I entered; 'and tell me if this be a likeness.'

He presented to me a small case, and I beheld the picture of Clement. I folded both hands over it on my bosom. I had not words to thank Mr. Valmont; but the tears that rolled upon my cheeks were tears of gratitude.

'I ordered Clement,' my uncle continued, 'to send me his portrait, done by an eminent artist; and his obedience has been as prompt as I could desire. You may retire, Sibella, and take the picture with you; but you are to bring it back to the library to morrow after my dinner hour.'

Only, conceive, Caroline, how I flew back to my apartment. Think how many fond avowals, how many rapturous caresses, I bestowed on the insensible image. While I eat, it lay before me; and while I slept, the little that I did sleep, it rested on my pillow.

I have counted the stroke of five, from the great clock. Now Mr. Valmont dines; and the picture is no longer mine. I have placed it in its case, ready for the hand of Mr. Valmont. I become dispirited. Farewel, precious shadow!

Farewel, also, Caroline to you!

SIBELLA VALMONT

I have torn the seal away from this letter! I am breathless with the tidings! Clement, my Clement, is to return! Oh, Caroline, Caroline, did you ever weep for joy?

LETTER X

FROM CAROLINE ASHBURN

TO

SIBELLA VALMONT

Certainly, a picture is at all times a very pretty toy; and I can readily imagine, that the picture of an absent lover must be indeed a precious blessing; but you will forgive me, Sibella, if I honestly confess that I have a hundred times, since the receipt of your letter, wished Clement had not been so willing, or his artist not so ready.

Oh, that Mr. Valmont had withheld the picture but one hour longer! Then would the womanish curiosity of Caroline Ashburn have been gratified. For, trust me, Sibella, your surprise at finding your enigmatical hermit in the Armoury could not exceed my disappointment at leaving him and you there without further explanation.

I have imagined and imagined; returned to the subject; and quitted it again, more wearied than before; and, though I did, after a time, discover that I never should, by the mere aid of suppositions, find of what materials your hermit is composed, yet I have persisted in comparing accidents, and combining circumstances perhaps totally remote from each other, with the vain hope of tracing him. Knowing how much your uncle worships mystery, I sometimes think it may be one of his stratagems; – sometimes that—— Psha! The folly of conjecture grows with me.

Pardon me, Sibella, you are above these things. Uniform in rectitude, you steadily pursue the path before you; nor mislead yourself to follow the swervings of others. In compassion, however, to the longings of your friend, hasten to communicate the remainder of this your adventure.

Our poor Indian is dead. She survived her reception at Barlowe Hall only about ten days; and, during the visits I made her, I never found her capable of sustaining any conversation with me. From her, as she was long a resident in the family, I hoped and expected to have been informed by what means my father amassed his fortune: for, the suspicions which I find generally attached to East Indian riches sit heavy on my mind. I do not love to encourage suspicion, for it is cowardly; nor can I indeed fairly give my opinions the name of suspicions, for I am persuaded, that in whatever clime or country it be found, the mind that grasps at such inordinate wealth must be vicious, and that there can be but little to choose among the degrees of vice wherewith it is obtained. Yet, being convinced as to that point, I still wish to know the employments of my father's life: for it is possible there may be some retribution to make to individuals. A voyage to India for such a purpose, Sibella, would be but as a pleasant summer day's excursion.

Your letter has been sent after me to Bath, for Barlowe Hall no longer retains her circle of gay visitors. The Ulson family have gone I forget where, and taken the Winderhams with them, while we, together with Sir Thomas, Lady Barlowe, and Colonel Ridson, arrived at Bath last week. The season is crowded, and my mother and the nabob think themselves fortunate in having been able to secure one large and commodious house for the reception of both families.

This arrangement Lady Barlowe and Mrs. Ashburn profess to find very pleasing. They declare a violent friendship for each other; and use it as a cloak for the workings of their secret malignities. My mother is the object of Lady Barlowe's envy: for the nabob's fears have made him covetous; he hoards his diamonds in their cases; and Lady Barlowe's glitter is out-glared by the happier uncontrouled Mrs. Ashburn.

On the other hand, Lady Barlowe has youth, and has beauty; and these attractions Mrs. Ashburn finds the lustre of the diamond will not altogether outshine, though there are many among the venal crowd, who daily offer up at the shrine of wealth the incense due to merit, wit, and beauty.

Sir Thomas, I believe, considers himself as bound to play both his own part and his nephew's; and to overwhelm us with the attentions and kindnesses, his ungracious Arthur with-held.

Did I not tell you, or rather did I not intimate, that before Mr. Murden made his appearance amongst us, the Baronet evidently bestowed him upon me? but, alas, scarcely had he arrived, when his uncle, remembering the value of a certain old proverb, left me to seek another lover; and gave or would have given his all-prized nephew to my mother.

It was highly whimsical to see the Baronet's labours to promote this end. He dared not be quite certain, that Murden, although dependent on him, would yield him an implicit obedience; and yet, according to his understanding, the scheme had so many and such important recommendations, that they were not to be hastily rejected. Fearing to be out-talked, if not convinced, should he at once resort to his nephew's opinion, the Baronet would not venture to do so; but, secure in the presence of numbers, he grew bold at hint, and soon made his plan fully comprehended by every person present; and put his nephew's ingenuity to the trial to find methods how to express his disapprobation, without being rude and offensive to the feelings of any one. I cannot say that Mrs. Ashburn appeared to think Sir Thomas very absurd in his designs.

After playing this game of hint, till the party talked of separating, the Baronet then acquired courage enough to make a direct attack on his nephew; the latter gave an explicit refusal to the proposal; and the former for some days lost his good humour and his patience.

It was, I suppose, in consequence of this marked displeasure from his uncle, that Murden thought of paying a visit to a friend at some distance from Barlowe Hall. At first, Sir Thomas opposed it not; but when Murden was actually on the point of going, the nabob relaxed his solemn displeasure, and earnestly requested Arthur not to leave him. Arthur, in his turn, became inflexible, and would not be intreated. He had written, he said to his friend, and go he must. At length, however, he condescendingly offered to hasten to join us at Bath; and, having thus accommodated their difference, the nabob and his nephew parted very good friends.

This serious altercation on the subject of Mr. Murden's quitting our party, took place in the breakfast parlour. Lady Mary Bowden invited me soon after to walk with her.

'Don't you think,' said she, putting her arm through mine, as soon as we had crossed the threshold of the Hall door, 'that Murden is very obstinately bent on making this excursion?'

'I think him determined,' answered I; 'and perhaps very properly so.'

'Thereby hangs a tale,' said Lady Mary.

'I don't love tales, Lady Mary.'

She looked at me, and smiled. 'Yet, I believe you are willing to hear this,' she said, 'and I am resolved to tell it you.'

Lady Mary certainly did not lay that to my charge, of which I was
undeserving; for I quietly suffered her to proceed in her story. It was
an accusation against Murden, that his pretended visit of friendship to
Mr. Villiers was in fact a visit of a different kind, to a female in Mr.
Villier's neighbourhood, of whom Lady Mary said Murden had not
been the original seducer; that she had been lured from her friends by
another person, and that having preferred the attractions of Murden,
she made a pretence of returning to her friends, in order to be the
more conveniently under his protection.

Lady Mary added a number of little corroborating anecdotes,
which gave the affair a striking appearance of matter of fact; and I
was inclined to believe it, till I recollected how much my opinion had
been misled by appearances in the affair of Peggy, of which I spoke to
you in my last letter. Warned by that example, I began to doubt the
representations of her ladyship; and begged she would join with me in
having better hopes of Murden, and endeavouring to discountenance
the unsupported assertions that were spread abroad concerning him.
Lady Mary willingly promised, and I dare say as readily forgot it the
very next instant.

As I told you, Sibella, my suspicions of Peggy, I will now tell you
her history at once, without going through the round of circumstances
that brought me acquainted with it.

In Murden's own words, you have learned, that the pleasant
farm was his house of call in the shooting season. The farmer is an
industrious and worthy man; and his daughter Peggy is, or rather was,
ere disappointment fed upon her bloom, a very pretty girl. Joseph,
Murden's servant, fell in love with Peggy, and Peggy with Joseph. He
was sober; he had some expectations from friends; and his master
thought very well of him; and all this together induced the father of
Peggy to consent. The marriage was settled as a certain thing; but a
delay of time was agreed on among all parties; and Joseph went to
London with his master. It so happened, that at Christmas Joseph's
father died; and, as he was a shopkeeper in a country town, Joseph
might, if he chose, succeed him, and marry Peggy directly. He consulted
Murden, who approved much of his designs, and likewise gave him
thirty pound to assist in forwarding them.

Thus, rich in pocket and in expectation, ere he commenced
shopkeeper, Joseph went first to stay a week at Peggy's farm, to
settle the time of marriage, &c. &c. Alas, the week began with much
happiness, and laid the foundation for much sorrow. Peggy became too

indulgent to her lover; and, in consequence, her lover cruelly forgot to come back, as he had promised, at six weeks end and marry her.

Peggy's father had a strong sense of honest pride; he disdained to solicit an ungenerous man. On the contrary, he exhorted Peggy to forget him, be industrious, and hereafter irreproachable. But while he was thus daily kind to Peggy, the poor old man, as he told Murden underneath my window, wept through sleepless nights for Peggy's naughtiness.

Murden knew nothing of these transactions. He had not called at the farm-house since he arrived at Barlowe Hall, when we met Peggy in the narrow lane. I can now well account for her blushes, and his surprize. He, struck with her appearance and her manner, left us to fish, and went to inform himself at the farm why Peggy was still in that part of the world. The father was absent; but the mother told him the whole story, and he promised to do all that lay within his power to restore the peace of the family.

It was Peggy's earnest longing to save herself from present pain at any future risk; and Murden thought it right to forward her wishes. He sent for Joseph, who was growing rich at five and twenty miles distance, but who not having more vices than his neighbours was willing enough to be ruled by a greater man than himself, and accordingly became either really or seemingly very penitent. The end of the whole is, that Peggy's present disgrace is salved by marriage. A foolish and impotent remedy, in my opinion; removing a partial evil, most probably to begin a lasting one.

How I misjudged Murden in this affair! – Others too may have misjudged him. I persuade myself they have.

Men, my dear Sibella, have not that enthusiasm and vigour in their friendships that we possess. I never could get Murden to talk much of Clement Montgomery, though I urged him to it repeatedly. As an incentive thereto, as well as to gratify my own feelings, I made you and your manners a perpetual theme of conversation when I held conversations with Murden. Perhaps my descriptions interested him, for he was never unwilling to listen to me, though he uniformly persisted in repressing my enquiries, if they led to the subject of his friendship for Clement, with an insuperable coldness. – Too vain, possibly, to praise the perfections of another; yet too honest, to deny their existence. Inconsistent being!

Inconsistent in all things that I know of him, except in his conduct to his uncle. There he is firm, settled and manly, respectful, but never fawning; he opposes Sir Thomas without petulance, and obeys him without humiliation. Such conduct will ever secure its proper reward. The Nabob feels his superiority, and still loves him.

Sir Thomas Barlowe rejoices, I am glad, while Mrs Ashburn and Lady Barlowe are neither pleased nor displeased, that tomorrow is the day of Murden's arrival. The other ladies of his accquaintance here, to whom I have been introduced, are not so indifferent as the two last mentioned to Murden's appearance; for, I have already heard some praise him indiscriminately as Lady Laura Bowden would, and others comment upon his attractions and his vices with as little true feeling of either as Lady Mary did. I am glad he comes to Bath, for I shall now see him amidst a multitude, where new faces, new forms will continually present themselves; where temptations will rush in crowds, and where the sober pace of reflection is outstripped by the flying speed of pleasure. If I do not now learn to appreciate his character, it will be owing rather to the idleness of my discernment than its want of space enough to practice in.

Do not imagine, dear Sibella, that because I have run through so many lines without a word of congratulation I am insensible to the joy which swells in your bosom on the expected return of your lover. I do indeed congratulate you. Your uncle becomes reasonable. His mysteries and his contradictions vanish. Sibella expects her Clement; and the heavy gates of Valmont Castle will fly back, that peace and liberty may enter.

Nevertheless, in the prosperity of your expectations, forget not the Hermit in the armoury, and the longings of your

CAROLINE ASHBURN

LETTER XI

FROM CLEMENT MONTGOMERY

TO

ARTHUR MURDEN

Dear Arthur,

Precisely such a command to return home, so sudden, and so unexpected as you received five months past from Sir Thomas Barlowe, have I received from Mr. Valmont; but the speed of your obedience bore no proportion to mine, for hither have I come with a rapidity which scarcely yielded to rest and refreshment.

Here I am already arrived almost within sight of the castle's prison like towers, and here have I been traversing the paltry room of an inn for one hour and three quarters. How much longer I shall stay here I know not, but by heaven were I to depart with a thorough good will, it would be to take the road back to the continent.

Arthur, Arthur, what a lesson it is that I have to get by rote! 'Fully assured, Clement,' says Mr. Valmont in his letter, 'that you cannot have departed from the rule of conduct I desired you to pursue, I do not doubt but that you will joyfully quit the haunts of treacherous sordid men, to enjoy with me the pleasant solitude of Valmont castle, &c. &c.'

No one knows better than yourself, dear Murden, how closely I have pursued Mr. Valmont's *rule of conduct*, and I think you can guess also how greatly I shall now *enjoy* the *pleasant solitude of Valmont castle.*

For a week, a month, perchance, the blooming Sibella will render the wilderness a world. Could I flatter myself, that Mr. Valmont recals me to give her to my arms, how I should bound over the distance which now separates us? No, Arthur, no such blessing awaits your luck-less friend; I am to look on her as a sister, says Mr. Valmont. Good heaven! and he recals me to stand perpetually on the brink of a precipice! For how can I hear her, look on her, touch her, and be a brother? Nay, the very first moment of my entrance into that castle may undo me, for she will rush to my embrace, she will cover me with kisses, and his chilling eye will be on me.

Had Mr. Valmont left me with the cottagers my parents, I had never seen Sibella; then I had dreamed through a stupid existence, without knowing life and love. Had he kept me the recluse of his woods, she had by this time infused her wild untamed spirit unto me, and I should have torn her from him, imagining we could live on berries, and drink water.

No more of that, Arthur. No! no! I now see the full value of my obedience to Mr. Valmont's commands; for I would, by heaven, rather this moment endure the rack, than be blasted to a life of hateful indigence, abhorred poverty!

Ay, ay, I must obey, must obey, Murden. Must, while my heart, my desires, my wishes, are still the same, must cloak them to please Mr. Valmont's eye; to fit his fashion I must be *a brother* to my charming Sibella; must abjure a world I adore, rail at men, curse women. – I invite you to the castle, Arthur, come and visit me in my disguise; come and by reminding me of times past, keep alive my hopes and expectations of times that may come.

Here, while I stay in this inn, I prepare for the first essay of my practice in the cynical science. I have been recollecting, as well as I could, the scraps and remnants of Mr. Valmont's harangue of man and womankind; and I think I have made of my memory a sort of common place book of this delectable jargon, from which I can pick and cull for all Mr. Valmont's occasions.

Half an hour or so, I stood before the looking-glass, to find what face was fittest to carry to the castle. The glances I have of late been used to, may do for the wood when Mr. Valmont is out of sight, but they will not suit the library. They speak a promptitude for pleasure. I must hide them under my cloak, and borrow something, if I can, of Mr. Valmont's sallow hues.

Yet these prudent necessary considerations found not an entrance into my mind till I came within six miles of Valmont castle. I was engrossed by a circumstance that hastened me to fly from the scene where I had known so much of joy and pleasure.

Abandoned, artful, cursed deceiver! I speak, Arthur, of Janetta, who has plundercd, duped, and jilted me. How well she feigned her passion! How artfully she drew me on continually to sacrifice to her avarice and vanity, till I was almost beggared; and with what management did she evade my first suspicions, and elude my enquiries, till at length an accident gave me proof too strong to be doubted or evaded, that she was falser than falsehood; that she was at once mine, and the mistress of her friend's husband! I would not trust myself to hear her plead in her defence; I would not stand the fascinations of her divine face; but having received Mr. Valmont's letter an hour before, I ordered my clothes to be packed up, and without taking leave of one single acquaintance, I set off post for England – Ha!

Was ever any thing more unfortunate than this. Ross, Mr. Valmont's steward, and one of the grooms from the castle have come into this inn, and know I am here. The groom I could manage, but Ross is not to be tampered with; and as sure as I live, he will inform Mr. Valmont of my passing half a day so near the castle. Had I possessed an atom of common understanding, I might have foreseen such an accident; and now, for want of this small share of foresight, I am panic struck. Ross was going from, not to the castle, therefore I will take one quarter of an hour to chill my looks into brotherhood, and then brave the worst.

CLEMENT MONTGOMERY

LETTER XII

FROM SIBELLA VALMONT

TO

CAROLINE ASHBURN

Hail, dearest Caroline! – Yes, peace and liberty, with every blessing for which Sibella pants, will enter when the 'heavy gaves of Valmont castle fly back' to receive her Clement.

I do not count the minutes, for that would be to make time more tedious, but I walk with a quicker step, with a firmer mien. I am ever seeking change of place, and sleep and I are almost unacquainted.

Yet other countenances wear the uniformity they did before. No matter! – but a short time; and, when I went to compare my own transports, I can look on the eye, or read the heart of Clement, and find them more than equalled.

My thoughts haste so pressingly to the future, that it requires an effort stronger than you can conceive, (you who expect no Clement) to turn them back to the detail you require.

I cannot be minute as to a conversation in which the hermit (as you call him) was chief speaker; for some parts of it I have forgotten, and others I did not understand.

He spoke with a rapidity which made him almost unintelligible; and his pauses seemed rather the effect of sudden anxiety, than of attention to my answers; he talked of escapes and accidents in a disjointed manner; so that, from his broken sentences, one might have supposed he meant I had placed him in hazard, and that I had conducted him to the Armoury. That which I remember most clearly was, the earnestness with which he urged me to lay no future restraint on myself. He said his interruptions were now ended – but, he added, and several times repeated, we should one day or other meet again; he then spoke something of dangers, but I know not whether they related to himself or me.

He was very pale, wildness and apprehension were marked on his features. He wore his hermit's hat and cloak, but the former was quite mis-shapen, and both disfigured by dust and cobwebs. Once, in the vehemence of his speech, he raised his arm, the folds of his cloak became loosened, and I saw a sword glitter beneath it.

I left him in the Armoury, nor have I entered it since. The wood is all my own again. No figure glides upon me but that my imagination loves to form.

On the day succeeding that in which I found the hermit in the Armoury, I saw Mrs. Valmont walking on the terrace. I went to her, and spoke of the circumstance. She appeared agitated by my words; she grasped my hand, and said the finger of heaven was in it; and she talked further in a strange way, of something that she called *it*, and *it*. She would not be me, she said, for worlds. I do fear the disorder has affected her intellects.

But a little little interval between me and perfect happiness! I cannot write. You know, Caroline, I love you, but now, indeed, I cannot write.

Dearest Caroline, adieu.

SIBELLA VALMONT

LETTER XIII

FROM CLEMENT MONTGOMERY

TO

ARTHUR MURDEN

'Tis all gone, Murden. The pinnacle of my hopes and expectations is crumbled to the dust. Where shall I turn me, or what consolation shall I ask? Arthur, do not bestow on me that insolent pity which only augments misfortune.

I am not the same Clement Montgomery you formerly knew, brought up in the castle, with homage and respect, afterward introduced into the circles of fashion, as Mr. Valmont's heir, and supported with an allowance equal to that expectation; no, I am only one to whom he gave an accidental kindness, on whom he bestowed temporary favours, and whom he now condemns to the abhorred life of care, and plodding with the lower orders of mankind.

Cursed be the hour in which I entered that inn, from whence I wrote you my last letter! in that hour my misfortunes began. When I arrived at the castle, Mr. Valmont was from home. Every creature rejoiced in my arrival. Even the insensible Mrs. Valmont lavished caresses on me, and praised the improvements of my person. Ah! but how can I tell you of Sibella's joy? I know nothing that describes it: so unrestrained, so exquisitely soft and tender, exquisitely delicate in all its effusions!

She appeared to me quite a new creature. I could not but acknowledge to myself, that her charms surpassed even the faithless Janetta's charms. I loved her the first moment I beheld her better than I had ever loved her before; and I in secret cursed myself for having sacrificed my innocence, and cursed you also, Arthur, who once said, *forget her in other arms*.

One hour I passed in heaven, and then Mr. Valmont returned home. Ross came with him. I saw them ride over the bridge, and I trembled with apprehension. Mr. Valmont did not leave me long in doubt; for, when I would have hastened to the library, I was stopped by his gentleman who denied me admittance.

Three days Mr. Valmont preserved his inflexible resentment; and these three days were passed with Sibella. She knew not why her uncle was in anger with me, and she reviled him and cheered me with her smiles, and sweet sounds of love, that I might not droop at my reception. She bade me talk of the world. Alas, it was an alluring theme, and I talked with more ardor than discretion of its abounding delights. I did not tell her though, Arthur, of all the delights I had tasted there.

On the fourth morning, a messenger came to summon me to the library. I turned pale, I loitered. 'Go! fly, Clement!' said Sibella: 'Cast away these apprehensions. Recollect, my dear dear Clement, that my uncle's favourite maxim is, that disappointment should be always the forerunner of pleasure. Who knows but Mr. Valmont at this moment waits to bestow happiness on us?'

I went. With very different forebodings from Sibella's I entered Mr. Valmont's presence. He received me like a stern haughty judge; I stood an abashed fearful culprit.

He bitterly inveighed against my want of duty, in resting so long in that inn so near his castle, after two years absence. He demanded the reasons of my conduct; and I stammered an incoherent something about want of horses, and having had letters to write. He saw I lied. He knew I lied.

'Well, Sir,' said he, after a pause, 'we will pass that by for the present. Now give me an account of your travels, and their effect upon your opinions.'

No matter what I said, Arthur. 'Tis enough to tell you of the manner. It seems I had not rancour enough for Mr. Valmont; I could not belie my feelings with sufficient warmth. I could not renounce enormities I had never known, and which have no existence but in his own inflated imagination.

Sensible, that the manner of my description, and Mr. Valmont's expectations, bore no sort of affinity, I became more and more confused; until one of those frowns and gestures, which at nine years old made me tremble for my life, now imposed on me a sudden silence. My sentence remained unfinished, and Mr. Valmont leaning upon the table, beat an angry tattoo with the fingers of his right hand. His eyes rolled from one object to another, without resting upon any thing.

It might be a minute or more, perhaps, in my estimation it was an age, that we remained thus. Suddenly Sibella opened the door and entered a little way, in a light and chearful manner; but seeing the state we were in, she hesitated, turned an enquiring look upon me, and then made a graceful bend to Mr. Valmont.

'How now, Sibella?' said he, 'who bid you come hither?'

'I came, Sir ——' she replied, in a sweet but irresolute accent, and then she again looked at me.

'I say, by what authority do you come, since you have not mine?'

While Mr. Valmont sternly asked that question, she kept her eyes fixed on my pale perplexed countenance.

'Ah, Sir,' said she anxiously, 'don't you love Clement now?'

Mr. Valmont made no reply for two or three seconds. I dared not look up to see whether he was more, or less angry.

'Tell me, child,' said he presently, to Sibella, 'what has that boy said to you, since he returned so *affectionately, so dutifully, so speedily*, to Valmont castle?'

Sibella paused: 'Tell me no falsehoods,' said he still more sternly.

'Falsehoods!' she repeated in a forcible tone, the colour mounting higher in her cheeks, 'Sir, I have nothing to do with falsehoods. I paused, because I thought I could not readily collect the matter of our conversations into the compass of one answer. I might, indeed have done it, for they have been uniform. We have talked, Sir, of our unchanging truth. Of times past, and times to come. Of the world, of its pleasures, and its virtues. Of——'

'Enough of it.' cried Mr. Valmont, darting on me a glance of extreme wrath; 'You talked, you say, of times that are to come. Pray, who endowed you with the gift of foretelling what times are to come?'

'Sir, our endowments are perfectly natural. We do not presume to tell of the future, except as far as it is confined to the feelings of our own hearts. We know, fully and entirely know, that our hearts must cease to throb with life, when that love is extinguished, which was born and nurtured to its growth, under the encouragement of your approbation – do not frown on me, Sir, – I – I——'

Mr. Valmont did not speak while Sibella made a faultering stop. She shortly went on again thus:

'I confess, Sir, that I do fear you. Habit is prevalent with me, and I still tremble at your frowns. I would not offend you, but I must expostulate. Oh be not, I intreat you, be not angry with Clement for loving me! He must love me. Our love is the very soul of our being. Give us then, Sir, new life! Unalloyed felicity! Say—— '

She seized my hand, and leading me close up to Mr. Valmont, she added, with rapid vehemence:

'Say now, that he is mine, and I am his for ever!'

Her emphasis made me tremble. I had neither power to brave him, and speak with her, nor attempt conciliating him, by withdrawing my hand from her's.

In a much less angry tone, although she had been so much more bold, than he had used to me, Mr. Valmont said,

'You are strangely presumptuous, child. Have I not told you, I have other designs. Have I not a right over you?'

'No, you have none!' replied Sibella, abruptly: 'No right to the exercise of an unjust power over me! Why dream of impossibilities, and talk of other designs? I tell you, Sir, I have looked on every side, and I find it is your caprice, and no principle of reason in you, that forbids our union.'

Had you seen him, Arthur, you could alone judge of the rage into which this daring speech threw Mr. Valmont. He sprang up, *My caprice!* he vociferated, and after bestowing on Sibella an execration, he rushed past us out of the library.

Sibella, neither abashed nor terrified, would have me go with her into the park, but I dared not; fearing that Mr. Valmont might think I joined in braving him if he saw us together. I endeavoured to persuade her it was necessary I should remain in the library, and proper that she should leave me. The lovely romantic girl called me weakly timid, and left me somewhat displeased.

I sat out the time of Mr. Valmont's absence from the library, full two hours, Arthur. When he came in, he said, 'Go, Sir. I shall have occasion for you by and by.'

So much prudence had I, that I did not go near Sibella, but shut myself, for the rest of the day, in my chamber, and sent her word it was by Mr. Valmont's order. My servant found her weeping, with her little favourite Fawn in her arms.

At six o'clock in the evening, I was again commanded to appear before Mr. Valmont, which I did with the most humble and submissive deportment I could possible assume.

Before he spoke to me, he ordered Andrew to stand without the door, to oppose Sibella, if she attempted to enter the library. Thus he began.

'Little did I expect, Clement, when I sent you from Valmont castle, guarded by the lessons of my wisdom and experience, that you would return with inclinations so different to those I would have had you possess. Your folly is excessive, and it will work its own punishment.'

And on this theme he laboured most abundantly; it would weary you were I to repeat it all. The second part of his subject commenced thus.

'You know, young man, (I am young man now, Arthur), that I have been a friend to you, a more than common friend. Such a one as you will not readily find among those people you admire, with equal mischief to yourself, and ingratitude to me. You——'

Pshaw! I have not patience to recount the dull monotony of his charges, let me at once proceed to the distracting summing up of the whole.

He told me, Arthur, that he was about to send me again from Valmont castle. Ay, but how? Not with affluence at my command, and honours in my possession, no, like a poor discarded wretch, condemned to disgrace and slavery.

Yes, by heaven! Mr. Valmont, with a brow and heart of marble, told me, he had determined, as the best means of promoting my happiness that I should go to London; and there choose for myself a profession, hereafter to live by it; and that his friendship and assistance would always be mine, according to the decency and propriety of my deportment. I thought I should have sunk upon the floor, Arthur.

The barbarian went on to torture me: In my castle you remain but one month from this day. And then I shall give you L.50 which will be sufficient for you, while you prepare your plans, and what future services you require, must be regulated by your deserts, young man.'

'I think,' continued Mr. Valmont, 'it is my lot to receive nothing but disobedience and ingratitude from those to whom I have shewn most kindness. You heard the insolence with which Sibella, to-day dared to arraign my conduct. Tell her from me, Clement, that she almost urged me to counteract the great good I intend her. But I will not be rash. Tell her, that implicit obedience, and humble submission may expiate her offence. I declare solemnly, that if she dares enter into my presence to plead for you, while you stay in the castle, she shall that instant be confined close prisoner in her chamber, and shall see you no more. If she becomes modest, temperate, and submissive, and things turn out as I expect, she will live yet to be very happy with the husband I intend her.'

Much longer did he enlarge upon Sibella's offence, his anger, her expected penitence, and his future designs for her. I heard him but imperfectly. The other part of his harangue had conjured up a horrible fiend. Dead-eyed poverty glared before me.

At length, he stumbled on a supposition, that Sibella would attempt to leave the Castle with me; and I readily promised, as he desired, that I would neither make, nor assist in the attempt, but would inform him if she resolved on so dangerous and mad an enterprise.

Not one consolating hint did my ready obedience purchase. He said, indeed, that the propriety of my present deportment merited commendation. And he dismissed me. After four hours of this cruel interviews' duration, he permitted me to stagger, sick, oppressed, drooping, dying, to my chamber, and seek rest, if I could find it.

I number the moments with more exactness than the sands of an hour-glass. One month is wasted now to one fortnight, and the end of that fortnight is wretchedness certain and endless.

I have not told Sibella, yet she sees misery in my looks. She hears it in my sighs, and the contagion has reached her. We meet but seldom. Complaint and remonstrance have usurped the place of transport and endearment. To her I attribute my sorrows to my jealousy of this rival, to whom Mr. Valmont dooms her. Alas, my jealousy has but a small share in them. Two years back, but to have dreamed another had gained possession of her charms would have driven me mad. Now I know it an inevitable certainty, and my feeble jealousy has none of the fierce characteristics of that raging passion: no, it is just fitting the groveling lover who is condemned to earn his abject livelihood.

She has seen him too. Mr. Valmont, in his own inexplicable way, has contrived two whimsical meetings for them. She does not conjecture this. Having related the circumstance, it is removed from her thoughts, and she mourns my supposed jealousy, as a cruel misfortune.

My impending fate she must know sooner or later, and this very morning, when she quits her apartments to go to the wood, I am resolved to follow, and tell her my despair. Perhaps she will join in seeming to renounce me, and thus so far conciliate Mr. Valmont, that some pity may arise for me in his obdurate breast.

You, Arthur, may perhaps be as insensible to the calamities of your friend as you have hitherto appeared to his pleasures. I have seen some letters that speak of you, and by them, I learn you are not less inexplicable to others than to me. Who is this Miss Ashburn that Sibella rapturously speaks of? I think I should not like her. She appears to have far-fetched ideas. I wonder Mr. Valmont should have suffered her and Sibella's intercourse. Are you, Murden, in love with this lady? Answer me these questions, and above all, assure me that you will not breathe a whisper of this change in my affairs to any living creature.

Sibella this instant crosses the lawn, I depart on my desperate errand.

I have performed my task, and gained nothing by it. No nothing. She will not, cruel as she is, she will not soothe Mr. Valmont, by pretending to renounce me. By heaven, I do not believe she loves me! Scarcely did she betray a particle of surprise, not one of grief. When I declared myself disinherited, I expected to have seen her frantic.

Well, then, it is all at an end! Ay, ay, she is wise. She talks of love to amuse me, and already prepares to yield herself to the wealthy lover Mr. Valmont provides. Oh, distraction! They will live in splendor and happiness, while I, an outcast, die contemned, unpitied, and forgotten.

Farewel! Would I could say for ever!

CLEMENT MONTGOMERY

LETTER XII

FROM SIBELLA VALMONT

TO

CAROLINE ASHBURN

Why in that moment should I turn coward, and rush from my purposes? Why did imagination cast an unusual gloom around me? Why did I sigh and tremble? Such alone ought to be the emotions of a guilty mind, and surely I am blameless.

I am about to do nothing rash, I obey no impulse of passion, I have not separated duty and pleasure. I have examined the value of the object I would obtain with calmness; and whatever view I take of the means, still duty points to the part I have chosen.

Oh, Caroline, could I once have imagined that I should require hours to deliberate whether I ought to become the bride of Clement!

No longer the animated noble Clement, whose love, the very essence of his existence, soared beyond murmurs, jealousies, and fears, whose eye ever spoke the fulness of content, he is now wan, desponding, as ardent, yet less chaste, misled by the wild creations of his distempered fancy, ashamed of poverty, brooding over imaginary evils; over doubts, fears, jealousies!

What a dark and fatal cloud must have overspread the mind of Clement, ere he could fear Sibella, for her love is not a mutable passion, it is incorporate with her nature. My love and reason have become one, my fancy only subservient to its predominant command. Clement still loves, and I know he would view the fairest beauty, the brighest grace, with an unmoved look, with an unpalpitating heart, for who that loved could be faithless!

But 'tis this cold, this cruel uncle has done it all. He heaps secret on secret, uncertainty on uncertainty, till the poor youth, bewildered, surrounded, overwhelmed, sinks the victim of conjecture.

He is no longer Mr. Valmont's heir, and he shudders at the prospect of earning his future subsistence. Mr. Valmont tells him we shall not be united, and forgetting that we are not the puppets of his power, even this useless threat, Clement loads with terror. Another separation too is about to take place, and he has not once looked forward to the hour, when we shall wash away the remembrance in tears of joy at our re-union.

And shall I be content merely to deplore my former Clement, giving nothing, to restore him? Oh, no! – I had written to him, I had even ascended the stairs to his apartment, when a sudden terror seized upon me. I hastily hid the billet from my view, and with the restlessness of an anxious mind, first sought the wood, and then my chamber.

The billet lies before me, I have examined its purport. It calls on Clement to become my husband. For ought I to withhold myself from giving him the fullest proof of my affection, from renovating him by this proof, because Mr. Valmont cruelly commands it? Surely I ought not. Mr. Valmont's presence and benediction might adorn with one more smile the nuptial hour, but 'tis our hearts alone that can bind the vow. If Clement's is not in unison with mine, if he feels the necessity of other ties, he will refuse the offer, and point out to me that I have erred.

My courage rises. The paleness of fear on my cheek gives way to the glow of hope. I shall forget that absence, misfortune, and pain, have intervened and live over again those hours of joy and peace, when our bosoms heaved no sigh, save the rich sigh of transport and confidence.

I go; and to-morrow will I, though now forbidden his presence, go to my uncle, and conjure him to convince himself that power and command are useless, when reason and conviction oppose them. Adieu.

SIBELLA VALMONT

LETTER XIII

FROM CLEMENT MONTGOMERY

TO

ARTHUR MURDEN

Read the inclosed, dear Arthur, and imagine my sudden transition from despair to rapture. I was sitting, mute in anguish, when the divine form of my Sibella appeared at my chamber door. She held to me a paper, and as I took it, she turned away sighing deeply. Read, read, I say, and partake if you can my feelings. But though I tell you, I have just arisen from her arms, with your cold killing indifference it is impossible you can form the shadow of a resemblance to those transports which wrap my senses in delirium.

Did you think I had not dared to follow? O, Yes! It was not to face the stern Mr. Valmont; no, it was in secret to receive Sibella to my arms, whom I love more than life. It was to outplot Mr. Valmont. To enjoy a glorious though secret triumph over this rival, this chosen, this elected of Mr. Valmont's favour. How could I, with youth glowing in my veins, love throbbing in my heart, reject the tempting offer, though multitudes of dangers threatened at a distance.

Avaunt, ye dark forebodings! Ye gloomy horrors assail not now the enraptured Clement! The hours cannot move backwards. The deed cannot be undone.

The moon and stars shone sole witnesses of our contract! But read, Murden. Write to me instantly, and say you have for once warmed yourself into delight, to find something like the state of

CLEMENT MONTGOMERY

N.B. Exquisite, but misjudging charmer! She would have told Mr. Valmont, that she had given herself to me. My arms my prayers could hardly restrain her from her wild purpose.

BILLET

FROM SIBELLA TO CLEMENT

Inclosed in the preceding Letter

When I would speak, I weep. New feelings, new ideas agitate my mind. A tremor that I cannot banish gives confusion to my thoughts, and all I now wish to express should be regular, forcible.

Once, had my heart conceived the design with which it now vibrates under a weight of apprehensions, it had been uttered without preparation: but you are not the same. Mr. Valmont's mysteries have acted on you in their full effect. You teach your brow caution. You learn concealments. You fear rivals!

Rivals in Sibella's love! Oh, no! no! no! But force you say. Mr. Valmont's power – Ah, Clement, Clement, turn your thoughts back, and find its importance.

But you cannot, Dread has seized up on you, and Mr. Valmont heightens the threatened evil, till it appears already arrived: it overwhelms you with its terrors, and there is nought left to Sibella but remembrance to paint her Clement.

Let Mr. Valmont dismiss you; that bears not the semblance of misfortune. But you shall not go to have your efforts chained down by despair, your vigour shall not be impaired by corroding doubts. When you seek delight, you shall remember your love, and the present short absence shall be the only pang her idea can inflict.

Come to my apartments. With pure hearts and hands, we will plight our fervent unspotted faith. Say I am your's, and you are mine, and sorrow and jealousy will vanish as a mist. You shall go the transported confiding husband.

LETTER XIV

FROM ARTHUR MURDEN

TO

CLEMENT MONTGOMERY

SIR

Your letters, one and all, I suppose, have come in safety to my hands. In your last you are urgent for my answer. It is this. Although you, Mr. Montgomery, amuse your spleen or your fancy, by talking of my *cold killing indifference*, I have such *feelings* as tell me your conduct is neither that of a lover nor a man.

Farewel, Sir. I renounce your friendship. I desire only to remain a stranger to your name and remembrance.

ARTHUR MURDEN

LETTER XV

FROM ARTHUR MURDEN

TO

CLEMENT MONTGOMERY

Montgomery

Call me mad, possessed. Curse me, reproach me, do anything, only that when you have had your revenge, forget such a letter as I wrote you last ever had existence.

Say it was strange, I say so too. Call it insolent, I will confess it; unaccountable, I still join with you. It was one of the sudden whirls of this vertigo brain of mine, almost as incomprehensible to myself as to you.

I have no excuses to offer, for the fit may come again upon me. Promise has no power with me, I am the creature of impulse. Alas! Alas! that reason and consistency should thus become the shuttlecocks of fancy!

Now taking it for granted, that I gain your pardon, next have I a long account to settle with myself. I would not partake of happiness of a common mould; lay it before me, and I disdained the petty prize, stalked proudly over it, and stalked on, prying, and watching, to seize hold on some hidden blessing, that reserved itself to be the reward of a deserving ventrous hero like myself – Oh! I have embraced a cloud, and the tormenting wheel rolls round with a rapid motion!

I know I am talking algebra to you, and if you take me for a companion, you must even be content to travel on in the dark. It is so, but why it is, I think your best discernment will not aid you to discover. Enquiry is useless, expostulation, a farce. Be patient, and forgive me this, and other transgressions, for I tell you, Montgomery, you have a potent revenge.

There is little probability that you and I should meet each other, as London will be the scene of your action, while I contdemn myself to wander north and south, in search of a few grains of that content I so wantonly gave the winds to scatter. I must have room to vent my suffocating thoughts. I cannot be pinioned in the croud; and I would rather seek converse with myself in a charnel house, than enter the brightest circles of fashion. I hate to be the wonder of fools. Already is my reputation raised, and I have now just sense enough in madness to play my antics alone.

Driven by winds and storms, I may seek an occasional shelter at Barlowe Hall. Whither, if you are so disposed, you may direct to
                                                        ARTHUR MURDEN

I believe, Montgomery, it is necessary that I say something more to you. The above conclusion is abrupt and harsh. That I feel inclined to treat you thus is the consequence of my own folly, rather than your deservings of me. Let it pass then. I wish you no ill, but as I told you before, I am become the tool of every changing impulse.

I sympathise in your change of fortune; or rather, I feel a concern that you should colour with such darkened hues, so unimportant a circumstance.

I too have counted upon heirship. But let my uncle the nabob put five hundred pound in my pocket, and set me down in London, Petersburg, or Pekin, and if I did not walk my own pace through the world, let me die like a dog, and have no better burial.

Five hundred pound! 'Tis a mine. Ah, sigh not to be foremost of the throng! Independence, peace, and self approving reflection may be, if you will, the companions of your new destiny.

Certainly Mr. Valmont managed his plan of making you a Hermit with wonderful ingenuity, to send you forth from your cave at that very age when the fancy runs gadding after novelty, and shadow passes for substance. He decked you too with the trappings of wealth, and expected every man to appear before you, with a label written on his forehead, of his souls most secret vice. – He had better have driven you out to beg with an empty wallet, and than perhaps when one had said – *Go work* – another had hinted – *Go steal* – and a third had passed you and said nothing, you might possibly have returned to a leopard's skin, and a hut of branches, the man after Mr. Valmont's own heart.

Be wiser and happier, Montgomery, than this man has been; shun his weaknesses and your own; you also have your portion of weaknesses follies, vices. Yes Montgomery the latter word is not too harsh, or I should not have had now to pity you for being duped by the contemptible Janetta L——. Other instances there are for me to cite: They press upon my feelings – they wound – they torture me!

Judge for yourself, Montgomery, upon the right and wrong of your conduct and intentions. I am ill fitted to become your adviser.

How could you so far mistake my character as to suppose I was the seducer of Seymour's mistress: I think one of your letters asserted so much. If to persuade a deceived girl to quit her profligate companion (I will not say lover, I should disgrace the name) and return to console the latter days of an aged grandmother be seduction, I am guilty. This I did to Seymour, and his invectives or the rumours he may spread are as unimportant and as little troublesome to my repose as the insects that are buzzing around me.

Montgomery, no more of your phrases, nor his accusations. Be assured I am neither your *soulless* marble, nor Seymour's *libertine*.

At a boyish age from boyish vanity I aimed to be called a man of pleasure. It was easy to imitate the air and manners of such a man, and not less by such imitation alone to arrive at the contemptible fame among persons equally ready to encourage the practice and accuse the practitioner.

I renounce the loathsome labours of the flatterers, the despicable renown of the libertine. Miss Ashburn is my monitress, she began her lessions at Barlowe Hall, and now continues the instruction at Bath.

Do not imagine it was done in devout lectures or pious declamations. No, it was the stedfast modesty of her eye, her intelligent condemning mein, which said, here shall thy proud boast be stayed.

She was the finest woman of our party; and all the rest prepared to meet me with the glance of approbations and the smile of encouragement; yet she having been forewarned of my renown preferred the hand or arm or speech of a silly old colonel of sixty. – Now she knows me better. No, she does not, I evade, I fly her penetration.

Montgomery, the worthiest feeling I know of you is, that you lament your having made your truth and innocence a sacrifice.

I am not in love with Miss Ashburn. I would give an ear, an eye, any thing I have on earth, except the full confidence of my heart, to call her my sister, my friend. I admire, seek, venerate her; but, Montgomery, I am not in love with Miss Ashburn.

END OF THE FIRST VOLUME

VOLUME II

LETTER I

FROM CAROLINE ASHBURN

TO

SIBELLA VALMONT

I have not answered your letter, my dear Sibella, as soon as you perhaps may have expected, because I was willing to dwell on the circumstances it contained, till the minutest shade was present with me, and till I discovered exactly wherein to praise, or wherein to blame. The time I have taken to deliberate has not been thrown away, for it has excited ideas in my mind that may prove of infinite service to us both: and should I in future find aught to add or diminish from my sentiments, I shall offer it as frankly as I now do my present decision.

Sibella, well might you, even at the door of Clement's apartment, retreat from your enterprise: for then, at that moment, you wandered the first step from your rectitude; and had you, instead of sitting down to detail your reasons to me, enquired narrowly into the cause of your sensations, you must have discovered that error was creeping in upon you, and that your native frankness and stedfast sincerity were making a vigorous effort to repel *secresy*, that canker-worm of virtue.

Have you forgotten, my Sibella, when you said – 'I am not weak enough to descent to artifice. Did I believe it right to go, I should go openly. Then might he try his opposing strength: but he would find that I could leap, swim or dive, and that walls or moats are feeble barriers to a determined will.'

This was noble; and I promised myself that, in you, I should find the one rare instance wherein no temptation could incline, or terror affright, into any species of concealment. I grant nothing could bring the temptation more strongly forward than the state into which Clement and you were forced: but still you should have resisted. Your every thought should still have flown to your lips. Your every intention should have been as public to those by whom you were surrounded as to yourself. No matter though it should dash aside a present project. Be openly firm in the resolution to do right, and, my life for it, the opposition of mistake and prejudice will bear no proportion in strength to your perseverance.

It is evident that this plain and necessary truth mixed itself with your ideas, although the tumults of hope and fear, and the croud of images that were then rushing on your mind, dazzled your perception; for you saw it in part, when you resolved to declare to Mr. Valmont in the morning all that you had done. Would you had previously declared it! I know how useless it is to wish over the past: yet I must again say – would you had previously declared it!

You pause, Sibella – you are convinced: but you instantaneously quit the regret of that error for selfcongratulation. I can enter into all your feelings; and I find you now dwelling with pleasure on the supposition that I condemn only the concealment, that I look on the contract itself as an act of justice, and that I am about to applaud you for the fulfillment of a duty. And herein it is that I have doubted. To this one point have I called every present and remote circumstance; and it is from the combination of circumstances alone that I have been able to decide. The distinction becomes nice between praise and blame, for I have both to offer: yet, if I judge aright, some praise belongs to you – to the blame Mr. Valmont has an incontestible title.

With such an education as he has given you, unless you had been a mere block without ideas, it was impossible you should not become a romantic enthusiast in whatever species of passion first engaged your feelings: and Mr. Valmont took care to make that first passion *Love*. Whatever cause can have led him to his present inconsistency, it is as evident to me as light and sensation – that it was his settled plan to render love for each other the ruling feature of your's and Clement's character. The contrivance was worthless; but the performance was admirable. Thus you and Clement loved from habit.

Youth is always ardent and lively; it inclines to fondness; and you had none of the constraints which society lays on the first expansions of tenderness. You had no claimants, from kindred or family, on your affections: for the forbidding Mr. Valmont excited only fear; and you sought shelter in each other's arms, from the terrors of his frown. It was not more natural to breathe, than to love – it was not more natural to love, than to obey its dictates. Thus you and Clement, secluded from the world with your every pleasure arising only from mutual efforts to please, could not fail to love from habit. Had Clement and you been educated in the world, Clement would still have loved from habit: because I suspect he possesses more of softness than of strength. He would have loved often; and it would have been a trivial love: neither arising to any height, nor directed by any excellence.

You, Sibella, would have loved from reflection, from a more intimate knowledge of increasing virtues, from the intercourse of mind: then call it friendship, or call it love, it would indeed possess those predominant and absorbing qualities you describe, and which you now feel. But, Sibella, depend on it Clement had never been the object.

Pardon me, I do not mean to wound you. I know you will not shrink from truth; and I must therefore tell you, that the alteration in Clement which you ascribe wholly to Mr Valmont's mysteries I ascribe to feebleness of character. Wherever your's rises to superiority his sinks. Had he been equal, and had there been no secrecy in the case, I would have hailed your *marriage*. I well know, my friend, that you did not mean to separate duty and pleasure. Motives the most chaste and holy guided you. No forms or ceremonies could add at atom to your purity, or make your's in the sight of heaven more a marriage – yet do I wish, with all the fervency of my soul, this marriage had been deferred – that you had previously informed Mr. Valmont.

'Tis past: and repentance is only of value as it guides us in our future actions. We must endeavour to rouse Clement from his inactivity. I do believe he is not vicious, though your uncle's conduct respecting him has the worst of tendencies: my Sibella's excellence must have placed a talisman around him from which vice retires hopeless of influence. This is one great step: and, as I understand from Mr. Murden he is to be in London, I will seek his friendship; give a spur to every lurking talent; endeavour to preserve him free from taint; and if I had judged too hastily, if he is beyond what I expect, with what delight shall I contemplate the merits of him whose fate you have interwoven with your own! – Ah, how close is the texture – with what firmness can you think – to what excess can you love!

The dark season of the year is arrived. The fashionable world haste to the capital. We are never hindmost of the throng; yet this once have I urged forward our removal to London with all my influence; for I apprehend the succession of its gay diversions, and the multiplicity of varied engagements which must then occupy my mother, will remove from her mind any inclination towards a second marriage. Here, opportunity is always at hand for that despicable race of young men who are ever on the watch to sell their persons and liberty to the highest bidder; and, as Mrs. Ashburn's immensity of wealth is the general topic, her splendor the general gaze, and her vanity not a whit more concealed from observation, the fortune hunters croud around her. At first the love of flattery appeared wholly to engage her and each was acceptable in his turn; till, at length, the elegant person of one youth became distinguished in a manner that alarmed me. Not but I should rejoice to see my mother yield herself to the guardianship of some good man, who had sense enough to advise, and resolution to restrain her lavish follies. Of such an union I have not any hope; and I must, if possible, prevent her being the dupe and victim of a misguided choice.

This young man possessed in a very emminent degree the advantages of person, air, and address; yet, when he directed his attentions wholly towards Mrs. Ashburn, there was such evident constraint in his manner, and his professions were so laboured, that almost any other woman would have contemned him. Mrs. Ashburn did not. She received, she encouraged him, she led him into every circle in open triumph, as her devoted lover: while his forced levity, at one time, and at another, his pale cheek, absence of mind, and half uttered sighs, told to every observer that he was a sacrifice but not a lover. I could not believe that the affair would ever be brought to so absurd a conclusion, till I found that the day of marriage was actually fixed on. I ought to have interfered before; for my interference has now saved them from the commission of such a folly.

I must, Sibella, reserve the history of this young man till another letter. I am called from the pleasing occupation of writing to you, by an engagement with a being more variable, more inexplicable, than any being within my knowledge, yet to me not less interesting than any. I mean Mr. Murden.

Never need I be wearied with the sameness of my thoughts, while I reside under one roof with Murden; for, let me turn them on the caprices of his conduct, and I shall find puzzling varieties without end.

Ever your's
CAROLINE ASHBURN

LETTER II

THE SAME – TO THE SAME

Henry Davenport is the young man of whom I am to speak. It was publicly mentioned here that he was related to several noble families; and at the same time was always hinted that he possessed no fortune. This I was ready to believe, from his addressing my mother.

Constantly surrounded with parties, and studious to avoid me, it was useless to attempt reasoning with my mother. I therefore wrote a card to Mr. Davenport, requesting an hour's conversation with him the succeding morning.

He came. He was light and gay in his habit and address. His voice possessed an unusual softness; and his cheek was flushed with an hectic colour, equally proceeding, I thought, from want of rest and intemperance.

'Mr. Davenport,' said I, interrupting his compliments, 'you will convince me most that you are pleased with this interview by answering the questions I shall propose with seriousness and sincerity.'

He folded his hands and ludicrously lengthened his visage; but of this I took no notice. 'Tell me,' continued I, 'frankly and truly, what is your opinion of my mother?'

His levity instantly disappeared; and he replied in a hurrying manner – 'I think Mrs. Ashburn a very charming – a very fine woman indeed.'

'What are your motives, sir, for marrying her?'

'Miss Ashburn,' said he, with great quickness and removing from the opposite side of the room to a chair next me, 'I do respect and admire you as much or perhaps more than any woman on the face of the earth. I would eat my flesh rather than injure you; and if Mrs. Ashburn give me her hand, I swear your interest in her fortune shall not be affected. I do not wish to be master of the principal. I only

want to share some of that income which is lavished on superfluities.
– O God! O God! how happy would the uncontrouled, independent,
present possession of some of those hundreds make me!'

You cannot conceive the force with which he uttered this; and it
seemed to recal a world of pressing ideas to his mind: for I found it
necessary to wait till his attention returned of itself.

'And the enjoyment of this income in marriage will make you
happy, year after year, all your life, Mr. Davenport?'

'Surely, Miss Ashburn,' and he looked at me stedfastly, 'you cannot
think I would ever use your mother ill.'

'Do you love her, sir?'

'I have told you, Miss Ashburn, I admire her – I think her a fine
spirited woman.'

'Do you love her, sir?' rejoined I with more emphasis.

'Love! why yes – no! – I have a great friendship for her, madam. –
But as to love 'tis out of fashion – it is exploded.' He rose; and walked
towards the window. 'Love is a romance; a cant; a whine; a delirium;
a poison; a rankling wound that festers here, here!' he layed his hand
on his heart, and leaned against the wainscot.

I sighed too: for the under tone of voice in which he pronounced
the last few words was inscribably affecting. He quickly started from
this posture, and threw himself on his knees before me.

'I confess it all,' said he, 'I am not more wretched than desperate.
This marriage is my resource from worse evils. Oh, Miss Ashburn! by
that benignity which irradiates your every action I conjure you suffer it
to proceed! – I will be grateful. – I will honor and revere your mother.
– More I cannot promise – I cannot. Allow me to depart, madam, I
cannot endure to be questioned.'

And thus saying, he would have quitted the room, had I not held
him by the arm, and with difficulty prevailed on him again to take
his seat, and to listen to me patiently while I pourtrayed the evils of
such a marriage, and the cruel injustice he was guilty of towards a
woman so chosen.

'I know all that,' replied Davenport. I have foreseen it a thousand
and a thousand times. I know I am a villain; but Mrs. Ashburn shall
never suspect me. I will be the obedient slave of her will. She shall
mould me to whatever shape her pleasure inclines. I will be more
docile than infancy. I will forego my very nature, at her command.'

'But you have not foreseen, Mr. Davenport, that the time must
arrive when her volatility and incessant eagerness after pleasure will

cease to relieve you. It is in the hours of age and infirmity that she will call on you for aid, will seek in your soothing voice, in your cheering smile a relief from pain: and how will you perform your task in those multiplied moments? My mother does not want discernment: and what will be your torture to see her dying perhaps under the agonizing reflection that the man on whose honour she relied, on whose faith and sincerity her hopes had towered to felicity, that, her husband had deceived her, perhaps had loved another.'

He became pale as death. I continued. 'But you shall not hasten to this destruction. I will prevent this marriage.'

'Miss Ashburn, for heaven's sake!' cried he: 'I have no other means –! must – marry.'

I took hold of his hand, for he trembled. 'I wish to be your friend, Mr. Davenport; indeed I am your friend, at this moment; it is far from my intention to tear from you this fallacious hope, without placing some certain and honourable advantage in its stead. Let me know your history. Neither conceal from me your wants nor your feelings, nor the situations they have throw you into; and I will undertake to do you every service that reason and humanity suggest.'

He attempted in vain to answer. Throwing himself back in the chair, he covered his face with an handkerchief, and shed tears.

I believe it was near a quarter of an hour ere he recovered from his agitation, and was able to speak as follows.

'My father was himself so enamoured of pomp that, although he allowed me, an only son, to share the magnificence of his town residence, yet he confined my sisters with their governess and two servants to a small house he possessed in a cheap country. I saw them only once a year; and the solitude of their abode was so irksome to me, that I was always eager to quit and unwilling to return at the usual period. However, about the time I was to set out on my travels, it was judged decent and necessary that I should pay them a visit of unusual length, as they were now almost women; and to my great surprize I found their old governess removed, and a young person with them as companion whom alas I did love to distraction.

'Weeks only were allotted to my stay, but I staid months. My father's mandates for my return were no sooner read than forgotten. All was enchantment and happiness. My sisters loved Arabella affectionately; and had so little knowledge of the world as to imagine our union altogether proper and probable.

At length, either surprised or alarmed at my continuance in the country, or having certain intelligence of my engagements, my father arrived one evening secretly and altogether unexpectedly. And, while we imagined our joys secure from interruption, he listened behind the little summer-house in which Arabella and I were interchanging vows of eternal constancy, till rage would not permit him to hear us longer. Then he burst upon us; and, as I defended my love with vehemence, he deprived me of present sensation by a blow.

'When I recovered I was confined to one room, and could obtain no tidings of Arabella, no intercourse with my sisters nor any intermission of the rigours of my imprisonment: although I obstinately refused all sustenance beyond the small quantity which irresistible hunger compelled me to eat against my will. In three weeks, one of my sisters found an expedient to let me know Arabella had been turned out of the house, and had taken shelter at the farm-house of a relation about five and twenty miles distance; that my father gave her the character of an abandoned strumpet, and vowed I should die in prison if I did not swear to renounce her for ever.

'From this time, I laboured night and day in contriving my escape till I effected it; and travelled the five and twenty miles with such speed in my emaciated state that I had no sooner thrown myself into Arabella's arms than I fell into fits. A fever succeeded; and, during this period, the people of the house, though excessively poor, strove with all their might to add comforts and conveniences to my situation. Arabella was my nurse. To them I was bound by gratitude – to her my ties became strengthened till they excluded reason, reflection, and prudence. The moments of returning health were devoted to my affection. Our days were passed alone. Our former distresses and future prospects were alike forgotten; and we became as guilty as happy.

'Scarcely had we begun to repent our error, when my father discovered my retreat; and once more tore me from my love. Guarded, fettered, and enduring every species of brutal usage from those employed about me, I was conveyed first to London, and then sent abroad, where I remained above two years – refusing to give her up, and refused upon any other terms to be allowed to return. My father's death gave me liberty. I flew to England; and found my Arabella pining under the accumulated distresss of extreme poverty, destroyed reputation, and a consumptive habit: all which miseries were rendered doubly poignant by the possession of an infant.

'I will not attempt, madam, to describe to you what I endured when I saw her and my child wanting absolute necessaries. All I could call my own was employed to procure medical advice for Arabella; and that all was a trifle. My father, to the astonishment of every one, had died insolvent. My sisters were taken into dependence by different relations; and I was turned adrift on the world without knowledge or means to procure myself one penny. To assist those who have no power to assist themselves, who have no claims but on me, me the author of their calamity, I have plunged myself into debt. The man of whom I have borrowed money pointed out to me the plan of marrying your mother; and, when I revolted at the dishonourable action, he shewed me the opposite picture – a jail. – What can I do, Miss Ashburn? Can I see them die – and consent to linger out my wretched existence in a prison? No! I am driven by extremity of distress; and must go on, or perish.'

'Does Arabella know you intend to marry?'

'O yes.'

'Where is she? May I see her?'

'She and her child reside at the distance of three miles from this place.'

I prevailed on Mr. Davenport to ride with me to the village in which Arabella resided; and, after introducing me to her, I also prevailed on him to leave us alone.

Arabella had beside her a tambour frame, at which she worked, when her cough and cold sweats would permit her. The little girl played on the floor. She received us with that sort of composure which seemed to denote the utter sacrifice of all her hopes and wishes, and that nothing was now left to excite agitation. I said, 'I am no stranger to your misfortunes, Arabella. In what manner did you support yourself, while Mr. Davenport was abroad?'

'By fancy works,' replied she, pointing to the frame. 'I endeavoured also to teach a school; but Mr. Davenport's father had spread such reports of me, which the birth of my child but too well confirmed, that scarce any one would give me the least encouragement.'

'What were your parents?'

'Poor shopkeepers, madam, who put themselves to numberless inconveniences to qualify me for earning my subsistence in a comfortable manner. Could I regain my health, and be removed to some place where no one knew my faults, Mr. Davenport should not be burthened with either of us; he should not——'

A tear rose, but quickly withdrew itself; and the serenity of a broken heart again took possession of her features.

'Why have you not urged Mr. Davenport to engage in some trade or profession?'

'Ah, madam, he has been brought up a gentleman. Trade would appear to him an indelible disgrace. He thinks he ought to respect the honour of his family, although they will not assist him. And as to a profession he has not the means.'

'And can you consent to live in possession of his affection and endearments, when he is married?'

'No, madam, no!' replied Arabella with firmness. 'The moment he becomes a husband, he is as dead to me as if the cold grave concealed him. He loves ease; he has been used to expence and pleasure – he will enjoy it all. I cannot live long, nor do I desire to live. I know he never will desert that poor babe – Don't you, madam, allow that innocent creature fully entitled to a father's protection?'

I had just taken the child on my lap. 'Yes,' said I: 'and you Arabella must live to see her possess it. My motives are not those of curiosity. I come to do you service; and I insist that you hope for better days. It shall be my part to devise better means than marriage for Mr. Davenport. I intend shortly to visit you again.'

I could not converse with Mr. Davenport any more that day, for it was necessary I should return and prepare myself to be partaker of a very splendid entertainment given by Sir Thomas Barlowe to all the fashionable people at Bath. I therefore engaged him to visit me again the next morning, and we separated.

Making mention of the entertainment brings Mr. Murden to my remembrance; and, as he played a part that very evening which attracted much notice and gave rise to speculation, I shall here relate it before I return to the subject of Mr. Davenport.

Ever since Mr. Murden joined us at Bath I have heard from his female acquaintance perpetual complaints of him. He was, they say, seducing, irresistible. No vivacity was ever so delicate as Murden's. No flattery ever so dangerous as from him. His look, his air, his voice, his gestures, all had their own peculiar character of persuasion. Thus captivating they say he was; and they lament, with all the energy of which they are capable, that he should now have become dull, lifeless and unbearable. I too, Sibella, have found him transformed. I see him negligent and inattentive to me and others; but he is neither dull nor lifeless. Some vision of imagination seems to possess him, to infuse into him as it were a new existence. I have seen his cheek glow, his eye beam. I have heard his breathings but half uttered; and, although at such moments I have suffered inconvenience from the want of his attention and assistance, I would rather have placed my safety in hazard than have disturbed his alluring dreams of fancy. So firmly has he become inaccessible to the temptations of dissipation and sensuality, that I revere his transformation and long for his confidence; but alas, I have to regret that he is secret and mysterious, and that while at Bath he has avoided me almost as constantly as he has neglected those damsels of fashion who have been calling forth all their enchantments to attract or subdue him.

To my great surprize, and some little satisfaction, no sooner was the Nabob's ball in preparation than Mr. Murden requested to be my partner. He had never danced here, though he had been frequently at the rooms; and I did expect to be honoured on this occasion by my fair friends with some very scornful looks and important whispers. – Hear the result.

The company assembled, a numerous and brilliant party. I had caught a previous glimpse of Mr. Murden elegantly dressed, and I expected every moment his appearance in the ball-room. That I was engaged I answered to several invitations; but to whom was yet in embryo, for the first, second, third and fourth minuet had been danced, and yet no partner for me appeared.

At length he came, but not with the smile of pleasure, not with the soft tread of politeness, the complacent mien of attention. No: he actually rushed upon us, his features almost distorted with some species of passion, his hair deranged, and the powder showered on his dress as if he had been dashing his head against some hard substance in a paroxism of rage. And in this strange manner did he, with eager long strides, cross the saloon, and throw himself into the vacant seat beside me, uttering a deep groan.

The eyes of every one were upon him; and astonishment imposed silence on every tongue. 'Miss Ashburn! Miss Ashburn!' repeated he twice very loud; then closed his teeth and murmured through them some words I could not understand, and several horrid imprecations. He sat thus a few minutes, his countenance varying from the deepest red to a most livid paleness, when Sir Thomas approached. 'Why, nephew! why Arthur! what, what, are you ill? – are you——?' and, without finishing his speech, the baronet retired abruptly; for Murden gnashing his teeth at that instant his uncle conceived he was mad; and I believe the baronet was scarce assured he had escaped the infection.

A bolder man now walked up. No less than the Earl of Ulson, of whom you have heard me speak. "Pon my soul, Murden, this is superlatively unusual! The ladies are actually terrified. Zounds! Murden, you must——'

We had not the good fortune to hear his lordship's advice to the end: for Mr. Murden, utterly inattentive to any thing but his own agitations, now snatched a crumpled letter from his pocket; and, tearing it into a thousand pieces, dashed the fragments on the floor. He there contemplated them a moment with a malignant smile; then carefully gathered up every fragment, and darted out of the room.

The band continued playing quite composedly; but the company assembled in separate groups, to communicate their various conjectures on the very extraordinary gambol this extraordinary young man had been playing. Sir Thomas's gentleman and a valet were sent in search of him and ordered to enquire into his malady; but we were presently informed that he was writing in his own chamber, and had bitterly sworn to blow out the brains of whatever person should dare to interrupt him. Brains not being a superfluity here, we e'en resolved to resume our dancing, and leave him alone to be as mad as he thought proper.

On the succeeding morning, I met him early and alone in the breakfast room. I was agitated with the expectation of hearing something painful and astonishing. I even intreated to be admitted to his confidence. He referred me to some future period. He spoke with calmness and resolution, but he seldom looked up. When the rest of the family joined us, my mother amused herself with affecting a ridiculous pity for him, Lady Barlowe painted her astonishment, while his uncle with much more sincerity laboured to impress us with an adequate idea of the terror he had suffered the preceding evening. Every syllable sunk into the soul of Murden. He preserved an inflexible and haughty silence: but I saw, in his agitated countenance, that he was frequently on the point of bursting into rage and madness. Sir Thomas Barlowe will on many occasions wind a shapeless circumstance round and round, till he has persuaded himself he has discovered something in it really insulting and injurious to him. He now conjectured, surmised, and talked of Murden's behaviour, till he had assured himself it could have no other design than to afflict him, the most affectionate of uncles; and, having for a short time indulged in the pathos of lamentation, he began to weep. Although I could scarcely forbear smiling at Sir Thomas Barlowe's folly, yet I was considerably affected by the sudden transition the baronet's tears produced in Murden. He forgot his anger and his dejection; he pressed his uncle's hand; soothed him with kind expressions: and, suddenly assuming an air of chearfulness, began to hand the cups and arrange the tea-table.

'You are in love with some creature you are ashamed of, Murden,' said my mother; 'I will swear it.'

'Do, madam,' replied he.

'Now do tell, me nephew Arthur,' said the baronet, 'why you tore it to pieces so unmercifully – tell me, dear Arthur, all about that letter.'

Why should he, Sibella, have fixed his eyes on me, while the colour rushed from his cheek, at the mention of that letter? Why did he groan? Why did he appear no more during the whole of that day? Why has he since been so uniformly pensive? Why seek me as a companion, yet reject me as a friend? Such are the enquiries constantly obtruding themselves upon me.

Adieu, dear Sibella. The remainder of Davenport's story must again be defered till another opportunity.

CAROLINE ASHBURN

LETTER III

FROM CLEMENT MONTGOMERY

TO

ARTHUR MURDEN

Sweet enthusiast! I loveliest romancer! sustained by thee, I could boldly defy the maxims of the world, could bear unmoved its taunting scorns, its loudest reproaches. Stimulated by thy visionary precepts, I could rush alone on its host of temptations, and attempt with the giantstep of fortitude to tread their legions into nothingness!

Methinks, Arthur, I see her now: and an increase of warmth glides through every vein till it reaches my heart, which glows and throbs more proudly and more proudly, that the arbitress of its every motion is Sibella Valmont. Let imagination dress up her most airy forms, let fancy exhaust the riches of her invention, the vision thus created may dazzle, may delude in the absence of perfection; but bring the all-radient charms of Sibella in contrast, and it sinks into vapour. Painting and language are alike incompetent to represent her. – Ha! that thought again shoots across my brain – I – I was inconstant! – Oh, I would give an eye, an ear, nay a limb, that I had never known other embraces! – Then I might have been all soul too: – what she now is, what I can imagine but never shall experience. – Yes, you gave the advice, Murden; and I , deserving almost damnation for the deed, stooped to gross allurements, and obeyed the calls of appetite, and I ought to have braved death in support of my constancy. Thank God! she cannot know it! And oh, may annihilation, or the worst of curses, fall on this head, rather than I again pollute myself, or entertain one thought within my breast that may not rank with her angelic purity!

Yes, Murden, I say purity. Ay, and she is as pure as angels, notwithstanding Clement has been admitted to her embraces. For I am her husband. She never heard of ties more holy, more binding, than those of the heart. Custom has not placed its sordid restraint on her feelings. Nature forms her impulses. Oh, she is Nature's genuine child! more lovely than painting can trace: yet robust as the peasant who climbs yon hill to toil for his hourly subsistence – soft as her lover's bounding wishes can desire: yet stedfast, aspiring, brave enough to lead an army in the field. No cowardly apprehensions enter her mind. She shrinks not from the wintry blast. Let the torrent descend, the wind howl, the lowering thunder roar: it affects not her peace. No trembling nerves has she!

Methinks I see her now: I hear again the harmony of that voice; now softening into the scarcely audible adieu; now rising into firmness, to instruct her Clement how to bear his destiny.

I had just quitted Mr. Valmont's study, where I underwent another torturing repetition of all the inconsistency of his designs for us. So freezing was his language, that it appeared to chill sensation; and when he presented me the 500l, which is to open my prospects in life, I was scarcely sensible either of its value or design. – I believe I never thanked him; and though I did not take his offered hand, its touch I dreaded more than the torpedo.

Languid, sunk, and overwhelmed, I crawled with feeble steps to my Sibella. – What a change! her vigour awakened mine; and as though hope, perseverance and courage had resigned themselves to her guidance, she commanded them to possess me wholly – commanded me to receive the noble inmates, and to vow I would be bravely independent, though a bed of straw were my portion and crumbs my fare.

I write this letter at my first resting place since I quitted Valmont castle; and the benignancy of my lovely Sibella has even chased my resentment towards you, but should an hour of lassitude perchance creep on me in my banishment, I may be tempted to enquire narrowly into the nature of your very mysterious epistles.

CLEMENT MONTGOMERY

LETTER IV

FROM SIBELLA VALMONT

TO

CAROLINE ASHBURN

Clement – my Clement is gone! All is silence around me. The trees have dropped their leafy ornaments; the wind sweeps through them in mournful cadence. Their foliage no longer intercepts my eye when it would extend itself around the vast horizon. I, now seated on the ivy-covered ruins of the hermitage, view this space; and tell myself it contains not one being to whom Sibella is the object of esteem, tenderness, or concern. Oh Caroline, Caroline! I am weary of this solitude. My mind bursts the bounds prescribed to my person, and impels itself forward to share the advantages of society. Compelled to return to its prison, it is disgusted with its own conceptions, and sinks into langour and dissatisfaction. Could it be my parents who doomed me to this slavery? Did they deem the benefits of intercourse a blessing too great for their innocent offspring? No: it must be Mr. Valmont's own plan; 'tis he alone who could wish to rob me of the faculties of my soul; and, finding I dare think, dare aim to extend them, dare seek to be happy, he shuns me with aversion or loads me with reproach.

Why, if he meant me to degenerate into the mere brute, did he not chain me in a cave, shut out the light of the glorious sun, forbid me to converse with intelligent nature? Then I might have expressed my wants in a savage way; have ravenously satisfied the calls of hunger or thirst; and, lying down to enjoy the sleep of apathy, have thought, if I could have thought at all, that this was to be happy. A being superior to this only in a little craft, did Mr. Valmont design to make me: a timid, docile slave, whose thoughts, will, passions, wishes, should have no standard of their own, but rise, change or die as the will of a master should require! Such is the height of virtues I have heard Mr. Valmont describe as my zenith of perfection.

He laments that he suffered me to share in Clement's education. Happy mistake! Then I found I was to be the friend and companion of man – Man the image of Divinity! – Where, then, are the boundaries placed that are to restrain my thought? – To be the companion, I must be equal – To be the friend, I must have comprehension and judgment: must be able to assist, or willing to be taught.

In the little intercourse I have had with Mrs. Valmont, she also has placed before me her picture of females: a picture as absurd and much more unintelligible to me than the other. She represents beauty as the supreme good; ascribes to it the most fabulous effects of power, conquest, and dominion. She represented me to myself as entering your world; and transformed me into a being so totally without description, that I ran from her to seek again my own nature: to find the friend and companion of man.

You, Caroline, are not such as either of these people describe. No: nor am I. Then shall I – but let me be content – a very short time and I shall join my Clement: shall aid his labour with my exertions. Oh, my Clement, my love, my lover, speed forward to the accomplishment of thy talk! Oh, be thy desires as bounded as my wishes! Thy Sibella covets no castles, no palaces. Seek for her but a shelter from inclemency, and take her therein to liberty, to thee!

Often, Caroline, have I imagined the useless parts of that vast building converted into little cottages such as I have seen from the top of its turrets. Fancy has instantly peopled the desert. I have believed myself surrounded by an active hardy race. I have arisen to enjoy the delights of communication: when, perchance, the rushing of a silent fawn through the thicket has awakened me from my trance; has reminded me that I too was one of the solitary herd; that the castle with its moats, walls, and battlements yet stood where gloom and silence hold their court, where Mr. Valmont presides and denies Sibella his presence, and where the inexorable key is turned on that library lest she should think too often or too well.

Andrew comes through the wood – he beckons – holds up a letter. –'Tis your's, Caroline.

I have pondered on the contents of your letter three days. What shall I say for myself more than you have already said for me? I feel, I confess, that inbeing secret I have deceived Mr. Valmont, have been guilty of vice. But how could I, tell me, Caroline; for my future benefit tell if you can, how could I devise a means by which I might have preserved my sincerity and saved my lover? – I can not. Remember it was my Clement's peace, happiness, and welfare, for which I made the sacrifice.

Yet now I feel it forcibly; for I hesitate to declare the rest; I, who knew no concealment, have by one deviation from my sincerity even become cowardly and irresolute in friendship. I fear your censures, Caroline; and dare think of eluding them, because too conscious that I cannot refute them. – I persevere in secrecy, in deception! Mr. Valmont is still unacquainted with our marriage. For myself, I had not done this – for myself, I could not perceive its value or necessity. I yielded to the ardent remonstrances of Clement; and promised to conceal our union, till his independence should have placed him beyond the mischief of my uncle's resentment. Ah! let me turn, to seek solace, in the end, for the means!

Be the means what they may, the end is effected. My Clement is restored. The energies of his mind are renovated. You will see him, Caroline: but you will see no feebleness in his character. You will find his love could never be *a trifling effervescence*; you will discover that we mutually love, from the *intimate knowledge of increasing virtues*; and no fabled or real oblivion can shed its influence on a love so elevated, so entire, so utterly beyond the reach of annihilation.

I conjure you, my friend, by your own words, to watch over my Clement – to preserve him free from taint; and to restore him, just such as he so lately quitted the arms of his, and your.

LETTER V

FROM ARTHUR MURDEN

TO

CAROLINE ASHBURN

MADAM

That I most ardently desire to possess your esteem is, whether you believe it or not, a fact I avow with all possible sincerity. Nor is it less a fact, that I quitted Bath so abruptly to avoid giving you my confidence: the only thing in the world by which I could be entitled to ask your esteem.

'Why do I then write to you?' – you are about to demand – Ah! madam: I have by me a long catalogue of such unanswered questions – Why do I do this? – and why do I do that? insolently treads on the heel of my almost every action.

Can you find a name more despicable than folly for the will that acts in opposition to acknowledged reason? If you can – apply that worst of names to me – to my incomprehensible conduct.

Oh, Miss Ashburn, almost without a motive have I pursued a dream, a phantasy! The offspring of my heated imagination. – Fancy lent her utmost delusions, and dressed the vision in such glowing charms that neither prudence, honour, friendship, nor aught else could stay me in my course – not even the heavenly ——

Whither am I running! – I would give a world that I could tell you – When! where! why! I dreamt and was awakened – not for a world's wealth though would I tell you.

'Tis past! 'tis done! the mischief is irretrievable. – The phantom remains; but the gilded hope that illumined her path is gone – despair casts its length of shade around me; and sunshine is no more.

Let me recollect myself. – When I began to write, I meant to request you would say something conciliating for me to Sir Thomas. The letter

I left for him was written in haste and from a sudden impulse, and probably expressed nothing I either meant or ought to have said – I beseech you, madam, do this for me. I know my uncle looks on me with affection; and I do not consider myself entitled to make so free with the happiness of others as I have done with my own.

If he has any expostulations to offer, any reproaches to make me, let him send them to Barlowe Hall. There I shall be some time. But let him not ask me to come to London.—— No: Miss Ashburn, the *ignis fatuus* is still in view; and, though I perfectly understand its nature and have no hope nor scarce a wish to overtake it, yet am I, lunatic-like, galloping after it over hedge, bog, and briar.

From this assurance, and from the many other things you know of me, you will believe I am in the right to subscribe myself the infatuated, miserable,

A. MURDEN

LETTER VI

FROM CAROLINE ASHBURN

TO

SIBELLA VALMONT

For the first time of my life, have I become the assiduous watcher of windows, the listener after footsteps; and have lived eternally in the drawing room. Yet has no Clement Montgomery appeared; and I have just now recollected that my desire of knowing him will not accelerate his approach, that so much time given to expectation is so much thrown away, and that to employ the same quantity of time in endeavouring to amuse you would be more friendly and of course more laudable.

Once more then, Sibella, we are in London, this great metropolis, alike the resort of him who possesses wealth and him who seeks to attain it. Here merit comes, hoping in the vast concourse to find the protector of talent; and hither the deliberating villain hastens, expecting the croud will be at once favourable to the practice of his crimes, and the means of escaping their punishment. What a field here is opened for the speculator, and the moralist! And often, Sibella, do I anticipate the time when we shall look on the chequered scenes of life together. When – but let me give you the remainder of Davenport's history while is is yet fresh in my memory.

Punctual to the minute I had named, Davenport entered my apartment. The same species of settled gloom I observed the preceding day in Arabella, marked his voice and gesture. He looked so familiarized, so wedded to sadness and misfortune that, desirous of expressing in my demeanour the kindness my heart felt for him, I approached and held out my hand to receive his. He lightly pressed it; and coldly bowing, retreated to a seat on the other side of the room. From that motion, I perceived he now viewed me as one who had saved him from the commission of an action which, although of evil and dangerous tendency, would have produced to him a benefit he knew not how, in any other way to procure; and that after rendering it impossible for him to marry, I was about to leave him with some general advice to the horrors of his situation. This he imagined was the utmost of my ability; he had convinced himself of the goodness of my intentions, and could not altogether call me his enemy; but he was now looking round, hopeless and despairing, for the almost supernatural means which could extricate him from his poverty and distress.

The power was mine; and I hastened to relieve him from the anguish he endured. I told him, he should render himself independent and happy; that my pecuniary assistance should go hand and hand with his endeavours; and enquired if he had any friends who could advise him in the choice of a profession.

'Not a creature in the world who would not rather advise him to end his miseries and disgrace with a pistol.' This was Davenport's answer.

I recollected that I had noticed some little intimacy between him and Mr. Murden; and, supposing the precariousness of dependence must have occasionally led Murden's thoughts to the same views, I concluded his judgment would be useful. 'Let us consult Mr. Murden,' said I.

'No: Miss Ashburn!' cried Davenport, reddening violently. 'Contrive it all yourself; I will obey you wherever I can; but do not command me to the revolting task of declaring to all the world that I am – a beggar. When Murden and I first knew each other, I was the expected heir to a good fortune; and, as I was descended from some of the first families in the kingdom, Murden moved in a sphere below me. He stands where he did; but I alas am fallen. – Yet I won't hear him exult and triumph in affected pity. – No: no! I could tell him that even a nabob's wealth cannot blazen him with the honours that cling to the name of Davenport.'

He spoke this with surprising bitterness.

'For pity's sake, Mr. Davenport,' said I, 'do not lay on high birth more infirmities than, from its nature, it unavoidably possesses. Were you ten times more honourably descended it could not alter Murden's ability to advise you, it could not degrade him or exalt you. I have seen you court his conversation: and did you imagine your poverty was then a secret? Oh, no! who could mistake the cause of your seeking to become Mrs. Ashburn's husband? In defiance of his uncle's displeasure, Murden refused this very marriage. At the same time, I must acknowledge, his firmness has not undergone the trial you have suffered; for he had no Arabella, I believe.'

Davenport threw his arms across upon the table by which he sat, laying his head upon them. The attitude prevented my seeing his face; but I thought he wept. A half supressed sob rose at intervals.

Thus he remained; for unwilling to press too hard on his prejudices, I relinquished the idea of consulting any other person, and sat silently examining plans for his future service. His age, his quickness of apprehension, and his manners which are pleasing to persons of every station, inclined me to think the study of physic would be well adapted to his capacity and talents. I made the proposal; named the sum I would give him yearly till he should be qualified to provide for himself; and his gratitude was expressed with the same vehemence which alike attends him on trivial or important occasions.

You will perhaps wonder, Sibella, that is, if the value of money is at all known to you, and if its importance ever occupies your thoughts, how am I enabled to make so lavish a use of it.

On our first arrival in England, my mother assigned me an annual income proportioned to the splendour of her appearance, and the immense fortune that I am destined to possess when her advantages in it shall be eternally proscribed.

That I do not employ this allowance in keeping pace with her elegance, that I do not blaze in jewels, and riot in the luxury of dress, displeases my mother; yet she continues me the stated income, flattering herself daily though daily disappointed that I will secure my own indulgencies by overlooking the errors reason tells me I am to condemn in her.

But to return to Davenport: on the subsequent morning, I ordered my horse very early intending to pass an hour with Arabella, when a servant informed me Mr. Davenport and a lady requested to see me. I hurried down stairs, to chide Mr. Davenport for suffering Arabella (supposing it must be her) to hazard an increase of her disorder, by coming out while the air was raw and cold, and the morning fog not yet dispelled. I opened the parlour door with the reproof almost ready on my lips, when Davenport, with his eyes glistening, his cheeks glowing, seized my hand and placed it within that of a young lady, who kissed it, and with mingled ardour and pleasure pressed it to her bosom. Surprised, I stepped back; and, looking alternately at her and at Davenport, a strong resemblance anticipated his introduction of a sister.

This sister, whom Davenport had forgotten in his misfortunes, was newly married; and had arrived at Bath the preceding evening, with her husband, a merchant of the name of Beville. Davenport had related the scenes he had passed through in those glowing colours whose use is so familiar to him; and the whole family were disposed to think I had rendered them an important service. Accepting Mrs. Beville's invitation to dinner, I was that day introduced also to Mr. Beville and Miss Harriot Davenport.

Davenport's feelings are ever alive to extremes. He was now in the bosom of his family. He saw his sister no longer the humble dependent of a proud relation, but the wife of an affectionate opulent husband, sharing her advantages too with his other sister. Then, how could Davenport look at them and remember either what he had been or might yet be. He was extravagant; sometimes brilliant, but always fanciful; and the incoherencies of his conversation formed an amusing contrast with the steady uniform bluntness of Mr. Beville. He was even too gay to be grateful; for, instead of thanking his brother-in-law for an offer of taking him into immediate partnership, in preference to the plan I had proposed, on terms so liberal as brought tears from his sister's eyes, Davenport began to ridicule and burlesque trade. He was determined for this afternoon at least to enjoy his mirth in defiance of the checks, instigations, or reproaches of the better inmates sincerity and common sense.

Poor fellow! The grimace, the laugh, the jest reign no longer; for Arabella cannot live! Perfectly satisfied with the prospects of her Henry, with his affection for her child, and the present attentions of his family to her, she calmly looks forward to that abode where *the wicked cease from troubling and the weary are at rest*; while he suffers ten thousand agonies in anticipating their eternal separation.

With Mrs. Beville and Harriot Davenport the remembrance of Arabella's former transgression now lies dormant, their former affection revives, gains new strength from the aid of pity, and instigates them to attend the dying Arabella as a sister. But I suspect from accidental hints they are yet infected with the worldly maxim that the guilt of such a sailing remains wholly with the female, from whom in every other instance of life we look for nothing but weakness and defect. Love more perhaps than reason has taught Davenport a better lesson; he would certainly have married Arabella, and Mr. Beville would have supported him in the resolution, knowing it to be now as much his duty as it was before their mutual duty to abstain from the transgression.

Thus have I saved Davenport. But not my mother. No – she will assuredly marry to prove to me her power and pre-eminence. She will pique herself also on chusing a husband, as handsome as engaging as the fugitive Davenport.

In the mean time flattery is flattery; and the dose being doubled from a female tongue approaches so near to an equivalent that the immediate necessity of a lover becomes less urgent. The happy Mrs. Ashburn – happy in her acquisitions – has lately gained a companion who can treble the quantity on occasion. In good English language, with the animation of French vivacity and French action, Mademoiselle Laundy deals out her bursts of admiration and exstacies of rapture from one of the prettiest mouths in the world. Shaping herself, most Proteus-like, to the whim of the moment, my mother sees not that she is young and handsome; and, could a painting be shewn to Mrs. Ashburn the exact but silent representation of Mademoiselle Laundy, unless previously instructed to look for the likeness, I am positive she would not recognize one feature of her companion.

This young person was born of English parents who were settled in France. Her father, being deprived of an enormous pension, by the change of government, chose rather to break his heart than live upon a contracted income, which could only furnish him with the necessaries of life; and such worthless accommodations as are beneath the enjoyment of a courtier.

After his decease, a ci-devant Durchess brought Mademoiselle Laundy to England, to try her fortune; and, most opportunely, chance threw her in our way at the very same time when my mother was seized with the rage of entertaining a companion. Money was an object with Mademoiselle Laundy, but none to Mrs. Ashburn; and the former knew how to hold off from the bargain till the latter's wishes and expectations were wound up to the highest. The pride also of enabling her companion to outdress half the fashionable young women about town was doubtless an additional motive with Mrs. Ashburn; and the enormous salary demanded was to me the first unfavourable specimen of Mademoiselle Laundy's principles.

Nor has the young lady improved on farther acquaintance. Supple as she is, she cannot accommodate the feigned artlessness of her countenance to the examination of my eye. Native simplicity would neither court nor retire; but Mademoiselle Laundy invites my favour, while she evades my scrutiny.

Resigning her personal pretensions to charm, and labouring incessantly to acknowledge the already inflated superiority of the people around her, she becomes the universal favourite; and 'tis hard to say whether the *dear, unfortunate, amiable*, Mademoiselle Laundy is more necessary to Mrs. Ashburn or to Mrs. Ashburn's acquaintance.

To her establishment here, however, I cannot object, because I should not be understood. Picking and stealing to be sure are very atrocious things; but who ever thought of calling selfishness, art, and insincerity by the name of vice? – Oh no! garret-lodgings philosophers may speculate, and dream over their airy systems; but we people of fashion know better things. We know self-love and insincerity to be useful and important qualities, the grand cement which binds our intercourse with each other. Born a superior race, we can bid truth and plain honesty depart; and, having dressed falsehood and guile in all the fascination of the senses, can bow down before the idol of our own creation.

'Tis all true, Sibella: although, in rambling about your woods, and looking into your own heart, and arranging the matter of your former studies, you may find what ought to be, you cannot discover one trait of what really exists.

Sir Thomas Barlowe is ill of the gout, and almost pines in his confinement for the society of his nephew; while the whimsical Murden, in defiance of command or intreaty, is capering about the country nobody knows why, nor nobody knows where.

Murden! Why cannot I name Murden without feeling a portion of that anxiety which so visibly preys on the happiness, and throws a veil of mystery over the actions of that inconsistent young man?

Various have been the endeavours I have used to understand the nature of his mind's disease; but he was wrapped an impenetrable fold of secrecy around his heart. At times, I imagined that acknowledgment was ready to burst from his lips; nay I even imagined at times I had caught some remote allusions that I thought I understood; yet in attempting to trace them to a source, I lost their original form, and became more and more entangled in the labyrinths of surmise.

As Sir Thomas and Lady Barlowe regulate all their jaunts and expeditions by ours, and as we have together made one household at Bath, it was natural enough that we should journey together to London. Mr. Murden of course was included in the arrangements;

and he neither breathed a syllable of doubt or objection to the plan. The evening before we quitted Bath, our party included only four or five visitors, but had there been twenty I must have directed all my attention towards Murden. The preceding day I had seen him petulant; and the preceding part of that day, I had observed him to be more than commonly pensive and absent. He did not appear at dinner; but joined us early in the evening, with smiles and gaiety. So sudden and so singular a change excited my wonder and curiosity! I perceived it was not the gaiety of force; yet it had a tinge of complacent melancholy; and, from his subsequent conduct, I am convinced it had its origin in some determination he had taken, whether for himself, fortunate or unfortunate, the sequel alone can explain.

He shook my hand affectionately, when he bade us good night; and, at breakfast the following morning, we learned that he had galloped away at day break. He had left a letter for his uncle, not filled with flattering apologies, never fear it, but containing a short harangue on the impossibility of his going at present to London, and a few cold wishes for the general safety of the party at large.

Since that time, I also have been savoured with a letter from him which, although it is not intended to elucidate any part of his conduct, has brought back to my mind, with additional force, a surmise I formerly dismissed as too improbable.

What a length of letter! You see, Sibella, how closely I consider our feelings as united; for, while I endure no weariness myself, I fear not the chance of inflicting it upon you. Adieu, my sweet friend: may principle alone, not personal fatal experience, teach you, that your present system of secresy is erroneous.

CAROLINE ASHBURN

LETTER VII

FROM LORD FILMAR

TO

SIR WALTER BOYER

What a life have I led these three days! An old house my habitation, built according to old customs, with its casements staring at one another across a narrow court, and the very offices turning their backs on noble prospects; two old men and one ugly old woman my companions. No young nor pretty face abides within these walls, for thy poor friend's amusement.

Called up at nine! and, what is still worse, sent to bed at eleven! Did you ever go to bed at eleven, Boyer? – There I wake, and dose, and dream – dream I hear the inspiring rattle of dice boxes – wake, and curse myself for ever having known their enticements, and then curse them for not being now beside me.

What, in the name of wonder, could have become of you the day I left London! Your valet was drunk when I stopped full of intelligence at your lodgings. Uc – and Hic – was all I could get from the fellow for a time – and then followed 'Yes, Sir, – to be sure, my Lord – I'll tell you at once – my Lord is gone, Sir, – in a post-chaise and four, my Lord.' –

'Where is Sir Walter gone, puppy?'

'Sir Walter, my Lord! – Oh yes – Sir Walter is gone – I don't know where he is gone, Sir Walter.'

Drive on, cried I; and home I went, to step from my carriage to the travelling chaise, in which with my dear father I was gently whirled down to Monkton Hall.

What a life have I led these three days! - A pestilence on your throat, I say! – There he sits, Walter, the bird of night and wisdom; and, with his quavering Hoo---oo---oo, calls on me to be solemn if I can't be wise. I hate wisdom; and, had I not a story to tell you, would sit down and rail at it.

Every clock from every steeple last Wednesday morning sounded seven as I with pledged honour and empty pockets drove home from——. The memento was insolent; and I was splenetic. I longed to throw stones at the steeples; and to knock down each sturdy porter who looked into the chariot, to inform me by his clear eye and vigorous step that he has passed the night in rest, and had arisen poor indeed but happy. Impudent scoundrel! He, a porter! I, a viscount!

I undressed and went to bed; where I had the felicity of ruminating till ten o'clock upon the vast increase of my knowledge and happiness since I became so intimately connected with Spellman and his associates. At which hour of ten, the Earl sent a servant to request I would breakfast with him. Qualms of apprehension stole upon me. I foreboded strange discoveries and severe remonstrances; and, as I felt too humbled in my own opinion to be insolent even to my father, I considered how to avoid the interview, till I had mechanically staggered into the Earl's dressing-room, where I was received with 'good morning to your lordship.'

'I hope you are well, my Lord,' said I; and throwing myself across the sofa we sipped a cup of chocolate in silence.

'I enquired for you last evening,' said the Earl. 'I believe, Lord Filmar, it was extremely late ere you came home.'

'It was extremely late my Lord,' replied I. As I so readily agreed in his opinion, the Earl was at a loss how to proceed. Twice he removed his chair, played with a tea-spoon, and we finished our chocolate.

After the breakfast things were removed, the Earl turned his chair more toward me. 'Hem,' said he, – 'Hem!' I arose and wished his lordship a good morning.

'Stay, Lord Filmar, a moment – pray sit down. Hem! I understand but too well – that is I suspect – I am fearful, the company you keep will do you harm.'

Now, Walter, this man, the Earl of Elsings! a peer of the realm of Great Britain! had not courage to say to his own son – 'Dick, thou art a fool, and wilt be a beggar. Thy companions are gamblers, sharpers, and knaves; and henceforward I command thee to abstain from their society.'

'You astonish me, my Lord,' answered I, with great apparent simplicity; 'I could not suppose I should displease you by associating with men of rank.'

'Oh certainly, not! By no means! Only I would insinuate that play is dangerous, and your income small.'

Small indeed, thought I. A considerable pause succeeded; and then my father's countenance brightened. 'I purpose going down this day to Sir Gilbert Monkton's,' said he. I wished him an agreeable journey. 'You must go with me, Lord Filmar.'

'Nay, pray excuse me, Sir. Consider the season, the place, and the society. How can your lordship plan such an expedition at this part of the year? You will inevitably bring on an ague, or a nervous fever. Dear, my Lord, don't think of it!'

'Indeed,' replied the Earl, 'nothing but a view to your interest could have determined me to make Sir Gilbert a visit now. Your interest, Lord Filmar, has strong claims upon me. Your present income scarcely exceeds 1000l. a-year; and you well know that, with all my care and prudence, I have not so far recovered former incumbrances as to be able to leave with the title of Elsings more than a clear 5,000l. per annum.' – The Earl paused, hemmed, picked up a scrap of paper, then hemmed again, and proceeded.

'You know, I think you know, Mr. Valmont.' I bowed assent; and the Earl looked as if he wished I had spoken; but I was resolved to hear him to the end.

'Yes, you do know, Mr. Valmont: a very singular man. He has strange ideas of education. In all our conversations on the topic, I never could be brought to coincide with him. Yet he is a worthy man too. He has a prodigious fine estate at Moor Down; and that estate round the castle is in excellent order. A strange Gothic dismal place that castle of his to be sure. I cannot remember how long it is since it was built; but it was a Valmont built it I know. It has never been out of the family. Yet I wonder he should chuse always to reside in it; and to keep his niece in it also. His niece – Hem! – You know, Lord Filmar, I am one of Miss Valmont's guardians.' I bowed again. 'I am told she is very handsome. She was a beautiful child. I have not seen her these ten years. It was very singular, indeed, I think to guard her so closely from every one's observation. Yes, Lord Filmar, Mr. Valmont's mode of thinking is certainly very singular. Miss Valmont's father was a most accomplished man; and one of my most intimate friends. He built a seat after the Italian manner, tasty and elegant as you can possibly suppose. He was very fond of Italy. Poor man, he died there. I wish I could have prevailed on Mr. Valmont to allow his niece a more enlarged education; her manners, I think, must be constrained and ungraceful: but certainly, as her father's brother, Mr. Valmont had a right to claim the sole protection of her person, and to bring her up as he thought proper.'

My father paused; and, though I could not immediately perceive the tendency of this ratiocination, I was resolved not to assist him, and remained silent.

'I was telling you, Lord Filmar, how much care and pains I have taken to redeem the Elsing estate. Let me advise you to leave off play, and to think of settling yourself advantageously. Would not a beautiful bride adorn the title of Lady Filmar?'

'I do not perceive,' answered I, 'that the title of Filmar wants any other ornament than it already possesses. Remember, dear Sir, I am scarcely two and twenty.'

Now, Walter, the Earl was not content with the simple recollections I had urged to him, but he began also to remember my profusion, my – my follies, (if you please) and my inadequate provision for them.

'Stop, my Lord,' cried I; 'and pray inform me what fortune my poor lordship has a right to expect as an antidote for matrimonial poison?'

'I think,' replied my father, 'that a lady of honourable descent, of good expectations, and possessing an unentailed six or seven thousand a year would be a very proper match for you.'

'And that lady is Miss Valmont.'

'No such thing! no such thing!' cried the Earl almost starting from his seat. – 'Will you dare, Lord Filmar, to assert that I said so?'

'Indeed will I not, my Lord. So far from it, I have heard you repeatedly declare she was left wholly dependent on her uncle. But why you should then be involved in the cares of guardianship, or why you should be inclined to saddle my encumbered estate with a wife without a fortune, I own appears a little mysterious.'

Be the true state of the case what it may (and we will talk of that hereafter) 'tis certain that every working muscle of the Earl's countenance betrayed the insincerity of his assertions, while he point blank denied that he had any reference to Valmont's niece when he proposed giving me a bride. I affected to be convinced; and, with a kind of lazy curiosity, played with my dog and asked questions about Miss Valmont, and wound my father round and round this dependent orphan, till I was nearly as assured as though it were on lawyer's deeds before me that six or seven thousand pounds a year is the lady's marriage portion.

A saucy triumphant smile at length betrayed me. The Earl reddened violently; and degenerated into such hints about certain affairs of mine that I suddenly jumped up, said I would attend him wherever he pleased, wished his lordship a hasty good morning, and drove away to deposit my burthen of confidence with you.

Well then, Walter; here we are at Monkton Hall, and Valmont's frowning fortress stands only at three miles distance; but still I am not one foot forwarder in the direct road of knowing why we came hither. In the bye-paths of windings and inuendo, indeed, I have made a little progress. I have discovered, Walter, that the Earl has a secret; but have not discovered the actual secret: only I can surmise a great deal. I surmise that the Earl and Mr. Valmont have laid a trap for me: and I surmise that I shall tumble into the trap, and be almost smothered with gold: and I further surmise that the gold will infallibly find its way out of the trap, and leave poor me behind it.

I am resolved to be perfectly obedient and resigned to my fate, and you may, if you please, wish me joy: for if the dear creature is but any thing like what her uncle intended to make her, with his wire-drawn principles about female weakness and female obedience, I shall be the least noosed of any married man in England. She will want no more than a cage, and a closet, and one smile a month from her sovereign Lord and master. Gloomy Hall, or gloomy Castle – some such name, I formerly gave that turret-crowned building. – Oh, the profaner! Why it is paradise! the court of Cytherea! where loves and graces sport on sideboards of massive plate, and intrigue with wanton zephirs upon every acre of Valmont's rich domain!

We are invited to dinner, Walter. This is Saturday. On Tuesday down go the draw bridges to admit me: me, me. The 'Squire and Earl settle preliminaries. The wood-nymph is introduced. She gazes with awe and astonishment, on her polished lover: while I forget her, to remember her fortune. At some future period, I shall subscribe myself your very rich and happy humble servant,

FILMAR

LETTER VIII

FROM SIBELLA VALMONT

TO

CAROLINE ASBURN

Imagine me, Dear Caroline, sitting down to write to you in the dead of night, by an almost extinguished taper: Somewhat chilled with cold; yet that sensation overpowered by the tremor of surprise, of curiosity, of emotions, in fine, which I cannot describe or explain.

And shall I boast of my strength, yet suffer my heart to palpitate, the colour to vary on my cheek, because an incident appears extraordinary? – Why did I not go back? Perhaps imagination was on the stretch, and I am self-deceived. Yet this writing! There must – but who would or could sigh with or for me, save one? – Foolish, weak Sibella! Art thou turned coward then? How can'st thou brave dangers, who hast fled from a sound? Perchance a fancied sound too! – Yes, I will return. I will not wait till day-light renews my courage; but go now to the wood, and examine this – Hark! – I hear a noise! – Good God! – Is it? – If it should be my Clem——

Oh no! that is impossible! – It was only the sweeping of the wind through that long gallery. But I won't go to the wood tonight, Caroline. I tremble more, and the cold increases. My taper too diminishes fast; but, while its light allows me, I will go over the events of the day and night, to discover if distinct recollection gives them a different appearance from what they now wear in the confusion of my ideas.

To begin, then, with the morning. While yet at breakfast, Andrew entered my room and intimated it was my uncle's orders that I should remain in my own appartments all day. – Strange as appeared the command, I sought no explanation from Andrew; but chose rather to submit to it in its present form, than encounter the teizing unintelligible signs of this silent old man. An hour had hardly passed, when I heard Mr. Valmont's footstep in the gallery; and as he approached nearer my door, I called up a firmness in my mein: for methought his visit to my chamber (a circumstance I never remembered to have taken place) foreboded something uncouth and unpleasant.

'So, Sibella,' said he, entering in a cheerful manner, 'you look quite well. You will oblige me particularly by not going into the park to-day. There's the armoury if you want exercise only be sure you go and return by the narrow stair-case. I would not have you seen for a moment in any other part of the castle. Perhaps I may bring a friend to visit you. A friend of your father's, child. You'll obey me, Sibella. And Andrew can inform you when you are at liberty to pursue your rambles.'

He withdrew. An address so familiar, with a voice and countenance so complacent, from Mr. Valmont to me, was food for reflection. The friend too! The friend of my father! – I felt not the necessity of exercise. I approached not the narrow stair-case. I thought not of the armoury. I remained in one posture; and Andrew's entrance, with my dinner, first broke in upon my reverie.

The meal ended and Andrew gone, it was resumed; and as long thinking will ever bring something home to the affections, I had left Mr. Valmont, his smiles, and his friend, to dwell on the image of my Clement – when my uncle led into the room a man somewhat older in appearance than himself, of an unmeaning countenance, whose profusion of dress sat heavy on an insignificant form. I turned away scornfully; for I thought it a profanation of the term to call this being *the friend of my father*.

How long he staid I cannot exactly tell – too long I thought then. He seemed to talk of me to Mr. Valmont; but to me he said little; and, owing perhaps to my dislike of the man, that little I did not rightly understand, and never attempted to answer.

When I saw Andrew in the evening, I ventured a few questions; and, with difficulty, learned there was company in the castle who were not expected to go away till late. I desired him to inform me as soon as they had departed; and, accordingly, a little, before twelve, Andrew opened my door, gave three distinct nods, shut it after him, and departed.

I understood his signal. Never had I passed a day in the house before; and I almost panted for the enjoyment of fresh air. The night was calm and serene; and the moon shone with a frosty brightness in a clear unclouded sky.

Wrapping myself in a cloak, I descended with a quick and joyful step. Neither light nor sound existed in the castle; and, unbarring the heavy doors, I sallied out in defiance of cold, to enjoy the lightness I then felt at my heart. The moonbeam directed my course; and I turned up the hill at the back part of the castle where no trees intercepted the partial light.

Standing on the summit, I looked around and my eye caught the glittering surface (made resplendent by the moon's reflection) of that small and beautiful lake which you may remember rises on the skirts of my wood. Thither I hastened; and, seated on the bank, I became enraptured with the scene. All seemed in union with my mind; only, that an undisturbed serenity reigned through nature; and, with the peace in my brest, a tumult of delight claimed its share.

I sang. I gave vent to my pleasure in words; in exclamations! – till at length the sound of two, from some very distant bell, floated through the air, and I rose to regain the castle.

Never in day time did I quit the park without visiting our oak; and now, when my heart bounded high with hope and pleasure, it would have been impious thus to have departed.

As I passed the rock, its dark shade, with the gloom in which the tall trees inclosed me, gave a new colour to my emotions. A pensive, but not a painful, tenderness stole on me. My breast began to heave, my lip to tremble: and, having reached the oak, I threw myself on the ground and sobbed. Still I felt no unhappiness. An impressive kind of awe took place of my former rapture, and dictated that I should dry my tears, and offer up a prayer for Clement.

At the foot of our oak, I knelt and audibly prayed. Still was I kneeling: still were my clasped hands raised: I uttered a deep sigh: and, close behind me, reverberated a prolonged sigh, if possible more deep, more forcible.

My taper emits its last rays. The moon is withdrawn; and total darkness compels me to seek rest – Adieu!

The sigh was distinct. It struck upon my ear. It almost reached my heart, Caroline. Dizzy, benumbed, I could scarcely rise; and, as I walked slowly along the open path from the monument, I really tottered. I believe I had proceeded fifty yards, and I began to tread with firmness and to consider if the sound could be real, when something whizzed past me and I perceived a little white ball fall to the ground and roll back as it was on the descent till it stopped at my feet. Equally surprised, but less affected, I turned quickly round. I looked every way: but the rock, the trees, the monument, and their respective yet mingling shadows, were the only objects I could discern.

I do not remember stooping for the ball; yet I felt it in my hand as I returned to the castle. I had left my light burning in the hall; but did not attempt to examine my possession, till I had shut myself in my own chamber.

The ball consisted of several folds of paper, with a small pebble in the middle, to give it weight I suppose. The inner fold contained lines, written with a pencil: the character neat, but uneven; and, in places, scarcely legible. These were the contents.

'Art thou instructed, beauteous nymph, that those planets to which thou now liftest thine eyes contain worlds whose myriads of inhabitants differ in their degrees of perfection according to the orb to which they belong? Some approach to immortality. Others are, as yet, farther removed: but all are in a progressive state toward the angelic nature. Even the lowest orb ranks above thy world.'

'From one of these latter planets, I descend – part mortal and part etherial. The former subjects me to pain and grief; but the latter can exalt me to bliss too extatic for the confined sense of mere mortality. – My spiritual nature places few bounds to my wishes, gives me invisibility, and brings the world before me at a view. I can see into the human bosom; and art cannot baffle me. In this world, I am permitted to seek a friend: and thee, hallowed inhabitant of this lower orb, I claim.'

'Set thy desires before thee. If they be many, chose the essential: if they be few, name all. To-morrow, after sunset, place the paper wherein thou hast written thy wishes on the tomb, and retire. If another mortal claim a share of those wishes, my power ceases; but if they relate only to thyself, fair creature, some one I may gratify. Thus may we communicate. To approach is forbidden. To be visible to thy eyes is denied me. Fly not then from the spirit, which *will* protect, but cannot harm, thee.'

Whither does recollection bear you, Caroline? – To the hermit of the wood and armoury, doubtless. The mysterious and whimsical stile of this written paper corresponds with the first address of that hermit. I wonder I did not remember it last night: but Clement's fears, and the mode to overcome them, have been objects of such magnitude in the heart of Sibella that curiosity has ceased to intrude its train of remembrances and suppositions.

Clement was right. Who, but through my uncle's means, could find entrance into this region of caution and confinement? Yes; Clement judged rightly! It is the man to whom Mr. Valmont says I must be united.

Will you, Caroline, give the inclosed to my Clement? Read it also; and judge with him for me. I wait your decision – but I wait unwillingly.

SIBELLA

LETTER IX

TO

CLEMENT MONTGOMERY

(Inclosed in the preceeding.)

Do we not create our own misery, my Clement, by this submission? – Mr. Valmont separates our persons, because he cannot separate our hearts. Oh! your reasonings were false, my love; and I was only misled when I thought I was convinced! – 'But a short time,' you said, 'and Mr. Valmont shall know it all, and we will be again united.' – Why not now? I cannot feel, I cannot understand these effects of his displeasure on which you dwell. Why do you dream of future benefits, when he tells you, that you are to have none of them? when he declares to you his wealth shall not be your's? And what of that! Will joy and felicity be less ours, because we are not rich? – We know it cannot. Did you possess wealth beyond what I can name, I should share its advantages; then if poverty or disgrace be your's, I demand to participate therein. It is my right; and twenty Mr. Valmonts shall not deprive of the inestimable privilege. Let me prove by actions the boundless love I bear you. Words are feeble. Where is the language that has energy enough to describe the croud of pleasures which rush upon my mind, while I am retracing our past scenes of happiness; or that can give its true colouring to my regret, when I call up the present separation, which bids them depart for a season?

Clement, you are dismissed that another may be introduced. The man of mystery, he whom my uncle has chosen, appears again. Say, my love! shall I tell them how useless are all their preparations? – that you and I have formed the indissoluble band? I am ready to do this. I wait but your consent. And then, if Mr.

Valmont resents our conduct and will not yield me to you and your freedom, I must and shall find means to shew him he has no more power over my person than my mind. I will escape him, and fly to thee.

Ever, ever, thy

SIBELLA

LETTER X

FROM LORD FILMAR

TO

SIR WALTER BOYER

Peaceful slumbers attend thee, Wat! The richer promising waking visions of expectation be mine! – A very pretty apostrophe that for a young viscount! I wonder if my father ever forgot to go to sleep when in bed, and sprang up again to write to some contemporary in same of his stratagems, intrigues, and toils? – Dear honest soul, no: – his sonorous breathings from the next chamber salute my ears in answer. – I certainly never was intended for the elder son of an Earl. Oh, I cry you mercy, Dame Nature! I read, I bow my head in obedience. A little twinkling star, Boyer, darting his ray throw the window, traces my destiny on this paper. '*When the heyday of the blood is past,*' says the oracle, '*thou art to be a statesman.*' So I will. Yes, a prime minister of Great Britain: and the more mischief I do before-hand, the better shall I be qualified for the duties of that high and important station.

The project I talked of in my last, have you not admired its tendency? Have you not rejoiced that the honours of the Elsing title is to have a fresh gilding from the Valmont coffers. If you have not already done this, I charge you neglect not a moment the duties of congratulation; for your friend, your happy friend Filmar, is assuredly, mind me *assuredly*, to be the husband of Miss Valmont. Therefore I will read you a letter, or at least a part of a letter, which came from her uncle to my father.

'Indeed, my Lord, to pursue this subject a little farther, it is only with a man who is prepared by such opinions as I have laid down to keep his wife in seclusion, that Sibella Valmont can be happy. I have purposely educated her to be the tractable and obedient companion

of a husband, who from early disappointment and a just detestation of
the miserable state of society is willing to abandon the world entirely.
And, not to mislead you in any way, such a one I hold in view.'

'You, my Lord, have acted with consistent delicacy throughout
our guardianship. You readily yielded to my plans, when our trust
commenced; and you have never attempted to counteract them by any
ill-judged interference; and I am therefore beholden to your prudence
and politeness. Of your Lordship's understanding I have so good an
opinion, that I cannot apprehend any offence will be taken on your
part for my declining the proposed alliance of Lord Filmar for my
niece. You must be aware, my Lord, how very unfit her education
has rendered her to be the wife of any person who does not in all
respects think as I do.

You must also suffer me to decline, for very good reasons, your
request that Lord Filmar may see her. The child has beauty; and the
interview for his sake is much better avoided. You, my Lord, have a
title to see her whenever you are so disposed; and I hope as a proof
that we understand each other, that Lord Filmar will accompany you
when you honour Valmont castle with your visits. From

Your friend and servant,

'G. VALMONT'

This letter, Walter, the Earl called me back to give me at his own
chamber door, after I had bade him good night. Do you not observe
how artfully Valmont had arranged the manner of his refusal; or are
you, as I was on its first perusal, a little chilled by the contents? I
perceive, by the Earl's delivering the letter to me at a time which
precluded all conversation on the subject, that he feels Valmont's
refusal to be unchangeable; now I dare not tell him that I have boldly
resolved to take the niece of Valmont whether her uncle pleases or
not, because what he calls his honour would stand between me and
my project. Honour will not pay my debts, Walter, So, *honour*, here
you and I part. Good by to you! – There: we have shaken hands: and
the musty fellow has marched off on yon straight road, while I turn
aside into this. Invention aid me! Stratagem be my guide! And do thou,
Walter, plot, contrive, and assist to make me matter of this prize.

Assuredly I will be the husband of Miss Valmont. This have I
sworn to myself: and this have I repeated to you. I read Valmont's
freezing epistle and I went to bed. Darkness and silence are admirable
auxiliaries to reflection. First, past in array before me my mortgages,

my debts, and the diabolical stake I lost to Spellman for which I have given notes that extend to the uttermost penny I can raise. Then, how gaily danced before me the visions I had indulged while I sounded my father about this hidden fortune of Miss Valmont, and while I reflected on the well-known wealth of her uncle. 'Ah but,' said I, 'her uncle has refused me, has already selected a husband for her!' And I shut my eyes; and sighed, Walter. That sigh proved my salvation: for it exhaled the dim vapour that had obstructed the operations of my confidence, my invention!

Then, how rapidly did my fancy teem with plan and project! How did I reject one, chuse another! Till, at length, I called for light and paper, that I might cool the fever of my hopes, by laying them bare to your inspection.

I well know what you are, Walter: a compound of contradictions. When you should believe, you are sceptical; where you should doubt, your faith is unshaken; and I expect when I tell you I am more and more convinced, by the recollection of many circumstances and by the Earl's aukward evasions, that Miss Valmont is her father's heiress – I expect, I say, that you will assure me I am deceived: and, as to my resolution of stealing her, you will assert that it is a project idle, vain, and impracticable. Yet, were I now to abandon the enterprize, you would wonder at my stupidity, would declare nothing could appear so certain as her fortune, and nothing so easy as its attainment. Therefore, dear Walter, I do not ask your advice; I only ask your attention. Six or seven thousand a year! The lady a minor too from the age of six, and no expences incurred upon her education! – Think of these circumstances, Walter; and, if you love arithmetic, cast up the accumulations of all these years; and to make the sum total of my future possessions, add the 10,000l. per ann. of her uncle who never had any other heir than this untutored Sibella! Would not such a sum convert even deformity into grace? But they say too she has beauty. Her ignorance and barbarism I will forgive; for I can at all times escape from a wife, though I cannot escape from the debts which are hourly accumulating to my destruction.

Marry a fortune or fly my country: there's the alternative. I chuse the former. As to flying one's country, I know of no country in which a man may drink, game, &c. &c. and spend his own and other people's money so easily as in that where, being born rather of one parent than another, the delightful privilege becomes as it were part of his legal inheritance.

It must be done too, if possible, time enough to prevent the necessity of a last mortgage to pay the notes I gave to Spellman. I was bubbled out of that money, but I was heated and the rascal so cool, I was unable to detect him; it becomes therefore a debt of honour and someway or other pay I must——Pshaw! Walter, thou wert always a dunce at school and at college. Now art thou turning over the page to seek the parting scene 'twixt me and honour. Foolish fellow! Didst thou never hear there are two sorts of·honour? Honour of principle, and honour of fashion. Honour of principle says – 'Do not steal Miss Valmont out of her uncle's castle; and pay thy poor tradesmen before thou payest the gambler Spellman.' – Here advances honour of fashion. What grace, what ease in her attitudes? How unlike is she to the aukward fellow who has just spoken, and who, without one bow, one smile, stood as upright as if he dared shew his face to the gods. But hark her mellifluous accents steal upon mine ear. 'Be,' says she, 'the accomplished nobleman for which nature in her happiest mood designed you. Exercise the elegance of your taste in the disposal of Miss Valmont's wealth. Above all, pay Spellman; or you forego, among the higher circles, the rapture of staking thousands on the cast of a die.'

It would be strange if a young man of my accomplishments did not know how much more useful and endearing a companion is honour of fashion than honour of principle! I will go and drink one bumper to the little solitary; then, I'll go dream. Aye: I'll dream that we are married; for I am upon honour there too. Adieu!

FILMAR

P.S.   Since I wrote the above I have given four hours to deliberation on the chances for and against my design; nor have I found any obstacle which may not be overcome, though I have not yet discovered the means. Do not laugh at me, for I think it no inconsiderable step toward success to have divined all the probabilities which may oppose my success.

To-morrow, I go to the castle. Griffiths shall attend me. He was once your valet too. Need I a more skilful engineer think you? Who knows what opportunities may occur to-morrow? A sigh, a glance, a word – Oh, but I forget! I am not even to look at her, says Don Distance. Well! well! we will talk of that hereafter. Twice have I perambulated around the park; but it is so walled and wooded and moated that the great Mogul's army and elephants might be there invisible.

A propos, in the second of these circuits, which was on yesterday evening, as I was leading my horse down a hill at the bottom of which Valmont's moat forms a sudden angle, I perceived a young man walking hastily up the narrow lane towards the moat. Hearing my horse's feet, he turned towards me; then, wheeling round, he fled out of sight in a moment. In one hand he held a long pole; and in the other a small basket. His figure was uncommonly elegant; and I imagined I had some knowledge of him, but there are no gentlemen's houses in this quarter, except the castle and Monckton Hall. The little valley where I saw him is unfrequented; and scarcely passable, it is so encumbered with brambles and underwood. Woods rise immediately on the other side of the moat, whose shade, with that of the high barren and black, which shews its rugged side to the valley, spreads forbidding gloom over the whole. Who could this youth be, I wonder; and where could he be going?

Adieu, Walter! Think of to-morrow.

LETTER XI

I charge you, Sibella, by the value you affix to my friendship, that you remain at present passive. It is a term of probation for Clement on which the colouring of your future days depends. – More of this hereafter. I write now with a kind of restless eagerness. Images, apprehensions, and even hopes, all finally resting on you, fill the place of soberer judgment. – This wood wanderer! This spirit – 'part mortal and part etherial,' – fascinates my attention. I see him gliding through the paths you had trodden. The tree which screened him from your view cannot conceal him from mine. I see him listen almost breathless to your prayer. The new-born colour on his cheek hangs trembling, daring not then to depart; and the throbbings of his agonized bosom collect themselves while restrained, and give force to that sign whose utterance has echoed a thousand times in my imagination. I see him dart the ball forward to meet your feet; and then he rushes into the thickest gloom to hide himself, if possible, even from himself.

This is no spirit of your uncle's choosing, Sibella. No: it is one who has refined upon romance; who can give, I perceive, as much enthusiasm to the affections, and carve misery for himself as ingeniously, as though he had passed his days under the safeguard of Mr. Valmont's walls and drawbridges. '*He will protect, but cannot harm thee.*' In truth, I believe it. Go to the wood then, Sibella. See him, if possible; and tell me, did symmetry ever mould a statue in finer proportions than his form can boast? His eye in its passive state is a clear grey, its shape long; and the finest eye-brow and eye lash that ever adorned mortal face, not excepting even your's Sibella, belong to his. Hold him in conversation and you will see that eye almost emit fire; it will dazzle you with its rays; or, if a softer subject engage him, it can speak so submissively to the heart that words become but the secondary medium of his theme. Observe how his hair, bursting from confinement into natural ringlets around his temples, contrasts itself with the fairness of his complexion – fair without effeminacy. His colour is of a doubtful kind; for it retires as you perceive it, or suffuses the whole of his fine countenance, just as you had begun to lament that he was too pale. His nose and mouth, though somewhat large, and perhaps irregular, yet admirably correspond with the harmony of the whole face. You probably will think Clement's glowing face handsomer: I do not. Chase but by one smile and dissatisfaction of your spirit, and there will a radiance, if I may so call it, beam upon you, that my best art fails to delineate.

I shall not underwrite the name till you have judged of my painting. Cease your astonishment, my friend, for I am no sorceress, and the spright is too etherial, too imaginative, to hold counsel with a mere mortal like me. To the means of his being with you I confess I have no clue; but if you read my former letters you will perhaps find mention of some few of the reasons and circumstances which incline me to infer I have discovered him.

You will find though what I am now about to tell you; for my heart only transmitted it to my understanding, where it remained to have its justice and propriety closely investigated. – Yes, Sibella, wild, variable, and inconsistent, as is this spirit of your woods, *I* could have loved him if – '*he would have let me.*' But 'tis past: 'twas a trace on the sands. Love shall never write its lasting characters on my mind, till my reason invites it: and where hopes rests not, reason cannot abide.

Clement's eagerness to cultivate our acquaintance is by no means flattering. I have known him but a week. It was at the opera that I observed Laundy's eye stealing to the adjoining box with something more than mere inquisitiveness. Mine followed. A party of young men occupied the box, all known to me except one: and from the position in which the stranger sat neither Laundy nor I could gain more than an oblique view of his face. Now I do acknowledge that even this oblique view gave promise of the whole being worthy of observation; yet my curiosity lulled itself to repose till the Dutchess de N—— (constantly of our parties) arose at the end of another act, to gaze around with that confidence which women of a certain rank deem infinitely becoming in themselves, though if perceived in a shopkeeper's wife or daughter downright impudence alone would be called its proper description.

'Ah!' screamed the Dutchess, 'Le Chevalier Montgomery!'

Clement, (for it was your Clement) starting from his former posture, bowed hastily; and having carelessly looked on the rest of the party returned to his seat.

Poor I, all flutter and palpitation, eager to know if this Montgomery was the identical Montgomery, was almost in despair that he should not avail himself of the Dutchess's recognition; but she was not to be so baffled. With some trouble, on account of the nabob's gouty toe, she displaced Sir Thomas and Lady Barlowe, and got close to the box. Already had she raised her fan to accost him with the tap of familiarity, when I heard Mr. Hanway his companion say – 'Mrs. and Miss Ashburn.' Clement's eye instantly met mine. A smile gathered round his mouth; and in two seconds he was in our box, regularly introduced by Mr. Hanway.

For the first minute, I was sure he resembled you; in the next, the likeness became indistinct; and in two more, I lost it entirely. His face, with all its advantages of complexion, colour, brilliant eyes, and exquisite teeth, has not the variety which your's possesses; though to say here that he is less handsome than any creature upon earth is almost a crime, and the ladies scruple as little to tell him he is a Phoenix as to think him one.

We had scarcely any conversation that evening; for my mother and the Dutchess vied with each other in their attention to Montgomery. Lady Barlowe could not claim a share of him, though Sir Thomas immediately recollected Clement and renewed their acquaintance with apparent pleasure.

'Don't you remember, Mr. Montgomery,' said the nabob, 'the day you and Arthur set out for the continent you dined with me? How much every body was delighted with my nephew's vivacity! That very day a gentleman said to me, Sir Thomas, – and a very great judge he was I assure you – Sir Thomas, said he, your nephew will make a figure in the world. If you bring him into parliament, what with his abilities and his relationship to you, Sir Thomas, he may stand almost any where in this country. Well, Mr. Montgomery, when I sent for him home so much sooner than I first intended, it was because this gentleman's advice appeared to me very good, and because he further told me no time was to be lost. Home Arthur came, and I could have bought him a borough the next day.' – 'No, indeed,' he said, he would neither buy votes or sell votes; nor did the conduct of parliament please him; nor could he – in short, he had so many faults to find and objections to make, that he out-talked me, and I couldn't tell what to say to him. But, thought I, he will think better of it; and I let the matter rest a while; and made another proposal in the mean time, and had he done as I wished he would now have been one of the richest men perhaps in the kingdom. Yet, upon my soul, he point blank refuses this too; and talked as much of principle and integrity and I know not what, as in t'other case! 'Twas damned insolent! and so I told him. – No, nor had he ever the modesty to ask my pardon; but took it all as coolly as you can imagine. – Well, and when I forgave him of my own accord, and behaved to him more kindly than ever, he has taken some new freak into his brain, and playing so many odd tricks of late that I am actually afraid of him.'

'Oh never was such an unaccountable!' said Lady Barlowe.

'The ball-night at Bath!' added my mother laughing.

'His letters are algebra to me;' said Clement, 'and I have been half tempted to forswear his correspondence.

'Last winter,' said Mr. Hanway; 'he made conquests by dozens. Some cruel fair one is revenging, I suppose, her slighted sex. – In love, no doubt!'

'I believe not,' replied Clement; and the conversation ended: for the Dutchess now chose to talk; and, never having seen this incomprehensible irresistible Murden, she could not talk of him, you know.

The party adjourned to sup at Sir Thomas Barlowe's: we and the Dutchess de N—, by a previous engagement, Clement and Mr. Hanway in consequence of the baronet's pressing invitations. Mademoiselle Laundy complained of indisposition, and returned home immediately from the opera. She, as well as her friend the Dutchess, had been acquainted with Clement in Paris; but, after the first cold bow, Mademoiselle Laundy remained unnoticed by him.

No man could be more gallant, more gay, or unrestrained, than your chevalier, as the Dutchess persists in calling him. At the nabob's table we met several persons of fashion, to whom he was already known, and by whom he was treated with attention. His person and manners are no trivial recommendation; and the belief which every where prevails of his being heir to Mr. Valmont supports his consequence with its due proportion of power.

I debated with myself to determine, whether or not this belief ought to pass without contradiction; and, foreseeing many injurious consequences that might arise to Clement from the expences and dissipation which it encouraged, I resolved to seek an early opportunity of conversing with and encouraging him to disown the supposition. No opportunity occurred during that evening; but, ere we separated, Clement was engaged to dine on the succeeding day in one of my mother's private parties.

I very seldom breakfast with my mother, our hours of rising and morning avocations are so different; however, I went to her dressing room that morning, purposely to talk of your Clement. I spoke much of your attachment to each other; and Mrs. Ashburn immediately declared she would take his constancy under her protection, as such elegance and accomplishments, she said, as those possessed by Mr. Montgomery would be assailed with more temptation than such charming candour and simplicity might be able to withstand. To Miss Laundy my mother appealed for her confirmation of Clement's praise; and she either did, or I fancied she did, give her assent with a languor and inattention not usual to her. I had no reason, however, to accuse her of inattention when I hinted at the change in Clement's expectations; for, although my mother suffered it to pass unnoticed, Mademoiselle Laundy thought proper to press questions on me relative to this subject. I resented her inquisitive curiosity on a point which could not in any way concern her; and, declining to answer her questions, I quitted the room.

To join *a private party*, my mother had invited Clement: that was fifteen visitors, placed at a table covered with the most luxurious delicacies served in gilt plate, and surrounded with attendants as numerous as the company. Mrs. Ashburn, less splendid, but more tasty than usual in her dress and ornaments, was studiously attentive to Clement; declared herself his guardian; and spoke with rapturous admiration of you, Sibella, but without naming you, Clement blushed, bowed, returned compliment for compliment; and, graceful in all his changes, assumed an air and mien of exultation. Sometimes he turned his eye toward Mademoiselle Laundy.

The evening had far advanced before I could engage him in any conversation. He then shewed me a letter from your uncle, wherein to my very great surprize Mr. Valmont desires Clement to be cautious in confiding his prospects or intentions to any one; bids him study mankind and despise them; tells him he does not mean to limit him to the sum he has already in his possession if more should be necessary; and advises him to be speedy in his choice of a profession; talks of the value of disappointment, the blessings of solitude, the duty of obedience, of his own wisdom, his own prudence and power; begins with the kind of appellation of – 'My dear adopted son;' concludes with the stern Valmont-like phrase of – 'Your friend as you conduct yourself.'

Here my interference ends. Henceforward, Mr. Valmont plans and Clement executes each in his own way. Your uncle has quite an original genius, Sibella; following no common track, he labours only to make a glare by strong opposition of colours, and to surprise by contrariety of images.

To Clement's murmers against Mr. Valmont, succeeded a little species of delirium: for I named you, and no impassioned lover-like epithet was omitted in the recital of your charms. – Whatever, Sibella, may be my own vanity and pretensions I could hear praises of your beauty from a thousand tongues without envy or weariness. Yet, from Clement, a slighter mention would have pleased me better. He is the chosen of your heart; and should prize the mind you possess equal to heaven. An Angel's beauty might be forgotten, when the present and future contemplation of such a mind could be brought in view.

Alas, your lover is no philosopher! He laments the energy which I idolize. – Allow me to indulge the percipient quality I suppose myself to possess, and sketch Montgomery when my messenger, presents him the letter you inclosed to me. No sooner does he behold that writing, than Sibella rises to his view in all her grace and loveliness. Could he give existence to the vision, that moment would be too rich in transport. He trembles with an exquisite unsatisfied delight: and, while the senseless paper receives his eager kisses, he could fight dragons, or rush through fire to obtain you. – At length he reads. – Well: the same Sibella is there – she whom he calls the most perfect and lovely of all God's creatures! – the same Sibella whose enchantments cast a magic illusion around the horror-nodding woods of Valmont! – The same Sibella, but poor and dependent, is now quitting those woods for ever and ever – she leaves behind her even the trace of wealth; and flies an outcast to Clement, who, involved in the same ruin, has neither fortune, fame nor friend! – Delightful expectations vanish. Torture succeeds. And the agony of this prospect to Clement could in no one instance be equalled, except perchance by the knowledge of your being in the possession of a rival and lost to him for ever.

I suspect there are some latent shades in this picture which will displease you: but remember, my ever dear girl, that early, even at the commencement of our intimacy, we reciprocally laid it down as a solemn truth that without full and entire confidence friendship is of no value. I have said that Clement and you love from habit. Nor let it wound you that I say so still; for I am willing to seek conviction, and though I cannot be more candid than now, nor ever more worthy of your affection than while I am offending your heart to inform your judgment, yet if conviction meet me, I shall be more joyful by millions of degrees in owning I had mistaken.

At all events, whether Clement approves or disapproves the intention, your leaving your uncle and his castle now would be decidedly wrong. Your education, constantly in opposition to that which a dependent should have had, unfits you for entering the world without protection. You have so much to learn of the manners of society, that perhaps any plan you might form would turn out the very reverse of your expectations. – Stay, patiently if you can: at any rate, stay, till Clement makes his final determination, and then I'll tell you more of my mind.

Be happy, my sweet my beloved friend! You have it largely in your power; and surely 'tis better to summons fortitude and walk boldly over a few thorns, than creep through miserable paths to avoid them, or sit down idly to bemoan their situation

CAROLINE ASHBURN

P.S. I have opened my letter, in consequence of a visit from Clement Montgomery. He came to me, Sibella, agitated and trembling. Your letter had conjured up a horrible train of fears and suppositions, and he was scarcely assured the evil he most dreaded had not already arrived. 'Rash, cruel Sibella!' he exclaimed, 'even now, perhaps, your have for ever undone me with Mr. Valmont!' I reminded him that you had said in the concluding lines of your letter to me that you waited, though unwillingly, for Clement's determination. 'O that is true!' cried he – 'and 'tis my salvation! Dear Miss Ashburn, conjure her, by your love and my own, to guard our secret faithfully from her uncle. Tell her, she cannot judge of the destruction she would hurl upon my head if she were now to betray me. Tell her, I intreat, I insist, that she make not one attempt to quit the castle. – Will you, dear Miss Ashburn, undertake this kind office? Will you turn the adorable romantic girl from her mad enterprize?'

'Certainly Mr. Montgomery,' I replied, 'I will deliver your own message exactly in your own words. As to my opinion, I have given it to Sibella already: it is against her quitting the castle.'

I should also have told Clement what were my motives for wishing you to remain with your uncle, had not my mother and Mademoiselle Laundy, at that instant, entered the room. Their presence, however, did not prevent Clement from thanking me with great warmth; and, the worst of his fears being now removed, his countenance again brightened into smiles, and he readily acquiesced in my mother's wish of his attending her to convey him to his lodgings to dress, and, as he quitted us, I bade him remember the purpose for which he came to London. Blushes covered his face, and he departed without speaking. Once more, adieu! Forget not the wood-haunter.

LETTER XII

FROM JANETTER LAUNDY

TO

CLEMENT MONTGOMERY

Wounded pride bids me forget the cold, cruel Montgomery; but fatally for the peace of Janetta, her love, betrayed injured and neglected as it is, still is more powerful than her pride. I have seen my family stripped of their honours and possessions by a band of ruffians. I have been left a destitute orphan: and compelled to seek subsistence in a strange country: compelled to descend even to a species of servitude! Yet how trivial such misfortunes, compared with the loss of thee, Montgomery! How could you leave me unjustified and unheard? How could you meet me as you did this night? Do you never remember, Montgomery, the sacrifices made to you by the undone Janetta? Do you never remember the hours of your solicitations, vows, and promises? and if you do remember them, can you thus kill with scorn and aversion her who solicits your return to your vows with tears of passion, love, and anguish?

I did not feign when I pleaded indisposition to excuse my attendance on Mrs. Ashburn to Sir Thomas Barlowe's; for, which in your presence and restrained by the presence of others from giving freedom to my emotions, I suffered indescribable torture. What dangers do I not incur by setting the messenger who shall give you this to watch your quitting the party? But you will not, Montgomery, dear adored Montgomery, if you do hate and despise me, you will not give me up to the contempt of others! My reputation is still sacred: and, but for you, the peace within my bosom had now been inviolate.

I must see you, I will see you, Montgomery! Do not drive me to desperation! I have woes enough already. Let me but once have an interview to explain that cruel mistake of your's, concerning the

Duke de N——; and, when I have proved my innocence, if you still bid me languish under your hatred, I will then suffer in silence. No complaint shall ever reach you. Should you again smile on me – oh heavens! the rapture of that thought!

Be assured I can prove my innocence. Be assured you were utterly mistaken. It was a scheme, a stratagem for purposes I can easily explain if you will but give me an interview. The Dutchess de N—— is to this hour my very best friend; it was she who brought me to England. Alas, what a sad reverse of situation is mine! thus to sue with tears and intreaty for one short hour's conversation to him who, but a few months past, languished for the slightest of my favours! Think what a preference I gave you over the many who followed me with their sighs; think what I was; what I have endured; and drive not to rage and despair her who is ever your's and your's alone:

JANETTA LAUNDY

LETTER XIII

FROM THE SAME

TO

THE SAME

Last night I obeyed the impulses of an unfortunate passion, renewed in its utmost violence and weakness by the unexpected sight of you. I now obey the dictates of prudence and reflection, and decline the interview I last night solicited.

Yes, Montgomery! I see evidently that I am sacrificed to some rival. Be it so. I am content to resign you. Content to endure this penance for my past mistakes. We will henceforward meet only as strangers. I am resolved. Never will I again trouble you in any way; nor ever again yield to that delusion which has brought upon me so much misfortune and misery.

I have but one request to make; and that, Sir, is a last request. Remember that I am friendless and dependent. Be generously silent. You are likely to be on terms of intimacy in this family, and Miss Ashburn is as severe as penetrating. Guard carefully a secret that would ruin me in my situation; and every service that gratitude can inspire shall by your's from

JANETTA LAUNDY

LETTER XIV

FROM CLEMENT MONTGOMERY

TO

ARTHUR MURDEN

Mr. Valmont, dear Arthur, has sent me to London with 500l. in my pocket to chuse a profession. 'Be not rash nor hasty in your determination, Clement,' said he when we parted. 'Associate with such persons as have already made their choice; and have from practice, from success, or disappointment, learned the exact value of their several professions. But associate with them as an independent man, one who seeks a variety of knowledge rather from inclination than necessity; and under these appearances, Clement, they will court you to receive their confidence, even their envy of your independence will increase the freedom of their communications.'

And do you dream, Arthur, that I am practising these grave maxims, and hearkening to the jargon of law, physic and divinity? No indeed, not I. The variety of knowledge I seek is variety in pleasures. My teachers are divinities whose oracles, more precious than wisdom, can lead the senses captive and enchain the will.

'Be secret,' said Mr. Valmont. Most readily can I be secret. I would have it remain a profound and everlasting secret, never to interrupt the delicious enjoyments which now again hover within my reach, which I must seize on. I have not the cold ability to chase from me the present smiling hour of offered delight, because a future hour may frown. Pleasure beckons, and I follow. I tread the mazy round of her varieties. Youth, vigour, and fancy conduct me to her shrine, the most indefatigable of her votaries. Alike, I abjure retrospect and forboding. As long as I can find means, will I elude the horrible change; and, if the fatal hour of darkness must arrive, why, Arthur, it is but to exert a little manhood, it is but to remember that all the charms of life are passed by, and boldly to plunge into everlasting darkness.

Imagine not, dear Arthur, by that doleful conclusion that I at all dread the possibility of its arrival; for, on the contrary, I believe my dismission is a mere farce, a something with Mr. Valmont to vary project and prolong inconsistency. I have compared his letters and his speeches; combined circumstances; and find them, though so various and contradictory, yet full of hope and promise.

One cause of dread, indeed, will assail me. I dread the rashness of Sibella. Could you suppose, Murden, that she has even talked of explaining the nature of our intimacy to her uncle, and of quitting his castle? Was ever any thing so violent, so absurd, so pregnant with evil at this scheme? When I had read her letter, I thought every chair in my apartment was stuffed with thorns. Nay, I endured for a time the torments of the rack. Thank heaven! Miss Ashburn adopted my sense of the extravagant proposition, undertook to dissuade Sibella, and restored me once more to gaiety, courage, and happiness.

Yes, Arthur, established in my former lodgings, courted, surrounded, congratulated by my former friends, I want but your society and the embraces of my divine girl to be the happiest of the happy. Thanks, Murden, for your silence on the subject of Mr. Valmont's threatened disposal of me. I am every where received like my former self. Oh! had I met one repulsive look , or supercilious brow, with – your servant, Mr. Montgomery – I surely should have run mad!

Miss Ashburn knows it all, and I hate her most righteously. I allow that she is a fine woman, but her beauty is spoiled by her discernment. I wish Mr. Valmont would refuse Sibella Miss Ashubrn's correspondence. The dear girl is already too eccentric. Yet could I now gaze on that lovely face, could I now clasp that enchanting unresisting form to my bosom! Had she ten thousand faults, I should swear they were all perfections. Murden! you never saw any one who can equal Sibella Valmont! Her charms cannot pall in possession. Ever a source of new desire, of fresh delight, adoration must ever be her lover's tribute! – Arthur, I will make her my wife.

Whom would you suppose I have, to my very great astonishment, found here, in Mrs. Ashburn's family? No other than Janetta Laundy! I first saw her at the opera, where I overlooked her with the most studied neglect. She quitted the party abruptly; and then the Duchess de N—— informed me of the cruel reverse of fortune in the Laundy family. Janetta, with so much beauty, she, who lately shone conspicuous in fashion, taste, and elegance, is now absolutely reduced to the mortifying state of a humble companion. Upon my soul I was shocked; and, notwithstanding certain recollections, I could not help feeling a strong degree of interest and pity for her. A brilliant party, whom we joined at the supper table of your uncle Sir Thomas Barlowe, banished Janetta and her misfortunes from my thoughts; but, as I was stepping into a chair to return home, after I had handed the Duchess and Mrs. Ashburn to their carriages, a man put a letter into my hand. The letter was from Janetta, written in the true spirit of complaint and fondness. She implored that I would see her; asserted her innocence with respect to the Duke de N——; and, recollecting the continued attachment of the Duchess to her, I was inclined to doubt the evidence of my senses, and half resolved to give her an opportunity of justifying herself. Again the circumstances came rushing into my memory, and brought conviction with them. I determined to contemn and despise her; and steadily to refuse the interview. She spared me the trouble; for, on the next morning, while I was dressing to dine at Mrs. Ashburn's, a second letter was given me, in which Janetta, with mingled love and resentment, bids me a final adieu.

At Mrs. Ashburn's table Janetta Laundy had no rival in beauty. She enforced the homage of many eyes; but she received it with so graceful a reserve, that those who would otherwise have been jealous of her attractions were irresistibly impelled to own her worthy of admiration. Toward me, her countenance expressed nothing but a frigid restraint. Once I approached her seat, and she found an immediate pretence for withdrawing; and, shall I confess it to you, Arthur, I was in a small degree mortified.

It has not been merely one day, or two, or three, that Janetta has upheld her determination. I have been astonished at her inflexibility and perseverance. I have almost doubted that she could really love me and be so firm. Scarce a day passes in which we are not together, for Mr. Ashburn is extravagantly fond of Janetta, and never moves without her. Mrs. Ashburn selects her parties as I best approve, and consults me on all her engagements. I attend her every where, and thus Janetta and I are frequently in the same apartment, in the same carriage, side by side; and, considering former circumstances, you will not imagine these can be very desirable situations.

It occurred to me one morning that I ought in justice to make Janetta a present, notwithstanding her allowance from Mrs. Ashburn is really splendid. Accordingly, I sent her a 50l. note, inclosed in a letter, written as I think with delicacy and propriety. The note was accepted, but the letter remained unanswered.

Two evenings after this, we were at Ranelagh, where Mrs. Ashburn joining the Ulson family, Janetta and I walked a round or two alone. She then, with more coldness than I could have thought possible, thanked me for my present, and hoped my generosity would prove no inconvenience under the alteration of my affairs.

By heaven, Arthur, her speech was a thunderbolt! I was dumb for the space of many minutes; and then stammering, incoherent, blushing with shame, and anger, I protested her meaning was an enigma that I could not unravel. Hanway at that instant came up, and every opportunity of further conversation was at an end.

And how do you suppose I aimed to settle the business, to prevent the cruel supposition from being whispered from one to another around the circles of my friends? Thus I did it. I took another bank note of 50l. and wrote another card, in which I alledged that I could only understand Mademoiselle Laundy's hint as a reproof for the smallness of the sum I had before sent her, and intreated she would now receive this an an atonement. I acknowledged the whole was scarcely worthy her acceptance, but I hoped she would consider I had less at command than in expectation. I added my fervent wishes for her happiness, but said not one word of love.

Still I have no answer. How wantonly cruel it is of Miss Ashburn to throw me thus in the way of torment and contempt! No one but herself could have told Janetta of the alteration in my affairs. 'Tis false! there is no alteration: for have I not four hundred pounds in my possession?

Where are you, and what are you doing, Arthur? By heaven, I never think of you without astonishment! You whom fortune favours, you so highly gifted to charm, to be sacrificing the age of delights, in a barbarous solitude! What, upon earth, can be your inducement? Your uncle pines for you. Certainly you must be either immoderately sure of your power over him, or desperately careless of your interest. All who concern themselves in your fate, apply to me for the explanation of your mysterious conduct; and, finding I am no more informed than themselves, they teaze me with their conjectures. Come, Arthur! come! banish melancholy and misanthropy till age shall have cramped your vigour and palsied your faculties! Then cast your dim sight upon the flying pleasures which you are no longer able to pursue, and rail, and be welcome! But now, while the power is your's, hasten to partake, to enjoy! The wealth of a nabob gilds the path before you! Beauty spreads her allurements for you! Come, insensible marble-hearted as you are, to the inticements of beauty – at least come to interest, if you cannot be interested; excite the sigh, the langour which you will not return! Be again as formidable as you once were; and let the meaner candidates, who triumph in your absence, sink back to insignificance and neglect!

Does not the prospect fire you? I know it does – or, you are unfit to be the friend of

CLEMENT MONTGOMERY

LETTER XV

FROM LORD FILMAR

TO

SIR WALTER BOYER

One, two, three, or four pages, by Jupiter! cried I, as I opened your packet, Walter; and I ran over the first ten lines with a devouring greediness: for, would not any man have expected, as I expected when I had so lately written you two letters upon the projects and hopes that dance in gay attire before me, that your epistle must have contained comments innumerable, hints useful, and cautions sage. Neither comment, hint, nor caution, could I find. Nothing but four sides of paper covered with rhapsodies which have neither connection with nor likeness of any thing in heaven above, in the earth beneath, nor in the waters under the earth.

Yet, negligent as thou art, still must I write on. My fancy is overcharged with matter, for I have done wonders: wonders, Walter! Yesterday at ten o'clock I talked with Lady Monkton's housekeeper; who once was Mrs. Valmont's housekeeper; and yesterday at four o'clock I talked with Mr. Valmont himself. Turn back to yesterday; and observe me, in Sir Gilbert's post coach, arrived with due state and precision before the venerable doors of Valmont castle, accompanied only by my father, and attended by Griffiths armed as all outward points like a beau valet, and like a skilful engineer within laying wait to spring a mine for his commanding officer.

With measured steps, Mr. Valmont approached us three paces without the drawing room door. He conducted us to his lady; who, on a rich heavy and gilded sofa, sat in melancholy grandeur to receive us.

'But the niece,' I hear you cry, 'Not a single glimpse of her, I suppose?'

'Yes, Sir Walter Boyer, I have seen her.
'Seen her! Why, I thought ———.'
Psha! what can a Baronet have to do with thought?

> Mark'd you her eye of heavenly blue!
> Mark'd you her cheek of roseate hue!

Do you still doubt? Then shall I proceed, and fire your imagination
with the graces of my goddess. *All enchanting! nothing wanting!* for I
have gazed my fill – yes – on her picture. – Why look you so, Walter? –
Am I not her predestined lover, and has she not 6000l. per annum?

'Pray, Madam, by what artist was this portrait done?' said I, to Mrs.
Valmont, while the 'Squire and Earl were gone to visit the nymph of
the south wing, with my imagination stealing after them on tiptoe.

'Not by any artist, Sir,' replied the lady. 'It was the performance
of Clement Montgomery. It is drawn for my niece –.'

'Then she must have the honour greatly to resemble you, Madam.
Upon my soul the likeness is astonishing.'

Up rose Mrs. Valmont. 'Why indeed, Lord Filmar, though I
never observed it before, there is something of me in the turn of
these features; but indisposition, Sir, the cruel hand of sickness, has
made sad havock with my face. – And she pushed a little backward
the hood which had almost hid her remnant of beauty.

In short, dear Walter, I dined at the castle. My father saw
the lady and I saw her picture. My father says, and so says the
picture, that she is very handsome. By the answers to a few questions
artfully arranged to Mrs. Valmont, but more certainly from the result
of Griffith's steady enquiries among the household, I learn that she
is a mere savage, and loves her fellow savage Clement as she ought
only to love me.

Loves her fellow savage Clement! you exclaim. Not less strange
than true, Walter; and, if you would know more, listen as I did to
the aforementioned housekeeper.

'Of all the youths my eyes ever beheld,' said Mrs. Luxmere,
'I think Master Clement Montgomery was the handsomest; and so
affable, my Lord! – He used to steal into my room once or twice
every day to eat sweetmeats, when Miss Valmont or his tutor did
not watch him.'

'But who does this Master Clement Montgomery belong to?' said
I.

'To Mr. Valmont, my Lord. I'll tell you exactly how it was. Nobody, as far as I know, had ever heard of this young gentleman till just after the 'Squire's niece came to the castle; and then the 'Squire took a journey, and brought home with him a fine handsome boy. And he gave a great entertainment; all the rooms were filled with company; and after dinner he led in Clement Mongomery, and bade every body look on him as his adopted son. Some people think, indeed, that he is the 'Squires——.'

Mrs. Luxmere affected to titter. 'You are of that opinion?' said I. — 'Certainly,' replied Mrs. Luxmere. Nothing can be more certain. Old Andrew has lived five and twenty years with Mr. Valmont; and he can't deny it. Beside, if you were to see Master Clement, my Lord, you would swear it. He is so handsome and so genteel!'

'And is Miss Valmont handsome, and genteel, and affable, Mrs. Luxmere?'

'I know very little about her, my Lord, although I lived in the castle nine years,' said the housekeeper, with much abatement of her warmth. 'Mr. Valmont ordered both her and Master Clement not to speak to any one of the household, and she never came into my room in her life. Master Clement used to come so slily! — and many a nice bit has he been eating beside me, when Miss Valmont has been roaming the house and grounds in search of him! She has a suite of rooms entirely to herself in the south wing, and is waited on by silent Andrew and his deaf daughter –'

'Where is Montgomery now?' said I, 'Oh dear, my Lord, you can't think what strange things have happened to him! The 'Squire sent him abroad and he staid two years and he came home they say so grown and so improved, it was charming to think of it! Yet that tyger-hearted Mr. Valmont has disinherited him, and sent him to London to work for his bread! Poor dear youth! I know it's true, my Lord.'

Enough of Mrs. Luxmere. It is true, Walter, that this dear and handsome youth was brought up in the castle with Miss Valmont. Every creature in it bears testimony to his good nature, for he would not only eat sweetmeats slily with Mrs. Luxmere, but he would slily ride with the grooms, tell stories with the butler, and so completely elude the vigilance of the 'Squire and his tutor, that his contrivances are still a famous topic in the servants' hall. Not so Miss Valmont. She never tempted the domestics from their obedience, nor invited them to familiarity, by that sacrifice of her integrity. I like this part of her character, nor am I at all inclined to give credit to the supposition which prevails among the servants of her being deranged in intellect. A little too hardy of nerve for a Countess, I confess, she roams, they tell me, in defiance of storm or tempest, in the woods, nay even in the echoing galleries of the terrific castle, at and after midnight. Some say she has conversed with apparitions, others only fear that she will one day or other encounter them; but all agree that, while he was here, she adored Clement. And since he has been gone she, to an old oak, for his sake, pays her adorations.

We talked of this Montgomery yesterday, at dinner. His being disinherited is all stuff. He is Valmont's idol. Valmont praised him to the skies, not what he is, but what he is to be when all the 'Squire's plans respecting him shall be completed. Yet he has faults, it seems. Wonderful! And cast in Mr. Valmont's mould too! What are his faults, think you, Boyer? Why, he admires the world. Lack a day! – at one and twenty! But he is to be cured of this defect. Oh, yes; Mr. Valmont possesses the grand secret! He is quack-royal to the human race; and possesses the only specific in nature to make a perfect man. Were I in Montgomery's place, I would wind Valmont round and round my finger.

Care I for the nymph's loving her Clement, think you? ne'er a whit! Did he win her by caresses, I'll not be behind hand. Or were sighs and flattery his engine, I can sigh and flatter too. Aye, surely the practice-taught Filmar may stand a competitorship with Valmont's pupil. In two months or less, she shall herself decide upon our merits, and acknowledge me the victor. None of your croakings, Walter. When did I fail of success where I chose to attempt it, even among beauties armed with cunning and caution? How then shall I fail with this unadvised, this inexperienced damsel, whom doubtless a man of less might than I could draw round the world after him in a cobweb. Should Uncle Valmont rave when I have secured the prize, I'll send him among the tombs of my ancestors for consolation. He loves family; and there he may nose out a long list of worm-eaten rotten heroes, whose noble scent can inform him that even the blood of the Valmonts may be enriched by uniting with the offspring of the dust of the Filmars.

My necessities are urgent, Walter. The day of sealing may last mortgage draws near; and, if my invention is not more fertile on that account, at least my resolution is more undaunted. Were time less pressing, I might grow coy with expedient. As it is, I must snatch at bare probabilities; and, in faith, be it the wildness of the design, be it ambition, avarice, or be the motive what it may, I grow more and more enamoured of the heiress of Valmont Castle, and more and more fearless of whatever risks I may encounter to obtain her.

Congratulate me, Walter, on my firmness; and believe me, in a very considerable degree, thine,

FILMAR

LETTER XVI

FROM CLEMENT MONTGOMERY

TO

ARTHUR MURDEN

I write again and again to you, Arthur, and you remain silent. Yet a fate so various as mine makes even communication enjoyment. Various, did I say? no, it was but my apprehension that were various. The fate was certain, established beyond the reach of change. Mr. Valmont ever designed to make me his heir, and designs it still. Yesterday brought me a welcome letter, and a more welcome remittance. 'I am known to be your protector, Clement,' says Mr. Valmont in his letter; 'and it is necessary for my honour that you should preserve a degree of consequence among men. Moreover, money is the master key to the confidence of men. Use it as such. Gratify their wants, real or artificial; and they, in return, will soon display the sordidness the ingratitude of their hearts.' Precious doctrines, these! And, Arthur, I being wiser than the sender, have dismissed them, to keep their fellow maxims company in a close shut drawer in my secretary, where they shall rest in peace until I turn snarling cynic also.

But the intimation, Arthur! – the cash, Arthur! I have not hoarded those in a drawer! you hear that it is necessary for Mr. Valmont's honor that I preserve consequence among men. Ah! dear Sir! leave me ever thus to the support of your honor among men! I will not complain though you preserve wholly to yourself the felicity of being locked within the walls of Valmont's castle! I yield the building, and am content alone to aim at preserving your honour and dignity with the valued produce of its rich acres.

This is the first time that Mr. Valmont's letters to me have failed to mention Sibella. Heaven avert the omen, if it be one! Yet surely, for Miss Ashburn advised and I commanded, surely she will be silent.

Murden, 'twas one of the blind mistakes of fortune that Sibella and I should love each other, directly in the teeth of Mr. Valmont's designs, and both so absolutely within his power. Heigh-ho! I have been just taking a view of her picture. – What a divine face! Some day I will make another copy of this miniature. The hair, beautiful as it is, falls too forward, and hides the exquisite turn of her neck. How can I endure to conceal the greater beauty, and display the less! Ah! Should those lips, lips promising eternal sweets, ever move to the destruction of my hopes, should they betray me to Mr. Valmont, then Arthur, must they never again give joy to mine; for, however Sibella's wild energy might inspire me, while reclined at the foot of a tree, to vow this and to promise that of fortitude and forbearance, here, in the centre of delights, I feel that Sibella is as much a dreamer as her uncle. A thousand wants occur, that I knew not in her arms – wants which possibly her refinements might call artificial; yet, to me, is their gratification so endeared, as to become necessary to my existence. Sooner would I quit life, than live unknown and unknowing. Misled by the power of beauty, methought Sibella spoke oracles while she talked to me of contentment and independence. Whither might not the thraldom of her enslaving charms have led me! 'twas wonderful I escaped ruin! Wonderful that I had strength to persevere in opposing her intent of declaring to her uncle the secret of that contract which crowned me with happiness, while it laid the foundation of a world of fears. Could you see her, and could you taste the enticements of her caresses, you would wonder too. Heavens! how will my happy years roll on, should I become securely the inheritor of the Valmont estates, for then will I reward my fairest, then will I make her my wife! Oh, that I could find some magic spell to charm her to silence, to deaden in her the memory of the past, so that I might peaceably enjoy the present without torturing apprehensions to assail me of Mr. Valmont's discoveries, of Mr. Valmont's resentments!

But enough of the name of Valmont. Faith, Murden, my thoughts are never so near the castle as when I write to you; and the reason is plain – I fly to my pen only when a cessation from pleasure threatens me with lassitude; and to such a cause, I am frank enough to tell you, you owe this my letter.

It is now one hour past noon, and I went to bed at nine this morning. My limbs acknowledged a most unusual portion of weariness; but the gay shadows of the night's diversions flitted before me in tumultuous rotation. I had moments of insensibility on my pillow, but not of rest;

and, after making a vain attempt of two hours to find sleep, I rose and ordered my breakfast. A thought of writing to you succeeded, for tempestuous weather will not let me ride, and haggard looks forbid me to visit.

Mrs. Ashburn's fortune must be immense; and, on my soul, I adore her spirit. She does not suffer time to steal by her unnoticed; nor wealth to sleep in her possesion. I believe her very dreams are occupied in forming variety of pleasures. Their succession is endless and perpetual.

Yesterday and last night, I made one of a brilliant crowd of visitors who thronged to Mrs. Ashburn's. Her new house was purposely prepared for this occasion; and no ornament that taste could devise and wealth approve was wanting to render it compleat in elegant splendour. – A suite of rich apartments were yesterday morning thrown open for the reception of near 300 persons. It was a breastfast worthy to be recorded among the enchantments of a Persian tale; and every mouth was filled with applause; and still would the breakfast and concert have been the universal theme, had not the more novel and splendid entertainment of the evening deservedly claimed the superior praise.

Mrs. Ashburn's cards had also invited the company of the morning to a masqued ball for the night. The masques began to assemble about eleven. Mrs. Ashburn had laid her commands on me not to appear till I judged the company would be assembled. No small tribute this her command to the vanity of your friend, Arthur. She had chosen my habit. She had added to it some brilliant ornaments. I will be honest enough to confess that to the utmost it displayed my advantages of person, and Mrs. Ashburn believed the effect of the whole would be striking. I represented a winged Mercury. My habit of pale blue sattin was fastened close around me with loops, buttons, and tassels of orient pearls. These, amounting to a value I dare hardly guess at, Mrs. Ashburn absolutely forced upon me for the occasion.

Thus resplendent I joined the throng. Buzzing whispers of – *the Mercury! the Mercury! Splendid! charming!* &c. &c. ran round the walls; but, if the Mercury excited their astonishment, his own surprise and delight was doubly triply excited by the enchantments which seemed to take his senses prisoner. Methought in the morning I had quitted a palace. What name then could I devise to express the fanciful grandeur of the present scene? Every thing was new. Such dispositions had been made that the form of the apartments appeared changed. How the pillars, lights, music, refreshments were disposed, you may amuse yourself, if taste will so far aid you, in imagining. As for me, I have no power of description; my brain whirls from one dazzling object to another, and leaves me but an indistinct crowded recollection of the various beauties.

Mrs. Ashburn was unmasked. Janetta Laundy had shone a bright star of the morning, but what cloud had now dimmed her rays I could not with the best of my endeavours discover. I detected the Duchess de D——; and essayed to gain some tidings of the recreant star, but she laughed me off without a tittle of information.

Suddenly the bands of music make an abrupt pause. Every one looks round, silent, and surprised. A pair of folding doors fly open. Streams of light burst upon the eye. The rich perfumes of the east pour forth their fragrance to the sense. The altar of taste appears, raised like a throne at the upper end of the temple. Rows of silvered cupids present offerings, and point to the goddess, who presides at her own altar.

I knew her form well: 'twas worthy of the goddess. Her robe fell gracefully behind, loose from her shape, which a white vest sprinkled with golden stars admirably fitted. Her plumes waved high over a coronet, of budding myrtle and the half blown rose. Her cestus glittered of the diamond. Diamond clasps confined the fulness of her robe sleeves a little above the elbow, and her fine arm borrowed no ornament beyond its own inestimable fairness. In short, Arthur, who could look on unmoved. 'Twas Mrs. Ashburn's triumph of wealth, but Janetta Laundy's uncontrollable triumph of beauty. I have many times wondered by what charm Janetta could arrive at such unbounded influence over her benefactress, for certainly Mrs. Ashburn has a plentiful share of vanity, and is ever aiming to excite admiration. How then can she forgive the youth and charms of her companion?

In vain Janetta last night assumed a double portion of that cold haughtiness of demeanour with which she now receives my advances to familiarity. She personated the goddess of taste; and men would pay their loud and daring homage to the divinity. Mrs. Ashburn became piqued. She spoke pettishly to Janetta, and endeavoured to disperse her admirers. At length she beckoned me from a distant seat, to which I had retired somewhat fatigued and dispirited, and delivered the goddess to my protection.

We danced together. We did not separate during the rest of the entertainment. 'This is as it used to be,' whispered the Duchess de N—— coming up to the sopha on which we sat. 'But you, Chevalier, are so faithless,' added she.

'Oh,' said I, fixing my eyes on Janetta, 'your Grace misplaces that accusation! I am constancy itself. You ladies, indeed, who know the power of your charms, are not to be satisfied with the homage of a single lover.'

'Your insinuation, sir,' replied Janetta, 'is easily understood; and if I am happy enough to escape interruption from the company, I shall take the present opportunity of freeing myself from your charges. The Duchess will condescend to aid me. I believe Mr. Montgomery will scarcely doubt of the testimony of the Duchess de N——.'

'Ah,' replied the Duchess, 'defend me from lovers' quarrels! For heaven's sake, my dear, do you suppose that you engross all the charms of to-night, and that poor I have no better employment than to shake my head, look grave, and bear a solemn burden to your serious speeches. Tell the story yourself, child; and, if the Chevalier can look on your face and mistrust you, make him a gay curtsy and follow me, my dear, into yonder circle.'

When the Duchess was gone, Janetta relapsed into her reserve; and, had I not become extremely urgent, would have deferred the explanation.

Yes, indeed, Arthur, I have wronged her most shamefully in my suspicions, but the story is too long for me to relate in my present record. I drag through one heavy sentence after another, intending that each shall be the last. Now, having by this effort brought on an increase of weariness, I'll e'en try what repose a couch will afford me; and then away to Mrs. Ashburn and Janetta.

CLEMENT MONTGOMERY

LETTER XVII

FROM LORD FILMAR

TO

SIR WALTER BOYER

Say, dear Sir Walter, to which of the gods shall my hecatomb blaze a burnt offering? Behold, entering within those gates, I see the Valmont coach!——I fly to greet the welcome visitants – more welcome to me than gold to the miser, than conquest to the warrior.——Lie still, thou throbbing mischief, down, down, ye struggling expectations! And let the for once spiritless countenance of Filmar conceal his hopes.

'Tis true, Boyer, as – as – as any thing that's most true. Here, in this very Monkton Hall, is Mr. Valmont, ay, and Mrs. Valmont too; and here I mean to keep them: – only to-morrow though.——To-morrow! Walter!—— Hail the dawn of to morrow! – Whips cracking, horses flying, and thy friend driving as fast as four can carry him into 6000l. a-year!

If you want cash, call on me any day next week. You, being a *particular* friend, I'll oblige. But to any one else – Somerville now for instance or Nugent – 'It will be curst unfortunate, but I shall have had a hard run of late – or, I shall be building, and want to borrow myself – or, there will be great arrears on my estates not yet paid up.' – But see, here comes a bowing cringing tradesman, who in my days of worse fortune has buffeted me with his purse-proud looks many a time and often. 'Really Mr.—— a – a – the amount of your bill seems a little enormous, but I can't fatigue myself with looking into these matters——the steward pays you, – Ay, ay, be not troublesome, and (throwing myself along the sopha) I may probably still deal with you. – Sibella, my dear, raise these cushions under my head – Psha, child, you are devilishly awkward – there – . Pooh! – throw that gauze shade of your's over me.—— Sit down, and watch, lest Ponto or Rosetta should leap upon or disturb me.'

By the bye, Walter, as I am determined to reform when I'm married, and become an obedient hopeful son and nephew, if uncle Valmont should think (and pray heaven he may) my wife's——

Oh, lord, what a shudder!——There! 'tis a radical cure, I assure you. – I seized a square piece of paper; and, writing thereon in large characters 6000 l. *per annum*, placed it exactly opposite me, and the qualm vanished. – Walter, you shall see wife written on my page – *my wife!* – Oh, I declare this scrap of paper is a charm of infinite value! –

If uncle Valmont, I say, should deem my wife's education incomplete, and desires to have her longer under his tuition, I will yield her up for one year, or two, or twenty, if he pleases. – There's forbearance, there's magnanimity! Dub me a hero, sir knight! and place me among the foremost! – Talk of conquering a world, indeed! Why philosophers of all ages have agreed that the truest heroism is to conquer self. – Dub me a hero, I say!

I grant you, this is all rattle (that is the manner not the matter, upon my honor), and poor forced rattle too; but I must be mad, for I cannot be merry, nor yet serious. My gadding spirits are whirling this enterprise round and round without ceasing. Sometimes tossing the dark side toward me; and then, ere I can make one retracting reflection, smilingly presenting to me its advantages. – At that still time of night (if my plan fail not) when graves yield up the semblance of their dead, my courtship is to begin. – Once begun, it must go on; and the second setting sun beholds me a bridegroom. – Close your door, Boyer; stir up your fire; and I'll tell you.———Not now though, for – enter Griffiths.

'The gentlemen have walked out to the grounds, my lord. Mrs. Valmont and Lady Monkton are alone.'

'Right Griffiths, I understand your hint.'

'My Lord, it will certainly take,' returning shrugging his shoulders and laughing. 'The butler hates squire Valmont, and enjoys the thought of playing him such a trick. The lads will have to strip and turn out to-morrow, I doubt not, for this day's frolic.'

'Then, I must provide for them! 'Tis our frolic, and not theirs, Griffiths. 'Should our plain fail——'

'It cannot fail, my lord,'

'Well, well – go – mind you give me more water than wine at dinner.'

And now, I steal from a back door, make a circuit round the house, and crossing the lawn join the dear good kind *informing* souls in the drawing room. ——You shall hear from me again presently, Walter.

I am gone, in reputation I mean, to seek the earl, the baronet, and the simple squire, but, in propria persona, returned to my chamber to tell you a story – a story of stories. The ladies were in the very heart of it when I entered. Luckily, I had waited a sentence or two outside the door, or I should have had no clue to bespeak a continuance of the subject. Mrs. Valmont was suspicious of me, but having persuaded her than I am a sober sort of youth, not at all given to hardheartedness and infidelity, she proceeded, and I had the good fortune to listen with wondering eyes and gaping mouth to the particular account of how, where, and when, Miss Valmont (my wife that is to be) saw a – ghost. – Stay, let me recollect – a ghost, is I believe a terrific animal, dressed in chains, howling, shrieking, and always withdrawing in a flash of fire; yes, that's a ghost. This was something more gentle and complacent. Mrs. Valmont makes nice distinctions. I remember she called it an apparition, of a spirit – first appearing in the shape of an old hermit – then in that of a young handsome beau – first walking, manlike, into a wood – next bouncing up, fiend-like, on a sudden in an armoury. – Ay, it was a spirit Sibella saw. – She, poor little barbarian, is no better acquainted with the qualities of an apparition than of a man; for, simply enough, she complained to Mrs. Valmont of the disturbance given by this said shifting phantom to her meditations.

To be sure, Lady Monkton,' said Mrs. Valmont, 'one must laugh at most of these stories; but we all know from good authority such things have been seen. Indeed, I did not altogether credit the very extraordinary accounts I had heard of the disturbance, the Valmont family had many years ago received from some thing that they say inhabits the Ruin on the Rock; and even when my niece, who, in such affairs is ignorance itself, told me her story, I would not be convinced till I had sent three men servants to search the wood and the Ruin. If any thing human had been there, it must have been discovered. The affair of the armoury I only mentioned to my own woman, for I well knew it was impossible that any substance of flesh and blood out of our own household could get into the armoury. What can be said Lady Monkton, but that it is to answer some wise purpose or other?

'Does, Mr. Valmont know?' said I.

'Surely, Lord Filmar, you must judge poorly of my discretion, to suppose that I would tell Mr. Valmont such an affair; for, besides that there is a shocking degree of impiety in people's disbelief when the thing is indisputably true, he would torment the servants incessantly, by sending them at night into those places, and perhaps he might abridge the poor child of her rambles around the park.'

'Isn't Miss Valmont afraid of being alone?' asked Lady Monkton.

'Afraid! – Ha! ha! ha! – why, she has not one idea, Lady Monkton, belonging to a rational being I assure you: She is not afraid of any thing. Well, really her want of understanding is not at all marvellous. Shut up in that horrid abode. – I preserve a part of mine, only by reflecting on former days.'

'The young lady's conversation, then, is not much relief to you, Madam?' said I.

'No, indeed, 'tis her absence is the relief, my lord. Mr. Valmont was much more kind than he intended, when he ordered his niece not to frequent my apartments. – It is a thousand pities; for the child has a fine person, and is – that is, had she any thing like manners, and were not such an absolute idiot, I do think she would be very handsome. &c. &c. &c.'

Some frolic of master Clement Montgomery's, I presume this apparition to be, Walter. Yet, surely she is not idiot enough to tell of herself in such a case! —— Ha! – woman! woman still! whether in solitude or society! – I well remember the fellow I saw tripping near Valmont's moat. – Yes, yes. He – Montgomery contrives to find secret admittance into that well defended place; and she contrives a rare finely imagined tale to turn the people's wits the seamy-side without, and throw a veil impervious as darkness around themselves and their pleasures. —— Yet, hang it! – no! – Montgomery, said Mrs. Valmont, was abroad on his travels when this affair happened. Beside, there is a degree of invention in the story which must have been beyond the capacity of so ignorant a girl. – Heyday! – Why I am anticipating eight and forty hours, and already beginning to feel myself accountable for my wife's adventures!

Peace be, then, to the apparition's ashes! – After the knot is tied, and I and my bride are travelling homewards to receive forgiveness and *golden* blessings, I shall probably want something to keep me awake, and the child must tell me the story in her own way.

Hark! – the dinner bell. – My part in the plot will soon commence. – Be content, Walter, to trace it in its several progressive steps toward the catastrophe. I have not patience to detail what is to be, and then sit down to relate what is.——Adieu, for a few hours.

So far, so good. – Nay, better than good, the very elements have conspired to my success. – Such a storm of hail, rain, and thunder, I never beheld at this season of the year. The darkness was tremendous, and Mrs. Valmont's shattered nerves felt its effects most powerfully, notwithstanding the pompous harangue delivered by her *caro sposo* against such terrors. – In the midst of this scene entered Mr. Valmont's gentleman; who, bowing reverently, in a low tone of voice begged to know if his lordly master would vouchsafe to be drawn home by one pair of horses, (he came, Walter with six) for that unfortunately the postilion was very drunk.

'Drunk!' exclaimed Mr. Valmont. Did you say, drunk?'

The man bowed and looked sorry; then ventured slowly to insinuate that he did not deem the coachman perfectly sober, though not absolutely drunk. He might be able to drive a pair of horses perhaps.

'I shall have my neck broken,' cried Mrs. Valmont, 'then all my sorrows will be at an end together; and you, sir, may be for once satisfied.'

'Madam! What mean you?' said the frowning *dignitary*.

The remedy was obvious. To remain at Monkton Hall for the night was proposed to Mr. Valmont with great earnestness by Sir Gilbert and my lady; and, at length, acceded to by him with due reluctant solemnity.——Mrs. Valmont smiled through her terrors.

To you, Walter, I give a sober straight forward history; but, in the opinions of my friends below stairs, I am fast approaching towards the honours which the squire's postilion and coachman have already purchased. I affected to grow very frolicksome, early after dinner; and am, at length, become, with the help of claret and burgundy, as properly intoxicated to all appearance as I find necessary to the carrying on of my plan. However, I am not yet retired for the night: – presently, I mean to descend, and give them such another specimen of my ability as shall make my departure so essential to their repose, that they will not attempt to recal or disturb me.

A messenger, Boyer, is gone to the castle, to give notice of its master's absence for the night. He carries other tidings there also: – tidings to me of great joy.

The servants of Valmont castle are held in such constraint by their proud master, that to enjoy the pleasures which are permitted in other households they are ever scheming. The squire's absence is a festive holiday; and Griffiths was invited by the butler, with whom he has purposely scraped an intimacy, to partake of the joy of to day. Why

the invitation was neglected you may divine. By the messenger now
sent to the castle, Griffiths informs the butler that, as Mr. Valmont is
safe at the hall, and Lord Filmar is safe in bed, the night is their own.
He begs they will prepare for mirth and gaiety, bids the housekeeper
and her damsels put on their dancing shoes, and promises to join them
early, accompanied by his brother, who plays an excellent fiddle, and
is the merriest fellow alive.

Such is the substance of Griffith's message to the domestics. Doubt
them not, Walter; they will jump at the opportunity, and swallow my
bait with all the greediness I can desire.

It is now past nine. My pulse begins to beat riotously, as if I were
drunk in earnest. – – Poor undiscerning souls! – I have looked in the
glass, Boyer. – All the uncertainty of my success trembles in my eye
– all the tumult of hopes and fears sits on my countenance: – yet these
animals cannot perceive it.——Would it were over!

The scene is almost prepared to shift. I am dismissed from the
parlour; and, as Griffiths tells them, am at rest. Now, I wait but his
summons. He is gone to hint among the servants here the advantage he
is about to take of his master's infirmity, and hypocritically to request
some one will make an excuse for him should *I by chance awake and
ring my bell before he returns*. – The coast securely clear, I quit the
house; join Griffiths at the lodge; and, at the corner of a little town,
only a quarter of a mile from Sir Gilbert's, we are to find Griffith's
brother waiting in a chaise. This brother, who would not have been
here if we hadn't sent for him, was only a common footman a week
ago, but the two days he has passed at the inn in our neighbourhood
has transformed him into a man of property; and he does not choose
to go four miles in the rain without a covered carriage. Had it not
rained, he would probably have received a sprain in his ancle, or his
knee. The grand business over, for which his assistance is required,
he puts on the Filmar livery, and becomes my footman. I was going
to say my wife's, but there's hazard in that. Gratitude may beget love;
and violently grateful will she be, no doubt, to the man that has helped
to make – her fortune.——Walter, I am no coward: yet, I say again,
would it were over!

I will put this paper in my pocket.——Should I get undetected
into the castle, I shall have many hours of waiting; and to write my
thoughts will certainly relieve me during the tedious interval.

I hear Griffith's signal.——I come.——Adieu.

——Safe in the castle!——'Tis just eleven o'clock. – Two will be the earliest I dare attempt to seize my prize.——Three hours! three ages, I may say, to undergo all the misery of expecting, in every blast of wind, the destruction of my project!——Wind enough!——how it rolls! – Floods of rain too! – A horrid and tempestuous night, this!——We must procure some covering, to shield her from the storm till we reach the chaise. I will mention it to Griffiths, that he may be quite in readiness. I should be sorry were she to suffer by the storm's inclemency. Does she go unwillingly, she suffers enough in going; goes she willingly, still she deserves not to suffer.——Why, thou cold whining Filmar, where is thy manhood? – Only the last stroke wanting, and that the easiest to accomplish, and thy scheme – thy darling scheme is – perfect. – Thy very valet claps the wings of exultation, and sings the song of triumph! Shame! shame! Rouse thyself! cast a look forward, Filmar!——

Yes, Walter, I am here happily supplied with a lighted taper by the dexterity and contrivance of Griffiths. – Securely stationed in one of the best apartments where even the mirth of the servants cannot reach me in a buzzing murmur, there is no hazard that any one of them should quit his diversions to wander among the mazy recesses of this mansion; and I do rejoice abundantly in my security. – Yet, Walter, I may rejoice, and feel the benumbing effects of this cold gloomy dwellings, too. – These old buildings are admirably contrived to fix odd impressions on the mind. – I do not at all wonder that every ancient castle is haunted in report. – Another such night, in another such place, and I could swear I perceived shapeless forms gliding around me.——I listen one minute to the variety of sound produced by the gathering winds; and, the next, find it hushed to so dead a calm, that the sound of my breathings alone interrupts the silence. Such – think of it, think of it, Walter – such are my employments!

I wonder whereabouts this armoury lays. Griffiths could tell. – The castle is amazing large, yet Griffiths is perfectly skilled in its geography. – He described to me, as we came hither, the situation of Miss Valmont's apartments. – They are nearer to where I am now stationed than to any other habitable part of the building.

The spacious gallery into which this room opens, runs the length of the whole front, expecting the wings and the towers. Narrow long passages connect the wings with the main building; and the passage nearest my side of the gallery, conducts you by a short flight of steps immediately up to Miss Valmont's abode. But this is not the road we are to take, because in a little room within that passage sleeps her attendant, silent Andrew; and we chuse not to pass so near him, lest perhaps these resounding walls tell him of our footsteps. – Our's is a more intricate path. The adjoining antichamber will lead us to a narrower stair-case; descending this, we shall cross some of the lower apartments; and, making a circuit, gain the bottom of the West Tower; from whence, alleys and winding stone stairs will introduce us to the end of Miss Valmont's gallery, opposite to that we must have entered had we gone in the straight forward direction. We deem it advisable to descend with our charge the same way, and to leave the castle by a little door in the West Tower. It is, to be sure, on the wrong side, and will oblige us to carry our burthen, if the young lady should not be disposed just then to make use of her limbs, so much the further.

Griffith's brother is a strong, bony, dark-looking fellow. Strength will be necessary, if persuasion should fail; and I cannot spare more than ten minutes to try the effects of my rhetoric. I will enter first; and, should a shriek of surprise or shriek of rapture (remember my person, Walter) escape her, the closed doors, distance of situation, and sleep of security, will prevent Andrew from hearing. Indeed, should he, mal-a-propos, interfere, it is only the extra trouble of *binding* him to good behaviour. It did once enter my thoughts to bribe this old fellow to our purposes, but the attempt might have wrought a discovery. Fearing nothing, he suspects nothing; absence of all care and a warm night-cap lull him to repose: – and pleasant be his dreams. – Ours all the hazard! Ours the reward! I have promised 500l. to Griffiths, and 100l. to his brother. My share of the plunder is to them a secret.

Now, though I allow the damsel one squall, yet I positively interdict any repetitions of the fort; and as, you know, I immediately became the arbiter of her fate, the sooner I accustom her to implicit obedience, the easier it will be to both in future.

Walter, I mend! My flagging spirits begin to bound and curvet. Oh! when we are once seated in that chaise and four, which now waits our coming in a retired corner, not above a hundred yards from the other side of the moat, how will my imagination outstrip the speed of the horses!

Dost thou talk of pursuit, Walter. – No! no! I mock pursuit! Supposing we get not away till three or four, we still shall have six or seven hours advantage in point of time. Then the old dons won't dream which way we are gone. – They do not know, what you and I do know, the great reward attendant on my deed; and, sorrowfully remembering the wickedness and sinfulness of their own youthful hearts, they will unrighteously judge of me, and sit down piteously to lament the loss of the lady's honour, whilst I, like a good Christian and worthy member of society, so far from diminishing am increasing her stock of honour, for the honour of a virgin is but a single portion, whereas, according to wise institutions, the honour of a wife is twofold – she bearing her husband's honour and her own. Pray heaven the cargo be not too mighty!

'Where is Lord Filmar?' says one of the party assembled at ten to-morrow morning to breakfast in Monkton Hall parlour.

'Tell Griffiths to let his lordship know we expect him at breakfast,' – says the earl.

'I told Mr. Griffiths, my lord,' replies the footman (one servant will always lie for another), 'but he says his lordship is asleep.'

This produces many pleasant allusions to last night's intemperance among the good souls; and they go to breakfast without me. Now, in the steward's room, one wonders Mr. Griffiths is not come home, a second wonders at my good nature and his faults, and a fourth wonders I do not awake. Amidst all this wit and wonder, another hour or two passes; and then two or three more probably in the surmises occasioned by the discovery of my absence.

The servants of the castle in the mean time are employed in their usual occupations, not at all surprised that their visitors had quitted them early unseen, because it had been so intended by them. Andrew, indeed, waits Miss Valmont's summons for breakfast, and deems it somewhat tardy. He concludes her walk to be unusually pleasing, and eats his own repast in peace and quietness. At length, his thoughts verge towards the extraordinary, and he inclines to seek further.

No, Andrew, 'tis in vain you search. No fair wood-nymph greets your eye. No voice answers to your call.——Ay! ay! assemble them: – hold your convocations in the great hall: – crowd, closer and closer: – whisper your suspicions, lest the dread ear of Valmont catch the tidings, that – *she is gone!* – Who shall carry these tidings to Mr. Valmont? – Not I! not I! not I ! answers every voice at once; and up to the hall door drives his coach and six. Away fly the pale culprits! – Jostling against each other, confusion retards their speed, and the dreadful secret is in part betrayed.

Fye! Mr. Valmont, fye! don't swear! don't call hard names!

Can't you hear him, Walter, declaring his rage, and threatening his vengeance? – I can.

Ill news fly fast. Mr. Valmont's horses are not unharnessed. –
Turn your eyes to Monkton Hall. See the squire enter – See the
earl turn pale; the baronet attempt to look sorry; and see them, as
I before observed, sitting in judgment on me, and putting their own
black constructions on my innocent praise-worthy intentions.

Assuredly, Walter, could I have commanded every circumstance
in my own way, it could not have happened more favourably. Mr.
Valmont's porter is ill, and has been removed from the lodge into the
house to be better nursed. Two grooms were deputed to take care of
the draw-bridge. Mr. Valmont absent, we found it down; and down it
remains now. — With what art Griffiths drew off the postilion, while
I got into the chaise! The lad had not a suspicion he carried more
than two – I crouched to the bottom, as they got out; and Griffiths
whip'd up the blinds in an instant. He gave me one compleat fright,
for we had agreed the postilion should follow them into the house to
be paid, while I freed myself; imagine how I trembled to hear them
discharging him on the spot, and he thanking and wishing their
honours good night.

'Stop my boy,' at length, cried Griffiths; 'hasn't thou got a wet
jacket?'

'Yes, indeed, master,' replied thc postilion, ''tis well soaked.'

'Why you griping old fellow, ' this was addressed to the butler, who
had come out to meet them, 'you grow as stingy as your master! – Why
don't you offer the lad a little inside cloathing? Come, postilion, come,
you shall go in and drink my health in a bumper. But first, my boy,
lead your horses under that arch, and they escape being wetter.' Then
singing, he led the whole train into the back part of the castle.

Now this thought of the arch was the luckiest imaginable; for,
had any of the grooms by chance staid loitering about the yard, the
chaise was then so effectually screened, they could not have seen me
descend from it. Turning on the right side of the arch, I crept along
the front of the castle, crossed the inner court, and the hall door, with
one gentle push, gave me admittance. Had the door been fastened, I
must have waited there till Griffiths could steal an opportunity to let
me in. In this part of the castle 'twas dark, as darkness itself; but as
I had been in this apartment before, and came by the great staircase,
I found my way hither without trip or stumble. Griff——I fancied, –
Nay, I'm sure, I heard a noise! – yet, all is silent again. – It was like
the creaking of a door, and like something falling.——Rat's probably;
the midnight tenants of the mansion.

Good God, how slowly the minutes move! only seventeen minutes and a half after twelve! – Astonishing! – that must be hail surely! I never heard rain drive with such impetuosity. – The casements tremble. I could almost fancy the building rocks with the tempest's violence.

What wonders will not education, custom, and habit accomplish! Miss Valmont, I dare say, feels no horror in listening to such sounds, nor tracing these murmuring galleries, lonely staircases, &c. I should not exist six months in this castle. – She must, indeed, be a strange unformed being! – Her portrait, that I told you of, hangs in this very room; and on my conscience it would persuade me she is an animated intelligent creature; but I know 'tis impossible; and now and then, when the 6000 l. per annum gets a little into the shade, I anticipate fearful things.

It is fortunate, Walter, that she has the advantages of person, for, on that account, I shall have a little the less reluctance in shewing her to the world, and a little more pleasure in attempting to humanize her. – Yet, I fear, it will be but gawky beauty neither, and that I abominate. – Robust health, no doubt; strong limbs; hanging arms; a gigantic stride; and the open-mouthed stare of a savage! – Oh, dear!

I must be fond too, I suppose, as we travel towards matrimony; but I don't feel the least inclined to fondness! – No! although I shall seize her unattired in bed, perhaps. – No: not one wild wish or mischievous thought will enter my bosom. – My pulse will continue to beat evenly. – My blood keep in its temperate course. I shall be a perfect anchorite. For me, she can have no enticements.——My——Merciful! Do I dream?——or——

Boyer, am I not in Valmont castle? – Did I not come hither to carry off the niece of Valmont? And was that bright vision the Sibella Valmont whom I have so traduced? – Hush! Walter! repeat not my crime, if thou hopest for peace in this world, or happiness in the next! It could not be her, her that I came in search of! – Yes, but it was her. Angel as she is in form, her heart is the heart of a mortal still. 'Oh, Clement!' said she, and, spreading one hand upon her heaving bosom, sighed deeply. – She addressed herself to that picture.

'Art thou safe, my love? – terrifying dreams disturb my rest!' She saw me not, for her back was toward me as she entered. 'Heaven preserve my Clement!' said she again after a pause.

She would have continued thus soliloquising, but I, to gain a view of her face, attempted to change my attitude. My cursed coat had somehow got entangled in the chair, and threw it against the table as I moved. She turned around; and I, as in the presence of a goddess, bowed lowly to the very ground.

She then approached nearer; and my eyes retreated from the scrutiny with which she viewed me. The examination lasted more than a minute; and all that time I was racking my invention to find words to address her, but I might as well have been born dumb: I had neither articulation, nor sounds to articulate.

'Mark me, Sir,' said she, and I, like the idiot I had been describing her, bowed again: 'Mr. Valmont may bring you here; may make this castle my prison; but my will is free. I tell you, Sir, I am beyond your reach. Remember it, I am beyond your reach.' – And away she glided.

'*Mr. Valmont may bring you here.*' Why, who the devil could she take me for? I thought Mr. Valmont brought nobody here! – '*I am beyond your reach.*' Say not so, sweet saint! – I would not have you now beyond my reach for a king's ransom. If she should alarm the house, Walter.——Hark!——No. – 'Tis nothing. – she knew me: yet knew me not. – defied me: yet is a stranger to my purpose. – What can all this mean? – Ha! then it may be true, that this frightful place has deranged her intellects! – Certainly that is the case. She looked a lovely lunatic, wrapped up in a loose gown, her hair streaming at its length; and arisen, in the dead of night, to apostrophize to her own picture!

Yet I am not deterred, Walter. I'll undertake her restoration. Expect me in London immediately. I unsay all. I would not yield her up to her uncle, no not for an hour!

Is she returned to her bed, I wonder? – Oh! my moderation is given to the wind! – The time draws near! – I heard the clapping of distant doors.——I cannot write. – I can hardly breathe.

Boyer, they shall neither of them touch her. – I will carry her myself.——I could not bear to see their arms encircle the sweet girl. – I'll enter her chamber first. – Her face they must behold; but, with the same zeal that I would feast mine own senses upon her other charms, will I hide them from the profanation of vulgar eyes.

The great clock striking two has just filled the turrets with its sound. – Griffiths has been with me. Their gayer sports have ceased. Punch bowls and story telling succeed the dance and song. Their animal spirits drooping with excess and fatigue, their old midnight habits return. – Mysterious tales of ghosts go round the circle; and each becomes desirous of seeking rest, though fearful to separate. A few more bumpers Griffiths says will at once bring them courage and sleep. He bids me assure myself of success.

Griffiths and his brother are to have a chamber in the front of the north wing. All the domestics, he says, except Andrew and his daughter, lie in the back part of the building.

'Within two hours, my lord,' said Griffiths as he quitted me, 'your triumph is complete.'

Two hours! Walter, two hours of yesterday were nothing: but two hours of this night! – now! – You do not know the length of hours, Boyer! how should you?

When you come to this line, my dear Walter, fill to your friend's prosperity. – My two agents are here. The light is already placed in the dark lanterns. – Not a sleepless eye in the castle but our own. All, even old Andrew, partook of the libations; and resigned their senses, to seal my triumph.

Griffiths has shewn me a gagg. It will not sure be necessary. Should it, I will heal those lips with kisses! My lines stagger. – No wonder! – I'm on the summit! – Now, I only stay to seal this letter. In the first town we arrive at after day-break, it shall be committed to the post. Go or send instantly, and stop all proceedings on the mortgage. Adieu! adieu! rejoice with

FILMAR

END OF THE SECOND VOLUME

VOLUME III

LETTER I

FROM LORD FILMAR

TO

SIR WALTER BOYER

DEAR WALTER,

Two days have I allowed you to wear out your astonishment at my ingenuity, address, and perseverance, and to exercise your imagination in following me and my bride from stage to stage of this admirably contrived journey. – Does the novelty of the adventure wear off? – Happy knight! – to have for thy chosen friend and bosom confidant, one who can ever open the field of variety before thee; and who, to cheer thy languid fancy, removes the pleasure on which thou hadst feasted to satiety, and places the pride-correcting view of disappointment in its stead.

Yes, indeed: old Andrew will find Miss Valmont where he left her; and I shall not be hanged for heiress-stealing. Don Valmont need not swear; and the trio will not sit in judgment on my deeds. – I have had my day of rage; and my day of sullens; and now, in the calmness of grief, I sit down to tell thee that, instead of being circled in my fair one's arms lord of her wealth, I am yet a poor broken-down gamester, and the guest of Sir Gilbert Monckton.

Heigh ho! – Had my plan been over turned when but half advanced, or had this family or that, even my father, or her uncle, detected me and torn her from my gripe I had forgiven it. But to be defeated in the moment of success by my own agents, my tools, tools for whose conscience and courage I had bargained – such tools I say, to be frightened by a black-gowned, bearded, nobody knows what – oh tis too much!

I swear when I wrote you that letter I would not have abated 500l. of my utmost expectations for the chances against me. How could I foresee I should have to deal with a knavish sort of a nameless something? – Who upon earth would imagine, in a seclusion so perfect, this girl could baffle a vigilant guardian, dupe a whole family, and with an art the most refined intrigue under circumstances and forms which sets discovery at defiance? – Nature-taught too!

But, my story. – Well: I described our intended route; and, in due process, we had crossed the antichamber, gone down the winding stairs, traversed the range of apartments below, and arrived at the West Tower, without the single creaking of a shoe to tell our progress. But, mind me: these brave fellows, who had so amply ridiculed the believing souls of the castle for their stories and their ghosts, now began to creep closer to each other. – And at every puff of wind that whizzed past us, they shrunk in circumference.

Thus I tell you we reached the West Tower: a tower long haunted in renown, and of which no apartment is either in use or preservation. We entered a rude kind of saloon, where we dimly saw mouldering walls, and unoccupied pedestals; scraps of its former carved ornaments were strewed upon the pavements; and here and there the faint rays of our lanthern glanced upon an headless hero. The saloon was cold and dreary; a wintry blast crept round us, with the hollow murmer of emptiness. We were treading ground, of which the apparitions of the castle had for time immemorial claimed the undisturbed possession; and the panic struck hearts of my companions were doubtless anticipating supernatural disasters, when slam went some door at no great distance. 'Lord, Lord have mercy on us!' cried Griffiths, seizing on my arm; while his yet paler brother, envying him the supposed protection, forced himself between us, and I have still the misfortune to bear tokens of his cowardly gripe. Enraged with the pain of this fellow's pinch, and the terror of being surprised, I shook him off like a fly; and, closing up the lanthern, I listened attentively at each door of the saloon, and became convinced we had heard only one of the accidental noises of an old and shattered building.

'Follow me, ye frightened fools,' said I, 'and at your peril——'

'Indeed, my lord,' whispered both cowards together, 'we were not at all frightened, and——'

With a look expressive enough I believe, for I was then mad with apprehension least their ignorance and credulity should ruin my project, I awed them into silence. I again bade them follow with the tone of authoritative command, and cowards are at all times most ready to obey.

Our next stage, and last except the stairs, was a winding, narrow, damp, stone passage.———The devil certainly owed me a grudge, since he incited me to enter it at that moment.———Ten minutes sooner, and I had probably secured the damsel, and had left the invisible night-walking inamorato to sigh, as it is now alass, Walter, my fate and fortune.

This passage was barely wide enough for three to walk abreast. I placed myself in the middle; and they clung to me with infinite zeal. I carried the lanthern; and our step was soft as secresy on my part and terror on their's could make it. – Turning an angle of this infernal passage, behold there came sweeping towards us a tall long bearded figure, in a black cloak, and carrying a dark lanthern likewise.

Zounds! What a howl from Griffiths and his brother! – The phantom fled. I pursued. – That beard never, never, grew on his chin, Walter. – He out-ran me; and I could only keep him in sight till, like a flash of lightning, he darted through a pair of heavy folding doors. – I expected nothing so surely as that he had secured them on the inside; and, now grown desperate, I resolved on a trial of strength. But the doors gave me admission as readily as they had done to him: and the long swords, helmets, truncheons, and other rusty weapons, and accoutrements, taught me I was in the *famed* armoury.

Now, Walter, heaven and himself only know to this hour what became of him. These eyes saw him enter, but neither eyes or hands could find him there. Four narrow casements gave light to the armoury; and these were most amply defended by cross bars of iron. That way he could not vanish.

You and others may talk of nursery prejudices till ye are hoarse with discussion, and I will still maintain it was not in the nature of man to witness the unaccountable escape of this spright without feeling his blood change its course. I honestly confess, drops of cold dew stood on my forehead, as I paced round and round this vast hall, holding up my lanthern at every fifth step to discover, and endeavouring from each crack and crevice to force, an opening into some other apartment. – None could I find. – A fearful awe crept to my heart. – I looked behind me and around me – even the void seemed to threaten me with something undefined and horrible.

Baffled in my search. I turned my thoughts from the phantom to Miss Valmont; and remembered with renewed courage that, as the

spright declined giving me an interview, there sprang no apparent
hindrance to my plan. – 'Take heart, Filmar,' said I to myself, 'haste
seek thy agents and complete thy bold undertaking.'

No sooner were the hinges of the closing armoury door silenced,
than I heard the passage resound with the audible voice of Griffith's
brother, repeating as follows: –

'Unto the third and fourth generation – I believe in the Holy
Ghost born of the virgin Mary, and in Pontius Pilate, crucified dead
and buried – But deliver us from all evil, the holy catholic church
and communion of saints, and lead us not into temptation, to be a
light to lighten the Gentiles, Father, Son, and Holy Ghost, as it was
in the beginning Amen. – I Believe in –.'

Charming! thought I – this will do exactly. These echoing vaults
will bear the tidings to Miss Valmont's chamber; and, presently, we
shall be all at prayers together. There was he kneeling when I came
up, his face close to the wall: nor would he open his eyes, nor cease his
unnatural jargon, till I had shaken, cuffed him, and actually stamped
and swore aloud for vexation.

Verily Knight, the saddest of sorrow's sons must have yielded
to laughter had he viewed the ghastly countenance this poor wretch
exhibited, and had likewise seen the half raised eye-lid, under which
he scowled a fearful examination of my whole person. – Perceiving I
had neither saucer-eye, nor cloven foot, cautiously and tremblingly he
ventured to lay three fingers on my arm – I did not vanish into air,
as doubtless he expected; and the fool, overjoyed to find me a real
man of flesh and blood, sprang up with open arms to embrace me.
Desirous to elude the kindness, I stepped aside. His clumsy elbow
came in contact with the lanthern, dashed it from my hand, and left
us in total darkness.

With the extinguished light expired my last hope. To go on
was impossible; and who would not, like me, have endeavoured to
wreak some little vengeance on the stupid destroyers of my scheme.
Fortunately for them, and perhaps in the end for myself, Griffith's
brother, fearing my escape, had seized me behind; and gaining strength
from his terror, pinioned me in spight of all my struggles and threats
till, as the price of my own freedom, I engaged to assist them in getting
safe from this assylum of accidents, apparitions, and harms.

Do not suppose, Walter, that here ended my provocations. No,
indeed; for Griffiths who had lain extended on the ground since the
black-gowned apparition first appeared, venting sighs, groans, and

tears in abundance, doubled his share of my torments, by refusing for a full hour at least either to be soothed or scolded into the use of his legs. Be assured I had left him to his repose, but the brother would not take of his embargo, till all the conditions on my part were fulfilled. The door which led to the terrace we had opened ready on leaving the saloon, and thither I rather dragged than conducted them. – We closed it after us. And then with a bitter curse, I bade them aid themselves; and walked on before, ruminating on my fatal disappointment, and its more fatal consequences.

Imagine what I felt when we came up to the waiting chaise, horses, &c. – money expended which I want; demands increased which I cannot pay. – And so near, so very near to – Well: I will not think.

It was past five when we got back to Sir Gilbert's – I threw myself on the bed; but slept not, Walter. At breakfast they, particularly Valmont and my father, wondered at the alteration in my countenance. I muttered curses at their inquisitiveness. They, doubtless, thought it was blessings for their consolations; and kindly increased them.

Not one syllable has Griffiths breathed on the adventure. We dress and undress as mute as mourners at a funeral. The brother is too much humbled by the affair of the lanthern, to appear before me at present. Eat he must, be my disappointment what it may. Do take him into your household, Walter. Then, if I catch a glimpse of future operations and find his aid needful, he would doubtless double his diligence, and call up his valour to retrieve a lost reputation.

Order Steele to go on again with the writings. I will be in town to sign by the twenty-eighth. Heigh ho! – One last sigh to the memory of my departing estate. – I –

Why, Walter, these fashionable damsels beat us hollow in the ease and gaiety of impudence. Miss Monckton (who arrived here the day following my disaster,) just now entered the library; and, coming up to the writing table, familiarity peered over my shoulder.

'A *lost reputation!* – Oh you wretch,' cried she, snatching the paper from under my hand, 'it is the volume of your sins! – Nay: – I protest, I'll read it.'

And she actually crammed it into her pocket.

'Madam,' said I passionately, 'I insist on your giving me the letter.'

'And I insist on keeping it.' Is not a lady's *insist* equal to that of a lord?'

'Madam –'

'Sir – Come hither.' she pulled me toward the glass. 'Look at yourself. – Guilty or not guilty? – Ah, Filmar, Filmar, from whom did you take your lesson of blushing? – But let me go, let me go. – I die to read the story, that I may know whether you have yet any chance for heaven!'

I don't perceive, Walter, why sex should be a security against horse-whipping. Such a revenge I could have bestowed with a warm good-will on Miss Monckton. – I took the next best, in my power; and had just forced the paper from her, when in walked my father, and the lady withdrew.

Would you believe it? The earl solemnly asked how I dared treat with such impertinence a woman of Miss Monckton's rank? – Did I think I was romping with some chambermaid?

'Be assured, my lord', answered I 'if I made a respectful distinction in this case, it is on the side of the chambermaid.'

My father looked his reply, (as well as he could Walter) and walked away.

Miss Monckton is a coquette, with all the finish of high breeding. She is elegant, though diminutive; highly accomplished in exterior: the rest a blank. – Yet her ease, grace, and vivacity, would have claimed more moments of admiration from me, were not my thoughts perpetually gadding after this Sibella Valmont: sometimes arraigning, sometimes acquitting, her. But my heart has no interest in the motive, Boyer. – No; she is quite an original, formed rather to constitute the business of a life, than the casual pleasure of a moment. I should hate uniformity even of happiness. Give me the zest of an occasional hour of rapture, snatched from a vortex of novelty, whim, and folly.

A blessed portion has Miss Monckton of these latter recommendations. But seven thousand pounds can't buy me. Six thousand pounds per annum! There's the bribe, Walter. And if I must have a counter-balancing evil, why e'en let it be the vice of nature, rather than a vice of education and art. – Ay: but I forgot. Miss Valmont has her art too; and a devilish deep-rooted art it is. – And now dare I not, with all my zealous wishes perpetually impelling me to the discovery, yet dare I not spoil their pleasures. To blast Montgomery is to betray myself.

By my soul, Walter, she is a most lovely creature. – '*Oh Clement! Clement! art thou safe, my love?*' – What! The hour of assignation was past, no doubt! Happy fellow! Favoured Montgomery! Who nightly turns the dwelling of horror into Mahomet's paradise with this Houri. Be in London, to meet me by the twenty-eighth.

FILMAR

This instant has it shot across my mind to ask Valmont for letters to his pupil. The lad can't be here and there too. It will afford me a fine and safe opportunity of setting scrutiny on foot. Adieu.

LETTER II

FROM ARTHUR MURDEN

TO

CLEMENT MONTGOMERY

Thou wilt make her thy wife.' – Good God what an implication! And
is her claim yet to be enforced! – *'I will make her my wife.'* – How
often, since I read thy letter, have I repeated those words – those
despicable words!

Trust me, Clement, I have no settled ill will towards thee.
No: by heaven, have I not – yet, there are moments when I hate
thee heartily.

The severity with which I speak may dissolve the bond of our
intimacy: – was it ever a bond of friendship? – Carry me back
to its origin. – 'Mr. Murden,' said the good natured Du Bois, 'I
have a young gentleman committed to my care whom I wish to
make known to you.' – And then he expatiated on the greatness
of your expectations, the astonishing privacy of your education, and
the singular naiveté of your manners.

Such as he described, you were; and I neglected all my
former acquaintance, to run with you through the round of town
amusements: – With what enthusiasm did you enjoy! With what fire
did you describe! No moment of disgust or lassitude assailed you.
The existing pleasure was still the best, the greatest. All to you,
was rapture, fascination, enchantment.

What a novelty, methought! How enviable and extraordinary!
– For, I had partaken of these pleasures without a particle of
enjoyment. Frequenting the resorts of dissipation from custom,
labouring to compel my revolting senses to the gratifications of
pleasure, struggling to wear a character opposite to my inclination,
seeking in public to seduce the attentions of women, from whose

hours of private yielding I fled with disgust, effectually removed from society which would have taught me the importance of mental pursuits, and living in the profusion of splendor, I almost prayed for wants, for a something, any thing, that could interrupt the routine of sameness, that could make me cease to be as it were the mere automaton of habit.

You charmed me. I longed to investigate the source of your never-failing satisfactions. You did not inform my understanding, but you greatly interested my curiosity. My uncle talked of my making the grand tour; and that was your destiny likewise. It must be amusing, thought I, to travel with one so volatile yet energetic; and such an arrangement was speedily resolved on.

We travelled. Sometimes you complained of my indifference, of the cold reserve that hung upon my character; but the avidity with which you perpetually hunted after variety, and the readiness wherewith I listened to your descriptions, reconciled you to whatever discordance you chanced to perceive between my feelings and your own. – Am I not right, Clement? Was not this rather intimacy than friendship?

While we viewed the Alps and Pyrenees, their sublimity oured into my mind a flood of enthusiasm. The laughing (as the French emphatically call it) country of Italy filled me with delight. But memory can often present such scenes with the warmth and vigour they first bestow; and even her attempts were repressed by the multitudes of follies that perpetually assailed us. I saw on every hand oppression, priestcraft, and blindness. Neither my tutor nor my companions were capable of stimulating me to inquire into the moral and physical causes of the evils I lamented; and, perceiving only the effect, I concluded they were without remedy, and dismissed the subject.

To one point, then, I chained my expectations; and that one point was love. And here, I quixoted my fancy into the wildest hopes. I wanted beauty without vanity, talent without ostentation, delicacy without timidity, and courage without boast. If I saw the semblance of any of these qualities, I hastened to search for the rest. Disappointment succeeded disappointment, without producing any other effect than to bring the visions of my brain before me with fresh allurements, with increase of attributes.

You, Montgomery, perhaps happily for yourself, have been a stranger to this species of refinement. You could have loved any where; and the utmost stretch of your powers of imagination, will not produce even a faint picture of that life of never-fading bliss I expected to enjoy, when I should have found my ideal fair one, for whose tenderness I preserved my heart a sanctuary, sacred, and inviolate. What, then, had been my faith, if, when the prototype of the ideal form did burst upon me in existence, I had been the chosen above all mankind of a heart corresponding in all things with my own.

Sir Thomas commanded me home. You I left without pain. To him I returned without pleasure. – Yes: I returned home – and soon – it was then, Clement – ay then it was –

You say I advised you to forget her in other arms. Montgomery, why did I advise? – And wherein was I competent to judge? – Had you not already prepared other arms to open for your reception? How could I divine that she whom you loved was not of the race of those beings to whom you were constantly lending the epithets of charming, lovely, exquisite angelic? Nought beyond a glance of transient admiration, or a temporary delirium of the senses, could they excite in me. I sighed to find something worthy of remembrance. You sighed to forget the worth, the inestimable worth you had known!

Wearied with the importunity of – 'would to God I could forget her!' – Forget her in other arms, I said. – Most readily did you yield to the advice; for which, as you have justly said in one of your letters, you deserved – 'tis your own words, Clement – you deserved damnation.

And what art thou doing now? – Now, even that she has sacrificed herself to save thee from despair? – That she has – Let thy heart tell thee her deserts – let it remind thee, that she is sorrowing for thy safety – preparing in mind and affection against thy return ages of joy, of felicity, such as never – merciful heaven! – And thou art – seeking reconciliation with Janetta Laundy.

Rememberest thou, Montgomery, the terrific and awful minutes we past on Vesuvius! Was not that a scene which, while it gratified curiosity and exhausted wonder, made nature shrink with repugnance from the situation? – Yet, in all the horrors of a night worse than that hour, lighted only by the flame of destruction, with showers of thundering dangers obstructing my footsteps, yet, had I been *thee* Clement! would I have climbed that summit – aye and precipitated myself into the gulph of ruin, rather than forever blacken the fair sheet of love, by sinking to the embraces of a prostitute!

Oh 'tis a stain indelible!

Will all great Neptune's ocean wash this blood
Clean from my hand? No; this my hand will rather
The multitudinous sea incarnadine,
Making the green, one red.

I seek not to quarrel with you, Montgomery. Careless as to your resentment, but willing still to possess your esteem, I am not more ready to declaim against your errors than to confess my own. Your's are recoverable. Make peace with yourself and heaven; while I go, not to expiate, but patiently to abide the punishment of mine.

This is the last time, Clement, that mystery shall cloud my words and actions. – In this very letter I meant to have cast if off. I thought I had torn myself for ever from the enchantment; and that reserve and secresy were at an end. But a strange unexpected circumstance, perchance productive of benefit to those for whom I would if possible sacrifice more than self, leads me once more to that scene where my dearest wishes lie buried – where I raised a funeral pile of all my hopes of happiness in this world – 'twas I conducted the fatal torch – I stood passive and witnessed their annihilation!

One day longer shall I remain at Barlowe Hall. I only arrived here yesterday. I may be absent a week; then I return again for a short time, to seek in solitude, a temporary recruit of spirits and resolution. Much indeed do I need them. You I have to meet. My uncle too. All who call themselves my friends: for, with this emaciated form, and mere emaciated mind, am I coming to London.

And what is my business there? – To take an everlasting leave of ye all. – To implore Sir Thomas Barlowe that he will allow me but a pat of the ample provision he has given me here, to supply nature's necessities in a foreign land. – I go abroad. Opposition and remonstrances are a feather in the balance. – I go, Montgomery, to find a grave. – Life and I are already separated! – I breathe: but I do not live! – Sleep and peace are vanished from me! – How swift are the ravages of an unhealthy mind, and who would not rejoice when the vague and fleeting scene shall have finally closed! – But a little time Montgomery and rumour will say, or perhaps some stranger affected into sympathy by my youth, will, as the least office of humanity, charge himself particularly to inform thee, that it was a sigh of resignation which liberated the agonized soul and, forever sealed the lips of

A. MURDEN

LETTER III

FROM SIBELLA VALMONT

TO

CAROLINE ASHBURN

Not write me one line! – Did you, Caroline, forbid him? – Prudence and safety required no such sacrifice! – Last night I dreamt – but why talk of dreams? When waking miseries surround us, why need we recur to those of imagination!

Tell Clement, if he meant a triumph, tell him he may congratulate himself. I would neither conceal nor deny, he has it most completely. – Here then I remain. – In full conviction that Clement has already learned a part of Mr. Valmont's lesson, I obey. – Yes: I suffer myself to be commanded into acquiescence, against which every fond affection of my soul revolts.

Tell Clement that – yet stay – ask thy heart, Sibella, that heart in which love and disappointment mingle the bitter poison which corrodes the very vitals of thy peace, whether this is not the momentary effusion of a perhaps unfounded resentment? – Tell him not, Caroline: or, if thou tellest him aught, and I do commit an error, oh may the tear which accompanies prove its atonement!

Caroline, I am incompetent to judge of his situation. Cares and tumults may surround him, and add to the anguish of separation. – And you, my friend, ah beware how you judge him rashly! The tender heart of Clement repels every approach of harshness. – While you seek to investigate, you forgot to soothe. – I detest your picture of my Clement's mind. – Oh! how ill do you appreciate that soul, wherein the image of Sibella lives immoveably, and eternally, undivested of her sway by any outward form or circumstance! – 'Tis true, indeed, Clement does attach to success and fortune in the world a value unfelt by me who know it not at all, and prized by you, only perhaps from its more intimate knowledge. But for whose sake is it, Caroline, that he dreads my uncle's resentment, that he would shrink to see me a pennyless outcast from Mr. Valmont's favour – is it not *mine*? – 'Tis I, that am, however distantly removed its effects from all but the discerning eye of love, I am his actuating principle! – Does he ever dismiss this one dear ultimate object from his thought? – 'tis because a lesser theme mixing therewith would degrade the loved idea. – Again undisturbed, self-possessed, his ardent mind returns to the dear remembrance of past, the still dearer anticipation of future, joys – when hourly, momentarily, they shall augment with the increase of years.

Oh Clement, that love at one and the same instant created on our sympathizing hearts! – sustained, with mutual ardor, through the uniform but interesting years of childhood! – at length spurred on by dangers and denial to form its firmest, chastest tie! – is there a temptation on earth, or a horror in futurity, which could bribe or bid that love seek to extinguish its smallest hope, its least particle of enjoyment? – No! No! Never! – An impassable gulph is placed between that love and diminution. – A chasm wide, deep, immeasurable, as eternity!

How dared I reproach my love! – How dared I decide, I whose mind is almost subdued by my situation! – Think Caroline! one hour heavily creeps after its fellowed hour; – day slowly succeeds to day, barely distinguished by another name; – the sun shines one morning, and hides his beam the next; – yon tall trees who bow their heads to the wind on this side to-day may to-morrow wave them on the other: and here ends the chapter of my varieties. – Night, indeed, brings variety amidst endless confusions! Broken sleep and apalling visions create debility of mind and body for the ensuing dawn! – It is but the fainting embers of my former animation that sometimes gleam upon the darkness of my soul. And, even now, now, while I acknowledge and reprobate my folly, I could return to the horrors of apprehension, could run through volumes of dire presages affirming while I disbelieved, creating as if to be interwoven in my fate fantastic, shapeless evils from which my better reason would turn, and would pronounce the worthless offspring of misrepresentation and falsehood.

And why, Caroline, should I be thus? – there is the question, that, as often as I impose on myself, as often returns unanswered. – I knew Clement was to go; and I know he *will* come again. What is new in my destiny is delightful to remembrance: it is the sacred union plighted by our willing hearts in the sight of heaven, the confirmation the everlasting bond of affection, which renders every blessing of this life subordinate, from which no change of circumstance could release us, nor not even death itself shall cancel.

I heard Clement speak one day of some ceremonials which would be deemed necessary to the ratification of this covenant, when we should enter the world. – Methinks I shall be loath to submit to them. The vow of the heart is of sacred dignity. Forms and ceremonies seem too trifling for its nature. But of the customs of your world, Caroline, I am ignorant.

I write at intervals – a giddiness returns upon me continually, and air is the only remedy. The last time I quitted my pen, I was almost overpowered, and could proceed no further than the great hall door. I sat on the step and leaned my head against a pillar of the portico. – It was not swooning, for I knew I was there.– I felt the cold wind blow on my face, but my limbs had lost their faculty, and my eye-sight its power. – A chill oppressive gripe seemed to fasten on my heart. – My uncle happened to pass in from the park. – He spoke, but I could not reply. I waved my hand, which he took in his; but, while he pressed it, he reproved me in an ungentle manner, for sitting on the damp stone, and exposed to the raw air – Tears unbidden and almost unexcited, roll down my cheeks. He called Andrew; and I was borne in, and laid on a sopha in the breakfast parlour.

After I recovered, my uncle, with a kinder tone of voice, noticed an appearance of ill health in my looks, and enquired into the nature of my indisposition. – 'You are too much in the cold, child,' said he. – 'Go; I give you permission to sit with Mrs. Valmont. I will join you there presently.' I replied I was engaged in my most interesting employment, that of writing to you? – 'Ah! child!' said my uncle, 'how much do you stand indebted to my indulgence for that liberty? – I rely on your integrity that you do not in any one instance, Sibella, abuse my confidence.' – I was going to answer, and began with your name.

'I know,' said my uncle, 'what Miss Ashburn is very well! Your friendship to her was formed by accident, and without my concurrence;

but I had never suffered it to continue, had I not found something to approve in Miss Ashburn. She has sensibility and affection; that is all you ought to learn. The rest is the sad licentiousness of her education. I could have made her a charming woman. And as it is, she has too much feeling, for the companion of women of fashion; and too little reserve, for the wife of a man of delicacy. I am giving orders to Ross, Sibella. He is sending a packet to Clement. Have you any remembrances for your friend and play-fellow?'

'Such, Sir, as most befits a wife to a husband.' Encouraged by the complacency of his eye, I threw myself at his feet; and assuredly reserve and concealment would in that moment have vanished, had not Mr. Valmont placed his hand on my mouth. 'Hush, hush, child! – You know I will be obeyed. – Happiness ceases to be a blessing, if disappointment does not precede, to stamp its value. Go, Sibella. Your fate in the husband I ordain for you may not be as desperate as you, at present, perhaps, imagine.'

Repeat this to Clement, Caroline, a thousand times. Let him fix his comment, and then judge of the throbbing expectation of my heart by his own.

How insensibly my pen glides into this dear engrossing subject! I began this letter almost for the sole purpose of telling you I am no longer a stranger to the '*wood-haunter*,' as you call him; and I have travelled through these number of lines without his idea having recurred to my memory.

From the night of the sigh and little ball, I sacrificed the first of my present enjoyments; and entered the wood no more. The opposite hill, from whence issues the parent spring of the lake, forms a shelter to the little park, a spot of ground left in its rude state to produce furze, &c. for the accommodation of our deer. Twice a day, for Nina's sake, I ascended the hill. Sometimes she appeared instantly, from the little park. – Oftner, after I had called loud, and long, she would come panting from the wood. But our meetings were less congenial than at the foot of our oak. – Nina would bound that way, suddenly stop, and look wistfully from me to the wood, thus as it were conjuring my return to that beloved spot where she used to share her fond caresses between Clement and myself, and spring from one embrace to be received in the other.

One afternoon Nina appeared on my first call; and, as I stooped to embrace her, I observed a folded paper tied to the plate of her collar. It contained only, 'your wood is free: farewell for ever.'

That Nina should become such a messenger must be, I concluded, by the order of Mr. Valmont, and the contrivance of a servant; for you, Caroline, experienced how inflexibly averse Nina is to strangers. Even to the domestics of the castle I never saw her more complacent. I felt grateful for the tidings; though I smiled to think my uncle should thus continually strive to perplex and mislead my imagination.

It was now near the close of evening. – Gathering clouds and fierce gusts of wind foretold a tempest. Instead of going to the wood, I returned to the castle; and scarcely was I housed, when the storm burst in its most tremendous violence.

You remember the apartment where my portrait hangs; and you have remarked the attractions of that picture for me. As the work of Clement, it is rather his image than my own. There I can vent the swelling sentiment of my heart, and find an auditor more interested than the dispersing winds. To this room and picture I resorted in the dead of that night, to harmonize my feelings and collect my thoughts, alarmed and scattered by a twice repeated dream full of terror and dismay.

There I met a stranger. I looked on him intensely; for I sought to discover the likeness of *the spirit*, whom you describe, I sought to recollect the features I had seen in the wood, and armoury: height and form agreed with your description, and my remembrance; but the countenance of this young man was devoid of softness and I thought possessed little interest. He had vivacious dark eyes, dark hair, and a full decided bloom. The impression of former circumstances was still powerful in my mind; I remembered the paper I had found on Nina's collar; and I concluded that this person could be no other than Mr. Valmont's chosen. I addressed him accordingly. I spoke of the weakness of his endeavours. I defied his utmost power. Twice the stranger bowed in silence; but he never attempted to answer me.

Early the succeeding morning, I decided on going to the wood. Should it be free – what a pleasure! Should the stranger be there – I had only to repeat, in a fuller manner, the sense of my last night's words and quit him.

Oh, Caroline, had you ever loved! – but love itself without separation could not have taught you the omnipotent value a lover's heart affixes to time, place, and memory! Who, in revisiting the hallowed ground of affection, can describe that slow eagerness of step, that still tumult of delight, which restrains while it impels, purchasing delay? – If these are not the happiest moments of life, at least, they are most worthy living for. The soul expands into a new existence. The body's encumbering mass seems no longer her organ.

Even now, Caroline, the charm returns, infusing itself through every vein, fending life's best blood in thrills to the heart, enkindling pleasure into agony!

I cannot proceed. – Will not Clement write me one line? – Another letter shall inform you, in what manner I discovered him; for the personated hermit is your Mr. Murden.

SIBELLA

LETTER IV

I know not precisely where to begin, nor how much of the adventure I told you in my last. Did I not say, that, while yet at my oak, Nina entered the wood a little below the tomb and without observing me began to climb the rock? But I think I broke off before I had mentioned her swift return at my call, and the irresolution she betrayed by running backward and forward from me to the rock, and from the rock back again to me. Desirous to know what her manner portended, I arose as if to follow, and away she bounded, taking the path up to the hermitage. As she ascended much swifter than I could, she waited on the outer side of the ruin till I also arrived; and then bent her course round to the farther part, which being the most perfect of the building I imagined she had chosen for the purpose of sheltering her young ones. It is called the chapel. Standing on a projecting point of the rock, it is difficult of access, for the path is cumbered with loose stones, from one to the other of which runs in perplexing branches the twining ivy. High grass and clusters of bramble choak the wild flowers that shed their inviting fragrance on part of the lower side of the rock, nor do I remember ever but twice before to have gone beyond the unroofed cell, where Clement and I, one happy spring morning, raised a seat of stone, and plucked away the weeds that new springing grass might mingle with our mossy foot-stool. There too we planted a woodbine, rose, and jassamine, but the cell refused nourishment to our favorites. Foiled in our attempt to make the ruin bloom a garden, it had no longer for us any attractions.

Nina's wistful look as she again stopped at the chapel's entrance now tempted me on, but it could tempt me no farther. At the stairs my curiosity or at least all inclination to gratify it terminated. In one corner of this small chapel where the wall is yet undecayed, remains a kind of altar. Some stones in front have fallen away and discover a slight of dark narrow steps, I concluded Nina had concealed her young in the vault below, for she would not return when I called: but I could not think of encountering I knew not what damp and darkness in the hope of finding them. Both suppositions were erroneous. The cell is superior in dimensions and dryness to those above ground, nor had my fawn any offspring there. This place, Caroline, was Mr. Murden's abode. Thence he ascended followed by Nina, and stood before me the original of your painting, and the same who once in the wood started from every appearance of feeble age into youth and vigour.

He named himself. 'Miss Valmont,' said he, 'I no longer bear a borrowed character. Henceforward, should you ever think of me, know I am Murden, the friend of Clement Montgomery, and the acquaintance (I dare not say more) of your Miss Ashburn. Already the victim of unsuccessful love, by all my hopes of heaven, I came hither only to seek your consolations. The world cannot find time to sooth a breaking heart. You in solitude might. But you have no pity, no friendship. An accident keeps me here this day, or I had now been gone for ever. Do not Miss Valmont, do not set your people of the castle to hunt me; for I am desperate.'

'Whose victim are you? said I.

'Whose?' repeated he loudly and wildly. 'Did you say whose, Miss Valmont?' Then turning away and sinking his voice, he said, 'Ay whose, indeed! Do you know,' added he, approaching nearer to me, 'that death is of icy coldness! The eye beams no tidings, for the heart feels no warmth! Such is my love to me! – Tell me, Miss Valmont, what would you do were Clement thus?'

'Alas! Die also!'

'Oh brave!' said Murden with a strange kind of smile: – 'bear witness, thou unhallowed gloomy mansion, for one, one moment of our lives are we agreed! – Miss Valmont, I shall never see you more. If I have created uneasiness in your breast, by my strange visits to this spot, forgive and forget it. Ask me no questions. In some hour of less anguish than the present, I will tell Miss Ashburn how and why I came hither. Another person there is also to whom I shall owe the detail. – Hold' – for I was going to speak. 'Do not name him. Your last words were, *Die also!* To me your last, choicest blessing. No! No! I will not hear you speak again. This is our final interview.

– In peace and safety, Miss Valmont, return to your wood; and when remembrances of love shall be no longer remembrances of happiness, then – *Die also.*,

And who, Caroline, could outlive their remembrances of happiness? I have placed myself one minute in the situation of this unfortunate young man: I beheld the tomb close upon the lifeless form of Clement, and in the wide world there was no longer room for me.

Murden descended to his cell; and I went home to weep for him. Will not you weep for him, my friend? and Clement too? I feel you will. Clement knows full well the value of requited affection; he will sooth his friend, but he will not ask him to live. It would be cruelty.

Nina looked kindly at me, but she followed Murden; and, since he quitted that ill-chosen abode, I often see her descending the rock. She even appears to mourn his absence; and she looks around expectingly, and starts at every gust of wind, as she used when Clement first bade us adieu.

Either to you or Clement I appeal for the further history of your drooping friend. Bid Clement write: be it only three words, '*Bless my Sibella*;' and I will wear it next my heart – a charm to hold disease and foreboding at defiance.

My dearest friend, farewel!

SIBELLA VALMONT

LETTER V

FROM ARTHUR MURDEN

TO

CAROLINE ASHBURN

When friendship and advice can no longer avail him, Murden intreats a patient ear to the history of his misfortunes.

Intreat! Did he say? – No, Madam; he intreats nothing of you: he demands your ear, demands your attention, your sighs, your sorrow: and little indeed is that, though your all of reparation, for the mischievous eloquence, which first instigated him to become the poor valueless object of pity, sighs, and sorrow.

To tell you that I love Sibella Valmont, is no more than Montgomery will tell you. But he loves her, in his way. – I, in mine. When present, her supreme and every varying beauty, makes his rapture; and, till he has been a day without her, he imagines absence would be insupportable. – Absent or present, alike she fills my every vein. I love her, Miss Ashburn, as – oh misery! – as she loves Clement!

Judge me not so absurd as to entertain hope, although I tell you I am again returned to the hermit's cell. Offer hope in its most seducing form; and still would I renounce it. Yes, Madam: possession of Sibella, were I an atom less to her than she is to me, must inflict torture worse than the present.

Nor deem, that I would dare assail her ears with my unauspicious love. I have spoken in mystery; and she thinks I mourn a buried mistress. – Alas! and so I do!

Montgomery, what dost thou owe me? Yet 'twas not thee I meant to serve; therefore thou owest me nothing. Thou canst find happiness any where: but, in the circle of thy arms and heart, centres the full measure of Sibella's wishes.

I would almost, Miss Ashburn, as soon have rushed into the fire, as again sustained the chilling beam of her eye. Yet I have come hither again, have endured this and more, to check the carniverous meal of anxiety already begun on her cheek's bloom.

I have been told, and have told Sibella, that instead of being a dependant on her uncle, she is mistress of fifty thousand pounds: with infinite astonishment she heard me, and is gone to demand an explanation of Mrs. Valmont. I requested her to forbear naming me, till I had made a safe retreat from the park; for Valmont is proud, insolent and cruel. And she bade me wait her return here, that according to Mr. Valmont's reception of the tidings, I, as Clement's friend, might yield her my prompt advice.

Yes! as Clement's friend, she said. Ah well may I talk of endurance!

When I first knew you, Madam, at Barlowe Hall, you won my admiration and esteem, by the uniform reserve, or I may say repugnance of your manners toward me. I adored your disdain of a character I equally disdained, while I contemptibly descended to wear it; and, though I could not instantly resolve to cast aside the unmerited fame of my licentiousness, yet you never moved or spoke, that I was not all eye and ear, however, you might contemn the abettor of impertinence and folly in Lady Margaret and Lady Laura Bowden.

One evening, you may remember, I abruptly shook off those interrupters, who wore gorgon-heads in my view, while they delivered their invidious suppositions concerning the lovely being, whose picture you had so animatedly given. – When your eulogium on Sibella Valmont ceased, I withdrew; flew to my chamber; and hastily locked the door, as if I had newly found treasure to deposit there in secrecy. I threw myself into a chair. 'And is not all this familiar to thee, Murden?' said I, after a pause. 'Hast thou not a thousand and a thousand times, in thy waking and sleeping visions, described a being thus artless, thus feminine, yet firm, such an all-attractive daughter of wisdom? – Ay: but I had never personified her in Sibella Valmont, though Clement had sworn ten thousand fathom deeper to her beauty.'

I could make no more nor less of it. My head ached; and my soul was burthened. I went to bed, and dreamt of a wilderness, and an angel; and the vision followed me through the engagements of the succeeding day.

Whether it was that I more industriously fought it than formerly, I know not, but soon an opportunity arose of conversing with you alone. It was easy to lead to a theme wherein your affections were as much engaged as my curiosity; and I heard every interesting particular of her mind, manners, and seclusion. Her love of Clement Montgomery, was also remembered. To me, his love of her never bore any striking features; and, somehow, her's to him seldom intruded amidst my chimeras. Strange wishers arose – tremulous expectations. 'It is all curiosity,' said I; 'and to overcome the obstacles that forbid thy knowledge of this Phœnix, is worthy the labour of ingenuity.'

When you, Madam, took the road to Bath, I unattended crossed the country to Valmont castle. Three days I passed in reviving and rejecting the scheme; and during that time, had stationed myself at a farm-house within a mile of Valmont. In the farmer, I recognized an old school-fellow of my day's of humility; and one whom I loved dearly too, before my uncle was a nabob. We met each other with an appearance of restraint and embarrassment. I, certainly conscious of an unjust neglect of him: he, perhaps secretly despising the man who preferred wealth to honesty. But reparation was then in my power; and the very critical moment at hand.

Farmer Richardson is rather given to endure than to complain. His simple statement of a few facts, which led to the service I rendered him, contained no invective. 'He told me he was an unfortunate man, to be sure; but Mr. Valmont was not obliged to know that.' – As to family concerns at the castle, after which I enquired, he said, 'he had occasionally heard more than he chose to relate. That the 'squire was perhaps proud and capricious, but he might have reasons for his conduct. Let every man act according to his own conscience, and the Lord have mercy on the greatest sinner.' Such is honest Richardson's creed.

The farmer's taciturnity was amply contrasted by the loquacity of his hind, formerly a domestic at the castle, and suddenly discharged with that pride and petulance for which its owner is famed. – John Thomas dwelt at Valmont-castle when Clement Montgomery was adopted; when Miss Valmont was brought thither – and though I always made him begin there, he constantly found means to shift his ground to the ancient mysteries of the domain. 'A sinful lord, turned penitent, enjoined to find money and materials for the structure, it pleased a neighbouring society of devout fathers to erect on the rock within the park. It was further necessary to his salvation, that this hermitage should be endowed on two of the most holy monks of the brotherhood, who would undertake to live longest by prayer and fasting. The event proved the choice admirably founded. Without the adventitious aid of victuals and drink, they dwelt I know not what number of years in this practice of piety, saw the society from whence they came broken and dispersed, and peaceably ended their days in the hermitage.' – Selfish fellows though these saints, according to John Thomas; for, dead, they will not yield possession to the living, but

> Revisit still the glimpses of the moon
> Making night horrible.

I essayed to gain information concerning Miss Valmont; and John Thomas's deduction from the little he had seen and the more he had heard was, that Miss had not a right understanding. He always thought Master Montgomery better natured of the two, and he would be a fine fortune when he came back from foreign countries.

Legends of the haunted ruin, on which John Thomas delighted to dwell, first suggested to me a hermit's disguise. Already, Miss Ashburn, you contemn the romance of my scheme; and its practicability seems impossible in expectation. Experience taught me how much a little ingenuity and great perseverance will effect. In all cases, whether of right or wrong, jointly they can almost work miracles.

Early misfortunes, a life of hard labour and little profit, had blunted that quickness of sensation in farmer Richardson, which might have led him to conjecture something mysterious of me. If I was there to claim my meals, it was well; if not, 'twas the same. I contrived to evade all enquiries into my absence, whether it were of the night or day, by fixing on myself the character of an excentric whimsical solitary.

Ah, Miss Ashburn! I smile to observe the precaution, and industry, wherewith I wrought my wretchedness! You allow me to be minute I know, for I know your sympathy and sincerity.

How this recapitulation of events has beguilded from me the consciousness of passing time! In this under-ground cell, where no ray of the sun's light ever penetrated, have I by my solitary lamp counted the lagging moments throughout a day. Yet now living over again in remembrance that preparatory fortnight when I was at farmer Richardson's was only restless, I have suffered hours to go by, without any additional torment of suspended expectation. Sibella is not returned. I thought I heard the sound of her feet in the chapel above; but, when I ascended, she was not there. I went on to the other side, but darkness has envelopped the castle, wood, and park. I shall not see her to-night then. Mr. Valmont may be from home, occupied or engaged; and she cannot gain an hearing. Nina too has quitted me; yet I am less alone than heretofore. The spirit of your friendship hovers round me. Be my friend, Miss Ashburn, while existence cleaves to me; and, when I am gone, double the portion of your love to Sibella. – Ah me! my heart has strange forebodings that she will greatly need it.

A continuation of my narrative shall amuse the sleepless night. Who will dispute that my claim to saintship is not more incontestible than that of the former fasting inhabitants of this mansion? The holy monks by their mysterious passages into the castle, could and assuredly did indemnify themselves at night for the forbearance of the day. But I, who have learned in this cell and its invirons to banish sleep, one of nature's greatest wants, where shall I seek the lulling medicine which can steal me from self? – can anticipate the tomb?

During the fortnight previous to my first seeing Miss Valmont, I reconnoitred day after day every inch of ground around the moat, and a first circuit shewed me that immediately beside the rock the moat, forming an angle, is not above a third part as broad as in any other place. This of course rendered it much easier to cross, but that facility was more than counterbalanced by the abruptness of the bank on the side next the lane, and the slippery steepness of the rock on the park side. Still this seemed the place, from its great privacy and difficulty of access, by which I must enter. Never but once did I see any creature approach it; and then I saw a gentleman on the opposite hill, who seemed to have lost his way. The exactness and solicitude of my observations a length pointed out a tolerable and easy method of descending the bank; for I perceived stumps of trees irregularly but artfully disposed, which I dare believe had been either purposely placed or purposely left there for the climber's assistance. At first, this surprised me: however, the whole business was fully explained, when measuring the depth of the moat in separate places, I discovered (and blessed the saintly contrivance of the starving monks) a mound raised across the moat, about two feet below its surface, on which large pieces of the rock were thrown, their edges just covered with water, so that with the assistance of my pole, I could pass from one to the other, suffering little more inconvenience than a wet shoe.

'Forerunners of your worthy successor,' exclaimed I, 'thankfully I receive the benefit of your labours! Your work, no doubt, is perfect in ingenuity; I shall tread in your steps up the mountain's rugged side, and nightly visit my shrine as you nightly deserted yours.'

Yes, Miss Ashburn, the ascent was attainable; and, though time has destroyed some of the useful works of the holy fathers, yet here and there, particularly in the more abrupt parts of the rock, I found steps formed. By diligent heed of these, and other aids, I certainly gained the only path by which I could have reached my destination. It brought me on the back of the heritage to the chapel's entrance, which if you have at all noticed its situation, you will recollect to be so placed, that any one may enter it without being discovered from the wood, or even from the park side of the rock.

I will not tell – no, I cannot tell you the swelling joy with which I hailed myself master of the ruin. It commands no prospect, save of the wood-path where stands Valmont's monument, and, a dearer object, Sibella's oak; yet, I bent my eager view through the chapel's cracked wall, and bade the winds bear to the castle's owner my proud defiance. This my first visit, performed at twilight, was only a visit of inspection. I discovered the stairs under the altar; but deemed it, at least improper, if not dangerous, to explore them without light.

All my apparatus were forthwith conveyed to the moat's-edge, where rushes afforded them an hiding place, till I had carried them to my station. A few biskets alone was my provender; but for the supply of my dark lantern I was abundantly careful. No monarch ever ascended a throne with more bounding exultation than that which filled my breast, when I took possession of this lower cell.

The next day, I saw her. – Good God! and you have seen her too – at the foot of her oak – her flowing hair – her modest drapery – a model for the sculptor! – A vision for the poet! —— I became neither! –

Were I to live ages, I could never describe her, for when her image is most perfect with me I have neither powers of mind, nor the common faculties of nature. The overwhelming sensation sinks me to the earth. Montgomery! – She may live in thy imagination, but not in thy heart, as in mine!

Surely I grow tedious in detail. These occurrences were few; yet they swell in relation.

Three days elapsed ere she came again to her wood. Doubtless, Madam, you have already heard of our conversation. – 'She feared me not' – She left me to inform Mr. Valmont. – In the first moment of our intercourse, I saw the firmness of her character. I saw she knew not how to threaten; she could only reason and resolve. I dared not quit the hermitage in day light, but I could provide for my safety within it. Walking backward and forward in my cell for exercise, one stone of the flooring had constantly resounded under my footsteps, and as I trod harder it appeared loosened from the rest. 'A grave or a treasure?' said I, and I raised the stone. There was only a flight of steps, three times as wide as those descending from the chapel. As I now trod the ground of mystery, this discovery excited no surprise; and, imagining myself securely and conveniently stationed in the cell, I had not the smallest inclination to explore further, till hearing the voices of people on the rock, who I doubted not were coming in search of me, I committed myself with my lantern to the subterraneous passage. Finding it well arched, dry, and wide, curiosity led me on; for I no sooner discovered it, than I conjecture its secret communication with some apartment of the castle.

It is unnecessary, Miss Ashburn, to dwell on the construction of this passage, its ascents, and descents, windings, &c. – Suffice it to say, that it seemed a journey of infinite length; that the crumbling fragments of one broken arch had nigh forbidden my progress; and finally that, this difficulty overcome, a sliding pannel of oak incomparably fitted, gave me admission into the armoury. From amidst the surrounding trophies of honour I snatched a sword, determined therewith to defend myself against any direct attack.

In the armoury I remained all that night; for I thought it possible that someone might be stationed to watch for me in the cell. Shall I not tell you that a feeling which surmounted my apprehensions of discovery chained me to the armoury? – I was under the same roof with Sibella!

The first dawnings of morn burst imperfectly through the high and grated casements; and I heard the creaking door of the armoury begin to open; I darted through my pannel, but the pannel shut heavily and with noise. Some person had already entered the armoury ere the pannel was quite closed. I shuddered for the consequences that might ensue; and I retreated a few steps, and grasped my sword. I heard the person in the armoury walk, and several times pass the pannel. The step was light and gentle. I heard a sigh. My heart took the prompt alarm. I looked through the crevice. It was – I had almost said – my Sibella – No: *Montgomery's* Sibella! I forced back the panel – flew to her – trembled – spoke – was wild, vehement, and perhaps utterly unintelligible.

And here let me pause, Miss Ashburn, to remark how strongly I discovered in her mind I had pictured and panted to possess. When I first approached her in the wood, tottering under a hermit's disguise, I could perceive, as it were, her collecting spirits embody themselves to repel my fraud. 'It matters little to me,' said she, 'who or what you are, since I well know you cannot be what you would seem.' Conscious rectitude forbade her to fear me, – it forbade her to mix me with her ideas in one shape – all her all prevalent love forbade it in another. – I saw her once – when the time, the place, the circumstance would have appalled me into agony! When, unseen, I echoed her bursting sigh, from behind the monument, I saw her a moment mute with surprize, then, call into her mien a dignity so firm so undaunted, that it might have spoken lessons to a hero.

After Miss Valmont left me in the armoury, I waited another hour; and assuring myself, from the still silence that prevailed, my passage was undiscovered, I returned to my cell, which I believe none had entered since I quitted. The succeeding night I revisited farmer Richardson's.

John Thomas, ever delighted to talk, came on me open-mouthed, with a tale newly brought from the castle: namely, that Miss Valmont had seen and spoken with the hermit's ghost in the wood.

And next, Madam, to prevent suspicion and enquiry, I deemed it proper to join you and my uncle's party at Bath. There, in the midst of the crouds, was I alone. I saw but one form. I heard but one voice. I began to despise Montgomery; to assure myself, against conviction, that she did not could not love him; and had promised my heart I know not what of success and felicity when – the contrast past; his letter came; and I, in the saloon, in your presence, before a crowd of witnesses, behaved like a fool and a madman. Pardon, Miss Ashburn, in consideration of my despair, any surprise or shock my conduct gave you. Never can you know what were the feelings of that night. Love had no concern therewith. It was a night of hatred, revenge and rage.

Adieu, Madam. I have filled up the last space of my paper, and my narrative must rest till I return to the farm.

The blessings of an uncorrupted mind ever, ever, be your possession.

A. MURDEN

LETTER VI

In continuation

Four and twenty hours longer of fruitless expectation did I endure
in that cell. No Sibella appeared. Did she then forget her request?
Painting her future delights with Montgomery, has she forgotten the
unblessed wretch, who for her sake could sustain hunger and cold,
watching and weariness, who to hail the same breeze that had saluted
her, quitted every indulgence of luxury for an abode that held comfort
at defiance, who stretched himself along the bare stone rather than on
a bed of down, because from that sleepless couch he could spring, to
gain an indistinct view of her bewitching form?

Ay, pour your contempt upon me, ye whose smiles I have beguiled
you of! – View him who bought your unprized tenderness with the
empty breath of flattery, view him, stealing slave-like into forbidden
paths only to gaze at humble distance, only to catch the echo of a sigh,
a sigh breathed to another!———He, Miss Ashburn, who lives without
hope – must *die* for consolation.

Yet, surely this her absence cannot arise from so more than common
an instance of insensibility; some accident may have prevented her
return; and I am capricious and cruel, while I dare to accuse her of
insensibility. John Thomas met me, as I returned to the farm. He
was carrying malt to the castle. I will throw myself in his way when
he comes home; and probably, amidst the abundance of information
he will be eager to communicate, I may find something which will
elucidate this strange absence of Miss Valmont.

Little remains, Madam, for me to add to my confessions. Sibella's
tender but romantic contract placed an eternal barrier between me
and the flattering illusions wherewith fancy fled my flame. I saw she
loved as I had wished her to love: had I been the object! – In the
first moments of phrenzy, I wrote Montgomery a mad letter; and no
sooner recovered a better frame of mind, than I dispatched one of

apology, which both made my peace, and quieted his astonishment, for he is not given to look beyond the surface.

Hours, Miss Ashburn, have I spent in wishing Montgomery worthier of his fate. Sometimes, have I calmed my swelling agony by reproaching her for loving him, then have humbled my proud heart to dust, to obtain her ideal pardon. Her seclusion, her enthusiasm, his reducing countenance, his vivacity of spirit, and above all his well expressed vehemence of love! Oh it could not be otherwise! She saw an outline: her imagination formed the rest.

No, not one single instance of self-reproach on Clement's account ever assailed me. When I first discovered that Montgomery's beloved was the selected friend of Miss Ashburn, I then knew they might be paired, but never mated. To rival him with one woman, methought could be little injury, when in her absence twenty others equally could charm.

After Miss Valmont had irrevocably given herself to Clement, I resolved to travel, for to the antipodes would I have journeyed, rather than met Montgomery. Yet I tutored my heart into the supposition that I still had a friendship for *him*, that Sibella had injured me, and was now not a jot beyond my friend, or my friend's wife. Dwelling on the delusion, it insensibly produced a desire, when Clement went to London, of returning to my hermitage, to her park, in order to behold her with firm composure, with almost indifference. – Self-devoted victim that I am.

'I can do her service,' said I to myself; 'and I can prevent her suspecting aught of the former intruder. Wishes she must have; something to alleviate the tedious uniformity of her existence.' And numberless plans to gratify and amuse her, without my having any apparent concern therein, I quickly resolved upon.

You recollect Madam, (perchance with disdain) my abrupt departure from Bath. – Farmer Richardson rejoiced to see me. John Thomas was yet brimful of Miss Valmont and the ghost. When these industrious labourers of the day retired to early rest, I betook myself to the now bleak and desolate hermitage. No sooner had I deposited my lanthorn and little basket, than I left my cell intending to revisit, not with rapture but regret, her selected paths.

It was I think one of the finest nights I ever beheld; and I must have wanted that fervour of soul which gave birth to my love, had I not been enchanted with the scene. The resplendent moon, now at the summit of her growth, silvered the wide spreading branches of

Sibella's oak, the fairest tree of the forest; her steady beam glittered over one half the tomb; the bending bough of a cypress on the other half, shed irregular darkness; the rock cast its pointed shadow up the path-way; light and shade no longer blended but were abruptly contrasted. No cloud glided into motion, no zephyr into sound. On the broken-down porch, I leaned. Imagination was alive. I will not conceal aught from you, Miss Ashburn, an excess of tenderness, even produced tears. And why need I be ashamed of that emotion? 'Tis not a property of guilt. And while I wept, I made a vow at the shrine of reason to abandon my mad enterprize, to quit for ever and ever this seductive rock.

Alas reason and resolution were instantaneously torn from me, by the sweetest sound that ever stole on the listening ear of night. You know the rest. Enraptured, I listened to her effusions; unobserved, was her shadow; scrawled with my pencil that inconsistent address; sighed to her sigh; and was more delirious than ever.

Prudent, cool, and considerate, she came no more. I enticed her fawn into the utmost degree of fondness; and when Nina returned to my cell from the caresses of Sibella, she brought me a pleasure which the universe to me cannot equal.

It must require all your faith, Madam, to believe that I lived thus without the shadow of a motive beyond sometimes seeing and sometimes hearing her: in the strictest sincerity, I assure you I had no other. Although I loved her to dotage, although I feel an internal testimony that I cannot live without her, yet was she, and is to this moment, more effectually banished from my wishes by her contract with Montgomery, than she could have been by age, disease, or any possibly deformity, circumstance or accident might inflict.

The sweetly soothing promise of speedy dissolution, produced temporary vigour. It enabled me to quit that vague and idle mode of life, unsatisfactory to myself and cruel to Sibella; to brave the censures of Montgomery; to ask your pity; and finally determined me to retire to a romantic and fit retreat for sorrow I once saw on the banks of the Danube.

One absurdity more, and I have done. By the little fawn I sent my farewel to your friend, and waited only for darkness to revisit farmer Richardson's. Night came and with it rain and such an impervious mist that I could not see my hand when I stretched it out, nor was I so lost to common prudence as not to foresee the danger of attempting my descent under such circumstance. Morning might afford me opportunity. The sword I brought from Valmont's armoury still lay on the floor of my cell; and a temptation arose of hearing it back to its original station: to be a last time under the same roof with Sibella, to offer a farewel prayer as near her as I dared approach. – Things so apparently unsatisfactory of themselves as these acquire an infinity of importance when the heart is assured they never, never can be reacted. The hour of night made me bold. I ventured beyond the armoury. I even intended seeking the room you once spoke of, and stealing from it her portrait. My beard and gown gave me the privilege of spirits, I thought to walk undisturbed; but hardly had I trodden ten paces beyond the armoury door when I met three men, and, what was still worse, considering the imagined security of my disguise, one of them pursued me. Apprehension gave me wings. I flew back; and had secured the pannel before he entered the armoury; then regained my cell with all possible expedition. This accident prevented my quitting the park by day-light, least I should be watched.

On the next morning, when Nina came panting down to my cell, I heard a voice calling her back, to which every nerve vibrated throughout my frame. I went up into the chapel. Sibella was there. I was shocked to see her pale and wan. – She heard me with patience, she looked on me with pity. Above all, she gave me very good advice. In the dusk of that evening, I left Valmont park.

As eager now to quit this place as I had formerly been to seek it, I would not even allow myself to rest one night at the farm; but, although the evening was dark and chilling, I mounted my horse and bade Richardson farewel. My strength failed me, my head became dizzy, and the bridle frequently dropped from my hand. When I reached the first village on my road, I stopped at an inn, and ordered a chaise to be got ready for me. They shewed me into a room where three or four other persons were seated at a table drinking. I drew a chair close to the fire and turned my face from them. For a minute after my entrance they remained silent; but observing, I imagine, that I did not appear disposed to give them any attention they resumed their conversation, and little should I have known of their subject had not the name of Miss Valmont struck upon my ear. I turned round involuntarily and found the speaker was a dark young man, smartly dressed; he was evidently in a state of intoxication, and his auditors not more sober than himself were the landlord of the inn and two countrymen.

'If I was to tell you all I know about it,' said the man, 'you would stare sure enough. And it is all true as the gospel – it is. My friend,

the nobleman I told you of, knows all the business as well as I do –
ay, ay, and he'll marry her too. Such a devilish fine girl deserves a
lord for her husband.'

This speech, interlarded with many oaths, had also frequent interruptions from the effects of his inebriety, so that my chaise was
announced just as he spoke the last word. I sat still, and called
for wine. They again recollected the presence of a stranger; another
silence ensued; and, while I lingered over my wine, the young man
and one other of the company dropped asleep.

My interest in that name would not suffer me to depart. I grew
restless and uneasy, I shifted my chair, stirred the fire; and in so
doing doubtless rouzed the sleeper, for he started up and vociferated
a great oath. 'Not see it,' added he, 'why I saw it myself, with my
own eyes, the Lord defend us! – no wonder! no wonder! I wouldn't
sleep in old Valmont's skin to have twenty fine castles. To cheat his
own brother's daughter out of such a fine fortune! 'Tis enough to
make the ghosts of all her grandfather's walk out of their graves.
Forty thousand is the least penny. – Well, well,' said he rising, 'I
shall see the day yet when a certain Lord that I know will have her
and her fifty thousand pounds too. Come, landlord, here's a safe
deliverance to Miss Valmont and her money out of the claws of her
old griping uncle.'

Having swallowed his bumper, he staggered out of the room, and
the landlord was instantly summoned to assist him to bed. From
one of the remaining guests, I learned that this man had lately
come from London; but his name was unknown to them. Finding
my intelligence at an end, I stepped into my chaise and proceeded
towards Barlowe Hall.

During my journey, I often, almost indeed perpetually, thought
of the conversation I had heard in the inn. And when I had arrived
at Barlowe Hall, and sat in the same apartment where I first heard
you speak of Sibella, I also recollected that colonel Ridson, who had
been in habits of intimacy with her father, expressed both doubt and
surprize when you said Miss Valmont was dependant on her uncle.
This recollection added new force to the assertions of the young man in
the village. I became persuaded that some injury was intended to Miss
Valmont; and resolved if possible to develop the mystery. I journeyed
back again to the village, where my suspicions had first been excited.
The young man had departed the day before; and no one could tell
me of his route.

I now determined to put it in Sibella's own power to demand an explanation of her uncle. Again, but without my hermit's disguise, I crossed the moat and ascended the rock. When I approached her in the wood, she looked on me sorrowfully; but, Miss Ashburn, there was no welcome in her eye. I had neither power nor inclination to hold her long in conversation. I briefly related to her my suspicions: and as I told you before, she bade me wait her return in the cell.

She returned no more. Have I then seen her for the last time? – I sicken. Never, never, never, to behold her! – Oh for a potion, powerful in its nature, rapid in its effect, that would overwhelm these dregs of existence, giving me but time to know the relief of dying when life has become hateful!

In continuation

The carriage, in which I instantly return to Barlowe Hall, stands waiting before my window. I do not fly through fear; but if Mr. Valmont knows my secret visits, and punishes her for my faults, he may release her when I am gone.

Write to me, I beseech you, Miss Ashburn, and say why Sibella suffers. She is a prisoner, madam. She has quarrelled with her uncle.

It is said he struck her. – Heaven forbid! It is said she attempted suicide! – But she will tell you all; and for pity's sake relieve my suspence, though you cannot quell my anxiety!

Respectfully your's

A. MURDEN

P.S. My authority is derived from John Thomas. – He was not, nor is any person but the family, suffered to cross the drawbridge. All the servants have been interrogated, and some discharged, for the supposed admission of a stranger. Sibella is not allowed to quit her apartment.

LETTER VII

FROM LORD FILMAR

TO

SIR WALTER BOYER

To the last hour I have lingered here, sometimes in hope, sometimes in fear, still bold in plan, but irresolute in attempt; and now, when the sun of my success begins to beam upon me, now must I come to London, to sign deeds to my shame and to pay money for my folly. Yet, Walter, though I *must* come to London, hither I mean to return again; for, as I told you before, the sun of my success begins to shine.

Know, dear knight, that things are all *en train*. We are in great alarm, great inquietude, and considerable trepidation: but as you may not be perfectly able of yourself to reconcile these assertions, be patient while I lent you my assistance.

Yesterday (being about to quit the country to-day) I thought proper to pay a visit of duty to my uncle elect. My footman rode up, and founded the bell of approach. – Roar, said the shaggy Cerberus on the other side of the moat; while the leaden-headed porter, crawling out of his den, bawled out for our business.

'My Lord Filmar to visit Mr. Valmont,' answered George. The porter walked away. – 'D – n the fellow,' said I, 'he has not let down the bridge!' – 'No, my Lord,' – replied George: and then I swore again.

In a quarter of an hour or something less the porter came back – 'Mr. Valmont's compliments to Lord Filmar, and he is engaged.'

Now, Walter, as you dote on discoveries, tell me what does your algebraic head make out of this?——'That he——.' No indeed, Walter.——'Then he——.' Nor that neither, Walter. Now I discovered it in an instant: keen-eyed, cool and penetrating, I saw at once that Mr. Valmont – did not chuse to see me. – 'Ay: but why?' – That's quite another matter.

'Lord Filmar,' said my father, 'you are the most impertinent prevaricating puppy I ever knew in my life.'

'My Lord,' replied I bowing modestly, 'I am told I have the honour greatly to resemble your lordship.'

'Sir, you – this is all going from the point, Sir.——Did – you – ever——.' beating time on one hand with a letter he held in the other, – 'directly or indirectly talk to any one about Miss Valmont?'

'Yes, Sir.'

'You did, Sir!' – fierce attitude – 'And pray what did you say?'

'I said, my Lord – that Miss Valmont – was a young lady.'

'Mighty well, Lord Filmar! – 'Tis mighty well! – Go on, Sir, – Ridicule your father for all his acts of kindness to you!'

'Ridicule, my Lord, is out of the question; but indeed I never shall be serious without knowing why, and your interrogatories of the last half hour are so vague, I cannot understand them. You ask me if I did ever talk of Miss Valmont? – As a young man naturally talks of a young woman, so may I have talked of Miss Valmont. The other day, for instance, I was riding with Miss Monckton – '*I should like of all things,*' said she, '*to see the wild girl of the castle. – Twice I have visited there with my mother; but Valmont won't suffer her to be introduced.*' 'The Earl,' replied I, 'declares she is handsome, and I too should be charmed to see her. – Perhaps, my Lord, I may have made a score such speeches, and if they are any thing to the purpose, I will endeavour to recollect them in form, and circumstance. – Let me see – Last Friday fe'night——.'

'Psha,' cried the Earl, 'they are nothing to my purpose.'

'Why then, will you be pleased, my Lord, to tell me what is?'

A pause succeeded, during which he appeared to seek instruction from the contents of the letter in his hand.

'If there is any thing in that letter, my Lord,' said I, stretching out my hand to receive it, 'which relates to me, suffer me to read it; then I can answer straight forward to the charge.'

It was not enough simply to refuse, Walter. – The Earl crammed the letter into his pocket. 'Hem! hem!' said the Earl. 'Before we came to Sir Gilbert's I remember, Lord Filmar, you thought fit to wind, and pry into the state of Miss Valmont's fortune. Now if you took upon you to assert any thing to any one, from that conversation, remember you told a falsehood, Sir, – an absolute falsehood. – She has no fortune whatever, Sir – not a penny.'

'No fortune whatever, Sir! – not a penny!' repeated I, slowly, and fixing my eyes on his. He had the grace almost to blush. – 'Be that as it may, I never told any falsehoods in consequence of that conversation, my Lord. – I might have said, if I had thought proper, that you deemed 5 or 6000l. a year a suitable portion for me, and meant to propose me to Miss Valmont.'

'Oh, Sir, if you mean to put your own construction on every unguarded disjointed expression a man drops in conversation, you may make something out of nothing, at any time.'

'True, Sir, the discourse was disjointed and unguarded enough; but the design was, I believe, perfectly regular. – I am sorry, truly sorry, the plan failed. – Has your lordship any further commands for me?' said I, rising.

'You are piqued, my Lord,' replied my father drawing the letter out of his pocket. – 'I have cause enough to be irritated, I am sure. My character as a gentleman is at stake. Mr. Valmont here makes charges against me which I don't quite understand.'

I held out my hand again for the letter, and he again drew it away.

'Nay, my Lord,' said I: – 'But perhaps you would rather read it to me. The best information and advice in my power is altogether at your lordship's devotion; and, if it is secrecy you require, I am dumb as the grave.'

The Earl looked somewhat doubtful. At length he suffered me to take the letter.

Now, Walter, read this letter, with attention.

TO THE EARL OF ELSINGS

My Lord,

As I took you to be a man of honour, I fully relied on your word, and never for an instant supposed you could depart from the strict performance of the promise you gave with so much readiness and solemnity of concealing from all the world the real situation of Miss Valmont's circumstances till the time when I, her uncle, guardian, and her only surviving relation, should no longer deem such a concealment necessary.

You knew, my Lord, I could have no sinister design in teaching Miss Valmont to believe herself dependent upon me. My well-known integrity forbids the possibility of such a surmise: and, my Lord, at once, in compliance alone with my own opinion of its propriety did I resign to you the entire care of her estate, reserving to myself the guardianship of her person and the direction of her education, to which cares the brother of her father had the most undoubted claim.

To the period when Miss Valmont should have attained the age of twenty, I limited your secrecy, my Lord; and this adds another proof, if another could be necessary, to the goodness of my intentions. By her father's will, she becomes independent of her guardians at twenty-one. At twenty, I intended that herself and her possessions should be given to the husband for whom I have purposely educated her; and from whom, for the security of their future happiness, I would carefully have hidden the knowledge of her fortune till that period.

My precautions were taken with such order and contrivance, that I have reason to believe it has not even been suspected by any creature that Miss Valmont is an heiress.

Do not slumber, dear Walter; read that line again – Miss Valmont is an heiress.

Yet now, my Lord, my niece herself is apprized of it; and has with more zeal than either judgment or duty demanded an explanation of my motives for treating her as my dependent. It is you only who can have conveyed this intelligence to her: you, my Lord, who, I am sorry to say, since you formed the design of uniting Miss Valmont to your son have forgoten honour and integrity.

I believe your son has found entrance into my castle by means a gentleman should scorn to use; but, neither in his own nor in his feigned name, shall he gain another admission. My vigilance is awakened; and, in his behalf, it shall not slumber a second time.

My Lord, I have returned the accounts you sent for my inspection, together with the necessary acquittals; and I request we may not meet any more, as the business till Miss Valmont is of age may be transacted by any agent you chuse to appoint.

I remain, my Lord, henceforth a stranger to you and your's

GEORGE VALMONT

'Is there not,' said I, and in truth, Walter, I did not very well know what to say, so dizzy had I become in reading Mr. Valmont's incontrovertible acknowledgement of his niece's fortune, together with the unlooked for charge against me of having stolen into his castle – 'Is there not,' said I, 'something like a challenge implied here, my Lord?'

'No indeed,' replied my father with sufficient eagerness. 'Don't you see he desires we may not meet again. – But I am rather in doubt, Filmar, whether we ought or ought not to send Mr. Valmont a challenge?'

'So am I, my Lord; but if your will allow me an hour to consider the case I will settle it if possible.'

'Do – do!' said the Earl. 'But what can he mean about you and the castle?'

'No one, Sir, but himself can decide that matter, I believe.'

The problem I had now to solve, consisted, Walter, of three parts. First, how Miss Valmont could have arrived at the knowledge of her fortune? – Secondly, how Mr. Valmont could know I had been in the castle? – Lastly, and of most importance, whether all circumstances duly considered it would be proper that I or my father should challenge Mr. Valmont?

My researches on the first part of my problem shewed me that it is highly probable I shall never know how Miss Valmont came by her information till she herself shall be in my power to tell me; and further that her knowledge of the affair will greatly tend to forward my projects, for no longer a dependent but a prisoner she will be rejoiced to free herself at any hazard from her uncle's galling tyranny. – Do you not perceive, Walter, how much my prospects are amended by this disaster? On the second part, I discovered that Mr. Valmont can have but an obscure and imperfect idea of my being in the castle, from his mention of a feigned name. I bore no name at all. Certainly my agents would not betray me. And Valmont must have spoken at random as to the means.

Out of the foregone conclusions arises the answer to the third part of my problems.

It would be highly improper for either me or my father to challenge Mr. Valmont.

What a blessing it is, Sir Knight, to find sympathy in our griefs! – From the moment my father confided to me this important business, he seemed to have forgotten its nature and my apparent concern therein. – He was lighter than Gossamer. – And valiant too! – talked big and bluff about honour, – and satisfaction – and could but just be prevailed on by my intreaties only to write the following pacific answer, in which, were he not a gentleman, the Earl of Elsings, and my honoured father, you or I might be bold enough to say – He tells *a falsehood, an absolute falsehood.*

TO GEORGE VALMONT ESQ.

Sir,

The charge you are pleased to make against me reflects infinitely more disgrace on yourself by its injustice than on me. Such an imputation deserves nothing but scorn, yet I will answer it so far as to say that neither my son, nor any person breathing has received from me the smallest intimation of Miss Valmont's fortune. My son never was in Valmont castle under any other name than that of Lord Filmar, where his behaviour kept pace with the dignity of his name, which will never suffer him to intrude himself or his alliance where it will not be rather courted than accepted.

I am quite as desirous as you, Sir, can be of dropping the acquaintance; and till the time you mention I shall (as I have ever done) sacredly guard my trust – wishing you may do the same, I remain, Sir,

Your humble servant,

ELSINGS

Didst thou never, dear Walter, see two curs pop unexpectedly on one another within a yard and half of a bone? – Er-er-rar – says one, softly setting down his lifted fore foot. – Er-er-rar, replies t'other; and each clapping his cowardly tail between his legs slinks backward a little way; then ventures to turn round, and scampers off like a hero. – If thou has wit to find the moral, thou mayst also apply it. – As for me, having reached the top round of my information, I beg leave to resign you to your cogitations and am as I am.

FILMAR

P.S. She is a girl of spirit! And, on my soul, 'tis infamous she should be thus treated! – Had the Earl a grain of kindness, he would rescue her; but no; he asserts he cannot possibly think of interfering. In two years, she will be of age; and then, if she should demand his protection, it will be a different matter. – Ah! – but I won't say what. – Your are to know, Boyer, that Griffiths has accidentally met his dear friend the butler. It was she herself spoke to her uncle of having seen a stranger; and what she further told him (which the butler does not know) irritated him to strike her. – Instantly, she rushed from his presence into the park; but, finding herself pursued, changed her direction which was toward her favourite wood, and flew to the other side of the park, where the wall not being very perfect she climbed it rapidly, and in sight of her pursuers threw herself headlong into the moat. She was taken up unhurt; and is locked within her own apartments. Either from disappointment, terror, or real indisposition, she confines herself to her bed, and preserves a perfect silence whenever Andrew or her female domestic approaches. Mr. Valmont has not seen her since. The prevaricating confusion of some of the servants made Mr. Valmont suspect them of being bribed to admit a stranger; but the butler, being *quite positive no one living soul more than he knows of* has been within the walls, he and others think Miss Valmont has seen the spirit again and is disordered in her intellects.

I am completely puzzled. – That hermit! – Miss Monckton has seen Montgomery, and calls him a fine elegant fellow, who makes love to every pretty woman he meets. If that's his forte, he would scarcely be content to creep like a snail out of his shell for a few stolen moments at midnight. – But what has set me to doubt and conjecture is, that Griffiths has heard of a very handsome man who lodges at a farm hard by, and wanders about the country night and day. The people say it is a pity such a sweet gentleman should go mad for love. Yet is it possible any one should know so well how to enter and escape, but those who had lived in the secrets of the castle? – Psha! –

In ten hours after you receive this letter, I hope to sup in your new lodgings.

LETTER VIII

FROM GEORGE VALMONT

TO

CLEMENT MONTOGOMERY

What does this mean, Clement Montgomery? Sibella talks of a marriage with you. – Have you dared, Sir, to form a marriage without my concurrence? I should dispute the possibility; but I find, from the avarice and ignorance of the wretches in my household, people have been admitted for one purpose, and perhaps others may have been admitted for another purpose. I command you instantly to tell me how far you have proceeded, Sir, against the obedience due to

G. VALMONT

LETTER IX

FROM CLEMENT MONTGOMERY

TO

GEORGE VALMONT

Dear Sir,

An attempt would be vain to express my astonishment at the contents of your last favour, or my concern at your supposing me guilty of so flagrant a commission of ingratitude to him, who has been my more than father.

Miss Valmont's mode of expression is strong and vehement. She may call the early union of our affections a marriage, for *I know of none other*. – No, Sir; however my wishes might urge me forward, however painful the struggle might be and was betwixt my love of her and my duty to you, I sacrificed my hopes in my obedience.

I flatter myself you will rely on this assurance, and consider the assertions of your lovely niece as romantic as they really are.

My time, Sir, had not probably been spent to as much advantage as it might have been, but I dare venture to pronounce it not totally thrown away. It is true, I have not yet attached myself to any particular profession, although you may expect I should tell you of my progress therein; but, without a guide or director, I feared rashly to engage lest I should afterwards discover my abilities unfitted to the part I had chosen. A general knowledge of the nature and professors of each, previously gained according to your advice, I deemed might hereafter save me the time at present expended. Thus have I been employed, Sir; and thus I plead my excuse for not having written to you sooner.

May I not presume to expect a continuance of your favours whilst I continue to deserve them? – I beg my dutiful respects to Mrs. Valmont; and, as *my sister*, I hope I may offer my best wishes to Sibella.

To you, Sir, I shall ever remain the most grateful and respectful of your servants.

CLEMENT MONTGOMERY

LETTER X

FROM CAROLINE ASHBURN

TO

ARTHUR MURDEN

Yes, rash and inconsiderate young man, I do accept your confidence, your offered friendship; but remember I cannot profess myself the friend of any one, to gloss over follies or vices. A friend, not blindly partial, but active to amend you, is the friend you must at once receive or at once reject in me.

I have heard myself called pedantic, inflexible, opinionated; I have been told, by some gentler people, that I am severe, misjudging, giving to those little foibles almost inseparable from human nature the name of vice, and this may be true; for you call yourself a foolish man – I call you vicious. – Nay start not, Murden; but lay your hand on your heart, and tell me, if you have well employed your time and talents? If you have done service to human kind, or if you have not in fraud and secrecy bubbled away your happiness? and if it is the part of a virtuous man to sigh with black misanthropy in solitude a few passive years, and then lie down in the grave unblessing and unblessed?

Yet I do pity you, for I have neither a hard nor a cold heart, nor a heart that dare receive a sensation it will not for your example dare to acknowledge. – Yes, I confess I have loved you! yet, because I could not possess myself of the strong holds in your heart, shall I sink down and die? – No! no! – I bade the vague hope begone. – I refused to be the worst of slaves, the slave of self; and now, my friend, more worthy than ever of your friendship, I am ready to do any thing in your behalf that reason can approve.

That service is to gain Sibella for you. Again you retreat. – Your false delicacy and false refinement fly to guard you with their sevenfold shield from the attack. – But hear me, Murden: – I would not unite you as you are to the Sibella Valmont whom you have loved with all the fervour the most impassioned language can describe, the erring Sibella while she sees neither spot nor stain in him with whom she has pledged herself in union: – No! I would first subdue the fermentation of your senses, teach you to esteem Sibella's worth, pity her errors, and love her with infinite sincerity, but not so as to absorb your active virtues, to transform you from a man into a baby. – You are but two beings in the great brotherhood of mankind, and what right have you to separate your benevolence from your fellow-creatures and make a world between you, when you cannot separate your wants also? – You must be dependent for your blessings on the great mass of mankind, as they in part also depend on you. – When you can thus love, I would unite you to Sibella, who in turn shall be roused from the present mistaken zeal of her affections. Her soul will renounce the union her mistakes have formed, when she knows Clement as unworthy of her as he really is. From a struggle perhaps worse than death, she will rise dignified into superior happiness: – Claim you as her friend, her monitor, her guide; and devote her life, her love to your virtues!

O yes, I know it well! – your imagination teems with the rhapsodies of passion! – I hear your high-wrought declamation, the dictates of a fevered fancy. I do pity you, Murden, from my soul; and if I did not believe you able to overcome all the misery you deplore I should not pity you at all.

I can scarcely picture to myself a life more negative, less energetic, notwithstanding your fervor, than that you would have led with Sibella had fortune placed you in the situation Clement stood with her. Do not let your burning brain consume you at the supposition; for, highly gifted as you both are, mind cannot always feel in that extreme: – the tight drawn wire must either snap or slacken. – Too happy, banished in rapture, age would have come upon you without preparation for its arrival, without proper nourishment for its abode. In vain you then turn to each other for consolation. – The spell that guarded you from every intruding care is broken: and you have lessons, wearisome tasks to learn, which would only have been pleasant relaxations intermixed with the abounding delights of youth.

You are both at present the victims of erroneous educations, but your artificial refinements being so admirable checked in their growth, now I know not two people upon earth so calculated, so fitted for each other as Murden and Sibella. – My resolution envigorates with the prospect! – Be ye but what ye may, and the first vaunted pair of paradise were not more happy! I perceive not only the value of the work I undertake, but the labour also; nor am I deterred by the firmness wherewith you hold your resolutions, not by the tedious scarcely perceptible degrees with which I must sap the foundation of Sibella's error. – Ah, Murden, I suspect, had she possessed equal advantages with yourself, she would have soared far beyond what you are as yet!

By her last letter, I find she discovers a deficiency in Clement's conduct which she struggles to hide from her own penetration. – He is my best auxiliary. I once thought him only a negative character, drawn this way or that by a thread. Now, I see he has an incessant restlessness after pomp and pleasure which nothing can subdue, and to which every thing must yield: Sibella in her turn – indeed, half her hold at least is gone already. – If he speaks of her now to me, she is not as before – his adored – an angel – superior to every thing in heaven or on earth – but one lady has an eye almost as intelligent as Sibella's – another, a bloom of complexion scarcely less exquisite – and a third, in form in graces moves a counterpart goddess! —— As you say, there is a vehemency and energy in his expressions, that, in the general apprehension, cloathe him with attributes which never did and never can belong to him. It is but very rarely that I partake of his effusions, for I am not to his taste. My mother is his confidante; and she is quite fascinated with the descriptions of his love. When he was first introduced to us, I thought it necessary, for a reason you perhaps divine, to mention the mutual attachment subsisting between Clement and Sibella. – Mrs. Ashburn declared she would take his constancy under her protection: yes, she would guard him from folly and temptation.

Alas, Murden, I am sick of the scenes that surround me! formerly, we were moderate and retired to what we are now. Our house is the palace of luxury. Every varying effort of novelty is exerted to fill the vacant mind with pleasure. Useless are my remonstrances. Eastern magnificence and eastern voluptuousness here hold their court, and my mother, borrowing from her splendor every other pretension to charm, plunges deeper and deeper in the vortex of vanity. Fain would I leave it all, but I dare not proscribe my little power of doing good. —— Come then, my friends, you who have already taken your station in my heart! – Murden and Sibella – live for each other – live that I may sometimes quit the drudgery of dissipation to participate of happiness with you!

If it really was Mr. Valmont's design (which I very much doubt) to give Clement up to a profession, nothing could be more unfortunate than his introduction here – where, with his natural inclination to do the same, he sees wealth lavished without check or restraint. So highly does he stand in my mother's opinion for taste, and so animated are his bursts of applause, that no overstrained variety is received or rejected without his sanction. – To be the confidante of a heart is a novelty with Mrs. Ashburn, who has had little concern in affairs of the heart; and perhaps to preserve him from sacrificing in her presence to the vanity of others may be her motive for encouraging him to speak of his passion for Sibella. – I have watched him narrowly; and, if he has any lurking wishes here, I am persuaded they fix on Mademoiselle Laundy.

I believe you never saw this companion of Mrs. Ashburn. She, or I greatly mistake, has of all persons I know most command over herself.

I had almost forgotten to tell you that Clement read me a few concluding lines of your last letter to him. What a decided melancholy have you displayed therein! – No, my dear friend, you must not, shall not die. – Clement was considerably affected by the representation of your feelings; yet he said you had used him ill in the foregoing part, and he believed he should never write to you again. – I find he has no suspicions of you; and I leave you to tell him at your own time, and in your own way.

Still I say nothing of Sibella's present distress, you cry. I have had no information of it, except from yourself. I have written again to Sibella, and look for an answer daily. With respect to her fortune, I think it probable that she should be her father's heir; but of that we can judge better when we hear what her uncle says to the charge. Alas, I know Mr. Valmont is vindictive, proud, and impatient of contradiction. – She resolute, daring to do aught she dare approve. – He might strike her. – As to suicide, I know her better: it would be as remote from her thoughts, under any suffering, as light from darkness. Oh, Murden, she is indeed a glorious girl! Mr. Valmont promised me an unrestrained correspondence with Sibella; and, while he is satisfied in the exercise of his own power over her person, he will as usual suffer her to communicate to me the croud of welcome and unwelcome strangers passing to and fro in her mind.

I need scarcely assure you that, whatever intelligence I receive, you shall share the communication. – Remain at Barlowe Hall; for, though your uncle is very desirous that you should come to London,

I am certain, in your present frame of mind, you would find yourself still more removed from ease in the society which Sir Thomas would provide for you than in solitude. – I should be sorry to depend for my happiness on that heart which could invite pleasure and gaiety to quell those griefs it could not banish by reason and reflection. Nor have I, Murden, so supreme an idea of your prudence, as not to foresee the birth of a new folly, should Montgomery and you meet each other.

Farewel! and may the blessing you bestowed on me rest also with yourself.

CAROLINE ASHBURN

LETTER XI

FROM LORD FILMAR

TO

JANETTA LAUNDY

In apartments opposite to Sir Walter Boyer's, there lives an Adonis. – A Paris, rather, to whose wishes Venus sends a beauteous Helen. Janetta, thou understandest me. – A chair – Twilight ——. As tradition tells us that the famed city was burned, and the famed family is I suppose extinct, I want to know from what Troy this Paris came, and what Priam was his father.

Thine, whilst I had love and money,

FILMAR

LETTER XII

ANSWER

My Lord,

Janetta does not understand you, and yet in another sense she understands you but too well. Once I thought you all tenderness, and generosity, but now you can both neglect and insult one whose love of you was her undoing. I neither know Sir Walter Boyer, nor any one who lives opposite to him, nor can in the least imagine what you would insinuate by twilight and a chair. If your recollection of former fondness does not incline you to treat me with more respect, at least her sad change of situation might preserve from your contempt, the unfortunate

JANETTA LAUNDY

LETTER XIII

FROM LORD FILMAR

TO

JANETTA LAUNDY

Undone! no charmer! Carry that face to the looking-glass, and ask if any thing but age or small-pox could undo thee! If thy mirror does not say enough to thy satisfaction, consult Montgomery. – Ha! have I caught thee? It was no stroke of Machiavelian policy amidst all thy profundity of practice, that the lodging opposite Sir Walter Boyer's should be so suddenly vacated.

But child, I do hold all my former fondness in my mind's eye; and thou art very ungrateful to refuse one little favour to him who has bestowed on thee so many. Can I more evince my respect of thy situation than by refraining to interrupt its harmony by my presence? What but respect, thinkest thou, made me order the horses back to the stable, when I had them ready harnessed to come and throw myself at thy feet for the little boon of information thou hast refused my letter.

I applaud Helen's taste. The Paris of old was a Jew pedlar to the present Paris of——street. Grace was in all her steps. Need I ask information of my eyes when my throbbing heart could tell me? – Oh yes, I should know my Helen's mien from a thousand.

I tell you, his name's Montgomery. Now you must tell me, if 'tis Montgomery of Valmont castle. If it is, you are directly to introduce me to him. – Remember, Janetta, in this I am serious; – remember also I am – *an old acquaintance* – now I hope you understand me.

FILMAR

LETTER XIV

FROM JANETTA LAUNDY

TO

LORD FILMAR

My Lord,

I did suppose, on the receipt of your first letter, that you alluded to my calling one evening on Mr. Montgomery; and had I not been withheld by the unwillingness I felt to disclose the secrets of another person I should certainly then have acknowledged that I paid a visit to Mr. Montgomery. But, my Lord, you compel me notwithstanding my extreme reluctance to make this confession; at the same time I must, to prevent your surmises injurious to myself, own to you that I called on Mr. Montgomery the evening you named by the order of Mrs. Ashburn whose very particular friend he is. The commission, my Lord, respected some business of a private nature; therefore you will perceive how necessary it is that you should keep secret your knowledge of this transaction. There is scarce any thing which Mrs. Ashburn would not sooner pardon in me than this breach of confidence.

With respect to my introducing you, my Lord, to Mr. Montgomery, a moment's consideration will convince you of its impropriety. In the unhappy and dependent situation which the misfortunes heaped upon my family have compelled me to seek, it is not the least of its afflicting circumstances that I am obliged to shape all my actions to the will or opinions of those by whom I am surrounded. That I should so suddenly claim an intimacy with a person of Lord Filmar's youth, graces, and accomplishments might appear suspicious to Mrs. Ashburn; beside, my Lord, how do you suppose I am to conduct myself in your presence? for, although you may have forgotten the time when you could not approach me without trembling, I can neither cease to remember nor cease to feel.

It is not possible for me to divine why you should insist so vehemently on my bringing you acquainted with Mr. Montgomery; nor is it easy to decline any request however hazardous the grant, when it is urged by one who has such claims, although now neglected, as you have, my Lord, on me. I have studied in what way, with any probability of safety to myself, I can gratify your wish; and find no other than your renewing your acquaintance with the Dutchess de N——, who is also at this time in London. Mr. Montgomery visits there frequently.

I think, my Lord, I need hardly remind you of the caution you ought to use, if by any accident it appears that we are acquainted. Mr. Montgomery was in Paris a short time after you left it. He was, like you, intimate with my father; but he did not, gain the devoted heart of the daughter. To wound my reputation now would be barbarity. Were you by any hint or jest to create a surmise in the breast of Mr. Montgomery, it would instantly be conveyed by him to Mrs. Ashburn; and my ruin would be certain. I intreat you will think of this with attention; and you would be well convinced of the attention it demands, could you know how scrupulously observant Mrs. Ashburn is of my conduct.

JANETTA LAUNDY

LETTER XV

FROM LORD FILMAR

TO

JANETTA LAUNDY

Female friendship still so constant! What, if French folks did surmise and say strange things of Janetta Laundy and the Duke de N—, the Dutchess well understands the value of a certain old proverb, *Keep my secret and I'll keep your's*. Amiable pair! Fear me not, Janetta. Filmar will not breathe a whisper that shall disturb thy peace; for he perfectly understands that Montgomery was in Paris after him.

Last night I supped with the Dutchess; Montgomery was there.

No wonder Mrs. Ashburn is *observant of your conduct*, Janetta; for she glared upon us last night in the fullness of her blaze, and I perceived in half an hour or less that she is tremblingly alive to every species of decorum. Whenever this *scrupulous* lady again chuses to *send* her pretty ambassadress on *private business* to *Montgomery*, he will still I doubt not continue to receive her with all the respect due to her *commission*.

Do not be angry, Janetta, but encourage the dimpling smile that so well becomes you. Montgomery dines with me; and I am, with him, to have the felicity of basking in the sunshine of bright eyes at Mrs. Ashburn's route this evening.

FILMAR

LETTER XVI

FROM CAROLINE ASHBURN

TO

ARTHUR MURDEN

How strange an animal is man! How prone to fall into habits, and how difficult it is to prescribe bounds to the growth of absurdity! I did not imagine Mr. Valmont would extend his absurdities so much on the sudden, nor do I know how far you will be inclined to follow his example, when I tell you that Sibella is so really a prisoner even my letters are denied access to her.

Yesterday I was honoured with a packet from Mr. Valmont containing my two last letters to Sibella, one written in answer to her's previous to the receipt of your's and the other written in consequence of the information you gave me of her confinement. Mr. Valmont, in his way, treats me with unusual respect; and I can only account for it, by supposing he was pleased with the freedom I used when at Valmont castle in speaking to him of his very improper seclusion of Sibella. My letters were returned unopened; and with them the following

Madam,
As long as my niece deserved the indulgence of your correspondence I, though against the principle upon which I formed her education continued to allow it. I herewith return your last letters. I would not open them, because I believe you to be incapable of abetting Sibella in the atrocity of her conduct, but I shall hold myself justified therein if you send any more letters after you receive this interdiction.

Truly sorry am I to say that Miss Valmont proves herself unworthy of the long illustrious line from whom she claims her name, and of whom she is almost the only surviving descendant. Unfortunate that house whose dignity is left to be supported by a female! Whether in solitude or society, I find the female mind still a mere compound of folly and mischief: greatly do I now regret I ever undertook its guardianship.

I have the honour to be, madam
Your humble servant,

G. VALMONT

Mr. Valmont scorns to flatter. Would you have been so candid with respect to the female mind? though once, perhaps, you enrolled yourself among those who endeavour strictly to check the growth of every seed therein except mischief and folly. My patience exhausts itself when I see men of even tolerable talents aiding to sink lower than the brute in value the fairest of God's creatures. – A horse! – Oh, a laborious horse deserves to be canonized in preference to the woman whose sole industry consists in the active destruction of her understanding, who smiles, moves, and speaks, as it were only to prove herself unlike every production of wisdom and nature.

The principle which moves this mischief is the error males and females partake concerning softness. – Bid them form a woman of an enlightened understanding, and with the learning of a scholar they never fail to associate the manners of a porter. – Talk of one, who scorns to sink in apprehensions, who would rather protect herself than sacrifice herself, who can stand unpropped in the creation, they expect a giant in step and a monster in form. – If reason and coarseness were thus inseparable, it were better to take both than to abandon both. But it is the reverse. Wherever coarseness exists with talent, it is because the talent is contracted; let it expand, and the dignified grace and softness of active virtue takes its place. – More of this hereafter. I wish rather to reason than declaim; and I have, at present, a heat of feeling that effectually precludes investigation, for the ebulitions of resentment.

Doubtless you have already exclaimed against my seeming unconcern for Sibella's situation. – You, who cannot detach yourself a moment from the concerns of your heart, can you forgive such a lapse in another. Of what avail, in our present darkness, to canvass it for an age? I must do something more. To-morrow morning, I set out for Valmont castle; and if at my desire you keep your station, you may depend on the speediest information from,
Your sincere friend

CAROLINE ASHBURN

LETTER XVII

FROM LORD FILMAR

TO

SIR WALTER BOYER

A pleasant journey be thine, Walter; but if this sudden trip be meant to evade the consequences of my wrath it was unnecessary. Truly I forgave you on the spot, in consequence of the very ridiculous situation you were in, turning with beseeching looks to me for pardon and stammering contradiction after contradiction to Montgomery, which served only to confirm the suspicions in his mind your foolish audible whisper had occasioned.

How guarded have I always been when Montgomery spoke of the Valmonts; and little did I suppose, though I knew your talent, when I urged him to shew you the picture you could forget your caution. Your shrug, your leer, your whisper struck Montgomery dumb; and to my explanation he appeared no less deaf. Yesterday he did not keep his appointment with me. – We accidentally met in the evening (where it had been better we had neither been) but he was distant and embarrassed.

Scarcely had Griffiths begun the honours of my head this morning, than Montgomery was announced and condescended to amuse himself with Rosette and Ponto in the drawing-room till the business of my sitting was at an end.

'Oh! by heaven,' he cried, as I entered the room, 'you would at this moment be irresistible! – Health, vigour, proportion, and the face of an Apollo! Luckless be ever the youth who shall presume to rival you' – I'll give you ten guineas for Rosette, Filmar. Will you sell her?'

'No, I will not, Montgomery; though you seem so well to understand our mutual value.'

He drew from his pocket the very miniature in the shagreen case: your stumbling-block, Walter.

'Do me the honour, Filmar, to accept this from me.'

'Miss Valmont's picture! – and of your painting! – You are delirious, Montgomery!'

'Faith, not I! – never more rational in my life, as this very action evinces. Exquisitely divinely charming as she is, who would stand a competition against your person, rank, and happy influence with Mr. Valmont.'

'Influence with Mr. Valmont!'

'Inimitable!' cried he. – 'You overwhelm me with your perfections this morning. How natural that start? nor do your forget the grace of the attitude, I perceive. It is too late, Filmar. Be candid. We will not quarrel; for, as you have so much the start of me in her uncle's approbation, I must resign with a good grace. Can I do more than even yield to my rival that resemblance of her enchanting face? All I ask in return is to oblige me in kind offices with Mr. Valmont. – 'Tis a curst strange business to be sure, but, on my soul, Mr. Valmont sent me to town to study! – I have no time to spare, as yet. – Mum! you know, as to my employments. – I shall reform ere long.'

'Send you to London to study! – Ha! ha! ha!'

'Yes by heaven he did! – To this emporium of delight! – A strange being!'

'And so are you; for, Montgomery, if I understand your meaning concerning Mr. and Miss Valmont, may I–.'

'S'death, my Lord, Sir Walter's strange speech and your confusion kept me awake two hours! Upon my soul, you have seen her! I know you have; and I am sure Mr. Valmont wouldn't suffer any man in the kingdom to look at her, except the one whom he designs for her husband. Everything corroborates the fact. You told me the Earl knew Mr. Valmont; but did you ever hint, in the most remote way, that you had been in the castle, till Sir Walter's question obliged you to have recourse to that portrait in the drawing room, to excuse the implication? – Ah, Filmar! – A divinity is destined for your arms, whilst I must sigh in secret over the remembrance of past hopes!'

'You won't sigh alone, Montgomery. You don't profess anchorism. There are other divinities.'

He smiled one of those enchanting smiles which will probably reduce many such divinities into frail mortals. And then he enumerated, in the way of exclamation, a number of his favourite beauties.

'No wonder you want to give up Miss Valmont,' said I, 'you that are the favoured of so many.'

'Want to give up Miss Valmont! Lord God, how can you talk so ridiculously, Filmar? Want to give up an angel, with whom it were life to die, to live from whom is death! Is she not torn from my arms? Am I not interdicted, and another elected? By heavens! my Lord, your secrecy was unkind, but this triumph is insulting!'

And thus, Walter, we passed away the morning:– he, affirming; I denying. I fairly overshot my mark in leading him to talk so often of Sibella; for he has tacked together such a number of scraps and ends, that, with the aid of his colouring, make proofs as strong as *proofs of holy writ*. – Well, and if he does speak of me in this way to Mr. Valmont? The man suspected me before, and all he can now do is to clap another padlock on his caution.

There is something unmanly in Montgomery's conduct. With studied vehemence of lamentation he recanted his many many former insinuations of his constant security in Miss Valmont's favour; and, unless it was a preconcerted plan between them, (which I do not think possible) his voluntary resignation of her picture stamps him a contemptible——. My fingers had a kind of tremulous impulse towards the picture; yet I positively refused to accept it; a double dose of prudence this morning made some amends for its total absence last evening. 'Tis too true, Walter; I left the club again without a penny. The Earl will not be in town till next week; and till I am in cash I cannot invent or contrive a probable means of saving my friend Montgomery the disgrace of being mistaken.

This youth makes a rapid progress in the sciences. He was as completely inducted last night as your humble servant. His tutor, Janetta Laundy, also is most admirably chosen; and if Valmont deems that to be a dupe with a beggared purse, and shattered constitution, is the antidote against society, Montgomery is going the high road to answer all his wishes.

Your hint, dear knight, respecting Mrs. Ashburn, was not lost upon me; but, though I would not marry for aught but money, I should like to have a wife thrown into the bargain whom I could love now and then. I acknowledge the widow is as young as any woman (of her years) I ever saw in my life; and in wealth I should be an emperor. But indeed, Walter, I could ruin myself as effectually, I feel I could, I have all the laudable inclinations necessary thereto, with a large fortune as with a moderate one; and then age will come, and gout, and bile, and ill tempers, and no sweet remembrances of smiles, of dimpling cheeks, of melting eyes, to cheer me! – Were the widow once turned of eighty, the charms of youth and beauty should not tempt me from her. – As it is, I could like her daughter better. – Ah, but Miss Ashburn's is a searching eye! She would enquire for thy passport of virtue and morality, Filmar!

You perceive plainly, don't you, Walter, that I have no alternative but taking Sibella Valmont with her 7,000l. per annum? You have now seen her picture, tell me, is she not unequalled? And may I not sometimes, without any violent effort of self-denial, condescend to toy away an hour or two with (though my own wife) a creature so perfect? Walter! Walter! Could I drench in oblivion that youth with the flowing beard, I should be proud to acknowledge how often I dream of this little seducer! – As it certainly was not Montgomery, who could it be? – and why came he there? This interrogation is constantly served up with my breakfast, it even attends my undressing, and has been, not unfrequently, my bedfellow – The very quintessence of politeness, however, it never intrudes further than the door of the tavern or gaming-house. For the former, I now leave it and thee.
Thine,

FILMAR

LETTER XVIII

FROM CAROLINE ASHBURN

TO

ARTHUR MURDEN

Can you, will you, my dear friend, undertake to rescue Sibella from the tyranny at present exercised over her? If you will, write me instantly three lines to London, where I am now returning. From that place I will relate the particulars of my visit to Valmont, which will also include my reasons for this request. – Now, I only write while I change horses at B——.

CAROLINE ASHBURN

LETTER XIX

FROM ARTHUR MURDEN

TO

CAROLINE ASHBURN

Madam,

When you bid me live, and live for Sibella, I shut my ears against the voice of the syren. – Name the possibility of my rescuing Sibella, and the light and sun again becomes of value to me!

ARTHUR MURDEN

LETTER XX

FROM CAROLINE ASHBURN

TO

ARTHUR MURDEN

Inexorable as you would persuade me you are, still I hope to conquer you. Yet, it must be a future work. Sibella's release is our present employment; and, though I am not surprised at your readiness to undertake it, I am truly grateful. In this case, I know your heart and your benevolence are separated; for, determined as you are to live and die without hope, every step that carries you toward her increases your anguish. – The sacrifice is great. I wish you would trust me, that in the end it may find a reward.

The inclosed letter you must yourself give to Sibella. Mr. Valmont may lock up the doors of his castle; but your cell and pannel is not under his dominion. Your hermit's cap and gown secure your own escape. Be sure you do not escape alone. Read the inclosed, and you will find I mean to join you on the road. You will there find also my reason for not being of your party, through the subterraneous passage and into the castle.

To yourself I leave the conduct of the business. Your brain is fertile in project; and on your faith and delicacy in execution I would rely as on my own soul.

When I reached Valmont park, Mr. Valmont sent an excuse for not admitting me. Message after message flew from the moat to the castle; and I was compelled to stipulate for not seeing any one but himself, ere the word of command was given for me to pass.

He received me with a demeanour cold, formal, and haughty. I assured him that a motive equal to the pleasure I had promised myself of seeing Sibella, had induced me to take the journey.

'I perfectly understand you, madam,' said he; 'but once for all, to save you the trouble of useless discussion, I will not relax an atom of my severity, till Miss Valmont has in some measure expiated her fault.'

'What is her fault, Sir?'

'Her fault!' repeated he, starting. 'I perceive madam, you are a stranger to the cursed business; and may you remain so, for your own, for her's, and her family's sake.'

'Is Clement Montgomery concerned?'

He bit his lip, arose from his seat, stifled anger contracting his brow.

'I see he is,' said I – 'and —.'

'Madam' said Mr. Valmont sternly, 'your understanding should inform you, that affairs which concern the honour of a family are only to be canvassed by the individuals immediately belonging to it.'

'You forget, Sir,' replied I, 'that I am a female; and, according to your creed, cannot possess understanding. – Is it owing to this deficiency that I am of opinion, the honour of a family, as generally understood, is a matter quite opposite to the virtue of a family. – In the present case, I think you clasp your honour and turn your virtue and justice out of doors. – If, when you use such terms, in speaking of Sibella, you allude to her contract with Clement, I acknowledge her in the wrong. To ratify that contract, Sir, would be a worse error: for he is undeserving of her. But all that, and the worst of errors she can commit, may ascribe their origin to yourself.'

'Madam, you are obliging; but you have not yet convinced me I am under any necessity of explaining myself to you. – Whatever offences Clement has committed against me, he shall not fail of his proper punishment – trust me, he shall not. – I – I – Will you take any refreshment, madam?' – rising – 'I regret Mrs. Valmont is too much indisposed to receive you. – Pardon me, our conference must end. – You will excuse me, but I cannot suffer you to see Miss Valmont. – It is indeed impossible.'

I declined the refreshment, lamented for Mrs. Valmont, and objected to putting an end to the conference. And this last produced an altercation too diffuse and passionate to be related minutely. I mentioned Sibella's fortune. He almost started with surprise. He said I could not have heard it from her, for he had refused her permission to write to me. – 'No,' I replied, 'I believe my informant was her's.' He called some Earl a lying scoundrel; and added, after a moment's pause, that now it was useless to keep it longer secret, that Miss Valmont was her father's heiress, since the object of its being concealed was utterly destroyed. He had planned the concealment for her benefit; and carried it into execution only to perfect her happiness. She had indeed a noble fortune, he said, ill bestowed. None of his should go the same way. And, as to the pragmatical puppy who took the pains to tell her of it, his scheme, by the disclosure, was effectually annihilated.

As you, Murden, have no striking characteristics of the puppy, I took the liberty of asking Mr. Valmont, if he knew the person to whom he alluded.

'Very well,' he replied, 'too well.' It was the son of Sibella's other guardian who wanted her wealth to amend his poverty

'I believe not,' said I.

'Madam, I am assured of it. He bribed some of the fools of my family to admit him.'

'Did they confess the charge?'

'Not absolutely; but they prevaricated and talked backwards and forwards in such a way as confirmed their guilt.'

'Talking backwards and forwards, Sir,' said I, 'sometimes proceeds from confusion and awe. I am very much inclined to believe your servants innocent in this affair, Mr. Valmont.'

'Miss Ashburn is extremely inclined to construe all I say or do in the way that best pleases her. But Sibella herself saw this person and herself gave me the information.'

'That I know too. And ——.'

'I know what you are going to advance, Madam. She might tell you as she did me, of his feigned name. He called himself some Mr. Murden; a friend of Clement's he persuaded her to believe him to be.'

'I, Sir, have a friend called Murden; and so had Clement Montgomery. Might it not be him?'

'No, Madam; it might not;' replied Mr. Valmont; 'for no person but her two guardians ever knew a whisper of Sibella's fortune. I tell you the Earl disclosed it to his son, because he wanted his son to marry her. – I refused their offer; and their residence lately in this neighbourhood confirms the rest.'

'Once more, you are mistaken, Mr. Valmont. Hear me out, Sir,' for his fiery impatience was again blazing forth. 'How the secret was first unfolded I know not; but, in the immediate agency of conveying this intelligence to Sibella, the guardian you speak of had no concern whatever. I am much better informed than you perhaps may imagine Mr. Valmont. You discharged your servants from passion not from conviction. I pledge myself to prove the truth of my affection, if you will let us make a compromise. Liberate Sibella. Give her to my care one month, and I will tell you who the person was; and, for your future security, how he gained admission into your park.'

'Cobwebs to catch eagles! I grant, madam, you are amazingly condescending; but as the days of enchantment are passed, I am as well instructed on the latter point as I wish to be. For my *future security*, I am also provided. The suspicious part of my household are gone; and I think I have secured the fidelity of the rest. Your request concerning Miss Valmont's passing from my care to your's madam, is not worthy of an answer.'

Somewhat indignantly I reminded him, that an abuse of power might be the forfeiture of power; and that the law, useless as it is for the relief of general oppression, might reach this particular instance.

'I despise your threats, madam,' said Mr. Valmont, 'as I do your intreaties. The will of the Hon. Honorius Valmont delegated to me the care of her person till the age of twenty-one. Then, whoever aspires to the protection of a disgraced dishonoured woman may claim it; but till then, madam, I swear that, in the solitude and confinement of this castle, she shall weep for her errors. Depend upon it, madam, whilst you favour us with your abode in any part of this country, the rigour of her imprisonment shall be tenfold.' And, so saying, he rang the bell furiously; and would have departed.

'Hold, Sir, one moment,' cried I – and then, after a pause, I promised to quit the country instantly if he would suffer me to converse one quarter of an hour with Mrs. Valmont.

'O! pray shew this lady to your mistress's dressing room,' said he, sneeringly, to the servant that appeared. 'It would be well in your wisdom, madam, to make Mrs. Valmont's influence of consequence before you attempt to gain Mrs. Valmont's influence.'

Mrs. Valmont, having worn out the variety of fancied indispositions, is now fairly dying of inanity. She was neither surprised at my visit, nor at all interested by that which she herself called the lamentable state of her niece.

Mrs. Valmont was attended by her confidential servant, whom I requested to remain in the apartment, for I judged I should from her gain more information than from her lady. And I judged rightly. She was not only willing, but eager, to tell me all she knew.

It seems Mr. Valmont has had two interviews with his niece. The first was on her leaving you in the Ruin, when Mr. Valmont was irritated, by her persisting to declare herself married, to strike her.

She did throw herself into the moat, but she received no injury. From that time, he ordered her to be confined. In the second interview, a painful circumstance, relating to Sibella, transpired, in consequence of which her uncle abruptly commanded her from his presence. The discovery he had made wounded him almost to madness; and his first transports of rage have subsided into a constant gloomy moroseness. At times he has been seen to weep. The circumstance I speak of has been whispered from one to another throughout the family; and in this way alone travelled to Mrs. Valmont – for mortified pride would choak Mr. Valmont's attempt, were he inclined to give the secret utterance. I can trace the operations of his pride, but I am lost with respect to his tears; for Sibella never possessed any of his affection.

My tears flowed without restraint when I learned this distressing circumstance, and heard also that our Sibella droops under her uncle's cruelty. She eats little, sighs deeply, but weeps seldom. 'Twas unnecessary to enjoin silence to her domestics, for she never attempts to speak to them. They frequently hear her talk of some letter which she holds up between her clasped hands, as she traverses her apartment in extreme agitation; and then she exclaims – *He never never wrote it!* Once a day she is conducted to the terrace; but her wood and all her beloved haunts are forbidden.

You, Murden, could not have borne the apathy with which these and other particulars were repeated; nor could Mrs. Valmont with all my reasoning be prevailed on to suppose that she who had been so long governed should now infringe on her obedience, and endeavour to give aid and comfort to her ill treated niece.

I had quitted Mr. Valmont in anger. I quitted Mrs. Valmont in sorrow. As I crossed the square court in front of the building, I stopped and looked up with an eye of tears to Sibella's windows. No pale melancholy form appeared to my salute. 'Does Miss Valmont,' said I to the servant attending me, 'inhabit the same apartments as formerly?' The man looked round every way, and replied in the affirmative.

Scarcely was I reseated in the carriage, when I began to accuse myself as wanting friendship and humanity when I foolishly promised Mr. Valmont to quit the country; Murden would not have done this, thought I; then Murden is the fittest person to repair the error; and before I arrived at B—, I had resolved to engage you to take her from this proud this cruel uncle.

I have only now to tell you why I hastened on to London – to procure her an asylum. The very term proves to you that Mrs.

Ashburn's house is out of the question. If you know Mrs. Beville, the sister of Davenport, you know a very amiable woman, who will open her arms and heart for the reception of Sibella. It is not my design to make either her retreat or the means used in her escape a secret; but, if it is possible to prevent Clement Montgomery's seeing her, that I will do. To shield her from Mr. Valmont, we must oppose authority. It was a strange oversight in me not to learn the name of her other guardian.

Let me beseech you, my dear friend, to arm yourself with fortitude. If the circumstance to which I allude in a part of this letter betrays its own authenticity to you, I know your heart will be rent with agony. Yet, persevere! – Ah! I need not say that! in itself, it includes every incitement to her relief.

Use no speed on my account, for I shall be unknown in that obscure village seven miles the other side of B—, where you must stop for me. Let me know when I may be there; and, in waiting for you, I can have no other impatience than of being assured you are in safety.

CAROLINE ASHBURN

LETTER XXI

FROM CAROLINE ASHBURN

TO

SIBELLA VALMONT

(Inclosed in the preceding.)

Your Caroline Ashburn, My Sibella, your own Caroline, who loves you with her whole heart, sends Murden to your relief. Need I add a stronger recommendation? Ah, no! Thus commissioned, you will instantly assure yourself he is benevolent, noble, just, and has not one fault in his nature, that counteracts the propriety of chusing him for your protector.

I have lately been in the castle, Sibella. I have seen your cruel uncle, your insensible aunt: but she for whose sake I encountered them was secluded from my view. I know every particular of your situation. Yes, my love, *every particular.* – There, you have endured enough. Come away! Follow the footsteps of your guide! They will conduct you to liberty. Happiness may overtake us by and by.

My own hand should lead you to the dreary hermit's cell – My smiles should cheer you – for Murden is not apt now to smile, yet, believe me, his heart will rejoice in your deliverance, though his eye may talk of nothing but woe – But I dare not come. Your uncle has spied. Were he to find me in the neighbourhood, he would suspect a plan to relieve you; and by some new manoeuvre counteract it. We have but this one means in our power, for your uncle is irreconcileable.

When Murden gives you this letter, commit yourself wholly to his direction. He will bring you, my Sibella, with all convenient dispatch to a little village called Croom, fifteen miles from your uncle's castle. There your Caroline's arms will receive you; and my affection tells me we shall never again be separated. A short farewel, Sibella.

CAROLINE ASHBURN

LETTER XXII

FROM GEORGE VALMONT

TO

CLEMENT MONTGOMERY

Sir,

On the very day I received your answer to my last letter, I discovered a circumstance which rendered that answer quite unnecessary, except to prove that you are not only a villain but a cowardly villain.

I should have given to myself the satisfaction of telling you thus much before, but I delayed for two reasons; the first, till I had completely banished every struggling effort of the affection I once had for you, almost the only affection I ever had in my life; and the second, perhaps a very consoling one to you, until I had executed the deed which comes herewith, by which under certain annexed conditions you are entitled to the possession of 200l. for life. However you may be obliged by the action, you have but little obligation to the motive. – I hate and detest you cordially; but I would not, for my honour's sake, give up to absolute beggary, *my own – my only son*.

Yes, sir, *my son*. Not legitimate, I confess, but *natural* in the strongest acceptance of the term. I cared not ten straws for your mother; yet, from your birth, I felt a strange propensity to love you. I schemed and planned for your advantage. For your sake alone, I contrived a project by which all the united wealth of the Valmont house would have been showered on your head. I intended, mark me, sir, *I determined* you should marry my niece, and take my name, burying the disgrace of your birth in the nobleness of my possessions. And, as I abhorred that a man who bore my name should abandon himself to the love of society, I sent you into the world as poor and adopted, that you might experience its disappointments and know how to value your proper happiness. – Amply have you rewarded my extreme love and constant labour!

I patiently undergo this statement, because I would have you see exactly where you might have stood, and where you stand now. – The conditions of your present independence are, that you never come into my presence: If you once intrude by letter or otherwise I wipe away the allowance and every trace of consideration for you: Also, the instant you form any species of intercourse with Miss Valmont, the deed is cancelled. Even this paltry sum, as it is mine shall not help to support infamy, ingratitude, and treachery. – Make the comparison, Sir, between 200l. and 18,000l. per annum! – Ha! does it gall you? – So may it ever! May rest fly from your pillow and contentment from your heart; and then you will know what I have experienced, since I discovered the indelible stain you have fixed on my family.

My equally worthless niece, perhaps, may, when she is her own mistress, be inclined to reward your conduct with her hand; for, if I may judge by her reception of your letter when I gave it her, she is not more the fool of inclination than of credulity. – Remember, she never possesses one penny of mine.

If you really have any friend of the name of Murden, pray offer him my very sincere thanks. But for his timely interference, I might have given you a part of your intended inheritance before I discovered your scoundrel-like conduct.

In the moment of acknowledging you my son, I renounce you for ever. I cast you from my affection and memory. And, should you henceforth think of me, know that you have an inveterate implacable enemy, in your father,

G. VALMONT

LETTER XXIII

FROM ARTHUR MURDEN

TO

CAROLINE ASHBURN

Madam,

I date my letter from the farm. Richardson is my confidant. He has a sincere generous mind. I stood before him confessed in all my folly. He will give me his utmost aid.

Do not again call me inexorable, dear Miss Ashburn. I have yielded greatly indeed to you. I consulted a physician at Barlowe-Hall. As we are so speedily to meet, it would be useless to conceal from you that, wherever it had its beginning, the disorder is not now confined to my mind. Youth, the physician said, was in my favour. The continent might do me service. He ordered some medicine; regulated my diet; and, when I told him of my leaving the Hall immediately, he shook my hand: – Conviction speaking from his countenance, that it was his last salute to me.

A few restorative medicines furnished me with strength to reach the farm. – Here my purpose nerves me. – But why do you bid me fortify my heart? Oh, my dear madam, it has been long since fortified! From the fatal night when she gave herself to the arms of Clement, my heart became callous, impenetrable to the dart of any new calamity.

And sometimes too I smile, Miss Ashburn. It is amazing into what familiar habits of intimacy I and the misery that abides with me have fallen.

Fear me not, madam. – In this enterprize, I have all the determination of will – all the vigour of health. – Everything is prepared – last night, accompanied by Richardson, who from his zealous apprehensions for my safety, would not suffer me to go alone, I visited the rock. – No interrupters have been there. The cell, the stone, and the passage are still at our devotion. – Richardson is too honest to make an improper use of the secret of this Ruin; nay, he was the first to remind me, it would be just when our purpose was effected to give Mr. Valmont its description.

Again I repeat, every thing is prepared – I only wait for you to inform me of the nearest connection between her apartments and the armoury. A blunder might be fatal. When you have given me this necessary information, quit London to meet us instantly; for the night succeeding the receipt of your letter Sibella shall bid adieu to her oppressor's dungeon. Direct to Richardson – Stantorfarm, W——.

A. MURDEN

N.B. You blame, with great justice, the little power I possess of detaching myself from the affairs of my heart. – Last time I wrote, it escaped me till my letter was gone, and now I have torn open the seal to tell you that Mademoiselle Laundy is an abandoned woman, Montgomery's mistress in Paris; and, though I have no positive proof, I venture to assert she holds the same station in London. If it suits you to inform Mrs. Ashburn of her companion's principles, on the authority of my name, it is wholly at your service.

LETTER XXIV

FROM JANETTA LAUNDY

TO

CLEMENT MONTGOMERY

I ought to reproach you; but, dear and irresistible as you are, your image, Montgomery, banishes every thing but sensations of pleasure. What can be the reason of your sudden gloom and distraction? I am sure the loss of your money cannot be all, because you know how easily you may be supplied by Mrs. Ashburn till you have further remittances. Why should you hesitate, when I assure you she would be obliged by your making the demand? Recollect her own words the evening she compelled you to use her pocketbook at the faro table; and, if you will not allow me to urge you on another point, at least be persuaded to spare yourself fruitless anxiety about your losses at play.

Still I fear there is something else; and will you not tell it to Janetta, to your own Janetta, who has sacrificed her peace to you, what it is that thus distresses you? Do you remember how you behaved last night? I was terrified to death at your appearance. I asked if you were ill. You struck your hand on your forehead, and said you were undone. 'Is the beauteous Sibella inconstant?' asked Mrs. Ashburn. – I shall never forget the manner of your answer. You spoke through your shut teeth. 'Damnation, madam! she has ruined me!' Then, whirling round, you caught my hand, and exclaimed, 'Oh Laundy! I am indeed undone!'

How I trembled! – I tremble now to think of it. For God's sake, my dear beloved Montgomery, be careful! The hated, the prying Miss Ashburn was by; and if she never suspected us before, I am sure she does now. You went up to Lady Barlow and asked her fiercely for her nephew.

'Mr. Murden, Sir,' said Miss Ashburn looking at you with such scorn I could have killed her, 'Mr. Murden, Sir, is at present a sort of wandering knight errant. Sometime within a fortnight you will hear certain tidings of him. He may be in London.'

It seemed as if you came only to ask this question; for you went away soon after; and, though you strove to be gayer, you sighed so deeply I could scarcely contain myself. I wept all night; and now I am writing instead of dressing. How dear to me every employment that has a concern with my charming Montgomery! – I know not what excuse I shall make at dinner for my melancholy appearance; but fears for my own safety are swallowed up in my apprehensions for you.

Luckily, the Dutchess is confined with a cold. – I will visit her to-night; and, on my way, call on you. So prepare to confide all your griefs to the sympathizing bosom of your Janetta.

Miss Ashburn, two hours ago, received a letter which seemed to give her great pleasure; and, while she was reading it, Lord Filmar came in. When she had finished the letter, she turned to him. 'Didn't I hear you speak of some one being ill, my Lord?'

'Oh, yes, madam, I was enquiring whether Montgomery came here last night to seek physicians or a nurse. I called on him yesterday morning and the servant said, his master was very bad, dreadfully bad, too bad to be seen. I sent after dinner, and he was worse. I drove to his lodgings, just now, to make my adieus, before I leave town, and still he was so bad I could not be let in. Yet I met Miss Trevors, who tells me he was of the party here last evening; a little out of spirits, indeed, but quite as handsome as ever.'

'That he is bad, my Lord,' replied Miss Ashburn fixing her eyes on me, I can very well credit. And, ere long, I shall endeavour to point out some persons who have the same infectious disorders.'

Unless you had seen her look, you can't tell half the meaning this conveyed. – After reading her letter again, she told Mrs. Ashburn she was going out of town immediately; and being asked where, she said, that could not be explained till her return. Her chaise is ordered; and I am delighted to think she can't interrupt us when she is away.

Dear, too dear Montgomery, except at nine, thy ever faithful

JANETTA LAUNDY

LETTER XXV

FROM CAROLINE ASHBURN

TO

ARTHUR MURDEN

The long narrow passage where you met those three men you spoke of connects the tower with the south wing. There you will find a flight of stone stairs, by which she used to descend to the armoury. Those stairs will conduct you into the gallery belonging to Sibella's apartments. Her uncle, fond of magnificence, appropriated to her use solely all the suite of rooms on that floor of the wing. She may be secured by lock and key, but I do not suppose any one is permitted to sleep near her. Of that you must run the hazard.

Do not wonder my lines are uneven, for I actually tremble while I follow you in imagination to that gallery. Were I writing to any one but yourself I should bid you blend boldness and caution. You have done it already.

Ah, my sweet friend, my Sibella! – but I forgot that you are a stranger, my Sibella, to nervous apprehension. – The first word of his errand will bless you!

No, Murden, mere assertion though aided by the authority of your name, will not convince Mrs. Ashburn of her companion's proflicacy. If I cannot fairly and fully detect her practices, I can never remove her. The affair must rest till my return; and then I will try my utmost. I thank you for your information, and I have this morning given Miss Laundy an information that I understand her. A surprising alteration is displayed in Montgomery. Mr. Valmont, I conclude, has begun his discipline. – Explanation is approaching; and do you, my friend, school yourself, before you and he meet, and then you will not cease to befriend him though he may cease to befriend himself.

Adieu! ere this arrives at the farm, I shall be at my station.

CAROLINE ASHBURN

LETTER XXVI

FROM CLEMENT MONTGOMERY

TO

JANETTA LAUNDY

And is it come to this? You urged the secret from me I would fain have withheld; and now do you also give me up to despair? Oh Janetta! Janetta! have I deserved it of you? What was there in that cruel letter of Mr. Valmont's which should chill the ardour of love? His anger has blasted all the fair promises of my life; but it could not transform me into age or ugliness. Still am I, though wretched and desperate, thy Montgomery; still adoring thy beauty, panting for thy charms.

Forgive me if these reproaches are injurious to your tenderness. If you yet love me, forgive me. Alas! you love me not! You turn from me with an averted eye. You repulse my caresses! You give me up to misery and despair; and the wretched Montgomery dies under your neglect.

Farewel, my Janetta! Oh farewel, farewel, then, to all the blooming pleasures which I gathered with an eager hand! My sentence is without appeal. Mr. Valmont – that a father should be so cruel! dooms me to poverty and disgrace. Can I exist in poverty? No, by heaven! Shall I languish in a sordid dwelling, with mere food and covering, and sicken over the remembrance of past enjoyments? Shall I live to crawl along with steps enfeebled by misfortune, and view the splendid equipages of those who were once my associates pass me unheeded? No, I cannot endure it. Some way or other I must end it. All the means of making life desirable are denied me. I blush at my unmerited disgrace. I would hide myself from every eye save your's, Janetta; and, when the fatal tidings are divulged abroad, I shall surely expire with torture.

Yet, be once more kind, my charmer: – if thou hast no kindness for the unfortunate Montgomery, this once, at least affect it. Thou hast known misfortune. Have pity on me! Come and listen to my sighs: let me breathe a sorrowful farewel on thy bosom. I shall not ask this indulgence a second time. I will fly, to bury in solitude the short remnant of a miserable existence. – Then come, and once more bid my heart throb with rapturous sensations! Bid me for a moment forget my doom, remembering only what I have been! – The blissful moment ended, farewel, Janetta! farewel to all!

CLEMENT MONTGOMERY

LETTER XXVII

FROM JANETTA LAUNDY

TO

CLEMENT MONTGOMERY

It is very strange I should express myself so ill as to have my emotions of sorrow and regret mistaken, by you, for coldness and aversion. It is cruel, Montgomery, thus to accuse your Janetta. Could I but describe the anguish I suffered both on your account and my own, you would pity me. Yes, Montgomery; 'tis I should ask for pity. I, who never till now knew how strong are the ties by which my rival held you. Barbarcus as she is, I fear you still love her. She thinks only how she can most effectually work your ruin; while you charge with neglect and unkindness the faithful Janetta, who is labouring to redress your misfortunes.

Montgomery, there is but one way. To talk of dying is absurd. You may feel a temporary languor, the effect of vapour and indigestion; but the bloom and vigour of a constitution like your's is not so easily undermined. Trust me, you will live to a good old age, even with the despicable 200l. per annum your hard hearted father bestows on you. But it is in your power, Montgomery, to live surrounded by riches and splendor, to command the perpetual succession of pleasures which riches and splendor can procure.

Remember the proposal I made you one day, half in earnest half in jest. Think of it. Embrace it. And send Mr. Valmont back his paltry annuity in disdain. You cannot be so blind, so mad as to reject this only means of your happiness. Renounce it, and I shall believe you reserve yourself for my rival, the faithless and barbarous Sibella. Accept it, and all the delights which Janetta's love can bestow are your's for ever.

Why should you hide yourself? That form and face were given for better purposes. Bloom in success and victory! And leave to those who possess not your advantages to mope in dull obscurity! You owe to yourself this triumph over the malice of Mr. Valmont and the cruelty of her who has so wantonly betrayed you to his wrath. Throw off your fables and your sorrow; and call up those alluring graces of your mien which are so irresistible. Exchange your sighs for smiles; and, aided by the advantages of dress you well know how to chuse, come here to dinner. I have contrived that we shall dine alone. Weigh well what I advise and its motives; and then ask yourself, if I deserve to be accused of unkindness – Ask yourself what that love must be which can content itself with secret confessions, and can yield its open triumph to another in order to secure your advantage. Consider these things with attention, dearest Montgomery: and convince me that you deserve all I am willing to do for you by your instant compliance. I cannot, do not, doubt you. Be here by six.

Ever your's, *if you wish me to be so,*

JANETTA LAUNDY

LETTER XXVIII

FROM GEORGE VALMONT

TO

CLEMENT MONTGOMERY

Scoundrel,

By means I cannot divine, Sibella has escaped me. I have no doubt you or some of your diabolical agents are concerned in the business. – The deed, Sir, I have burned. – Your draught of it must help to amuse you.

It delights me to think she is not yet nineteen, and that you are pennyless Beg at my gates if you dare! – The worst of indignities are better than your deservings. – You seal your union under happy auspices. – I give you joy. – Would I could give you destruction!

GEORGE VALMONT

LETTER XXIX

FROM CLEMENT MONTGOMERY

TO

GEORGE VALMONT

Since, Sir, you have extended my punishment to the utmost, I can incur no heavier penalty by thus intruding myself before you.

I could offer many excuses, Sir, for my first fault; but it is now too late. Only, I must say your harshness and severity drove us to that measure, which, in justice to myself, I must also inform you Miss Valmont proposed, and with which I but reluctantly complied.

But, Sir, your further charge is without foundation. I have neither any concern in, nor any knowledge of Miss Valmont's flight; and, further to prove that I would have obeyed you if I could, I shall refuse to protect her. – Indeed, Sir, your last letter has driven me immediately to ratify an engagement that precludes the possibility of any further intercourse with Miss Valmont.

I remain, Sir,

Your unhappy and repentant son,

CLEMENT MONTGOMERY

LETTER XXX

FROM ARTHUR MURDEN

TO

CAROLINE ASHBURN

There she is, Madam! – She walks and sighs: – and one little room, a small circumference, contains *only* Murden and Sibella. When the waiter shut the door and withdrew, I would have given an eye to have detained him. – She knows not I am writing to you; for she would have taken the office on herself, and that would not satisfy me. – It is a relief, madam, to write – tho' any thing upon earth would be preferable to hearing – I mean, *seeing her.*

Miss Ashburn, till I saw her, I did not understand you. – Well might you warn me!

It will be three hours before we reach you. – I send this letter by a man and horse; because, in knowing that we are safe, you will have at least half an hour of less anxiety.

The place where we are now is only a village, five miles out of the road to Valmont. – Richardson advised me to make this sweep for fear of a pursuit. – He brought us here through cross roads on his own horses. I have sent him back; and the only chaise this little inn maintains is engaged for a two hours airing for some invalid in the village. – Have patience, madam. – Your friend is safe.

Richardson and myself possessed ourselves of the cell at half past nine last night. – Then in our disguises we prowled around the castle till about eleven, and heard the locking of doors, and saw in the upper windows light after light die away as their possessors yielded themselves to rest.

We would not venture too early. I believe it was past two before we left the armoury. – All was hushed. – The stairs! – the gallery! – her apartments! – I seized Richardson by the arm, as he attempted to turn the lock. – It seemed profanation. I feared every thing! – I would have gone back. – Richardson forbade me.

We entered the antichamber. We crossed two others. The door of a third stood open. – In that there was a fire, a candle, and a bed. – The curtains were undrawn; and I caught a glimpse of her face. Instantly, I drew the door so close as only to admit my hand, holding out your letter. – I gasped. – 'Speak for me,' I said to Richardson; 'Say, Miss Ashburn.'

'Rise, dear Miss Valmont,' said he, 'Miss Ashburn sends you this.' I heard her start from the bed. – 'Who? – What?'

'Miss Ashburn,' repeated Richardson, 'Miss Ashburn, it is a letter from Miss Ashburn.'

She took or rather snatched the letter; and, as I withdrew my hand, she shut the door hastily.

I heard her utter an exclamation – I could hear her too burst into sobs and bless you. – I heard her also name another.

At length she asked, without opening the door, if I was indeed Mr. Murden, and if I could take her from the castle.

'O yes, yes,' said I, 'Come away,'

'Stay,' she replied.

She was dressed in an instant. She opened the door. She came out to us. – 'Ah! what, what is the matter?' cried she, extending her arms as if to save me from falling. – Why were you not more explicit in your letter, Miss Ashburn? – I recoiled *from her*, from the remembrance of her Clement – and, as I leaned on Richardson's shoulder, I closed my dim eyes, and wished they might never more open upon recollection.

'Shame!' whispered Richardson, 'you are unmanned!'

And so I am, Miss Ashburn. I think too, I should love revenge. I feel a rankling glow of satisfaction, as she walks past my chair, that I have so placed it I cannot look up and behold her.

I recovered strength and courage while my horror remained unabated. – She saw I could hear, and she began to pour forth the effusions of her gratitude upon you and us. – She knew you had been in the castle. Her cruel uncle had informed her of it. – 'And then,' said she, 'I fancied I must die without seeing any one that ever loved me.' – As she spoke, I turned my eyes from her now haggard and jaundiced face to my own, reflected in the mirror by which I was standing. 'Moving corpses!' said I to myself – 'Why encumber ye the fair earth?'

'He shewed me a letter too,' added she. 'He said Clement had renounced me. – Ah, Mr. Valmont! deceiving Mr. Valmont!' – and she waved her hand gracefully – 'had you known Sibella's heart as she knows Clement's, you ——.'

'Come away!' said I.

'Have you no other preparation to make, madam?' asked Richardson; 'the night is very cold.'

This reminded her of a cloak. – She enquired if she must swim across the moat; and said she was sure she could swim; – for she knew why she had failed before. – I bade Richardson lead her.

I expected to have seen her much more surprised at the strange path through which she had to go. – From the armoury to the cell she never spoke. Her mind was overcharged with swelling emotions. – At times we were obliged to stand still. She even panted for freer respiration. The——

I heard wheels. – I expected our chaise. – It is some travellers who have stopped to bait.

After we had safely crossed the moat, she alternately grasped our hands in a tumult of joy; named you, named me, but *talked* on the never-failing theme of *her* Clement.

She rode behind Richardson. – I see she is much worse for the journey; yet her burning eye and vehement spirits would persuade me otherwise.

She kindly ceased her torturing questions concerning Clement, imagining, by my abrupt answers, I was too ill to talk. – She says you will heal me – for you have healed her. – Miss Ashburn, how ardently she loves you!

I find you will receive this letter an hour before we come. – Won't you thank, and praise me? – It is written with a shaking hand, and throbbing temples. I know it would be difficult to keep Sibella from mounting the same horse, if she were informed of the messenger. When we enter the chaise, I will tell her what I have done.

A. MURDEN

LETTER XXXI

FROM THE SAME

TO

THE SAME

Why should I have the rage of distraction without the phrenzy? Dare they tell me I am a lunatic? – She is gone, Miss Ashburn? I have lost your treasure! – Some villain, lured by the vestiges of her transcendent beauty, has taken her from me. – They have forced me into a bed! – The barbarians confine me here. – Won't your order me to be released? – Oh sweet Miss Ashburn, won't you tell them I must be released?

Now I recollect I wanted to tell you all the particulars.——Ha! they fade from me, and I dream again!——

Madam,
I keep the Blue Boar at Hipsley; and the poor unhappy gentleman who wrote the above came to my house with his lady yesterday morning. As long as ever I live, I shan't forget the poor gentleman's ravings, when he discovered that his lady had ran away from him, and he only came to his senses about an hour ago, when he ordered us to send for you, and he wrote till his raving fit returned; and it would melt your heart, madam, to hear how he is bemoaning himself and calling by the kindest names the ungrateful wicked lady who served him so badly. – I saw her jump into the chaise myself; and she went willingly enough, though he won't believe it. My son brings you this, madam; and I hope you will tell us what we must do for the poor gentleman. From
      Your ladyship's humble servant,
                                      MARY HOLMES

LETTER XXXII

FROM CAROLINE ASHBURN

TO

ARTHUR MURDEN

Ah my friend, my beloved Murden, if an interval of memory, happily, now is thine, read these lines which thy friend pens to thee in agony. – She follows on the instant. You once demanded my consolations and friendship, as a reparation for the mischievous error into which I had led you. – Will you receive them now as such, against the manifold mischiefs I have brought upon you?

Ah! what, what had I to do with secret escapes! – I, who exclaimed from the beginning against Valmont's secrecy, and prophesied its fatal consequences! – Must I too conspire to make Sibella the victim of secrecy? – Unhappy sufferer! Yet more unhappy Caroline! She, debarred the use of her judgment, erred only from mistake; I, alas! have sinned against reason and conviction!

Clement, I suspect, has watched our footsteps. I fear he has secured her. – Ah, miserable fate!

Console yourself, my dearest friend. It will please you to know that, even before I come to you, I am going to B——, to send messengers in search of Sibella. And if money and vigilance can bring us tidings of our lost friend, I have the power of employing both. – Prepare to receive me with calmness. – Already, I have the aggravated distress of your and Sibella's feelings to endure. – I am pained beyond description.

CAROLINE ASHBURN

LETTER XXXIII

FROM LORD FILMAR

TO

SIR WALTER BOYER

I can truly say, I neither sit, stand, walk, nor lie: – that is, the complete *I*, body and soul together; for, let the former attempt its mechanical motions as it will, the other in a quite opposite direction is striking, curvetting, capering, twisting, tumbling, and playing more tricks than any fantastical ape in nature.

Therefore, dear Walter, you must send me instantly a hundred guineas. Yes really, if you want to quiet my conscience, you must send me a hundred guineas.

Nothing will quiet my conscience but matrimony.

I cannot marry without a hundred guineas. – Ergo, if you don't send me a hundred guineas, and I should die, and be ——, the sin will lay at your door, and you will die and be —— likewise.

As I have much consideration for you, my dear Walter, and as I know that people who have very weak heads, have sometimes also very weak nerves, I would advise you to lay down my letter, unless you are seated in some safe place, for, should your situation be dangerous, and should the surprise I am preparing for you rob you of apprehension, down you drop and leave me in utter despair – lest your executors should refuse me the hundred guineas.

Well – are you settled to your satisfaction? – Here it comes like a thunderbolt!

Miss Valmont is mine, and I am her's – your hundred guineas will buy a parson and a prayer book; and then the *L.7000* a year is mine also.

You know, dear Walter, that resolved to obtain the heiress of Valmont Castle, I left London to return to Monkton Hall, with a heart full of promise, and a head full of stratagem. Fortune, that dear blind inconstant goddess, who formerly was almost within my grasp, now dashes the projects of others to the ground, to give my wishes their triumph. Some Merlin, with more potent spells than mine, broke the enchanted castle, bore off the damsel, and, directed by fate and fortune, brought her on the road, to meet me, to the very spot where it was decreed his success should end, that mine might begin. And begun it has.

Last night, I slept at B——; and intended breakfaking with Sir Gilbert Monkton: this morning I ordered the driver to leave the high road, and cross the country, by which means I should save six miles of the journey. Griffiths had been unwell some days; and he now appeared so cold, and so much indisposed, I thought it prudent to give him a breakfast on the road. The postilion, by the luckiest of all chances, drove up to a pretty little white-washed inn, that I shall love dearly for six months to come.

The landlady, a curtsying civil woman, was mighty sorry she had not a better room to receive my honour in; but her best parlour, she said, was already taken up with a lady and gentleman, who had arrived at seven o'clock in the morning. And she showed me into a little place, which had two excellent properties, namely, perfect cleanliness, and a good fire.

By this good fire I had sat five or perhaps ten minutes, when Griffiths entered. 'My Lord! my Lord!' said he, and turned back to shut the door; 'I have seen the strangest sight, my Lord! I have seen a gentleman ——' At that moment a tea-kettle was brought into the room; and Griffiths grew downright pettish with the damsel who bore the kettle, because she did not quit the room with sufficient speed.

His information, Walter, amounted to thus much – that in the passage he had seen the gentleman who occupied the land-lady's best parlour; and that this gentleman, of whom Griffiths had had a very distinct view, certainly was, or Griffiths was much deceived, the very identical spright who reminded some of us of our devotions in the narrow passage of the west tower at Valmont castle. ''Tis impossible!' said I.

'My Lord, 'tis true,' said Griffiths. I should know him among a thousand. I know his eyes and nose as well as I know your's, my Lord.'

This you will allow, Walter, was but a very vague sort of a supposition to ground any belief upon; for, as eyes and noses are the

common lot of all mankind, it may happen now and then that two or
more may be greatly alike. Yet, so diligent is hope and imagination,
I could not persuade myself these eyes and this nose had any owner
but the spright of the castle. – It was Miss Valmont and her hermit,
my fancy said. I blessed my stars. I cursed my stars. I wondered how
and why they should come hither. Then, I remembered, that fancy,
though sometimes a prophetess, is rarely an oracle, and I thought it
might not be Miss Valmont and her hermit. – I consulted much
with Griffiths; and, at length, had recourse to the waiter, a dapper
shabby–coated fellow with a wooden leg.

They came, he said, on horseback before seven o'clock. A man,
who conducted them, did not alight. They were impatient to be gone.
They waited for a chaise. They had ordered a breakfast which neither
of them had tasted. The lady did not appear, he thought, equipped
for travelling. The gentleman was melancholy, and the lady restless
and agitated.

Miss Valmont: whispered I to myself.

'They are a fine couple,' said the waiter.

I asked if he thought they were a married pair. He answered, he
was sure she must be a married lady. I enquired if the gentleman
seemed to be very fond of her.

'Not at all,' replied the waiter. 'The gentleman sits writing, Sir,
with his back to her. She walks about the room, muttering to herself.
When I carried in the breakfast, he leaned his head against the wall,
and groaned with his eyes shut.'

It cannot be Miss Valmont and her hermit, thought I.

'Is the lady handsome?' I asked.

The waiter thought she was too pale to be very handsome; but he
added that in all his born days he never beheld such a head of hair.

'Of what colour is it?' I asked.

It was neither black, nor brown, nor as red as Jenny's; – he
thought it was not any colour, but it shone as if gold threads
were among it.

Miss Valmont: whispered my forward heart. I rose and walked
hastily across the room.

'What did they talk about?' said I.

'They don't talk at all, Sir. The poor gentleman seems very bad;
and as I told your honor before, she walks about muttering. When
they first came, as I was lighting a fire for them, the lady pulled off
her hat just as if she was in a passion, and then she shook her fine

waving locks, as though she was wond'rous proud of them. And she said her head ached with that – cumbrance; and she said something more about customs and cumbrances, but I forget what, your honor. While she talked, the gentleman looked so kind and pretty at her it did my heart good to see him; but he is either very ill or very whimmy, for, immediately, while she took off her cloak, he laid his head on the table with his face downward and sighed as if his heart was breaking.'

I asked if he had heard her call him by any name, and the waiter replied he had heard her twice name somebody as she walked about the room; but to my great disappointment at that moment, his memory had not retained the name.

At this part of our conference, the parlour bell rang, and the waiter disappeared; not, though, till I had sealed him mine by a bribe, and given him orders to return instantly. However, Griffiths, who was most zealous on this occasion, thought proper to follow him. Fortunate was it that he did; for, my waiter, dull at a hint, had received a letter from the guest in the parlour, which, without consulting my will and pleasure, he was quietly bearing to a courier ready mounted and waiting for it at the inn door. Griffiths with a careless air took the letter from his hand. It was addressed, Walter, to – *Miss Ashburn*.

I began to stalk, to exclaim, to ejaculate. Go on, Filmar, cried I, and prosper! Henceforward be plot and stratagem sanctified! for Miss Ashburn deigns to plot.

Griffiths prudently reminded me that it would be quite as well at present to think of Miss Valmont, and leave Miss Ashburn alone till another opportunity.

'Right,' said I.

''Tis folly! 'Tis madness, but to think for a moment of such a project!', said I, ten minutes after, and turning myself half round in my chair, throwing one arm across its back and one leg over the other. No! no! I'll have nothing to do with it!' and I fell to shaking the uppermost leg furiously. 'It might be very easily managed though,' said Griffiths; 'and then your Lordship——'

'Would have nothing to do but to digest Montgomery's bullets and Miss Ashburn's harder words. – Oh that Miss Ashburn can find words to lash like scorpion's stings! Say no more of it, Griffiths, I have give her up.'

'As you please, my Lord.'

'Ay! ay!' muttered I to myself. 'Let her go to her Montgomery! There are men who perhaps are worthy of being loved as himself, and might perhaps be more capable of constancy. There are other women too in the world, thank heaven! – Strange,' continued I, 'that Miss Ashburn with her understanding, and who must know the imbecility of Montgomery's love, could dream of joining in any plot whose object was to bear Miss Valmont to Montgomery!' For, Walter, I had by this time concluded that the quondam hermit was some righteous go-between of Miss Valmont and her lover; and I felt inclined to be mortally offended with her, because Montgomery had so well concealed from my penetration their mutual intelligence. I shifted to the other side of my seat; and I did not sigh; but I blew my breath from me with much more force than usual.

I mused during the greater part of an hour. 'Your chaise is waiting, my Lord,' said Griffiths; 'and, as you have quite done with this affair, if your Lordship thinks proper it is as well not to keep the horses in the cold. – Well, I must say 'twas a fine opportunity!'

'Do you think so, Griffiths?' said I mildly.

The rogue exultingly smiled; and, to change my wavering into downright resolution, he recapitulated all the probabilities that awaited my attempt, and noticed the trifling hazard that would accrue (provided I adopted his plan for the purpose), should the attempt fail: nor did he forget an oblique glance or two at certain prospects which he knew put no inconsiderable weight into the balance.

'Away! away!' I cried, 'give the driver his directions; let him draw up close to the door, before the other chaise; and let him be sure to keep his chaise door open, but not the step down.'

Signifies it to thee, Walter, of what Griffith's plan consisted? Surely not. Nothing could be more easy than, at the instant of their departure, to request a moments conversation with the gentleman; nothing more simple than to invent a tale of a pursuit, to be delivered into the attentive ear of Miss Valmont's guide: nothing could promise fairer, and surely never did fulment better follow promise.

Our casement looked upon a garden, and there the melancholy conductor of Miss Valmont came to walk for a few minutes. There needed no screen to hide us from his glance. His arms were folded, and his eyes intensely fixed on the earth. His hat shaded the upper part of his face, so that I could see no part of his said resemblance to the bearded youth of the armoury; but I observed with pleasure and thrilling expectation that he and I were nearly of one stature, both booted, and both wearing dark blue great coats. This only difference existed, one of his capes he had drawn round his chin, all mine lay on my shoulders. – Walter, I could button mine up on occasion.

George had ridden my grey mare from town. I felt no way inclined to make him a party in the transaction; and I also wanted the mare for Griffiths. I therefore ordered him to return to B——, and take a stage for London, waiting there my further orders. Griffiths saw him mount a post horse, and led the grey mare round the house, and fastened her to some rails in readiness.

It was exactly two hours and one quarter from the time of our arrival, before their chaise came to the door. The horses were to have a feed in their harness; the guests were impatient to be gone. I shuddered: and, as I traversed our little room, the echo of my footsteps seemed to be blabbing tell tales. I shall never, Walter, know such another minute as that. All in future will be the dull uniformity of peace and plenty.

It was done. The waiter delivered Griffiths message in the best parlour. I, from a distant peeping station, saw the gentleman walk to our room. I heard the door shut – the waiter stump away. Thrilling, throbbing with hope and fear, I walked up the passage to their parlour. Wrapped in her cloak, the hood drawn over her head, her hat in her hand, stood the fair expectant. 'O come,' said she, 'do let us hasten!' The day was gloomy, the passage was dark, I had drawn up my cape and drawn down my hat. My hand took her's. She tripped along. No creature was in sight. I caught her up in my arms, lifted her into the chaise, and we whirled off, just as the landlady came bustling up to the door.

I had my cue of silence and reserve in the intelligence I had received from the waiter. During the first three miles, I neither spoke nor looked up. She, the while, clasping her hands and *muttering*, as the waiter called it. I heard her pronounce the names of Miss Ashburn, of Montgomery, and of some one else. For three miles, I say, we interchanged not one word: then, Walter, the first word betrayed me.

And now what a list of sobs, tears, screams, prayers, and lamentations you expect! I have not one for you. She sighed, indeed, and a few drops forced a reluctant way; but she neither prayed, threatened, nor lamented. She demanded her liberty. She reasoned for her liberty; reasoned with a firmness collected, vigilant, manly, let me say. She remembers seeing me in the castle, and takes me for her uncle's agent. In truth, Walter, I suffer her to think it still; for I do not find, when carefully examined, that my own character and motives in this business possess much to recommend them.

In a little glen, between two hills of which the barrenness of one frowns on the cultivation of the other, stands a farm, embosomed hid in secrecy and solitude. No traveller eyes it from the distant heath. No horses, save its own, leave the print of their hoofs at its entrance. But even more than usual gloom and dulness now reigns around it. The lively whistle of the ploughman and hind no longer chear the echoes of the hill. The farm yard is emptied of its gabbling tenants. The master is dead, the stock sold, the tenants discharged, and one solitary daughter, with one solitary female domestic alone, remains to guard the house till quarter day shall yield it to a new tenant.

'Tis neither fit employment for my time to relate, nor for your's to read, the trifling adventures by which Griffiths became acquainted with this fair daughter, her circumstances and abode; nor how he wooed and won her love during our residence at Monkton Hall. At Griffith's instigation, hither I brought Miss Valmont; and here, till your cash arrives, as in a place of trust and safety, do I mean to keep my treasure, although I am little more than three leagues distant from Monkton Hall, and scarcely four from Valmont castle.

A less ready imagination than even thine, Walter, might picture to itself the manner in which Griffiths deluded Miss Valmont's knight-errant with a tale of pursuit and discovery. The youth checked his surprise, and renewed his vigour. He hastened to secure his lovely ward; and Griffiths, mean while, stole round the inn, mounted the grey mare, and was out of sight and sound of the consequences.

I hear her walking. A slight partition divides her chamber from mine. No more of those deep-drawn sighs, my fair one! I thank heaven I am not an agent of Valmont's neither. He must have used her cruelly. She is excessively pale; and strangely altered.

I stand, Walter, the watchful centinel of her chamber door, which I presume not to enter. Till I had her in my possession, my thoughts, in gadding after the enterprize, possessed all the saucy gaiety which youth and untamed spirits could impart. Nay, when I began to write this letter, they wore their natural character. I must shift my station from this room. Those deep deep sighs will undo me! Hasten, dear Walter, make the wings of speed thy messengers to bear to me a hundred guineas, that we may fly to the land of blessings ere I forgot that her cupids have golden headed arrows. – Hem! – *Seven thousand per annum* – O 'tis an elixir to chear the fainting spirits!

And now, as sure as I have possession of the rich and beauteous prize after which I have so long yearned, so sure will I recompense her present uneasiness by a life of tenderness, attention, and, to the best of my present belief, of unabated constancy.

But marry me she must and shall, by G–d!

FILMAR

LETTER XXXIV

FROM CAROLINE ASHBURN

TO

LADY BARLOWE

Dear Madam,

By a strange concurrence of accidents I am at present attending Mr. Murden, who during many days has lain dangerously ill in a small country inn nine miles from Valmont castle. I must leave it to your prudence to acquaint Sir Thomas Barlowe (to whom I know it will be most distressing tidings) that his nephew is in danger, but it is necessary that Sir Thomas should know it immediately, for I have made preparations for bringing Mr. Murden to London, that he may have better accomodation and better advice. Though I speak of advice, I dare not encourage any hope in Sir Thomas, for I have watched the progress of his nephew's disorder, and I believe he is only lingering – abide he cannot.

Sir Thomas Barlowe loved this young man as a son; and, to receive him scarcely a shadow of his former self, will create distressing emotions. Yet, I beseech you to urge Sir Thomas carefully to avoid any strong expressions of sorrow when his nephew arrives, for I have the grief to tell you that Mr. Murden's reason is shaken: and dreadful paroxysms may follow the slightest agitation.

Nought but the power I have long laboured to obtain and have in part obtained over my sensations could have preserved any degree of fortitude in me under the most trying events of my life, events which have lately befallen Miss Valmont and Mr. Murden. On them I had bestowed the warmest tribute of my affections. In the enjoyment of their virtues and happiness, I expected daily to augment my own. But, alas! it is gone; and my wretched hopes still wear their beautiful and alluring form while sinking in disappointment.

I am aware, Madam, that Mr. Murden's misfortune cannot create more concern in your breast than the circumstance of my being with him will raise wonder and curiosity; nor have I any other than a full intention of making you acquainted with the circumstances that drew us both hither, whose sad termination has operated so fatally on Mr. Murden. But I am obliged to defer the relation till our arrival in town, both on account of its length, of the preparations I am making for Mr. Murden's ease and safety on the journey, and the continual anxiety of watchfulness which possesses me for the sake of Miss Valmont, to whom I have been unhappily the cause of evils possibly worse than that which has befallen Mr. Murden.

I cannot name the day when you and Sir Thomas may expect us, for the time consumed in the journey must be regulated by the abatement or increase of Mr. Murden's disorder. He shall travel in a litter; and I hope it is unnecessary for me to assure Sir Thomas nothing shall be wanting to his accomodation that I have means to procure.

I remain your Ladyship's well wisher and servant,

CAROLINE ASHBURN

LETTER XXXV

FROM CAROLINE ASHBURN

TO

GEORGE VALMONT

Sir,

By the messenger of mine, who, on his search for my lost friend, came to your gates a few days since, you were informed that it was through my means Sibella escaped from your castle; and, however stern may be the anger you entertain against me, be assured, Sir, it cannot exceed the vehemence of that self-reproach and sorrow which now assail me, for having been the contriver of so unjustifiable an undertaking.

I send you, Sir, a pacquet containing all the letters I have received from Sibella, and also the letters that have passed between Mr. Murden and myself. I lay them before you, with the confidence that you will afford them a patient and temperate perusal; for I think they will serve to convince you, as they have already convinced me by the unfortunate event to which they have led, that, however plausible and even necessary in appearance, yet artifice and secrecy are dangerous vicious tools.

Your secrets were the preparatory step to the errors of Clement and Sibella. Had Sibella never departed from strict truth and sincerity, she had never formed her rash engagement with Clement. Had Murden never (with his dangerous refinements of fancy) longed secretly to view this rare child of seclusion, he had not battered his life and happiness for a sigh. And lastly, had I not given way to the fatal mistake that secrecy could repair the inability of reason, I had, instead of availing myself of the ruin on the rock, ere now perhaps released Sibella by convincing you. And we had all been comparatively happy.

Murden's unfinished letter from the village of Hipsley will shew you his deplorable situation, and all that we know concerning the loss of our Sibella.

I have six agents employed to discover her. But they wander blindly, for I have neither trace, nor supposition, to guide them. What can I do, Sir? if you have any advice to offer, I hope you will not withhold it, from animosity to me. Excessively do I love the friend I have helped to sacrifice, yet I can readily and sincerely forgive you the errors of your conduct towards her. Oh then, Sir, pardon mine, and in pity to the anxiety of my heart aid me with your advice and assistance.

I do not even hate Mr. Montgomery; though I do despise him altogether. You suspected him of taking Sibella from the castle. I suspected him of stealing her from Mr. Murden. He was otherwise employed.

I arrived in town, with my poor patient under my protection, yesterday evening, and resigned Mr. Murden to the care of his uncle, Sir Thomas Barlowe. When I drove up to my mother's door, I found it more than usually crowded with carriages and servants; hung upon the pillars; and, when several of my mother's footmen stepped from among the crowd, I perceived they were in new liveries adorned in the highest stile of elegant expence. Though it was impossible not to notice the uncommon glare of splendor that saluted my eyes, yet our changes have always been so various and profuse, I never thought of enquiring into the cause of the present. Unfitted by my dress, but still more by weariness of limbs and depression of mind, to encounter company, I retired to my chamber and to bed.

This morning my maid attended me; and, with the natural hesitation of good nature in relating disagreeable tidings, she informed me – Mr. Montgomery was married to my mother.

Sir, it is the fact. Last Saturday, my mother became the bride of your son; and the parade I witnessed last night was to do honour to the first complimentors of this extraordinary hymeneal.

The tidings stunned me, for I was no way prepared from the conduct of either to expect such an event. Uninvited and assuredly unwelcome, I visited their apartment the hour of breakfast, and my mother collected the utmost of her haughtiness and Mr. Montogmery his gay indifference, to repel the reproaches they expected I should be prompted to bestow on them. But, Sir, they mistook me. I went only to deliver to them a plain history of the mischiefs I have heaped on Mr. Murden and my Sibella, to remind them how early, and, alas! how severe a punishment has followed my deviation from rectitude.

I saw Montgomery's countenance become pale and ghastly. It was, Sir, when I spoke of Miss Valmont's independent fortune. Then, I believe, all the force of his situation was present with him. May it often recur, and be the preservative against future follies.

Allow me, Sir, to say a word or two of him who most loved your niece and best deserved her. Mr. Murden intruded on your domain, and destroyed some of your unripe projects; yet I persuade myself you will feel a pity for his misfortunes. His life pays the forfeiture of his curiosity and secrecy. A romantic love of Miss Valmont sapped its foundation, and his nights of watching amidst the chilling damps of the Ruin hastened the progress of its destruction. Sibella's unaccountable escape from him at a time when his high toned feelings were wrought upon, in a way that I cannot express, by the *alteration* in her person, drove him to madness. Then it was that I saw him who once possessed every advantage of manly grace and beauty changed to a living skeleton, whose eyes starting from their sockets glanced around with wild horror and insanity. Oh, Sir, it was indeed a scene that called forth all my fortitude!

As his delirium had no mischievous tendencies, it was judged better to remove him to London; and whether change of air and place had the salutary effect, or the delirium had exhausted its force I know not, but he became perfectly restored to reason before we reached London. That restoration was almost beyond my hopes; and there hope rests, it dares not presume further. The most certain indications of speedy dissolution now appear; and all my time must be given to the endeavour of tracing my beloved Sibella, and consoling the anxious Murden for her loss. On his own account, consolation pains him. All his wishes centre in death; and the irrevocable union will soon take place.

Will you be kind enough to inform me of the name of Sibella's other guardian? – Adieu, Sir, may that peace which is only to be purchased by rectitude become an inmate of your abode.

CAROLINE ASHBURN

LETTER XXXVI

LORD FILMAR

TO

SIR WALTER BOYER

Faith, Walter, I have secured a rich prize, indeed. Hear but its estimate.

In the first place, a very lovely and adorable woman.

In the second, a fine estate.

In the third,——an heir (in embrio) to inherit it.

True, by the Gods! – Nevertheless, stop your rash conclusions, for I have heard her whole story, therefore I tell you that Miss Ashburn is an angel, Mr. Murden a fine fellow, Mr. Valmont an ideot, Sibella a saint, and Montgomery – a scoundrel: though on my soul she talked so movingly of his *never fading faith* I could not for my life persuade myself to tell her my true opinion of him.

From the little she knows of Murden, (her hermit and deliverer) I long to know more. I burn to tell you of her wonderful escape, of the marvellous Ruin on the rock, but I have resolved to wave explanations till I come. – I charge you, by your friendship, breathe not a whisper of the adventure till you see me. I am going to restore her to her friends; her eloquence did part, but truly her condition did more. – I never bargained to pay off such a mortgage. I could love her dearly; but then you know my name is Filmar, and as a Lord I am bound in duty to love and cherish no son but a son of my own begetting.

I have dispatched two messengers, one for carriages and another to that inn at Hipsley *(which I don't love at all now)* to make enquiries after Mr. Murden. I wonder how he and I shall adjust our accounts. – I fear there is a long balance in his favour.

You perceive, Walter, all my secret plottings and contrivings have brought me to a fine heritage at last! Murden cannot call me any thing less than a *thief*, and will say I deserve a thief's punishment. Valmont too will want a peck at me, neither for the credit of love nor integrity but only because Sibella is the great great great granddaughter of some one or other of his *great* grandfather's. Montgomery may pretend the honour of *his wife* (her own phrase) impeached by her residence with me, and if he won't believe that until two hours since I never forced myself into her presence, why I shall be obliged by all the laws of honour and gentlemanship to prove it by the length of a sword.

Heigh ho! and this pretty wisdom-speaking mortal has actually prevailed on me to endure the brunt and carry her back to Miss Ashburn! She has offered high bribes, – solid comforts, – made up of duty and justice; – but I have a sickly palate – spoiled by other viands, – I want a modern seasoned fricassee.

Alas! I have no alternative – unless I shoot her and bury her under a tree. I don't know what of that sort I may be tempted to for myself! for when I have no longer her and her concerns to think of I must turn to my own – a pretty prospect!

Do you know, Walter, any way that a Lord turned plain man can get a living? for unless I *get it* heaven knows I must go without it.

You are admiring my forbearance in keeping such a distance, Walter; but the fact is, I was a coward. Daily almost hourly Miss Valmont intreated she might speak with me, and I as constantly with a great many civil excuses declined the conversation. What could I have said but what had amounted to this: 'Miss Valmont, I ran away with you, because I wanted your estate, for want of a better. – As to yourself, I know nothing about you, therefore how can I care for you?' Methought, Walter, when I had your cash in hand I should be bold. Your cash came; I pocketed it; and I proudly strutted up to Miss Valmont.——The former pages will tell you the result.

The plot thickens, and I am more of Montgomery's fort than I believed I was. – Mr. Murden is dying. – Good God, Walter! who would have thought on this? – They told my messenger that he has been raving mad! and that a lady took him away for London yesterday morning. – I dare not relate to Miss Valmont these cursed tidings. – I am impatient to yield her up. – We shall travel as fast as I think her condition may allow without danger.

FILMAR

LETTER XXXVII

FROM GEORGE VALMONT

TO

CAROLINE ASHBURN

Madam,

I am certainly obliged to you for your intentions; and though I allow you have sometimes reason on your side, I think you make too little allowance for the proper obedience due from children to parents. As a parent I certainly stood both to Clement and Sibella, and they ought implicitly to have obeyed my commands. However, she poor child suffers sufficiently, and I am willing to forgive though I can never be reconciled to her. Her pregnancy will now be known to the world; and, were I again to receive her, I should co-operate in disgracing my family. I heartily wish your search may be successful; and I am ready to reimburse your expences; and also, if you find my niece, to allow her a proper establishment.

My Lord of Elsings, joint guardian with me in the trust of Miss Valmont, resides at present in this neighbourhood. I have had an interview with him on the business; but I do not discover that either himself, or any one related to him, is any way concerned in taking Sibella.

Will you take the trouble, in my name, to wish Clement Montgomery all the *felicity* he may expect to find in his union with old age, folly, and affectation?

Madam,

Your very obedient servant,

G. VALMONT

LETTER XXXVIII

FROM LORD FILMAR

TO

SIR WALTER BOYER

Your Pardon, Walter, that I should pass your lodgings as I drove out of town without stopping to say a single how-do-ye. But, let pity and humanity plead their cause with ever so much eloquence, yet the prejudices of custom are so potent that a man becomes ashamed if his eyes give their tribute to the feelings of his heart. Truly, Walter, I should have blushed to-day at my insensibility if I had not wept yesterday. Yet, for weeping, I coward-like drew up the blinds of my chaise, and, to hide myself from the finger of scorn, bade the driver carry me with all expedition to my aunt's retreat at Hayley lodge.

I must suppose, for your own sake, Boyer, that when you wrote me your hasty letter to the farm, you were uninformed of Montgomery's marriage with Mrs. Ashburn. Haste could not excuse such an oversight, as little as you knew of Miss Valmont. No! no! it was not possible you could be informed of it and not send me the tidings.

I am an ass, I have not the common discernment of a school boy, or I had never talked of accomodating her condition by tardy travelling when I was bearing Miss Valmont to her beloved though perfidious Clement. Speed, flying speed, was alone necessary to her safety. I spared neither money nor command, yet to her foundered. Not that she complained. Never! She even thanked my zeal, when her gasping sensations would give way to utterance. But I saw it, Walter, in her eyes. I saw the speed of her affections in the convulsive swells of her bosom. Do not call me ridiculous, but upon my soul there were moments of the journey that while gazing on her I was on the point of grasping her in my arms, lest her very form should dissolve into feeling and vanish from my protection.

Once I refused to proceed unless she would take refreshment. She did not plead; and taking from me a cup of chocolate, her shaking hand raised it half way to her lips then returned it untasted to the table. I drew a chair, and deliberately seated myself, as if resolved to put my threat in practice. After a short silence, 'Sir,' said she, 'have you ever known what it is to love?' I was looking on the fire; and, recollecting some odd sensations that had occasionally crept to my heart, was about to reply in the affirmative, but turning my head and meeting the full gaze of her eloquent eye, an honest and prompt reply sprang to my lips – 'By my soul and salvation, never, Madam! – Griffiths, see the horses instantly put to the chaise. We alight no more, till we alight in London.'

Montgomery shewed you a silly portrait that he painted. To say it was the likeness of Miss Valmont was a falsehood. 'Twas a mere passive representation of fine features. Let him paint me their energy, their force, the fulness of hope that beamed from them yesterday morning, and I will say he is worthy of Miss Valmont's love! – He cannot do it, Walter! He could as soon be a god! She never was beautiful till then. Not, in the fullest bloom of her vigour and prosperity, did she ever equal herself such as I saw her yesterday morning.

'This, Madam is Miss Ashburn's residence,' I said as we drove to the door.

'I shall see my Caroline first then,' said Miss Valmont: – 'next my Clement.'

Agitated as I was at the time by her impatience and expectations, I cannot suppose I enquired for any one else than Miss Ashburn. Whether the servant imagined she was of the party or concluded my visit must be to his mistress I know not, but he announced Lord Filmar in the drawing room; and I led in the loveliest spectre with golden threaded hair to an apartment where Montgomery lolled negligently on one sofa and his portly bride on another.

Shall I tell you how they looked? No! for their best looks are worthless! But I will tell you that Miss Valmont looked ardor love and truth. – She raised her clasped hands one instant, then rushed into the arms of Montgomery, which involuntarily opened to receive and were compelled to sustain her. A confused suspicion of something more than usually wrong in Montgomery darted upon my mind. I looked wistfully around the apartment, as it were for a relief from danger, and my heart bounded as I saw Miss Ashburn enter the room.

– Charming woman! She could make astonishment yield to better feelings. With admirable presence of mind, she instantly approached Miss Valmont, saying, Sibella, dearest Sibella, have you no tokens for your Caroline?'

'Oh yes,' replied Miss Valmont, 'many, many! Love and gratitude also for my Caroline! happy happy world! I will live with you in it for ever!'

Miss Ashburn endeavoured to retain Sibella in her embrace; and began hurryingly to enquire of her where she had been, and by what means she had got hither. But Miss Valmont knew nothing of the past. She was alive only to the present, to her own anticipation of the future. She turned back to him.

'I say for ever, Clement!' – She would have given herself a second time to his arms, but an averted look and staggering retreat forbad her.

Good God, Walter, methinks I see her now! Never shall I cease to remember the changes of her countenance – from rapture to astonishment – from dumb astonishment to doubt: – and from doubt, the quick transition, to despair!

Thus spoke to her the hesitating cold blooded villain – 'Miss Valmont, you have used me very ill —— once – I – I could have – it was barbarous of you who knew your uncle's severe disposition——a little longer concealment might –'

He paused. Miss Ashburn's tears began to flow for her friend, who showed no symptom of common sorrow. Miss Ashburn endeavoured to take her hands; but Sibella shrunk as if the kind emotions of her nature were congealed. A tear that had lingered on her cheek, the last of her tears of happiness, died away. Her asking eye still fixed itself on Montgomery, nor could he forbear answering to it.

'You know, Miss Valmont——'

'Hear me! listen only to me!' exclaimed Miss Ashburn. Sibella pushed her firmly aside, and bent forward to him.

'I would, Miss Valmont –' continued he in the same irresolute, cowardly, cruel tone, 'I should be glad to serve you. – It will be best that you return to your uncle. It might have been otherwise – but you were always rash and premature. – This is not time for explanations. I am sorry, but I cannot now give you any protection, for I – I am, indeed——Yes, Madam, I am married.'

'Are we not both married?' said she, with an emphasis that thrilled him. – 'What is this? – speak Clement!'

'Nay, now, Miss Valmont, you are childish,' said Mrs. Ashburn coldly (Montgomery's bride I mean). 'What man of taste marries a woman after an affair with her?'

'I can bear this no longer,' cried Miss Ashburn. 'Silence, Madam! – Sibella, dear Sibella, turn your eyes on me! Let not their pure rays beam on a wretch so worthless!'

Devoured by emotions over which friendship had no controul, she was still deaf to Miss Ashburn. Still those pure eyes bent their gaze on Montgomery, who now trembled, who now could not ever articulate his broken sentences, who, fainting with guilt, supported himself by leaning on the back of that couch on which he had so lately reclined in the ease of his basely purchased triumph. Suddenly starting from this posture, he rushed towards the door.

'Whither, whither, Clement!' exclaimed Miss Valmont. 'Oh, you'll take me with you, Clement!' – And while, without daring to look on her, he disengaged his hand which she had seized, she rapidly uttered in a softened tone of voice – 'Clement, lover, husband, all!'

The door shut upon Montgomery, she shrieked. Miss Ashburn would have embraced her, but she would not suffer it. She sunk upon the floor. She crossed her arms upon her bosom, with a violent pressure, as if to bind the agony; her teeth grated against each other; and every limb shuddered.

I had approached her with Miss Ashburn, and, scarcely less affected than Miss Ashburn herself, I was turning away to hide my emotions when she sprang upon her feet in an instant; and, grasping my arm, you shall not go without me,' she said. 'Come, Sir: I have told you the way, carry me back to the castle.'

'Then you have forgotten your Caroline, forgotten the kind Murden who hazarded so much to save you?'

'No,' replied Miss Valmont, 'I never forgot any one.'

She took her hand from my arm, and lifted both hands to her forehead. She stood immoveable in deep musing for some time. 'Take me to the castle!' at length she exclaimed, without changing her posture or looking at any person. 'Bid Mr. Valmont provide a dungeon where I can die. I will not go to the wood! Oh, no! nor to my chamber!' She groaned and started. – 'For whom is it that you weep, thus?' she asked, abruptly turning round to Miss Ashburn.

'For my Sibella.'

She bent forward; and gazed intently in Miss Ashburn's face, as if in search of something.

'It is Caroline!' said she, drawing back. Spreading her arms wide, she looked down upon herself: 'Sibella!' – then, every muscle of her face convulsed with anguish, she bent her eyes upon the door – 'and that was Clement! – Oh!'

In short, Walter, a thousand tender touches followed which wrung my heart to pity – while that——woman had the insolence and brutality to call herself Montgomery's wife. But Sibella did not understand her, or if she did, 'twas nothing. His look, his tones had compleated the work, and her mind could feel nothing beyond. Other dreadful agonies followed, but under the suffering of those she was patience itself. She was conveyed to her friend's chamber; and in three hours delivered of a dead child.

I waited the result alone in Miss Ashburn's library, canvassing over all the exquisite concern I had in producing such misery to this injured Sibella. Had I been buried in a quick sand on the road to Hipsley, her noble minded Caroline and the tender Murden might by due preparation have robbed Clement's perfidy of half its sting. But to come upon her thus, to hurl her down such a precipice from the felicity of her expectations – Oh, no wonder her life should be in danger! And think, Walter, what I must have felt when they came to tell me so.

In such a moment, who could palliate? Not, I indeed! I did not conceal from Miss Ashburn an atom of the truth; and she talked like an angel, for she not only told me I should amend but taught me how to amend.

One little satisfaction, indeed, visited me under that roof. I saw Janetta Laundy disgracefully dismissed. She it was, I doubt not, that made this match to satisfy her own grasping avarice by Montgomery's folly. Would you believe that she had so far imposed on the credulity of Mrs. Ashburn that she dared sneer at my assertions? Luckily, I had some letters in my pocket-book lately written by her to me, and such proofs could neither be denied nor parried. As the letters pretty fully displayed the commerce with Montgomery, Mrs. Ashburn poured on her a torrent of abuses; but scarcely had Janetta withdrawn when she complained that her daughter had made her house odious to her, had brought a rival to insult her; and finally she ordered a servant to enquire if Mr. Montgomery would attend her to the opera. Mr. Montgomery was no where to be found.

And, next, Miss Ashburn gave me a commission. No less, Walter, than to relate my worthy exploits to Mr. Murden. By the interest of

Miss Ashburn's name, I was admitted to his chamber. When I saw the wasted form and heard the hollow voice of Murden, and knew, for Miss Ashburn had told me, that love of Miss Valmont had brought him thus near the grave, I shuddered at the idea of my commission. He heard me with a composure which shocked while it astonished me, till I mentioned our entering Mrs. Ashburn's drawing room. 'Hold Sir,' cried he, 'has she then seen him?' I replied, 'she has indeed.'

'Enough, Sir,' said he, 'I know all that remains already.'

Not another syllable passed between us, till I rose to go. He then offered me his hand, and said if I would promise not to pity him he would ask to see me again.

And so he shall. I will, if possible, see him before he dies. My messenger, who brings you this letter, travels for tidings respecting Miss Valmont. Adieu,

FILMAR

LETTER XXXIX

FROM CAROLINE ASHBURN

TO

GEORGE VALMONT

Sir,

Our Sibella is found. – I write at her bed-side; and, if after one hour's cool investigation of the past, you can lay your hand on your heart and say, *though Sibella offended me I was ever just to her*, I will yield up the earnest wish I have, that you should come to London to extend the forgiveness you have already granted, to see, to bless her, e'er she dies. Those convulsive starts tell me nature cannot long support the struggle.

She was the only child of your brother, Sir, and one among the fairest among the daughters of men.

You complain, Sir, that my opinions pay too little deference to the obedience due from children to parents, and in answer to that I must observe, I know not of any opposing duties, and wherever the commands of parents are contrary to the justice due from being to being, I hold obedience to be vice. The perpetual hue and cry after obedience and obedience has almost driven virtue out of the world, for be it unlimited unexamined obedience to a sovereign, to a parent, or husband, the mind, yielding itself to implicit unexamined obedience, loses its individual dignity, and you can expect no more of a man than of a brute. What is to become of the child who is taught never to think or act for himself? Can a creature thus formed ever arrive at the maturity of wisdom? How is he who has never reasoned be enabled in his turn to train his offspring otherwise than he himself was trained. Proud of sway and dominion, he gratifies every impulse of caprice, blindly commands while they blindly obey;

and thus from one generation to another the world is peopled with slaves, and the human mind degraded from the station which God had given to it.

You sent Clement into the world and you commanded him to hate it, but you never told him why it merited this abhorrence, only he was to hate because it pleased you that he should hate the world. Clement Montgomery saw every thing new, every thing fascinating; and the more he remembered he was to hate, the more he loved the world. Then you bid him make himself independent, and you had not given him one lesson of independence of mind, without which he must ever be a tool and dependent. Indeed, Sir, you have no right to withhold from him your forgiveness, for you taught him by your own example to say one thing and intend another; in your own mistakes, you may trace the foundation of his vices.

Mr. Montgomery has, indeed, heaped upon himself an infinite load of mischiefs; and you, Sir, in the bitterness of your resentment, could not wish him a severer punishment than, I believe, he at present endures. My beloved and sacrificed friend was unhappily led into his presence on the first moment of her arrival. She claimed him as her own; and, he must have been marble itself, had not that interview and its sad consequences to the deceived injured Sibella stung him with remorse. Yet his repentance has more of frenzy than feeling. Several times he attempted to force his way into Sibella's chamber; and, finding me immoveable resolved that he should not see her, he gave way to the most violent bursts of indignation and inventive, whose chief object was my mother. At length he quitted the house; and it is said that, in grief and distraction, he also quitted the kingdom. But I understand his feeble and wavering character; his sorrow will abate; he will be again reconciled to himself, and live abounding in all things but esteem.

In consequence of Mr. Montgomery's departure, my mother has vowed an everlasting enmity to me. She has chosen another abode, and forbidden me her presence. It is, Sir, no uncommon case for persons who would fly from the consciousness of their follies to shelter themselves under resentment, and accuse others of malignantly creating those misfortunes for them which were the unavoidable consequences of their own errors. How vain and futile are such endeavours; and how strongly do they help to prove the value of rectitude, which brings its own consolation under every afflicting circumstance of life.

To press you further on the subject of your coming to London, or to relate the particulars which have befallen Sibella, would be only to give you unnecessary pain. Suffer me, however, to remind you once more that the moment approaches rapidly upon us when resentment cannot agitate nor forgiveness soothe her.

I remain, Sir, your sincere well wisher,

CAROLINE ASHBURN

LETTER XL

FROM CAROLINE ASHBURN

TO

LORD FILMAR

My Lord,

I scarcely recollect the verbal message I sent in answer to your letter of yesterday; for I was then under the dominion of feelings more powerful than reason – yet not more powerful; it was reason had yielded for a time her place.

I will fortify myself for the relation of the events of yesterday, because I think it will do you a service. I am sure you are not incorrigible; and one example of the wretched consequences of error has often more power than a volume of precepts.

It was half past eleven yesterday morning when an attendant silently beckoned me from Sibella's bed. In the antichamber, Sir Thomas Barlowe's gentleman waited to inform me that Mr. Murden was in my study. I could scarcely believe I was awake; it seemed so impossible that he should be there. 'Alas, Madam,' said the young man, 'every persuasion has been used to prevent his rash design. And since Sir Thomas Barlowe, by the advice of the physicians, positively refused his coming to visit Miss Valmont, he has neither taken rest nor sustenance. What could we do, Madam, but indulge him?'

How indeed could they act otherwise! He was brought, my Lord, in a chair; and had fainted once by the way.

Much affected by the nature of his enterprise, and by the resolution with which he persisted in accomplishing his design, I could not restrain my tears when I joined him in the study. He was gasping for breath; and seemed ready to drop from the arms of the servant who supported him.

As I approached him, and took his hand, he turned his head away from me; an increase of anxiety and something of ill nature contracted his brow, for he expected a decided opposition on my part to the design which he had resolved never to relinquish.

'Murden, my dear Murden,' I said, 'I——'

He interrupted me in a peevish tone. He came, he said, to see Sibella – He *must* see her. And, if I refused to let him see her, he would crawl to her chamber door, and live there whilst he did live.

I would have spoken again, but he waved his hand to express that he would not hear me; and rested his head on the servant's shoulder. The hand which I still held, though he had twice attempted to draw it from mine, began to endure a consuming heat. A deep hectic colouring overspread his cheek; and I imagined disappointment was committing more ravages on him, in one way, than indulgence could, in another.

Strongly incited to lead Murden instantly to my friend's chamber, yet unwilling to hazard so much merely on my own judgment, I retired to consult with Mrs. Beville, who has kindly given me her society and assistance since my mother quitted the house. Mrs. Beville suggested to me an idea which determined me to permit the interview, unless Sibella herself should object to seeing Murden.

I must tell you, my Lord, that from the fatal day when you was a feeling witness of her agonies, Sibella has been perfectly or rather horridly calm. Never has she named Clement; nor has she ever wept. She insisted on having the corpse of her infant brought to her before its burial; and, while she pressed it to her burning bosom, she said – 'Poor senseless earth! In quitting life so soon, thou hast not lost but gained! What art thou? nothing! thy members will not swell into strength and proportion. Life will not inform them. Thy heart will never beat, and it shall not feel.—— Babe, thou art gone for ever! None laments for thee. She who should have been thy mother weeps not for thee. – Go, babe! go to thy cold shelter! soon will that shelter be mine. But I cannot afford thee warmth: for I shall be cold, senseless, dead, as thou art!'

As she spoke her eye had no moisture; and she delivered up the infant without shedding one tear; but the oppression she endured for want of this salutary relief was dreadful to behold. Mrs. Beville was of opinion that the altered and pity-moving countenance of Murden, the recollection of his kindness, and his sufferings for her would surprise, affect her, turn her consideration from herself to him, and call forth a sympathy which must produce tears.

I had less hope of the success of the experiment in this way to Sibella than Mrs. Beville entertained; yet, I had hope and I also persuaded myself that a kind word from her would give to Murden a renewal of vigour, and prove the chearing companion of his few remaining days.

Sibella was at this time more composed than usual; and, on being informed of Mr. Murden's desire, she expressed an earnest wish to see him.

I returned to the study. 'You are come to lead me to her,' said Murden, impatiently. 'Yes,' I replied, I am. Sibella herself desires it.'

'Give me – give me—— ' said he, stretching forth his hand, and his servant presented some liquid he held in a glass; but Murden pushed it from him. 'Carry me there,' said he, 'all my strength is gone.'

I saw that he trembled excessively, and gladly would I have retracted my consent; but it was too late. I could nothing more than hasten the interview, that the expectation of it might not prey on him thus dreadfully. We prevailed on him to taste the liquid; and then his attendants carried him in their arms to the chamber door, where at his own desire they stood still for a moment or two.

When he was borne into the room, he suddenly assumed a strength which had before totally failed him, and tottered to the seat beside her. – Neither spoke.——He gazed, till he could gaze no longer; and, leaning back his head, burst into a violent flood of tears. Sibella was not moved. She put out her hand towards his; I lifted his, and gave it her.

'Mr. Murden,' said she, as she pressed his hand, 'you have been very kind to me – tell me how I can thank you?'

'You were once unkind to me,' replied Murden, sobbing, – 'you hated me! you shunned me!'

'True, for I did not know you.——Yet, I fancied myself infallibly discerning.' She turned her head away.

'Oh do not, do not turn from me! – Miss Valmont, I once talked with you in the Ruin – Do you remember it?'

'Yes. – You were not so ill then, as you are now.'

'And you, Miss Valmont, was well.'

'I did think so,' she said, and sighed.

Murden comprehended the fullest force of her meaning. He looked wildly around the apartment. 'Let me go, let me go,' said he eagerly, withdrawing his hand from Sibella and attempting to rise. I beckoned in his two attendants, who lifted him from his seat.

'Will you go, and not bid me farewel, Murden?' asked Sibella.

He started at the plaintive tone. – 'Stand off!' cried he, 'would ye dare take me from her ere my errand is compleated?'

'It is compleated, my dear Murden.' said I. 'You have seen Sibella. Bid her farewel, and part.'

'Yes! yes!' said he, sitting down again beside her. 'We shall part – we are now on the very verge of parting. – Oh dear, good Miss Ashburn, bless you for ever!' As he spoke, he pressed each of my hands alternately to his lips. – 'Dear dear Miss Ashburn, fare you well!'

'Indeed, Murden, you must go,' said I. 'Must,' repeated he – 'must! why I know I must. – I have no choice, Miss Ashburn. But allow me a little longer: – won't you,' – turning to Sibella – 'allow me a very little longer?'

'Certainly, I will,' replied Sibella; 'if it will give you satisfaction.'

'Satisfaction!' said he.

After a pause, during which he gazed intently on Sibella, his countenance underwent a striking alteration. He made a motion for something to be given to him; but, when the servant approached, he put him aside. His head dropped against the side of the chair; and the hand he had just lifted to his forehead fell upon the bed. Sibella placed it between both of her's.

He drew his breath slowly and heavily. Once I thought he had fainted, and offered to support him. 'No! no! no!' he said; and shortly after, I believe he slept.

At that time all who were in the apartment observed a profound silence. Sibella in deep thought continued to hold his hand. Sometimes she looked upon Murden; and, in those expressive looks, I read the anguish of her heart. She could not, as Mrs. Beville had supposed, separate his sufferings from her own. I perceived that her emotions were kindling into agony; and I arose from my feat, undetermined which way I could relieve her, when a loud and dreadful groan from Sibella roused Murden from his short interval of forgetfulness.

'Oh! have pity!' said Murden.

Sibella uttered a second groan.

'Miss Valmont!' exclaimed Murden.

'Give me not a name' – cried Sibella. 'I own none! What am I? a shadow ! A dream! – Will you oblige me?' added she, vehemently grasping Murden's hand – 'Carry to him the name you used to me.

Bid him murder that also. – Oh! your touch is ice!' – she exclaimed, throwing his hand suddenly from her; 'you have chilled my blood!'

A moment after, she recollected herself. 'Poor Murden!' said she, 'Warm! warm yourself! Why are you so cold?'

'Because I too am but a shadow,' replied Murden. 'Hear me, Miss Valmont. I must call you so. – It was when you came to seek your fawn in the Ruin, that you talked with me there. Do you remember it?'

'I do.'

'Oh, Miss Valmont, Miss Valmont, methought you never looked so lovely, never was so gentle as while you spake two words – Only two. And can you not remember that I said to you – When remembrances of love shall be no longer remembrances of happiness, then – *Die also.*'

'Great God! Do you reproach me with living!' cried Sibella, starting up in the bed in a phrenzy. 'Know you not I expired when – Oh! Am I not dead dead already?'

'Then, let the same grave receive us!' Bending forward, he locked her in his arms, and sunk upon her pillow, never to rise again.

It is easier, my Lord, for you to imagine than for me to describe the consequence of yesterday's event to my beloved and dying friend. Her convulsions become each hour more and more rapid and exhausting. Yet she has intervals of composure and even of rest, and these serve to detain a little longer her bursting spirit within the fading form. Oh, cruel those who have been the means of thus early separating a mind and form so worthy of happiness, so mated to each other! As for myself, I have endured much, and have much yet to endure, for remembrances of Murden and Sibella, of their virtues and misfortunes will live with me, will be the cherished, tender companions of many hours; nor shall that which the world calls pleasure, ever buy me from one of those hours with the richest of her temptations.

Last night, while Sibella slept, I would have slept also, but the scene of yesterday lay a cumbrous load upon my heart. I rose and passed to the chamber where the corpse of Murden is deposited. His faults fled from me. I saw only Murden, I remembered him living, and now I looked on him dead. – My Lord, my Lord, what a contrast! – What a pang!

A smile of something more than peace illumines even now the face from whence animation is gone for ever. It was his last smile, the smile he had so dearly purchased. His heart indeed dictated that smile, for it expanded with joy when he felt he should die with her for whom he died. Fatal end of an ungoverned passion – virtuous in its object, but vicious in its excess!

The corpse still remains in the house. Why should I part with it? None loved him better.

A sleep almost like death still locks up the faculties of Sibella. During her last interval from pain and convulsions, she gave her final directions, and you my Lord are concerned therein.

Mr. Valmont is sick, sick at heart. He could not come to London; but he sent his steward with forgiveness, blessings, and an earnest request that Sibella would make her own disposition of her fortune, by which he has resolved most faithfully to abide. There is a sum in hand of near a hundred thousand pounds, out of which she has desired that your debts may be discharged, my Lord. Her request to you is, that you will in future refrain from the pernicious practice by which they were incurred. I have no doubt but you will; and certain am I, my Lord, that you may find means of disposing of your time, that in real pleasure will beggar all comparison with those to which you have been accustomed.

I am summoned to Sibella's chamber.

Again Sibella doses. – Her fits have ceased, and death becomes gentle in its preparation. 'Now, my Caroline,' said she as I approached her bed, 'Come and let me bid you farewel. I find there is something yet for me to feel in leaving you. – Methought – ' she added after a pause – 'sensation had been dead in me – I have had strange feelings, Caroline. And now I seem awakening from a fearful dream. I have lost the raging fire which consumed me – early scenes recur – and here,' laying her hand on her bosom, 'something swells as if – as if I yet had – affections!'

So saying, the melting sufferer burst into tears; and my fond hopes would have persuaded me, that these tears were the beginning of her restoration. No, my Lord, it is only fondness that could for one moment entertain the supposition.

'Do not let us weep,' said she, 'Caroline, there is a person – 'tis, I desire it, Caroline – whom you must forgive, pity, and befriend. When you meet him – Clement' – the name hung upon her quivering lips – 'tell him to be sincere. Tell all the world so, Caroline. – My uncle's secrets could have done me but temporary harm, it was mine own secrets destroyed me – Oh that fatal contract!'

A long pause succeeded; but she neither wept not sighed. She had folded her hands upon her bosom, and she looked intently upward.

Again raising herself, she embraced me; and then she said, 'Poor Murden! he had his secrets too, and he has died for them!'

My Lord – it is over. – She expired in my arms.

Yes, they shall be entombed together – the dearer parts of my existence. – I loved them both as I never loved man nor woman beside.

FINIS

MOTHERS
OF THE
NOVEL
....
DALE SPENDER

*100 good women writers before
Jane Austen*

"Quite simply, and in the face of the verdict of the men of letters, it is my contention that
women were the mothers of the novel."

While Jane Austen was one of the many women writers in her own day, she
has since been cast in the role of instigator rather than inheritor of a rich and
diverse tradition of women's writing.

In this wonderfully comprehensive and readable study, Dale Spender
reclaims the many women writers who made significant contributions to the
literary tradition. She describes the interconnections among the women
novelists, their lives and achievements and the public response to their work.
She explores the ways in which the records have since been rewritten so that
women's contributions to the history of the novel have been largely ignored.

"What Dale Spender does convincingly is emphasise the radical qualities of
writing in these novels and the sheer productive energy of many of these
writers. One of the merits and excitements of her survey . . . is the way it
focuses attention on a whole new area of books."
– *The Times*

"A feminist standpoint allows Spender to be an infectiously enthusiastic
champion of these writers."
– *The Irish Times*

". . . exhilirating, highly readable."
– Emma Tennant, *The Sunday Times*

"Spender, as usual, is pure gold . . . *Mothers of the Novel* is one of the most
important literary remakes of the era."
– Jane Blue, *The Women's Review of Books*

Price £4.95 net
ISBN 0-86358-251-6

THE HISTORY OF
MISS BETSY THOUGHTLESS

....

ELIZA HAYWOOD

Introduced by Dale Spender

In which the lovable heroine, Betsy is shown the error of her thoughtless ways and after many adventures marries Trueworth.

First published in 1751, this long and extraordinary novel gathers into its net a multitude of sexual and social concerns; abortion, divorce, marriage laws and the double standards governing men's and women's behaviour in the eighteenth century.

Betsy's growth to maturity is played out against the realisation that the institution of marriage is a personal as well as a social commitment for women, who must try to take control of their own lives – overcoming chauvinistic social conventions. But despite its more tragic episodes, this is a happy book: witty, adventurous and touching.

Price: £5.95 net
ISBN 0-86358-090-4

MEMOIRS OF
MISS SIDNEY BIDULPH

·····································

FRANCES SHERIDAN

Introduced by Sue Townsend

First published in three volumes in 1761, *Memoirs of Miss Sidney Bidulph*
portrays the ill-fated and unconsummated love of the heroine for her
devoted but misunderstood suitor. A witty but passionate story, full of
intrigue and hapless events, it was well received by critics of the day and
enjoyed widespread popularity on the continent.

Although Frances Sheridan wrote this, her best known novel, furtively
between household chores, it became a literary model for her
contemporaries and for later women writers. Her son Richard Brinsley
Sheridan, appropriated several incidents from the novel for his own play,
The School for Scandal.

Price: £5.95 net
ISBN 0-86358-134-X

HELEN
....

MARIA EDGEWORTH

Introduced by Maggie Gee

In which the heroine, Helen, finds her honesty and integrity pitted against the well-meaning but morally ambiguous behaviour of her friend, Cecelia. The conflicting loyalties of the two young women, caught between patriarchal authority, with its moral absolutes, and their affection for one another, are played out against the broader political ideals of the wise and tolerant, Lady Davenant.

First published in 1834, Maria Edgeworth's comedy of social and sexual manners was greatly admired by many later writers, including Elizabeth Gaskell, who used it as a model for her own *Wives and Daughters*.

Price £5.95 net
ISBN 0-86358-104-8

PATRONAGE
....

MARIA EDGEWORTH

Introduced by Eva Figes

An ambitious work, and Maria Edgeworth's most commercially successful novel, *Patronage* is an astute and humorous portrayal of the British class system and the different ways in which men and women make their way in the world.

Written in 1814, this magnificent novel is not only a comedy of manners but also a meditation on the concept of 'patronage', both financial and sexual. The plot revolves around two families – the Percys and the Falconers – whose fortunes mirror and contrast each other. The Falconers accept patronage from Lord Oldborough but by the end of the book it is the Percys who are perceived as possessing the greater moral worth and wealth by dint of their own efforts.

Price £6.95 net
ISBN 0-86358-106-4

BELINDA

······································

MARIA EDGEWORTH

Introduced by Eva Figes

Like her contemporary, Jane Austen, Maria Edgeworth concealed beneath a seemingly effortless lightness of touch and humour, an awareness of the poignancy and sadness of everyday domestic existence.

Written in 1811, this is the story of Belinda and the two men who court her.

Around this conventional literary cliché, Maria Edgeworth has woven an extraordinary complex and powerful narrative, so that a romantic comedy of manners becomes, in her hands, a rich and subtle counterpoint of themes – love, fidelity, passion, cynicism and the position of women in society – with characters all equally memorable, whether virtuous like Belinda, 'wicked' like Lady Delacour or feckless like Vincent.

Price £4.95
ISBN 0-86358-074-2

THE O'BRIENS AND THE O'FLAHERTYS
A NATIONAL TALE
....

LADY MORGAN

Introduced by Mary Campbell

Lady Morgan (Sydney Owenson) brings her passionate interest in Irish history and politics and her own life experiences together in this story of two families, and the different ways their native land has treated them. Both the O'Briens and the O'Flahertys are dispossessed and uprooted by the Penal Laws; the O'Flahertys have survived by going abroad whilst Terence Baron O'Brien (now Lord Arranmore but born Terry the bastard, the child of an illicit union between the two families) changes his religion and allegiance to enter the world of the Ascendancy and beat them at their own game. But underneath it all he remains a Catholic and treasures the idea of a Gaelic Ireland. He heaps his ambitions upon his son, Murrough, who is educated at the nominally Protestant Trinity College but secretly by the Jesuits.

Enter the Abbess Beauvoin O'Flaherty, a true Morgan woman; independent and free, patriotic and liberal, and a campaigner against religious bigotry wherever it might appear.

A rich and complex novel, *The O'Briens and the O'Flahertys* was first published in 1827 and ran to three editions in the first year. It is Lady Morgan's strongest and best work: a brave and highly engaging story in which she tries to come to grips with the reality of the political situation in Ireland in her own times.

Price £8.95 net
ISBN 0-86358-289-3

EMMELINE

THE ORPHAN OF THE CASTLE

....

CHARLOTTE SMITH

Introduced by Zoë Fairbairns

Emmeline was so spectacularly successful when it was published in 1788 that by June of the following year it was well into its third edition. Emmeline Mowbray, the ostensibly illegitimate orphan who grows up in an ancient castle in a remote part of Pembrokeshire, becomes engaged to her wealthy cousin Delamere only because he threatens to kill himself unless she consents to be his future wife. But the same instability and emotional excess leads him to doubt her honour and, although she is a virtuous and modest young woman, Emmeline then decides to set the terms of her own life.

Charlotte Smith's first novel caused something of a sensation because of the dangerous code of conduct it appeared to condone: not only was she writing about illegitimacy, broken engagements, dishonest aristocrats and a dissolute husband, she also failed to punish her guilty characters. Yet the Bluestockings Mrs Carter and Mrs Montague sang the author's praises and sent her their best wishes, hoping that the income from the sale of *Emmeline* would secure Charlotte Smith's freedom from her vile husband – which indeed it did.

'We remember well the impression made on the public by the appearance of *Emmeline, the Orphan of the Castle,* a tale of love and passion, happily conceived, and told in a most interesting manner.'
– Sir Walter Scott, 1834

Price £7.95 net
ISBN 0-86358-264-8